Praise for Ann Charles'

NEARLY DEPARTED IN DEADWOOD

"Full of thrills and chills, a fun rollercoaster ride of a book!"
~**Susan Andersen**, New York Times Bestselling Author

"Smooth, solid and very entertaining, Nearly Departed in Deadwood smartly blends all the elements of a great read and guarantees to be a page-turner!"
~**Jane Porter**, Award-winning Author of *She's Gone Country* and *Flirting with Forty*

"Nearly Departed in Deadwood is a delightful mix of on the edge suspense and laugh-out-loud humor. An impressive debut. Ann Charles is a star in the making!"
~**Gerri Russell**, Award-winning Author of *Seducing the Knight*

"An intriguing mystery laced with a wicked sense of humor. The dialogue sparkles, the characters are quirky fun, and the storyline keeps you turning the page to see what is going to happen next. Watch out Stephanie Plum, because Violet Parker is coming your way."
~**Deborah Schneider**, RWA Librarian of the Year 2009 and Author of *Promise Me*

"Both barrels loaded with offbeat charm, Nearly Departed in Deadwood aims to entertain and never misses the funny bone."
~**Terry McLaughlin**, Author of the Built to Last Series

Charles' debut novel and she couldn't have started it off better. This is a must read that I highly recommend."
~**John Foxjohn**, Bestselling Author of *Tattered Justice*

"Vicariously living Violet Parker's escapades through Deadwood feels like being with a best friend. You fret, you nod, you laugh out loud, and the secrets you find out might put you in the grave, too! Yep. I'm completely addicted."
~**Amber Scott**, Author of *Irish Moon*

"Ann Charles has truly done it. She plunges you into the story from the very beginning and keeps you there every page. Even at the end you're begging for more! It's no wonder *Nearly Departed in Deadwood* was chosen as best overall for the 2010 Daphne Award!"
~**Susan Schreyer**, Author *Death By A Dark Horse*

"Mystery, humor, and romance—a fabulous book from a talented author that you'll be hearing about for a long time!"
~**Jacquie Rogers**, Award-winning Author of *Much Ado About Marshals*

"This gem has a bit of everything … mystery, romance, comedy, suspense, and even a bit of the paranormal. Ann Charles has done a terrific job showing how difficult it is for a single woman to juggle life at work and home, while still having a bit of time to date. I cannot wait to see what the future holds for Violet and the eccentric residents of Deadwood. Ann Charles has a winner in Violet Parker. I have a new favorite author in the mystery genre!" ***** FIVE STARS!
~**Huntress Reviews**

Also by Ann Charles

Deadwood Mystery Series
Nearly Departed in Deadwood (Book 1)
Optical Delusions in Deadwood (Book 2)
Dead Case in Deadwood (Book 3)
Better Off Dead in Deadwood (Book 4)
An Ex to Grind in Deadwood (Book 5)
Meanwhile, Back in Deadwood (Book 6)

Short Stories from the Deadwood Mystery Series
Deadwood Shorts: Seeing Trouble
Deadwood Shorts: Boot Points

Jackrabbit Junction Mystery Series
Dance of the Winnebagos (Book 1)
Jackrabbit Junction Jitters (Book 2)
The Great Jackalope Stampede (Book 3)
The Rowdy Coyote Rumble (Book 4)

Goldwash Mystery Series (a future series)
The Old Man's Back in Town (Short Story)

Dig Site Mystery Series
Look What the Wind Blew In (Book 1)
(Starring Quint Parker, the brother of Violet Parker from the Deadwood Mystery Series)

Coming Next from Ann Charles

Deadwood Mystery Series
A Wild Fright in Deadwood (Book 7)

Dear Reader,

Once upon a time, I thought my crush on Deadwood, South Dakota was going to be just a summer fling. Boy, was I wrong. I had fallen head-over-heels. Deadwood had gotten under my skin. Its golden history filled my mind with daydreams; its promising future spurred tales that needed to be told.

Nearly Departed in Deadwood is a contemporary mystery full of colorful characters that have been taking root inside of my noggin for almost three decades. The seed was planted when I was a young teenager sitting on the bench outside of the old Prospector Gift Shop on Main Street, waiting for my mom to get off work. Over the years, the seed sprouted as I hiked all over town, strolling around Wild Bill Hickok's and Seth Bullock's gravestones at Mount Moriah Cemetery, sitting on the steps outside the Deadwood Public Library, walking up and down Main Street, perusing the tourist shops.

As times changed, so did Deadwood. The drugstore where I used to buy candy, the clothing store where I bought my favorite Levi's, and the Prospector Gift Shop are all gone now. At first I was sad to see them go, but then I realized that Deadwood had to transform and grow in order to survive. Just like I did.

A couple of years ago, I was driving down Strawberry Hill on my way into Deadwood when an idea hit me. It was a "what if" moment that sparked the fire of a story in my head. This time, the "what if" involved a single mom, living in Deadwood, struggling to make ends meet with two kids—twins—for whom she had to provide. I had one young child and another on the way at the time, so taking care of kids was front and center in my mind (and my body).

As I drove through Deadwood that day, memories ran rampant in my mind, and the story you hold in your hands began to take shape. I could see it clearly. I'd name the heroine Violet, an old-fashioned name. I could hear her voice; see her in her favorite purple cowboy boots. I knew exactly the location of the realty office where Violet would work, the street she'd live on, and how I'd pull Deadwood's past into the story and intermingle it with the present.

Over the following month, I plotted this story. My poor husband was forced to listen to my ideas morning, noon, and night; there was no shutting me up. Then he caught the Deadwood bug, too, and he joined me in brainstorming and planning. Before I even wrote the first line, I knew that one book was not going to be enough to tell this story, but I had to start somewhere. Finally, after months of writing, I reached "The End" of *Nearly Departed in Deadwood*, the first book in a series, with much hooting and hollering in celebration.

Now, after several rounds of editing and a lot of polishing, I want to share Violet's story with you. If you have half as much fun reading it as I had writing it, you'll close the book when you're finished with a big grin on your face—especially since you know there is more fun to come.

Thank you for joining me in this adventure. Hold on to your hat!

Welcome to Deadwood.

Ann Charles

www.anncharles.com

N~~D~~EARLY DEPARTED IN DEADWOOD

ANN CHARLES

ILLUSTRATED BY C.S. KUNKLE

NEARLY DEPARTED IN DEADWOOD

Cover Art by C.S. Kunkle
Cover Design by Kathy Thomas, Mona Weiss, and Sharon Benton
Editing by Mimi Munk

First Edition
First Printing, 2011
ISBN: 978-1-940364-14-8
Published by: Ann Charles

To the memory of Robert "Buck" Taylor, who taught me to explore, take crazy risks, and figure my way out of whatever calamity in which my sorry ass landed. You left the party too soon. The Black Hills aren't the same without you.

To the memory of Harvey Harvey, who I never had the pleasure of meeting in person, but whose family has shared so many of his jokes and tales of adventure that I had to try to capture a small sample of his charisma in print.

You were two wild and crazy guys who inspired this story with your bigger than life personalities. I thank you both and dedicate this book to you.

Acknowledgments

This is going to be a long one. You know the saying, "It takes a village"? Well, that is the theme for the story of this book's creation. I have a village worth of people to acknowledge and thank. I'm hoping I remember to mention all of them, but being me, I'll forget someone important and have to beg and plead for forgiveness later.

First, thanks to my husband, for sticking with me; helping me to brainstorm; critiquing even the love scenes; keeping Beaker, Chicken Noodle, and me fed and clothed during the whirlwind of book production; and listening to me talk on and on and on about writing, marketing, and promoting. You deserve five-acres and a workshop.

Thanks to my brother, Charles Kunkle, for scaring the crap out of me repeatedly during childhood with tales of monsters just waiting to eat me. Your artwork graces my cover, website, and more, and I love telling the world how masterful you are with a pencil and paints.

I'm indebted to Margo Taylor for helping to spread word about this book to the world, and to Dave Taylor for chauffeuring her all over God's green earth to do it.

Also, I couldn't have done this without my parents and their unending support, both emotionally and financially. Only a parent will let you drone on about something without telling you to shut up. Love you all!

Thanks to Mary Louise Schwartz for your friendship over the years.
Thanks to Mimi "The Grammar Chick" for keeping me from looking like a fool in print.

Now, let's get down to the mechanics. Thanks to all of my readers and critique helpers: Wendy Delaney, Beth Harris, Marcia Britton, Mary Ida Kunkle, Amber Scott, Deborah Schneider, Paul Franklin (who also helps me with my research), Kathi Tidd, Jody Sherin, Renelle Wilson, Robin Weaver, Marguerite Phipps, Joby Gildersleeve, Denise Garlington, Jim Thomsen, Shelly Zachrich, Louise Edwinson, Stephanie Kunkle, Thea Taylor, Sharon Benton, Heidi Mott, Susan Schreyer, Pam Seiler, and Margo Taylor

Special thanks to Adam Wilson from MIRA books for helping to make this book stronger and trying to pull me into the fold.

Thanks to Christy Karras of Proof Positive for bending over backward to help me catch the attention of the press.

Thanks to the RWA Kiss of Death Chapter and the Daphne du Maurier contest coordinators for the hard work that goes into putting on their contest.

Thanks to the wonderful reviewers who took the time to read and comment about this book; and to the awesome authors willing to give me a cover quote before I had a contract in my hand.

Thanks to Jacquie Rogers, Wendy Delaney, and Sherry Walker for years of friendship and patience with me. Thanks to the columnists and crew at 1st Turning Point for sharing their knowledge so willingly. Thanks to Gerri Russell, Joleen James, and Wendy Delaney for keeping me on task.

Thanks to Amber Scott for continually picking me up, brushing me off, and sending me on my way again. Let's keep thinking BIGGER.

Thanks to my "tribe" for cheering me onward. You guys rock!

Thanks to Clint Taylor for always being the fall guy—literally. I'll always cherish those memories.

In Deadwood:

Thanks to Ken Reder for his answers about real estate in South Dakota.

And finally, thanks to the town of Deadwood for all of the years of wonderful hospitality and great memories. This one is for all of you!

NEARLY DEPARTED IN DEADWOOD

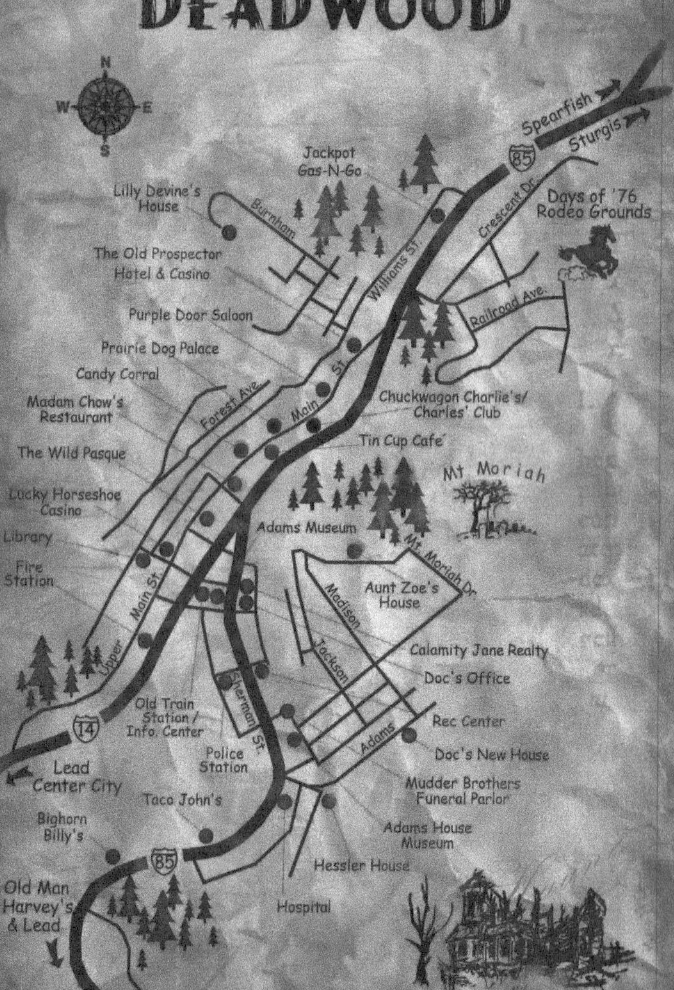
DEADWOOD
N
W
E
S
Spearfish
Sturgis
85
Jackpot
Gas-N-Go
Lilly Devine's
House
Burnham
Days of '76
Rodeo Grounds
Crescent Dr.
Williams St.
The Old Prospector
Hotel & Casino
Railroad Ave.
Purple Door Saloon
Prairie Dog Palace
Candy Corral
Main St.
Madam Chow's
Restaurant
Forest Ave.
Chuckwagon Charlie's/
Charles' Club
Tin Cup Cafe
The Wild Pasque
Mt Moriah
Lucky Horseshoe
Casino
Adams Museum
Library
Mt. Moriah Dr.
Fire
Station
Aunt Zoe's
House
Madison
Main St.
Upper
Calamity Jane Realty
Jackson
Doc's Office
Sherman St.
Old Train
Station /
Info. Center
14
Rec Center
Adams
Doc's New House
Police
Station
Lead
Center City
Mudder Brothers
Funeral Parlor
Taco John's
Adams House
Museum
Bighorn
Billy's
85
Hessler House
Old Man
Harvey's
& Lead
Hospital

KUNKLE

Chapter One

Deadwood, South Dakota
Monday, July 9th

The first time I came to Deadwood, I got shot in the ass. Now, twenty-five years later, as I stared into the double barrels of Old Man Harvey's shotgun, irony was having a fiesta and I was the piñata.

I tried to produce a polite smile, but my cheeks had petrified along with my heart. "You wouldn't shoot a girl, would you?"

Old Man Harvey snorted, his whole face contorting with the effort. "Lady, I'd blow the damned Easter bunny's head off if he was tryin' to take what's mine."

He cocked his shotgun—his version of an exclamation mark.

"Whoa!" I would have gulped had there been any spit left in my mouth. "I'm not here to take anything."

He replied by aiming those two barrels at my chest instead of my face.

"I'm with Calamity Jane Realty, I swear! I came to …"

With Harvey threatening to fill my lungs with peepholes, I had trouble remembering why I'd driven out to this corner of the boonies. Oh, yeah. Lowering one of my hands, I held out my crushed business card. "I want to help you sell your ranch."

The double barrels clinked against one of the buttons on my Rebecca Taylor-knockoff jacket as Harvey grabbed my card. I swallowed a squawk of panic and willed the soles of my boots to unglue from the floorboards of Harvey's front porch and retreat. Unfortunately, my brain's direct line to my feet was experiencing technical difficulties.

Harvey's squint relaxed. "Violet Parker, huh?"

"That's me." My voice sounded pip-squeaky in my own ears. I couldn't help it. Guns made my thighs wobbly and my bladder heavy. Had I not made a pit stop at Girdy's Grill for a buffalo burger and paid a visit to the little *Hens* room, I'd have a puddle in the bottom of my favorite cowboy boots by now.

"Your boots match your name. What's a 'Broker Associate'?"

"It's someone who is going to lose her job if she doesn't sell a house in the next three weeks." I lowered my other hand.

I'd been with Calamity Jane Realty for a little over two months and had yet to make a single sale. So much for my radical, life-changing leap into a new career. If I didn't make a sale before my probation was up, I'd have to drag my kids back down to the prairie and bunk with my parents … again.

"You're a lot *purtier* in this here picture with your hair down."

"So I've been told." Old Man Harvey seemed to be channeling my nine-year-old daughter today. Lucky me.

"Makes you look younger, like a fine heifer."

I cocked my head to the side, unsure if I'd just been tossed a compliment or slapped with an insult.

The shotgun dipped to my belly button as he held the card out for me to take back.

"Keep it. I have plenty." A whole box full. They helped fill the lone drawer in my desk back at Calamity Jane's.

"So that asshole from the bank didn't send you?"

"No." An asshole from my office had, and the bastard

would be extracting his balls from his esophagus for this so-called *generous referral*—if I made it back to Calamity Jane's without looking like a human sieve.

"Then how'd you know about my gambling problem?"

"What gambling problem?"

Old Man Harvey's eyes narrowed again. He whipped the double barrels back up to my kisser. "The only way you'd know I'm thinking about selling is if you heard about my gambling debt."

"Oh, you mean *that* gambling problem."

"What'd you think I meant?"

Bluffing was easier when I wasn't chatting up a shotgun. "I thought you were referring to the … um …" A tidbit of a phone conversation I'd overheard earlier this morning came to mind. "To the problem you had at the Prairie Dog Palace."

Harvey's jaw jutted. "Mud wrestling has no age limit."

"You're right. They need to be less age-biased. Maybe even have an *AARP Night* every Wednesday."

"Nobody told me about the bikini bit 'til it was too late."

I winced. I couldn't help it.

"So, what're you gonna charge me to sell my place?"

"What would you like me to charge you?" I was all about pleasing the customer this afternoon.

He leaned the gun on his shoulder, double barrels pointed at the porch ceiling. "The usual, I guess."

No longer on the verge of extinction, I used the porch rail to keep from keeling over. Maybe I just wasn't cut out for the realty business. Did they still sell encyclopedias door-to-door?

"This ranch belonged to my pappy, and his pappy before him." Harvey's lips thinned as he stared over my shoulder.

"It must hold a big place in your heart." I tried to sound

sincere as I inched along the railing toward the steps. My red Bronco glinted and beckoned under the July sun.

"Hell, no. I can't wait to shuck this shithole."

"What?" I'd made it as far as the first step.

"I'm sick and tired of fixin' rusted fences, chasing four-wheeling fools through my pastures, sniffing out lost cows in every damned gulch and gully." His blue eyes snapped back to mine. "And I keep hearing funny noises at night coming from out behind my ol' barn."

I followed the nudge of his bearded chin. Weathered and white-washed by Mother Nature, the sprawling building's roof seemed to sag in the afternoon heat. The doors were chained shut, one of the haymow windows broken. "Funny how?"

"Like grab-your-shotgun funny."

Normally, this might give me pause, but after the greeting I'd received today from the old codger's double barrels, I had a feeling that Harvey wore his shotgun around the house like a pair of holey underwear. I'd bet my measly savings he even slept with it. "Maybe it's just a mountain lion," I suggested. "The paper said there's been a surge of sightings lately."

"Maybe. Maybe not," Harvey shrugged. "I don't care. I want to move to town. It gets awful lonely out here come wintertime. Start thinking about things that just ain't right. I almost married a girl from Taiwan last January. Turned out 'she' was really a 'he' from Nigeria."

"Wow."

"Damned Internet." Harvey's gaze washed over me. "What about you, Violet Parker?"

"What about me?"

"There's no ring on your finger. You got a boyfriend?"

"Uh, no."

I didn't want one, either. Men had a history of fouling up my life, from burning down my house to leaving me knocked up with twins. These days, I liked my relationships how I liked my eggs: over-easy.

Harvey's two gold teeth twinkled at me through his whiskers. "Then how about a drink? Scotch or gin?"

I chewed on my lip, considering my options. I could climb into my Bronco and watch this opportunity and the crazy old bastard with the trigger-happy finger disappear in my rearview mirror; or I could blow off common sense and follow Harvey in for some hard liquor and maybe a signed contract.

Like I really had a choice. "Do you have any tonic?"

Chapter Two

Later that afternoon, I whipped into the parking lot behind Calamity Jane Realty and found a late '60s, black Camaro SS with white rally stripes hogging my parking spot. I glared at it long and hard, telepathically leveling plague-laden curses at the nitwit who'd ignored the Private Parking sign.

Years ago, around the time my butt wound up peppered with BBs thanks to my best friend's little brother, Deadwood had been a quiet town, struggling to survive on its golden past. Historic buildings lined Main Street and parking spaces were abundant.

Then came the gambling.

As thousands of new tourists and millions of new dollars poured in, casino after casino crowded the main drag with bright window signs promising big bonanzas. The only thing abundant these days were slot machines, and finding an empty parking spot on a hot summer day was tougher than lining up triple red sevens for the progressive jackpot.

Swearing, I cruised through one parking lot after another, finally sliding into a too-tight spot three blocks from the office. The meter ate every bit of spare change from my ashtray.

By the time I yanked open Calamity Jane's front door, I'd shucked my jacket and sweat beaded my upper lip. A whoosh of cool air sprinkled with a hint of jasmine swirled around me as I stomped to my desk and flung my jacket on it.

Mona, my coworker, new-found friend, and mentor all wrapped in one stunning, flame-haired package, placed a Post-It on my phone. Another stronger whiff of jasmine hit me. "You okay, Vi?"

"No." I glared around the office. "Where's Ray?" Should I poke the jerk in the eye or bust his kneecap for sending me out to Harvey's without mentioning the old man's ardor for his gun?

"He's showing the place on Dakota Street to that cute young couple who were in here the other day."

"You mean the Rupps?" I flopped into my chair and snarled at Ray's empty seat.

Mona smiled. "They're so sweet, the way they're constantly giving each other those googly-eyed stares."

Pushing fifty, Mona had yet to land her happily-ever-after. Her rose-colored glasses rarely left her face, for her true love might be the next man she met … or the one after.

"They came in looking for you, but Ray couldn't reach you on your cell."

That's because I was out in the sticks playing spin the bottle with a loony old kook.

"So he took them out himself."

"Wait a second!" I sat up straight, suddenly realizing what she was saying. "Those were *my* clients."

"The house is a real fixer-upper. I doubt they'll be interested."

For Ray's sake, I hoped she was right. I picked up the Post-It and stared at Mona's writing. "What did Layne want?"

"He said something about finding a skeleton in the backyard and needing you to pick up a jar of worms on your way home."

Some days, my son made electroshock therapy sound

appealing. I reached for the phone.

Ray Underhill burst through the front door, his face furrowed, his fake tan two shades redder than usual.

"Who in the hell let them put this shit in our front window again?" He ripped free a piece of paper taped to the plate-glass and held it out.

Missing: Nine Year Old Girl it read in bold letters. A slightly fuzzy, black-and-white picture of a blonde with a smile too big for her face took up the bulk of the page; a local phone number and "$10,000 Reward!" filled the footer.

It took me a breath and a blink to realize this wasn't the same Missing poster I'd seen stapled to poles and stuck in store-front windows for the last few months. This was new—a different girl, a different amount, but the same story.

Mona crossed her arms. "I taped it in the window."

"What are you thinking?" Ray wadded up the sign and tossed it in the trash on his way to the coffee maker. "We're trying to convince retirees and families that Deadwood is a safe place to live. Pictures of missing girls don't exactly encourage these suckers to cough up a down payment."

I dropped the receiver back in its cradle and scooped the wadded-up sign from Ray's garbage. "When did this happen?" I asked, my chest tight; my blonde, nine-year-old daughter spurring my sudden dizzying spell of anxiety.

"Vi, are you okay?" Mona asked through a tin can on the other end of a string—at least that's what it sounded like as my vision tunneled. I felt a warm hand on my shoulder. "Honey, sit down."

I dropped into a chair that somehow ended up behind my knees. My hand trembled slightly as I held up the picture. "When?"

"Two days ago."

"What's with her?" Ray said as he passed behind me.

"It's not her kid."

I took a deep breath, something I found myself doing often these days when Ray was within a five-mile radius. If there was an award for the World's Biggest Horse's Ass, Ray's desk would be littered with grand-prize trophies.

"You okay, Vi?" Mona asked, her hand squeezing.

I nodded and flashed her a smile. It weighed heavy on my lips.

Ray was right, it wasn't my kid. It was, however, a second child gone missing. In a town as small as Deadwood, one girl was a worry. Two was an epidemic.

"From here on out," Ray's chair griped with a squeal as he dropped into it, "only MLS listings go in our window."

I stuffed the Missing sign in my purse and tried to push my apprehension aside for now. I still had to sell a house.

"The boss approved, so get over it," Mona said.

A blaze of curses fired from Ray's mouth.

Mona examined her manicured nails, her feathers apparently ruffle-free. She once informed me that after working with the blockhead for over a decade, she'd developed a callous exterior when it came to Ray's bullshit. That didn't stop her from dumping an extra helping of Benefiber in his daily glass of orange juice every now and then, as I'd witnessed several times.

"I take it the Rupps weren't interested, Sunshine." Mona also liked to give Ray cute nicknames just to needle him.

"You're wrong. They're going to sign an offer letter."

"What!" I was out of my seat and in his face before I realized it. "They were *my* clients."

Ray patted me on the head. The smell of his sweat under his plaster of Stetson cologne made my stomach churn. "You snooze, you lose, Blondie."

Ray used nicknames, too, his purpose a bit darker.

"I wasn't snoozing. I was facing off with a shotgun."

"So, Harvey was feeling feisty today? I warned you."

"You said to use honey instead of vinegar, not wear a Kevlar vest and carry a concealed weapon."

"Some customers are tougher than others. You're going to have to buck up, little girl, if you want to make it in the realty business in this town." His chair creaked again as he kicked back, his hand-tooled, Tony Lama boots acting as paperweights. "Leave Old Man Harvey to me."

"You stay away from Harvey. He's my client."

"You got him to sign a contract?" Mona sounded surprised.

I plucked the contract from my tote and held it up.

Ray snorted. "There's no signature on that, Sweetheart."

"There will be after tonight."

"What's tonight?" Mona asked.

My cheeks heated. I mumbled my answer as I stuffed the contract back into my tote.

Mona leaned forward. "You're doing what with Harvey?"

"Going out to dinner."

Ray's laughter rumbled throughout the room.

"Oh, Vi. Do you think that's a good idea?"

I wasn't used to seeing Mona frown. "It's just dinner, that's all. He's a lonely guy."

"I'm a lonely guy, too, Blondie. Stop by my place after dinner and I'll give you a lesson on finishing the deal. Wear something tight and low-cut."

I'd sooner drink Drano. "I'll pass."

"Your loss." Ray nodded at the calendar hanging on the wall. "With your time just about up, I guess I should call my nephew and tell him to have his interview suit dry-cleaned."

Ray had made it no secret that he'd been ticked Jane hired me back in May for the newly-created Associate position, instead of waiting another month for his nephew to finish realty school. As Deadwood's reigning King of

Schmooze, Ray wasn't used to rejection, but no amount of dining—or whining—had convinced Jane to take on a fourth employee.

I lifted my chin. "I'm not out of the game yet." I had a Hail Mary play left in me still, I was sure of it.

With his trademark smirk in place, Ray sat forward as if he had a secret to share. "Harvey isn't going to sign any contract, Sweetheart. He's just dangling a carrot, hoping to get some young tail. Did he tell you that he got kicked out of the Prairie Dog Palace Casino last week for wagging his Johnson at a busload of pretty old maids from Canada?"

That wasn't true—well, not exactly, according to Harvey. Besides, it didn't matter if it was. I needed a sale, even if it cost me a little dignity and a lot of antacids.

"Sunshine," Mona said, "your asshole meter is red-lining."

Ray waved off Mona. "Face it, Blondie. You're like Wild Bill and Potato Creek Johnny around these parts—history."

I picked up my stapler with every intention of imprinting 'Swingline' on Ray's forehead via blunt force trauma.

The front door whisked open and a tall, sandy-haired Don Juan zeroed in on me with a white-toothed grin that saved me from a potential assault charge.

"Hello, Miss Parker."

I lowered the stapler, a little starry-eyed by Don Juan's dazzling features. "Have we met before?" I was sure I'd have remembered him.

He held out a postcard I recognized by sight.

A month ago, I'd had the harebrained idea of making up postcards using a family picture to help round up some business. The whole "look at me, I'm just a friendly mom who wants to help you sell your house and make all of your dreams come true" kind of card. It had drained my dwindling savings account of several hundred precious dollars.

"Ah. You got my postcard. How can I help you?" *Please say you want to sell something.*

"I want to sell my house."

Yes! I offered Don Juan the seat across from me and grabbed paper and pen. "Let's start with your name."

"Wolfgang Hessler."

"Hessler? Spelled the same as the jewelry store in town?"

"Exactly. That's my store."

"Oh. That's a nice store." That was like saying the Hope diamond was a "pretty stone."

Hessler's Jewelry Designs was one of the two primo jewelry stores on Main Street—heck, in western South Dakota. There were none of the usual Black Hills Gold grape-leaf pieces in his store window, only original designs that took my breath away. Not that I could afford even a single earring from his shop, let alone two. But I often drooled in his store's window while scarfing down chocolate from the Candy Corral, located a few doors down.

"You're Wilma Hessler's kid?" Ray rolled his chair over and joined the conversation in spite of my eat-shit-and-die glare.

"Wilma was my mother, yes." Wolfgang's articulate use of the English language seemed out of place.

"I thought you moved to San Francisco." Ray knew everything about everyone in town. That's probably what had made him the top salesman every month for the past five years, and possibly the only reason that Jane put up with his chauvinistic ass.

"I did."

"Are you going to sell the jewelry store, too?" Ray asked. If I'd had a Kleenex, I'd have given it to Ray to wipe the drool from his chin.

"No. My mother would roll over in her grave if I did that. It's been in the family for generations." His cobalt eyes locked onto mine. "I'm just here to sell my mother's house."

If I smiled any wider, my forehead would cave in. Here it was, finally! My big, gorgeous fish.

"What's the address?" I tried to keep the giggles of glee out of my voice.

"55 Van Buren Street."

That was near the old Adams' house-slash-museum in the historic presidential neighborhood, just a short hop from downtown Deadwood. I glanced at Ray and could have danced the Charleston at the sight of his clenched teeth.

"When would be a good time for me to come over and take a look around the place?" I was available now, yesterday, and the day before.

"Are you free right now?"

The phone on my desk rang, interrupting my shout of *Yes!* I looked at the number of who was calling and recognized it. "I'll let that go to voicemail."

Wolfgang smiled. I smiled back. Hell, the whole world was smiling at that moment. We should have all joined hands.

"Let me just check my calendar to make sure I don't have any other appointments this afternoon."

A muffled guffaw came from Ray's direction. Mona cleared her throat.

The phone stopped mid-ring as I dug through my tote for my daytimer.

"Here we are." I flipped open to July, happy I'd taken the time yesterday in between twiddling my fingers and twirling my hair to add a few fake appointments to my book just to cheer myself up.

Mona's phone started ringing. She picked it up on the

second ring.

I ran my finger down the page. "I'm taking a client to dinner this evening but other than that, my schedule is open."

Wolfgang stood. "Perfect. You can follow me."

"Excuse me, Vi?"

I looked at Mona.

"I have a call for you." She mouthed my son's name.

Damn it, Layne! "Can you take a message for me?"

"Ummm, he sounds like this is kind of important."

If this was about those stupid worms … I turned to Wolfgang. "Could you hold on for just a second, please?"

He nodded.

I walked to Mona's desk and took the receiver from her. "I'm a little busy. Can I call you back in a bit?"

"No!" Layne yelled. I'm pretty sure they heard him over in Montana. "You have to come home right now! It's an emergency!"

"Layne, calm down."

"Now, Mom! Hurry!"

"Where is—" The line clicked, and then silence.

My heart thudded hard against my ribs.

"What's wrong, Vi? Is he okay?"

"I don't know." Layne had a history of crying wolf. His so-called emergencies often turned out to be minor predicaments fixed by applying or removing super glue. But if I didn't go and something really was wrong, well, that was the Catch-22, wasn't it? "I need to go home." Then I remembered my big fish. "Uhh, Mr. Hessler—"

"You want to reschedule?"

"I'm so sorry."

"Don't worry about it." He reached in his back pocket.

"I could go with you, Mr. Hessler," Ray volunteered, standing. "If you'd prefer to get moving on this today."

"That's okay. I'll be in town for a few more days." He

handed me a business card. "Call me. I'll be at the store tomorrow morning." With a nod goodbye, he left.

I grabbed my jacket and purse. "Mona, I'll call you later. Ray, you're a dickhead. I hope you choke on a cheeseburger."

My boot heels clomping, I rushed out the front door. My eyes were on my cell as I dialed home again. I cut the corner and tripped over a box full of books. The cell phone flew from my hands. I landed on my palms and knees, which saved my nose from catching a sidewalk rash.

"Ow!" I sat up, the smell of sun-baked pavement all around me. My knee burned. Then I noticed the big hole in my green slacks. "Crud!"

"Shit. I shouldn't have left that box there." A deep voice said from over my head. "Are you okay?"

I looked up from my scraped knee into a chiseled face with dark brown eyes and a cleft chin. "No. These are my favorite pants."

"I'll buy you another pair."

"You can't. They're a couple of years old."

Mr. Brown Eyes held out his hand to help me up. "How can I make it up to you?"

I accepted with a grunt, wincing as his hand found the sidewalk burn on my palm. "Don't worry about it."

"Here's your phone," he said and held out both pieces. "Are you bleeding?"

"I'm fine." I brushed my hands off on my ruined pants, took the phone, and popped the battery back on. A scratch appeared to be the only visible damage. That made two of us.

"Does it still work?"

It powered up. I nodded, stuffing it in my pocket, and then glanced down at the box that had sent me sprawling. One of the books on top had a two-inch thick spine. I lifted it up. "*The Life and Times of James Butler Hickok*," I read under my breath. A glance at the other books revealed more prose about Wild Bill. "You're not from here, are you?" I asked.

"What makes you say that?"

"Because anyone raised in the Black Hills general area had enough Wild Bill history crammed down their throat in elementary school to last a lifetime."

"Maybe I'm just a big fan of history." He took the book from me and dropped it back in the box.

Ten bucks said that dinner conversation with this guy would require toothpicks to prop my eyelids open. I hoisted my purse on my shoulder and peeked in the office window that shared a wall with Calamity Jane Realty. Boxes, a ladder, and two paint cans sat next to a lone desk.

"You must be our new neighbor," I said, noting the keys in his hand. "I work next door."

"You're a Realtor?"

"Uh-huh."

Taped to the outside of his plate-glass window was the same Missing Girl sign about which Ray had thrown a fit. One corner was loose, slightly crinkled. I flattened it against the glass.

"I don't think she's just lost in the woods," my new neighbor said. Something in the tone of his voice made me look up at him. He stared at the girl's picture with an intensity that made me shiver.

I hoped he was wrong. The urge to swaddle my own kids in bubble wrap reminded me that I had a so-called "emergency" at home. "I gotta go."

Brown Eyes grabbed my jacket from the ground and handed it to me. "Let me give you some cash for the pants."

Tempting, but I wasn't that desperate. Yet. "Thanks, but no. I'll see you around."

"What's your name?" he called after me.

"Violet," I yelled without turning around. I limped as

fast as I could the three blocks to my Bronco, replaying Layne's call in my head. He had better not have burned his eyebrows off again with another exploded chemistry experiment. Super glue wouldn't fix eyebrows.

Chapter Three

I skidded to a stop in front of the old Ponderosa pine tree that shaded my Aunt Zoe's 1870s Victorian house, the place the kids and I currently called home. After worrying I'd find a police car or ambulance in the drive, I scratched my head at the sight of my daughter sitting near the sidewalk behind a table with a *Pet Teeth Brushing—$2* banner taped to it.

"Hi, Mom." Addy waved at me as I climbed out of my Bronco. Apparently, her brother had not informed her of his so-called emergency. "How was your day at the office?"

"Okay."

As I shut the car door, the scent of warmed pine cocooned me—a bonus with living in the tree-covered hills rather than on the dusty prairie. I hesitated, listening for screams, cries, or shouts of pain; something other than the scratchy *caw caw* from the lone crow on the power line overhead.

"Did you meet any nice men?" my daughter asked, unwrapping a pink sucker.

Addy had two goals in life these days—to become a veterinarian and find me a husband. While I could live with the occasional broken-winged jay and road-kill squirrel, I drew the line at her creating a profile for me on a website that specialized in helping ex-cons find their true loves.

"Nope, not a single one," I lied, pushing aside the image of the sandy-haired, potential knight in shining armor who had chosen me to sell his mother's house.

"That's too bad. But don't worry, I have a plan." She popped the sucker in her mouth.

That made me worry, but not as much as Layne's call. I stooped to drop a kiss on her upturned forehead. Her soft skin tasted like Coppertone sunscreen. Smart girl. "Have you seen your brother lately?"

"Sure." She said around the sucker. "He's in back. Why?"

"No reason." I took a step toward the front porch and stopped, then reversed to take a closer look at the items on Addy's table. "Is that my toothbrush next to the phone?"

"Ummm no. It's … uh … one from the cupboard." Addy's pink face matched her sucker.

"Adelynn Renee, I told you after I found that cat whisker on my mascara brush to stop using my stuff on your patients."

"It was an eyebrow, not a whisk—"

"Mom!" Layne burst through the wrought-iron side gate so fast it didn't have time to squeak. His favorite fedora hat and black bow-tie were dusted with dirt crumbs. "You have to come in the backyard now! Hurry!"

Back through the gate he zipped, disappearing behind the house.

I pointed at Addy. "We're not done here, child."

"But Mom—"

I held up the hand of silence and jogged after Layne.

When I rounded the house, the smell of fresh earth and a blast of heat hit me at the same time. Aunt Zoe's backyard had no shade by late afternoon, except for the thin slice angling off the side of her glass-studio workshop. In the far corner, Layne was elbow-deep in a bathtub-sized hole in the ground.

I slowed to a walk, dropping my purse on the grass next to the swing set that had moved with us to Deadwood a few months ago. "Layne, we need to get something straight."

He didn't even look up as I approached.

"An 'emergency' means blood, broken bones, and an immediate trip to the hospit—"

"Look what I found, Mom!" Layne sat back on his heels, one of Aunt Zoe's paint brushes in his hand. His eyes shined so bright they practically glowed.

I did as he commanded, then dropped to my knees next to him on the crispy grass. Or maybe my knees gave out, I wasn't certain. It wasn't every day that I came across a huge, elongated skull in my backyard.

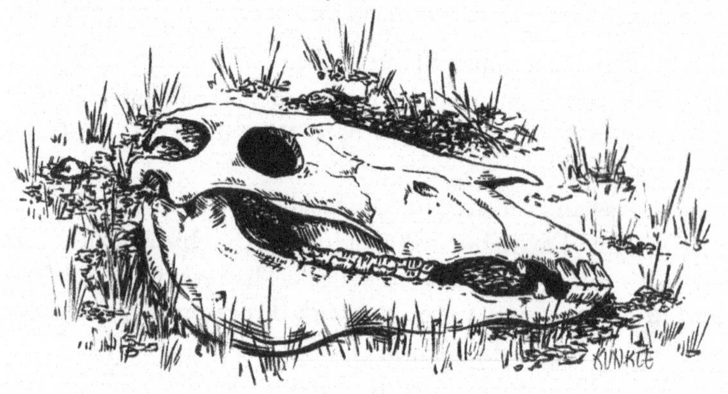

"Isn't it cool?" Layne's voice was higher than usual.

"Yeah." I leaned close, shifting slightly to take weight off my scraped knee. A small hole pierced the frontal lobe of the skull. "Very … uh … cool."

A shadow fell across the skull. "You're home early."

I shielded my eyes. Aunt Zoe, backlit by the sun, had her long, silver-streaked hair tied back with a strip of leather.

"Layne called," I explained. "He's found a skull."

"Do you think it's a dinosaur?" Layne asked as he sat up and wiped sweat from his brow, leaving a stripe of dirt behind.

Aunt Zoe peered at the skull. "Oh, no, honey. That's

just a horse. With that old cemetery up the hill, you'd be surprised what they dig up around this neighborhood."

Aunt Zoe's place sat about fifty yards downhill from Mount Moriah cemetery, the dirt home of Deadwood's famous legends, like Wild Bill and Seth Bullock.

Layne's smile drooped. "Just a horse?"

"Yes, sir." Aunt Zoe crouched next to Layne. "But look—that's a bullet wound. This horse may have been murdered."

"Awesome!" Layne's grin returned twofold and he dove back into the hole.

Aunt Zoe glanced at me over Layne's upturned hiney. "How was your day?"

"Pretty good." My gut clenched at the idea of telling her I was less than three weeks away from getting shit-canned if I didn't sell a house. Aunt Zoe's heart rivaled the size of Mount Rushmore. Not only had she called in an old favor and landed me the job at Calamity Jane Realty, but she'd also opened her house to me and my two children, rearranged her gallery hours so she could be home to babysit, and allowed my kids to dig up her yard and perform toad autopsies on her front porch.

"I'm taking a client to dinner tonight," I added, which was kind of the truth, even if Harvey wasn't officially a client yet. "And I have an appointment to look at a house tomorrow for another client." I preferred to think of that one as a prediction, rather than a lie.

"Congratulations." She squeezed my shoulder, but the slight wrinkling of her brow made me wonder if she could smell my *Eau-de-Rat Parfum*. "Do you need a babysitter tonight?"

"No, I have it covered."

While wooing Harvey might have been easier without the twins, I wasn't going to ask Aunt Zoe to close her gallery this evening.

She stood and wiped her hands on her jean shirt. "Then I think I'll go shower and head to the gallery early."

I wanted to talk to her about the kidnappings, voice my worries aloud, search her face for signs of fear for Addy's safety, find some validation that I wasn't overacting. However, now was not the time, not with Layne's ears this close.

"I have some new pieces to sell. Cross your fingers they're big hits." She headed for the back door.

"I'll keep my toes crossed, too." I called after her. Whatever it took. Aunt Zoe had refused to accept any money from me for rent or utilities. I owed her my firstborn, but since my kids came as a two-for-one deal, she'd settled for letting me buy groceries.

"Are you going to dinner with a man?" Layne asked, staring at me with a narrowed gaze.

"Yep."

"Do you like him?"

"He's kind of nice." When he didn't have a shotgun pointed at my nose.

"Does he like you?"

"I hope so." Enough to sign on the dotted line, anyway.

"Are you going to marry him?"

I grinned. "No, of course not."

"Good, because we don't need a man around here."

I couldn't agree more, but I wanted to hear Layne out. "We don't?"

"All you need is me. I can fix stuff and take care of you."

"I'm sure you can, but don't you get tired of being stuck with three girls?"

He shrugged. "Sometimes, like when you guys are all yelling at me to put the toilet seat down. But it's no big deal."

"I'm glad to hear it." I lifted his hat and kissed him on

top of the head. Even his hair smelled like dirt. "I agree with you—we don't need any other man."

His dimples showing, Layne grabbed his hat and shoved it back on. "So who's babysitting us tonight?"

"Me. You two are coming along to dinner." Old Man Harvey hadn't specified that I had to come alone. Besides, I could use the bodyguards, just in case Harvey really was after my tail.

"Hey, Mom?" Addy called from the side gate.

I looked over my shoulder. "What?"

"There's a man on the phone for you."

"Who is it?"

Addy shrugged. "He says he's replying to your ad."

I hadn't placed any ads, just sent out those postcards. Besides, how would he have gotten Aunt Zoe's number? "What ad?"

"Probably the one that says you need a boyfriend."

* * *

Tuesday, July 10th

"Addy did what?" Mona's nails stopped clacking on her laptop keyboard. Her bronze eye shadow sparkled as she grinned at me.

"She used the money she earned last week giving neighborhood pets a bath to place a singles ad for me. See for yourself." I tossed her the Sunday copy of the *Black Hills Trailblazer.*

Mona slid her rhinestone-studded reading glasses higher on her nose. "Pretty mom looking for a nice man to wash her Bronco and give her the loving she needs. Must like kids and pets."

I slumped into my chair and covered my eyes. "Can you believe her?"

"Well," Mona's attempt to hold in her laughter made her voice vibrate. "Addy's heart is in the right place."

"There were ten messages on the answering machine last night when we returned from dinner. After the first one, I had to shoo the kids upstairs. Nothing but a bunch of perverts detailing the 'loving' they planned to give me. One spent thirty seconds alone on the topic of spanking."

"Give it a week and things will quiet down, especially when you don't return their calls."

"At least Addy didn't include our address."

Unease over the missing girls had made my hands clammy through much of the evening and into the wee hours of the night. By morning, I'd made the decision to educate myself on the two girls, to prove that Addy's commonalities were few.

Nails clacking again, Mona yawned. "Hey, how did dinner go? Did Harvey sign?"

"Dinner, right." My heartburn bubbled at the memory. "Let's see, for the appetizer, Addy dissected her Cornish game hen on the linen napkin."

Silence again issued from Mona's keyboard.

"For the main course, Layne took one bite of his elk burger and spit it back on his plate, declaring to all of Deadwood that it tasted like poop."

Mona's grin was wide. "I've never been a big fan of elk."

"And as a grand finale, Harvey leaned over to pinch the waitress's butt while she was lighting my Cherries Jubilee and his beard caught on fire."

"Is he okay?"

"Just a little singed. You know, that's the first time I've been kicked out of a restaurant."

"Well, at least you have a signed contract now."

"No, I don't."

Mona peeked at me over her glasses as her fingers

returned to work. "Why not?"

"Harvey said he wanted to read it at home where he could let it all sink in."

"So now what?"

"I wait until tonight."

Her pearl-drop earrings jiggled as she shook her head. "Don't tell me."

"Dinner is on him this time."

"He's really milking you on this. Want me to watch the kids?"

"Nope. They're invited, too. We're picnicking at the Dinosaur Park down in Rapid."

My phone rang. A number with a 415 area code greeted me instead of South Dakota's usual 605. Who was calling me from out of state? I picked up the receiver. "Calamity Jane Realty, Violet Parker speaking."

"Hello, Miss Parker. How are you this sunny morning?" Wolfgang Hessler's whiskey-smooth voice brought a smile to my face. He must have been calling from his cell phone.

"I'm wonderful," I bluffed, "and you, Mr. Hessler?"

"Ah, you know my voice. I like that in a relationship—business or personal."

Personal? Dear God, please tell me he didn't get Sunday's paper.

"Are you still interested in showing me your mother's house today?" While the guy's handsome face could make a girl want to put on a little black dress and a coat of red lipstick, I had a one-track mind these days.

"Will you be able to meet me at the house around noon?"

"Of course."

"Splendid. Do you like shrimp?"

Only when it was battered, deep fried, and tasted like chicken, but for a signed contract, I'd eat a fermented egg. Or an elk burger. "Sure, why?"

"Bring your appetite. I'll see you soon, Miss Parker."

He said my name like I was one of those James Bond babes. I hung up and looked at Mona. "Cross your fingers. I have a lunch date with a jeweler."

"You're getting popular," Mona said right as Jane was stepping out of her office.

"Violet's getting popular?" Jane headed for the coffee maker. The fruity floral and vanilla scent of her favorite perfume floated across my radar. "Does that mean you have good news for me?"

Mona and I exchanged winces.

"Not officially," I said, unwilling to admit defeat to the woman who would be signing my commission checks someday.

Jane turned, coffee in hand, and smiled at me. Since the first time I'd met her, her resemblance to the mom on the Partridge Family made me feel like chestnuts were roasting on an open fire.

"Violet, did you see the note on today's To-Do list?" She pointed a manicured pink fingernail at the white board next to the coffee maker.

The picture of professionalism from the tips of her frosted dark blonde hair to the toes of her Manolo shoes, Jane loved lists, whether they were full of to-dos, goals, or pros and cons.

"No, sorry." I'd been a little too distracted by my daughter's latest plan on how to find me a man.

I walked over to the board and grabbed the yellow Post-It next to my name. *Call DR Nyce: 605-555-1971*

"Do either of you know this Doctor Nyce guy?" I asked Mona and Jane.

They shook their heads in tandem.

"Did he say he wanted to buy or sell a house?" *Or buff my Bronco?* Had he read Addy's ad and tracked me down?

"No, just that he wanted you to call him back," Jane

said.

"I bet he got your postcard." Mona winked at me. "That was a great marketing idea, don't you think so, Jane?"

Jane grinned. "Mona, you couldn't be more obvious if you were wearing a blinking neon sign. Violet, please tell me you have at least one signed contract in the works."

"I do. Two of them." Lying was bad, I reminded myself. I held up the Post-It. "Maybe even a third."

"Good. It will make today's lunch more tolerable."

"What's going on at lunch?" I asked, sweat forming in all of my usual nervous spots.

"Ray insisted on taking me out."

Mona closed her laptop with a click. "He's not still trying to get you into bed, is he?"

Jane was in the midst of wrapping up her third nasty divorce. Being the vulture that he was, Ray kept circling, waiting for her to stumble and fall into his arms.

Jane's laugh seemed hollow. "No. He wants to introduce me to his nephew." She perked up at the sound of her phone ringing. "Oh, that's my lawyer."

I watched her stride back into her office, my lungs in lockdown as panic ran amok. Ray's plan to replace me with his nephew was no longer just a mouthful of hot air.

"Vi, honey," Mona's voice sounded like she was talking to me through a double-paned window. "You're turning blue."

I gulped. "I'm so screwed."

"Not necessarily. It's just lunch."

I stared at the phone number on the Post-It. This Doctor Nyce better not be another freak interested in "twiddling with my radio dials." I picked up the receiver and punched in the numbers, counting the rings. After the sixth, I hung up.

Pushing to my feet, I grabbed my purse. "I'm going to head out a little early and take some pictures of area houses

I can use for price comparisons."

"That's my girl."

"If this Doctor Nyce calls back, will you give him my cell number?"

"Sure thing."

"Thanks." I took a deep breath and smiled at Mona. "I'll be back after lunch. If Ray's here, I'm going to stuff my signed contract down his goddamned throat."

Chapter Four

I gaped at the Hessler house.

Like many of the other houses in the historic Presidential neighborhood in Deadwood, the place was a nineteenth-century Victorian with a multi-gabled roof and two-plus stories. However, unlike the surrounding houses, it suffered from loneliness—evident by the peeling paint, missing roof shingles, and rusting front gate. It was going to take some serious nursing to remove the Norman Bates curb appeal.

My right eye began to twitch.

The front gate's hinges screamed at me as I opened it. Scraggly patches of shin-high grass drooped over the walkway, snagging at my nylons. The paint-starved floor boards groaned underfoot when I climbed the steps onto the veranda-style porch.

No doorbell to be found, I pulled open the wooden, gingerbread-style screen door and yelped when the whole thing broke off its rusty hinges. If I were a believer in omens, this one would be up there with croaking crows and howling hounds. Now all I needed was a black cat.

I laid the screen against the wall, wiped my hands on my soft suede skirt, and knocked on the front door.

Thunder boomed, low and distant. I peeked around the porch's roof. Cumulus clouds billowed in the western sky. The hills were thirsty, but in a land littered with dry tinder, lightning kindled nightmares.

Footfalls thumped toward me from inside the house. I turned to the door as it swung wide.

"Miss Parker, welcome to my humble abode." Wolfgang's smile could have charmed the stockings off a preacher's wife. Lucky for me, my pantyhose were control-top.

I tried to crack a grin in return, but my cheeks would have none of it. Denial was a defense mechanism on which I couldn't waste time. I had to accept fact—there was no way in hell I could flip this house in three weeks. "Hi," I said around the sob swelling in my throat.

"Are you okay?" Wolfgang asked.

His question snapped me out of my poor-me party. The last thing I needed was to bawl all over a potential client.

"Yes, but I broke your screen door."

He shrugged off my admission. "I'm just glad the whole house hasn't fallen down yet."

Oddly enough, his words weren't exactly the wind beneath my wings—more like a baseball bat to my knees.

He stepped back so I could slip by him. Which I did, in spite of an urge to run back to my Bronco, race to the Candy Corral, and bury my head in a vat of dark chocolate.

Musty with stale varnish and dust bunnies, the vestibule's warmth made it hard to breathe. Or maybe it was just grim reality tightening its choke hold, I couldn't be sure.

Wolfgang closed the door behind me, throwing us into shadow. "Let's start with lunch. Then I'll drag you through the rest of the house."

I'd be kicking and screaming the whole way if the inside was as bad as the outside.

He slid open a set of rolling doors to my left, and shafts of light beckoned. I followed after him, my heels echoing on the mosaic tiles.

We crossed a formal sitting room with a hardwood floor. Sheets covered everything, filling the room with ghosts of all shapes and sizes. The walls might have been green or tan—the drawn blinds made it tough to tell. A rolled-up rug lay along one wall, in front of a boarded-up fireplace. The hippo sitting on my chest shifted at the sight of an ornate marble mantel.

Through another set of rolling doors was a dining room, the table and chairs also under wraps. A chandelier trimmed with spider webs hung cockeyed. To my right, a narrow door blended in with the wainscoting. The air smelled fresher in here. The light was brighter, too, thanks to a pair of French doors to my left. The end of the tunnel drew near.

"Here we are." Wolfgang opened the French doors.

I stepped into a screened-in breakfast nook. Shafts of sunlight splayed across the floral-covered bench seat lining the southern wall. A small round table held a bowl overflowing with salad, shrimp, orange slices, and croûtons. Lemon wedges filled a saucer next to it, and two empty salad plates accompanied by silverware sat across from each other.

"Make yourself comfortable." Wolfgang pulled out a white wicker chair for me. "I'll be right back with something to drink." He disappeared through the French doors and I heard the creak of another door opening.

I dropped my purse on the bench seat, then grimaced at the dust that poofed up. The chair looked rickety, but was sturdy as I lowered into it.

Outside the screened windows, a battered cedar fence imprisoned the backyard. Waves of dry grass bristled in the slight breeze. A gnarled oak filled the southeastern corner, the remains of a swing dangling from one of its limbs. The rusty skeleton of a trellis leaned at a 45-degree angle over a stone bench. Next to the detached garage, a blood-red water pump and handle protruded up through the weeds.

Sighing, I shoved a loose curl behind my ear. It was a regular Eden back there, the broken concrete birdbath a fitting centerpiece.

The ceiling creaked overhead, as if someone was walking around upstairs. I looked up, expecting paint chips to sprinkle onto my face, happy to be disappointed for once.

"Choose your poison." Wolfgang's voice tore through me with a jolt. My chair grunted from my sudden shift. How had he gotten back downstairs so lickety-split?

"Lemonade or beer?" He held a glass and a bottle out toward me.

"Beer, please." Lemonade wasn't going to cut it today.

He placed a sweaty bottle of Black Hills Nugget in front of me. After dishing up some salad for both of us, he joined me at the table. "Well, what do you think?"

"Ummm, it's …" I tried to choose my adjectives carefully.

"A mess?" His grin reached the corners of his eyes. "A rattrap? A sty?"

"Yes, but I mean that in a good way."

He laughed, the tone warm, friendly. My shoulders sagged in relief, and I suddenly realized how hungry I was. I dug into my salad in spite of the shrimp and practically purred over the tangy vinaigrette dressing.

Small talk about Deadwood filled the time as forks flew and croûtons crunched. I swallowed the last of my beer, ready to press on and see what other surprises the house held.

The kitchen revealed two secrets upon entry. The first, the delicious lunch had been take-out. The second, Wolfgang's mother had loved clowns. From the clown-popping-out-of-a-barrel cookie jar to the clowns-pouring-out-of-cars wallpaper, the room crawled with painted faces with cavernous, sinister smiles. Had I walked into the room on a stormy night with a lit candle in hand, I would have peed my pants.

The clown theme continued throughout the downstairs as Wolfgang tore off dustcovers and exposed decorative plates and paintings, stacks of clown-covered magazines, and pieces of clown-themed ceramics. Good thing furniture didn't come in clown.

The second floor consisted of four rooms—three similar-sized bedrooms and a bath. Luckily, the clowns didn't follow us up. Two of the bedrooms had flowery themes, one pink roses, the other purple violets. While the wallpaper had faded and the furniture veneer had dulled, the rooms were almost pretty.

In the rose room, after a quick peek in the empty closet, I noticed a framed black-and-white photo of a young blonde girl in frilly clothes sitting next to the bed. I picked it up, reminded of the missing girls' posters for a gut-twinging moment. I looked up to find Wolfgang's gaze on me, his eyebrows arched. Silence stretched like taffy. I held up the frame. "Is this your sister?"

"Actually, that's me. My mother had a penchant for lace."

"Oh." My neck warmed. I removed my foot from my mouth and tried to skip over my blunder. "Sorry. I just assumed you had a sister."

"I do."

"Does she live close by?"

"No. She died shortly after that picture was taken."

I placed the picture back on the stand. "I'm sorry," I apologized again, wondering at his choice of verb tense.

"Mother never quite got over Wilda's death. She'd always had a fondness for girls."

Unsure whether I should sympathize with a touch or frown or words, I stood there staring at the lines wrinkling his brow.

He brushed his hands together. "Shall we move on?"

I led the way out. The third bedroom had hunter green

paint on the walls, with horses and groomsmen on a strip of wallpaper trim. This room must be Wolfgang's, but the dust layer on the embroidered duvet looked like it hadn't seen the south side of a derrière in years.

"You're not staying here, Mr. Hessler?"

"Oh, no," he said with a grimace. "I have a room at the Buffalo Ranch."

The Buffalo Ranch was a not-so-cheap resort outside of Deadwood's city limits. I'd only been in the lobby once, and I hadn't dared to touch anything.

Like the rest of the house, the bathroom needed some remodeling to catch it up to the twentieth century, let alone present day. At least the porcelain shined and the plumbing worked—with a groan from the old pipes. A rust-stained sink advertised a leaky faucet.

"Is there a basement?"

"Yes, but it's overflowing with mother's boxes and trunks."

And clowns, I'd bet. "Is the garage usable?"

He nodded. "Although the door creaks. It's on its way out."

We tromped back downstairs and onto the front porch.

Thunder rumbled, this time loud and close. Dark, threatening clouds blocked the sun. I hadn't noticed the change in lighting in the shut-up house, too lost in my world of "what-ifs" and "oh, shits."

"What do you think, Miss Parker? Can you sell it?"

Sure, but not in three weeks, and therein lay my problem. Unmarketable, "as-is" houses sold quickly in a seller's market; but Deadwood was mired in the buyers' pockets right now.

However, with a little—okay, a lot—of elbow grease, this place had the potential to be a big-ticket sale. Maybe I could convince Jane to keep me on longer with the promise of a high commission. Or even all of my commission.

What the hell. I had nothing to lose. "Yes, I can sell it, but under one condition."

"Name it."

"You sign the listing agreement today." If I was going to put sweat equity into this house, Ray wasn't going to steal it out from under me.

"Deal." He held out his hand to seal it. "But only if you start calling me Wolfgang. 'Mr. Hessler' was my grandfather."

"Okay, Wolfgang." I clasped his hand and squeezed. "No more Miss Parker, either."

"Violet, it is." He squeezed back and gave me another one of his de-pantser smiles. "Has anyone ever told you that you have beautiful hair?"

* * *

The black Camaro SS with rally stripes had stolen my spot again. Two blocks later, my windshield splattered with fat raindrops, I found a parking spot. Halfway to the office, the clouds split open with a loud crack and dumped buckets of icy cold water over my head. I swam through Calamity Jane's front door, my pink silk blazer soaked, my hair a drippy mess. The place smelled like permanent ink and jasmine, a lovely bouquet.

"Oh, good, you're back," Mona said as she capped the marker she'd been using to write on the whiteboard.

"Do you know who owns the black Camaro that keeps stealing my spot?" I strongly suspected it was one of Ray's buddies.

"No." Mona handed me a tissue. "Your face is running."

I wiped away the rain and half of my makeup.

"You missed some." She placed another tissue on my

desk. "Did your Ken doll sign a contract?"

"Yep." I pulled out the comb holding the remains of my French knot in place and shook out my waterlogged curls. The peachy scent of my shampoo surrounded me.

"Congratulations!"

"Don't buy any party poppers just yet."

"What do you mean?"

"Wolfgang's house is a mess. I'm not sure I'll be able to have it ready to show within three weeks, let alone find a buyer."

"Damn."

I grabbed the Yellow Pages and scooted up to my desk. "Do you know the name of any good contractors?"

Twenty minutes later, I'd found plenty of contractors, just no available ones. Deadwood winters were often harsh and snow-filled, so summer was the busy season for building, remodeling, and anything else that required a hammer and nails. Same went for gardeners, too, as it turned out.

My hair frazzling more by the minute, I gave up on the outside of the house and focused on the groaning pipes and leaky upstairs faucet. The soonest I could get a warm body lined up was two weeks from now. I booked the plumber and called the cleaning company we used when preparing for a showing.

"Margo, it's Violet from Calamity Jane's. I'm in need of your magic touch."

"You're out of luck," Margo said.

"Can't you spare even a day?" I'd take any crumbs.

"Sorry. The biker-week rush started early this year. We're booked solid through the end of August."

I hung up, rubbing my eyes. My fingers came away with black smears from my cheap eyeliner—the waterproof stuff was too pricey for my budget these days.

"Mona, do you know any other cleaners?"

"Let me make a call."

I pulled out my compact as she dialed and grimaced at the face staring back at me. The clowns at Wolfgang's house weren't as scary.

My cell phone trilled. I dug it out of my purse. Aunt Zoe's number showed on the screen. "Hello?"

"Mom, can I bring a friend tonight?" Addy asked, her breath quick and shallow, her voice an octave higher than usual.

"Sure." The more the merrier, as far as I was concerned. I was happy to hear Addy was making friends. "Is it one of the neighbor girls?"

"No, I met her at the pool today."

Deadwood had a Rec Center just down the hill from Aunt Zoe's house. It had been there since long before I'd splashed around in the pool during my childhood summer visits to Aunt Zoe's. These days, my kids liked to hang out there when they weren't hiking through the graves at Mount Moriah or peddling their bikes around Deadwood.

"I look forward to meeting her."

"Thanks, Mom. Kelly's been really sad since her best friend disappeared last summer. I thought it might be fun for her to see the dinosaurs with us."

I raked my fingers through my hair, trying to make it look less Tina Turner-like. "Disappeared? You mean moved away?"

"No. She went missing and they never found her."

My fingers froze, goosebumps spreading up my arms. "If you're joking, Adelynn Renee, that's not funny."

"That's what she told me, Mom, I swear." There was a loud crash on the other end of the line that left my ear ringing.

"What was that?"

"Layne! Stop it right now or I'm telling Mom!"

"What's he doing?"

"Gotta go, Mom. Bye." Addy hung up on me.

I sighed and closed my phone and tossed it on my desk. Addy's comments about her new friend left an acidic taste in my mouth. Disappeared last summer? Addy must be confused. The first girl went missing this past winter—January, if I remembered right.

"Thanks, anyway," Mona said into her receiver and hung up. She gave me a lopsided grin. "Sorry, Vi, but every cleaner I know is too busy to take on another job right now."

Everyone in Deadwood but me was making money. I guess if this realty gig didn't fly, I could always clean houses. Rather than stomp around and cry about it, I changed the subject. "Addy just said the oddest thing."

Mona stuffed her laptop in her briefcase. "What?"

"That a girl went missing last summer."

Frowning, Mona grabbed her rain slicker from the office coat tree. "Was that a year ago already? Man, time flies faster the older I get."

My stomach churned. "So, three little girls have disappeared from Deadwood in the last year?"

"Well, technically, this last one was from Lead, not Deadwood."

Lead. Deadwood. The same thing. The two towns sat so close together they were practically Siamese twins. "What month did the first girl go missing?"

"It was last August, I think." Mona slipped her arms into her jacket. "I can't believe you haven't heard about it. Where have you been, Vi?"

In Russia, of course, leading the glitzy other half of my double life as a world-class spy. "I've been a little busy lately, thank you very much. Just explain, please."

"The reason Ray got so pissed about the Missing Girl sign is because this third incident has rumors flying all over town that Deadwood has its very own serial snatcher."

"Oh, Jesus." I wrung my clammy palms together. What had I done, moving my kids here? Life down on the prairie had been filled with ruts over the last few years—especially deep ones when it came to my crappy-ass job and lack of satisfying love life, but long unpaid hours at work and a slew of really rotten blind dates didn't put my daughter's life at risk.

"Talk about bad publicity," Mona said. "This town doesn't need this kind of problem. Deadwood's history has been bloody enough."

"Do the cops have any suspects?"

"None so far." Mona grabbed her keys. "I gotta go. I have an appointment down in Rapid this afternoon. Jane and Ray haven't come back from lunch yet, so you're on your own."

Good. I could use some alone time to shake off the heebie-jeebies.

Mona headed past Jane's office toward the back door. "Good luck tonight, Vi." The back door slammed shut behind her.

Why hadn't Aunt Zoe told me two girls had gone missing in the last year before I relocated my children into a kidnapper's lair? I chewed on a pencil, brooding. Would it have mattered?

My need for change had been cracking the whip hard, pushing me into taking risks I'd have run from in the past. Working for over a decade at the car dealership had been draining me dry, and after being groped for the final time by the drunken owner at last year's summer barbecue, I'd given my two weeks' notice, applied to realty school, and moved in with my parents to save up my money.

Aunt Zoe's invitation to try life in the hills with her had been my gift upon finishing with school. I hadn't even hesitated before yelling, "Yes, yes!" and crushing her in a hug. Since I was a kid, Deadwood had held memories of sunshine and fun. I didn't want to let some monster steal that away from me. I'd worked too hard to make it here.

In the remaining silence, I could hear rain pounding overhead. Gloom penetrated the office, shrouding me in doubts about my ability to provide a safe haven for my kids.

My cell phone rang again. It was my boss. "Hi, Jane."

"How did it go? Did Hessler sign?"

"Yes." No lies this time.

"Good. Now you just need to find a buyer."

I heard what sounded like Ray's usual guffaw in the background and wanted to reach through the line and clock him.

"Listen, Ray and I won't be back in today, so I need you to close up the office."

"Sure."

"And will you do me a quick favor? Go into my office and read me the number that's on the Post-It next to my phone?"

Her office fluorescents flickered and hummed overhead. The Post-It note was stuck to a *July Goals* printout. I read the phone number to Jane and she hung up with a "Thanks."

As I started to turn away from her desk, I saw Ray's nephew's name, Benjamin Underhill, on a folder that was partially buried under the Goals printout.

It took just a second for curiosity to win the arm-wrestling match against ethics. I pulled the folder out and flipped it open. An 8-by-10 color picture of a younger version of my favorite asshole looked up at me, his eyes icy blue, just like his uncle's. Benjamin's smile was identical to Ray's, down to the last chemically whitened tooth. I glared at the Sharpie in Jane's pencil holder and fought the temptation to blacken a few of Ben's choppers.

His resume followed his picture. I scanned his credentials, sagging against Jane's desk as each one reduced my own qualifications to a burger-flipping level. The next page was a recommendation from a realty broker in Rapid City. Words like "highly organized," "go-getter," and "extremely intelligent" filled the gold-embossed paper.

Snapping the folder shut, I wanted to crawl under Jane's desk and nurse my bruised ego back to health with a bottle of Southern Comfort.

"Hello?" A male voice echoed through the empty office.

I nearly dropped the folder in surprise. "Be right with you." I slipped the folder back in its place.

Straightening my damp camisole, I forced my cheeks into a smile and stepped out into the front room. "How can I …"

Our new neighbor, the cleft-chinned Wild Bill groupie, stood pasted against the wall next to the To-Do whiteboard. His gaze was locked on the coffee maker, his lips pressed tight, his rugged face visibly pale. I glanced at the coffee maker, looking for a mouse or a rat or a flying-purple-people-eater. Something other than just a glass decanter half-filled with brown liquid.

"Are you okay?"

His dark eyes flicked my way. "I will be in a second."

"Can I help you … somehow?"

"I just need to catch my breath."

Funny, he didn't seem winded.

As the seconds ticked by, his cheeks regained some color. "I'm Doc Nyce, by the way."

Nyce? How did I know that name?

"I left you a message earlier this morning."

"You're Doctor Nyce?" Judging by his jeans and faded black T-shirt, I wouldn't have guessed that M.D. followed his name.

"Yes, but I'm not a doctor."

Puzzled, I crossed my arms. "Then why do you go by

doctor?"

"I don't. I go by 'Doc.' My name is Dane, but my initials are 'D.R.' Nyce."

Well, there were ten seconds of my life that I'd never get back. I indicated to the chair across from my desk. "Do you want to have a seat, *Doc*?"

"I'll just stand here, if you don't mind."

"Okay." I hesitated, uncertain if I should follow his lead or sit.

"You have something on your …" He circled his face with his open palm.

Shit! I'd forgotten about my clown makeup. My cheeks burned so hot that my ears sent up smoke signals. I grabbed another tissue and swiped at my eyes. "Is that better?"

He winced. "Not really."

I gave up and sat. "What can I do for you, Mr. Nyce?"

"I want to buy a house."

A buyer? Holy crap. I tried not to drool as I smiled. "Do you have a house in mind?"

"No." His gaze whipped back to the coffee maker, his nostrils flaring.

"An area then?"

"Close to Deadwood." He sniffed, twice.

"How close?" Was the coffee burning? I sniffed, too. Nope. "Like a five-mile radius?"

"Sure."

Wolfgang's house came to mind, but it wouldn't be ready to show for a few weeks, if that. I opened my notebook containing our current listings and scanned for Deadwood addresses. "How many bedrooms are you interested in?"

"I'm easy."

"How many baths?"

"Two." His voice sounded further away. I looked up to find him pressing against the front door, his focus now on

Mona's desk. What in the hell?

I sat back and scratched my neck. "Are you sure you're feeling okay?"

"I'm just a little nauseated."

He was making me just a little nervous. "Would you like a glass of water?"

"No. Fresh air will help." His body tensed visibly, his face creasing for a blink of time. "Can we look at some houses tomorrow?"

"Sure. Morning or afternoon?"

He shoved open the door and practically fell outside. "Afternoon," he hollered in at me.

I stood up, unsure if I should follow him out. "You want to meet me here at twelve-thirty, then?"

"No. You come to my office instead."

"All right. Then I'll see y—" He was gone before I could finish. I dropped into my seat, feeling like a hit-and-run victim.

A pounding on the front plate glass made me jump out of my chair. Mr. Nyce waved at me and slid an envelope through the brass mail slot in our door. He disappeared around the corner again before I had time to frown.

Heart pounding, I picked up the envelope and tore it open. Inside was a piece of paper and a hundred-dollar bill. I fished out the paper: *Sorry about your pants—Doc Nyce.*

In spite of the whole Marx Brothers routine with Mr. Dane 'Doc' Nyce, I grinned. I had a buyer.

Now I needed a house that wasn't on the brink of being condemned.

Chapter Five

Wednesday, July 11th

Jane once told me she believed that blinds were bad for business. Which meant squinting was my only solution for the mid-morning sunshine ricocheting off the SUV parked in front of Calamity Jane's.

I sat hunched at my computer. I should have been combing the Internet for a cleaner or a contractor within a fifty-mile radius. Instead, I was hunting with little success for crumbs on the first girl who'd disappeared last summer. A trip to the library might be in order soon.

At the next desk over, Ray polished his Tony Lama boots while chatting with his nephew on the speaker phone. The smell of stinky feet and leather had my stomach bucking.

"You have nothing to worry about, Ben," Ray told his nephew. "I could tell Jane liked you by the way she drilled you on that condo project going up in Sturgis."

I tried to breathe through my anger in spite of its strangle hold on my windpipe. An hour ago, Ray had danced into Calamity Jane's with a victory smile so wide it looked as if someone had stuffed a banana in his mouth sideways.

"I hope you're right," Ben's husky voice crackled slightly as it came through the speaker phone. "I forgot to tell you, the owner of Moonbeam Lodge is almost ready to sign with me, but he'd prefer I was backed by a broker."

"Tell your seller you'll have a broker in three weeks."

Ray snickered while slipping on a boot. "There is definitely nothing happening in Blondie's ballpark."

"She might hit a home run in the last inning."

Ray's laughter echoed off the plaster-covered walls. "The Queen of Strike outs? No way."

My molars grinding, I glared at Ray.

He blew me a kiss.

I flipped him off.

It was one of those warm, fuzzy moments they wrote about on Hallmark cards.

"Listen, Ben," Ray tugged his other boot on. "I have to go show a place. I'll see you tonight at the poker game." He disconnected the call and spun my way. "Was that an invitation, Sweetheart? You interested in putting our differences to bed?"

I aimed a second bird his way.

The front door whooshed open.

I jammed my hands under my desk.

"You two sharing your love for each other again?" Natalie Beals asked, placing an iced latte on my desk.

I smiled at my best-friend-since-childhood. Natalie's cousins, the Morgans, were my next-door neighbors while growing up down in Rapid City. Her cousin, Claire, had introduced us while playing kick ball, and the rest was history.

Ray made a gargling sound in his throat—his version of a tiger growl usually reserved for Mona on her tight-sweater days. His gaze slithered up Natalie's body before settling on her full lips, a focal point for most testosterone-driven suckers. "I wouldn't mind sharing some love with you, Cupcake."

"Give it up, Ray." Natalie sank into the seat across from me. "There isn't enough alcohol in town to make you look good."

Ray's face darkened under his fake tan. He wrinkled his

upper lip at Natalie and then sneered at me. "Two-and-a-half weeks and counting, Blondie."

He left grinning.

If I'd had a bow and arrow, he would have left limping.

I groaned and leaned back in my chair. "I'm so screwed."

Natalie nudged the sweating coffee toward me. "Have a hit of caffeine. It will make it all better."

I took a drink. Icy sweet. "Yum, caramel. I owe you one."

"No, you owe me five." Natalie stretched out her long, bronzed legs and crossed them at the ankles. Her cutoff jean shorts, tennis shoes, and dirt-smudged tank top were typical for a pavement-sizzling summer day. "I got your message. How can I help?"

There were five people I could lean on when life kept smacking me with a flyswatter. There was Aunt Zoe, but she had already done too much; and Quint, my older brother, but he was somewhere in the Great White North taking pictures of polar bears and snow; and my parents, who were vacationing in Maine until the end of the month. That left Natalie, the sister that my real sister was too busy to be.

"I have a house to flip." I took another swig of caffeinated courage before diving into my request. "But it needs some serious work. The kind involving the tools that you carry around in the back of your pickup."

Natalie spent most of the year playing caretaker at a popular resort just south of town.

I leaned forward. "I've called every contractor and handyman in the area. Only one guy could fit me in, but I would've had to sell some naked pictures to *Playboy* to afford him, and I know how you feel about your privacy."

She grinned. "How long do you think this will take?"

"A couple of weeks." Or more. I crossed my toes since

she could see my fingers. "I'll give you half of my half of the commission."

Natalie stroked her chin. "Forget the money. Make it one favor owed—no questions asked."

"Deal."

"When do I start? This afternoon?"

"Sure, but aren't you going out with Mr. Clean tonight?" Natalie's current boyfriend was draped with muscles, had a shaved head and a hoop earring.

"No. Mr. Clean cheated on me with some face-pierced whore with a tramp stamp."

I grimaced. "I'm sorry."

"Don't be. He was just another in the long line of losers I keep winding up without. I swear to you, he's the last one. I'm taking a year sabbatical from men."

"Me, too."

"No, your year is over."

The absolute tone in her statement made me blink. "What do you mean?"

"I found the perfect guy for you."

"You mean he likes poor, desperate, chubby mothers who mooch off their friends and families?"

"You're not chubby."

"Okay, flabby."

"Either put up the cash for a tummy tuck or shush up." Natalie's grin took the sting out of her words. "Anyway, you'll love him. He collects Star Trek stuff."

Ever since I wore pigtails on a daily basis, I'd had a crush on James Tiberius Kirk. Natalie had always confused my adoration for Captain Hottie for an all-things-Trekkie passion. Big difference.

I shook my head. "No blind dates. You know what happened last time."

"How was I to know he had that open sore?"

Just the memory of it made me want to scald my hands

clean. "Nat, you know I'm not interested in a relationship right now."

"Who cares about relationships? I'm talking sex here. You need something to take the edge off."

"That's what yoga is for." Not that I did that anymore. Lately, my morning sun-salute ritual involved a middle finger and several curse words as I fumbled for my sunglasses.

"Yoga is for a different set of muscles."

"Why are you pushing me on this?"

"I want you to stick around town."

"You think me going out with this guy will accomplish that?"

"No, but helping you find the *one* will. We have to start somewhere."

She didn't get that there was no "one" in my life, only "two," and they didn't leave me much time for sex. "No. Absolutely not."

"You owe me a favor, remember."

I could tell by the firm set of her lips that I'd have better luck stapling pudding to a wall than winning this battle. "Fine. Give the guy my cell number and have him call me."

"I will, but I think he's leaving soon for some comic book convention, or something along those lines, so don't expect him to call right away."

Never would be too soon. I sucked down the last of my latte.

"How did your date with Old Man Harvey go last night?" Natalie asked.

"It wasn't a date, just a picnic."

"Did he try anything funny?"

"No, not with three kids present."

In spite of the biting flies and the sweltering heat rolling off the prairie, everything had gone well—except for the "dinner once a week until the ranch sells" clause Harvey had insisted upon adding before signing the contract.

"What do you mean three kids? Did you pop out another since I saw you last weekend?"

"Addy brought her new friend, Kelly."

"Kelly who?"

"Kelly Wymonds. Addy met her at the pool." I frowned at Natalie. "What's with the silly grin on your face?"

"I dated Kelly's dad in high school. He couldn't focus on anything besides football, even while we were naked in his back seat."

Natalie had been born and raised in Deadwood. She read through the local white pages like it was the *National Enquirer*.

"Exactly how many guys have you slept with?"

She grinned. "Deadwood is a small town. A girl gets bored."

Another reason for me to send Addy off to a convent—that and the serial snatcher roaming Deadwood's streets. Which reminded me … "Kelly Wymonds' best friend was the girl who disappeared last summer," I told Natalie.

Her eyes locked onto mine, all traces of humor gone. "Did Kelly talk about it at the picnic?"

"No." Which surprised me. I guess I'd expected Kelly to spill bits of information about the kidnapping in a juicy, more-at-eleven, news-trailer format. "I didn't ask. But last night, while the twins were getting ready for bed, Addy told me that Kelly talks about her missing friend a lot."

"Even after all this time, huh? That's sad."

I nodded, remembering Addy's solemn voice as she frowned up at me from her pink pillowcase and prodded me for more information on the kidnappings than I wanted to spill. I had no problem talking to my kids about life's grim realities, but this was nightmare fodder.

I massaged the back of my neck where tension lingered,

tightening. "Kelly told Addy that she and her friend, Emma, had been out riding bikes when the girl disappeared. They'd stopped at the Piggly Wiggly for milk and baby food for Kelly's little brother. Emma stayed outside to watch the bikes. When Kelly came out of the store, the bikes were still there, but her friend was gone. That was the last time anyone saw Emma."

Natalie shuddered visibly. "Jesus, that's creepy."

"Makes me not want to allow the kids to ride their bikes around town anymore."

"Understandable, but they'd be miserable stuck at home."

She was right. As much as I wanted to lock my twins in the house and not let them answer the door, I had to show some trust in their judgment when it came to strangers.

"Kelly said Addy reminds her of the missing girl. Do you think Kelly's parents took her to a counselor after the whole thing happened?"

"Who knows? Kelly's dad works for the county on the road crew. He's not the most sensitive guy. His brains got rattled a few too many times back on the football field."

"After what Addy told me last night, I wanted to nix any future friendship with Kelly, but I can't do that. Addy will just say I'm out to ruin her life—again."

"Maybe Kelly just likes to talk about this," Natalie said. "You know, an attention-getter now that she has a baby brother."

"She didn't come across as needy, more melancholy." The little waif seemed to have a black cloud behind her eyes the whole time she and Addy had clambered around the huge dinosaurs. "I sure hope Addy has the sense to back away if Kelly gets weird."

Natalie patted my hand. "You never had that sense when it came to me."

"Yeah, but you started out weird."

A shadow blocked the glare glinting off the SUV. I peeked over Natalie's shoulder.

Doc Nyce beckoned me through the plate-glass window.

The sight of his ruffled black hair and long legs made me do a double-take.

I made eye contact.

He pointed at his watch, then held up his index finger.

I gave him a thumbs-up.

Doc's gaze dropped to Natalie, and I realized she had turned and was waving at him. He gave her a nod, then me, before exiting stage left.

Natalie whirled back to me. "Who was *that*?"

"Doc Nyce."

"He's gorgeous. Is he an OB-GYN?"

I wrinkled my nose. "You're positively ill, Nat."

"You're right, I should see a doctor. Do you think Doc Nyce is available?"

"He's not a doctor."

Obviously ignoring me, she glanced back at the window. "How do you know him?"

"He's my client. We're going house-hunting this afternoon."

"Lucky you! So Doc's sticking around town, then?"

I could see where this was leading. "You're on sabbatical, remember?"

"Damn it. That's right." Natalie stood. "What time am I picking you up later?"

"Five-thirty. The kids are coming, too." I had no choice. Babysitters didn't exactly grow on pine trees.

"Okay." Natalie backed toward the door, her dimples showing. "Give Doc Nyce a 'Welcome' kiss for me."

"Not on your life." Although my mind veered to Doc's mouth, pondering. What would it be like to grab him by the ears and taste-test?

I shook the thought from my head. I had a handful of principles, and one in particular had something to do with not mixing work with play. Besides, his actions yesterday were just not normal, no matter how I tried to spin it.

With a wave, Natalie stepped out into the sunshine, leaving me alone with a ticking clock.

* * *

A minute before my appointment with Doc, I stuffed the listings I'd printed into my tote and headed for the front door. My cell phone trilled as I stepped out into the afternoon heat.

Aunt Zoe's phone number showed on my screen. "Hello?"

"Mom," Layne sounded winded. "Will you pick up some ammonia on your way home tonight?"

I stopped just short of Doc's door. "What do you need ammonia for?"

"For boiling the skull, of course." He said it as if we boiled skulls for supper every night. "Do we have any peroxide?"

I covered my eyes with my free hand. "You're going to cook the skull in ammonia and peroxide? I don't think that's safe, Layne."

"No, Mother." His tone held a nonverbal "duh." "The peroxide is for bleaching."

Something meowed in the background. Aunt Zoe didn't own a cat. "Was that a cat, Layne?"

"Gotta go, Mom. Don't forget the ammonia."

I swore under my breath as I snapped my phone shut. I sure hoped Aunt Zoe had fire insurance.

Shaking off Layne's phone call, I pushed open the door to Doc's office and noticed he had company.

A shirtless man with curly gray hair smiled at me from his perch on the edge of Doc's desk. Behind him, Doc peered at his bare back with a magnifying glass.

"Sorry." My cheeks lightly toasted, I turned my back, pretended to stare out the window, and tried to find something to do with my hands. It's not like I hadn't seen a bare-chested man before. Hell, I ogled the tanned torsos of road construction crews along with every other sex-starved female south of the Arctic Circle. I just hadn't expected to come across so much exposed flesh and chest hair in Doc's office at one o'clock on a Wednesday.

"I'm pretty sure it's just a mole," Doc's baritone voice sounded extra loud in my fidgety brain.

"Thanks, Doc."

I heard a pair of boots hit the wood floor. I turned my head just a bit and peeked at the two men.

The older guy slid his plaid shirt back on and picked up a book from the chair opposite Doc's desk. "I'll see you next week."

I tried to read the name of the book as he nodded at me on his way out the door, but his hand covered the title.

As soon as the door closed behind Doc's visitor, I whirled around. "I thought you weren't a doctor."

"I'm not. He was confused."

So was I. "But he's coming back next week?"

"He needs my help." Doc grabbed some keys from his top drawer. "Ready to go?"

I nodded, but didn't budge when he held open the door for me. "Who are you really, Mr. Nyce?"

"I'm just a man trying to buy a house, Ms. Parker."

I may not have dated since acid-wash jeans were in style, but I knew a brushoff when I heard one. With a mental sigh, I crossed the threshold. "I'll drive."

Two hours and two houses later, we bounced along a steep hillside street in Deadwood's northern Forest Hill neighborhood. My knuckles were white as I clenched the steering wheel, but not due to the steep dropoff on my left.

There was definitely something odd about Doc. Something that made my sweat cold in spite of the hot gusts swirling through the gulch this afternoon. I'd been analyzing it since we toured the first house and I'd caught him sniffing in an upstairs closet. Not sniffing coke or Elmer's glue, just sniffing.

I'd kept my mouth shut. After all, I had been standing alone in an empty house with a man whose forearms alone looked muscled enough to snap my neck like it was dried spaghetti.

He sniffed every room, every corner, every nook and cranny, everywhere. He was like some human version of a bloodhound. I'd half-expected him to turn around and sniff me at some point.

After inhaling his way through the house, he'd declared that he would pass on the place. When I pressed, he shrugged and just said, "Too big."

A thorough sniffing of the second house inspired a "too small" from him.

Now, as I parked the Bronco in front of the last house I'd opted to show him today, I could tell by the vertical wrinkles lining his forehead that he was already thinking up another enlightening two-word reason why he didn't like this home.

"How old is this one?" he asked while tailing me up the sidewalk to the front door.

I checked the listing paperwork. "Early 1900s." I punched in the code to unlock the lockbox and pulled out the key, expecting him to tell me to forget it, but he didn't. I held the door for him to enter.

"You first," he said and waited for me to lead.

This was the third time he'd insisted I enter a house before him. I couldn't figure out if he was being a gentleman or if this was another of his strange tics.

I stepped inside a well-lit foyer, lined with hardwood flooring. Stained-glass windows in the interior walls shed pink and blue-tinged light into a wide hall from rooms to the left and right. Arched thresholds to adjoining rooms added to the open feel, and a staircase anchored the opposite end.

I beat him to the first sniff. Pine-sol and Lemon Pledge filled the air.

Doc inhaled and grunted.

I couldn't tell if it was a good grunt or bad grunt, being that I was rusty on my Caveman vernacular.

He tapped one of the stained-glass windows. "I like this."

I coughed in surprise.

We sniffed our way through a carpeted living room with sage-colored walls to the kitchen. Stainless steel appliances, glass-paned cabinets, and can lighting gave a modern but cozy feel to the room. Whoever had had this place before put some money into it.

While the dining room was small, French doors leading to a well-manicured backyard encased by a split-rail fence gave a false impression of more space.

The downstairs bathroom had a polished granite sink top, a black toilet, a heated stone floor, and a mosaic of the sun tiled into the shower wall.

I paused at the base of the stairs. "You want to continue?"

"Sure." He smiled for the first time since we'd left his office. The transformation made me do a double-take.

There were three rooms upstairs—an office, a small bathroom with a shower instead of a tub, and a master bedroom. I stood inside the doorway of the latter, waiting for Doc to finish his inhalation of the bathroom.

I heard him come up behind me. "This is just perfect,

don't you think?" I asked. A coined phrase I learned in a one-day seminar about using positive voice inflections to acquire a sale.

In actuality, the house was an ideal bachelor pad. Doc could even set up a computer at home and skip the three-mile commute to the office if he wanted.

"The toilet has a new shut-off valve," he said.

To which I couldn't think of a single response, so I just nodded.

He sniffed. "Do you smell that?"

I smelled something flowery, probably carpet freshener—a nice touch by the real estate agent. I'd have to remember that. "Smells like gardenias."

Doc gasped, coughed, and then wheezed.

I turned toward him. His face had a pale, blanched tone that made his dark brown eyes seem larger. "Are you okay?"

He leaned over, nearly retching now, his neck tendons showing.

I grabbed his shoulder, not sure if I should smack him on the back or poke a hole in his windpipe with a pen. "What is it? Are you allergic to gardenias?"

His whole body began to shudder. He broke free of my grasp and raced out of the room. I heard him clomp down the stairs, then the front door banged shut. Through the window, I watched him lean against my Bronco and wipe at his mouth.

What the fuck?

It took a couple of minutes for my adrenaline to stop shooting through my limbs with fire-hose intensity. I swabbed the sweat from my forehead and headed downstairs, locking up behind me.

I climbed into my Bronco and started the engine, waiting for the air conditioning to kick in before looking at Doc. His skin had returned to its normal olive color, his eyes no longer watering, his breathing quiet and rhythmic.

"I take it you're going to pass on that one, too?"

"I think I want to come back again."

My mouth fell open. I couldn't help it. "You do?"

"Another day, though."

My mouth still gaped. "What happened up there?"

"I don't like gardenias."

"You need to seek medical help for that."

"We should probably call it a day."

A flesh-and-blood buyer or not, I was tempted to call it a life and say our "goodbyes" right then, but I really wanted to keep my job.

The short trip back to the office was broken only by the whir from the vents.

"Could you drop me off at my car, please?" he asked.

The sooner I could put some space between us, the better. "Where are you parked?"

"Behind the building." He cleared his throat. "Are you available tomorrow afternoon?"

No! "Sure. One o'clock?"

"I have an appointment then. How about two?"

Appointment with whom? I wanted to ask what exactly he did besides inspect moles and read books on Wild Bill, but since he'd brushed me off earlier, I decided to save it for another time. "I'll find a few more houses to show you."

"Maybe something a little older," he suggested.

Older? If that's what he wanted, Deadwood was perfect for him. It didn't get its ghost-town label for nothing.

I bounced through a set of potholes into the parking lot behind Calamity Jane Realty.

"Right there," he said, pointing out his car.

I stomped on the brakes. My tires screeched in protest. Doc braced himself on the dashboard.

"You're kidding me." My teeth ground as I stared at his late '60s black Camaro with rally stripes. "That's *your* car?"

"Yeah." He raised his brows. "Not a Camaro fan, huh?"

Not for the one that parks in my spot.

First the box of books, then the whole gardenia incident, now the car. As much as I wanted to play praying mantis and bite Doc's head off in one swift chomp, I squeezed my lips together. I needed him. "Do you always park there?"

"I didn't at first."

"But you do now."

"Your co-worker, Ray, informed me last week that the building owner enforces assigned spots and this one's mine."

Jane owned the building. The only assigned spots were for her employees.

"See you tomorrow." Doc shut the passenger door.

I sighed. One of these days, I was going to poison Ray's orange juice.

Chapter Six

The sight of Wolfgang's house still made my eye twitch.

"That's it right there," I said to Natalie as I pointed at the rundown Victorian. "You can park in the drive."

In the weakening glow of the late afternoon sun, the overgrown yard teemed with fat flies and gnat swarms. I dreaded wading through the tall weeds with Natalie and learning all of the house's hidden trials and tribulations. The smell of a neighbor's freshly mowed lawn drifted through the open pickup window, mocking me.

"You've got to be shitting me," Natalie parked and killed the engine. A lawnmower droned in the distance. "You didn't tell me you were talking about the Hessler house."

I pushed open the passenger door. "Do you have a problem with working on Wolfgang Hessler's house?"

"No. It's just a little weird, that's all."

"Why weird?"

Layne and then Addy squeezed out from behind the seat and leapt down onto the cobblestone next to me.

Natalie shut her door and leaned on the bed of the pickup. "It's like being asked to remodel a haunted house."

"This is a haunted house?" Addy asked.

"Awesome." Layne whispered. "Let's go check it out." He took off up the drive. Addy raced after him.

"Layne! Addy! Get back here!"

They both disappeared around the back of the house.

I growled in my throat and slammed the pickup door.

"You okay?" Natalie asked while pulling her thick brown hair back in a ponytail. "Your eye keeps twitching."

I swiped at the sweat rolling down the side of my face. "I'm fine. Just hot and tired." Not to mention frustrated with Addy about the two stray kittens I found hidden in her closet after work. I stared at Wolfgang's house and noticed a shutter missing from a second floor window. "Please tell me this place doesn't have a reputation for being haunted."

"Well, not officially. It's not listed on the Ghosts of Deadwood tour or anything like that."

A big, bloated, unspoken "but" hung there between us. I fell back against the side of the pickup. "Wonderful. Not only is the place a wreck, it comes with a 'haunted' label, too."

"Nonsense. That's just child's play." Natalie rounded the pickup, grabbed my forearm, and led me up the drive. "It was only a rumor that spread because of Mrs. Hessler's long nose, pointy chin, and black hair. None of us really believed she was a witch. At least not in the daylight."

A witch and a haunted house. Even better.

In the backyard, Layne and Addy were playing tag in the shin-high scraggly grass.

Natalie shaded her eyes from the late afternoon sun and stared up at the house. She blew out a long, slow whistle.

That didn't sound good. "Nat, you can fix up this place in two-and-a-half weeks, right?"

She spared me a shielded glance, but said nothing and swished through the grass toward the breakfast nook in which I'd eaten yesterday.

I watched her brush over the peeling paint around the window casing, then pull her leather gloves from her back pocket, slip them on, squat, and start picking at the mortar in the exposed-stone foundation. The frown lines I could see on her normally smooth forehead made my chest tight, as if a boa constrictor was giving me a cozy hug.

I turned my back to her and focused on the two hellions fighting over something Addy currently held in her cupped palms up out of Layne's reach.

"Hey, you two. That's enough!" God, I hated it when I sounded like my mother.

I strode toward them, my hand held out. "Give it to me."

Addy opened her cupped hands, and something warm and smooth fell into my palm.

When my brain finally made sense of what I was looking at, I flinched. "Ewww!"

"Be careful, Mom." Addy leaned over the bald, limp, baby bird. "It's still squeaking."

Layne moved in close to peek at it, too. "I found it over by the garage. What should we do with it?"

I carried the baby bird toward the garage. "Show me where you found it. The nest might be nearby."

Layne zipped in front of me, leading the way. Addy crashed through the weeds behind me.

"Mom?" Her voice was hesitant.

So was mine. "Yeah?"

"Can I spend the night at Kelly's tomorrow?"

I grimaced, keeping my back to her so I wouldn't have to look her in the eyes. "You've only known her a couple of days, Addy. Isn't it a little soon?"

She sighed with the drama of a nine-year-old going on fifteen. "I knew you'd never let me."

Not if she kept up that tone. I took a deep breath before replying. "I'm not saying 'never.'"

"When, then?"

"I don't know." Not until the police had whoever was snatching up little girls locked up tight behind bars. There was no way in hell my daughter's face was going to be on a Missing Girl flyer.

"When will you know?" Addy pressed.

"I need to meet Kelly's parents first." I wanted to find out what kind of counseling she's had. While I felt sorry for the girl, allowing Addy to spend more than an hour alone with the sad-eyed waif made the hair on the back of my neck prickle.

"This is where I found it, Mom." Layne stood near the back corner of the square, brick garage.

We spread out and searched the overgrown lawn for a nest.

"Hey, Mom," Layne called out. "Where does this door in the ground go to?"

"What door?" I glanced his way.

"Layne!" Addy yelled from behind the garage. "Come look at what I found."

Layne tromped out of sight. I followed.

"It was sticking out of the dirt over there." Addy was pointing toward the garage's back wall as I rounded it.

"What is it?" I asked.

Addy held out a small, metal toy train engine. "I wonder how old it is."

I leaned closer. "Is there anything on the bottom?"

Layne took it and flipped it over. The bottom was bare except for rust and patchy remnants of black paint.

"Hello, Violet," a familiar male voice said from behind me.

My breath caught. I spun around, my face burning, very aware that I was sweaty, dusty, and trespassing with my two kids in tow. "Hi, Wolfgang."

Sunshine spotlighted his wind-ruffled hair and emphasized the hard lines of his cheekbones. His white, button-up shirt allowed a peek of tanned chest, and his spicy cologne left me a little lightheaded, like I'd hung upside down on the monkey bars too long. Damn, the man knew how to crank up the sex appeal.

His gaze fell on Addy, then Layne, a smile forming on

his cheeks. "One has your hair, the other your eyes."

"These are my kids, Addy and Layne."

He held out his hand to Layne, "Nice to meet you."

Layne hesitated, casting a glance my way. Upon my nod, he shook Wolfgang's hand.

"Wow, that's a strong grip." Wolfgang turned to Addy and squatted down to her level. "I bet you're the older twin."

Addy's eyes widened. "How did you know?"

"It's written on your face."

I mentally rolled my eyes. Addy would be spending even more time in front of the mirror now.

"Is your name really Wolfgang?" Layne asked, emphasizing the 'wolf' part. He grunted as Addy elbowed him.

Wolfgang nodded. "Sure is."

I stepped between the kids as Layne made to hit Addy back. "Wolfgang used to live here, guys. That's probably his train."

"What train?" Wolfgang asked, still eye level with the kids.

Layne held out the rusted toy.

"Layne and I found it." Addy lifted her chin, using her more serious, older-sister tone. "Is it yours?"

Wolfgang looked at it. "Hmmm, I don't think so."

"Can I keep it, then?" Layne's palm closed around the train, already taking ownership.

"Layne," I said, reprimanding. "You don't—"

"Sure, consider it yours." Wolfgang stood and glanced down at my hand. "What did you find?"

I'd forgotten about the bird. "We were searching for its nest, but not having much luck."

Wolfgang's forehead creased slightly. "We could make a nest for now and stick it up high, out of reach of predators. If its parents are nearby, they'll hear it crying."

The round-eyed look Addy bestowed upon Wolfgang mirrored one of those crazed, poodle-skirted Elvis fans of the late '50s. I couldn't blame her. The way he was warming up to my twins had my bobby socks in a twist, too.

"Violet?" Natalie rounded the back corner. "We have a little prob—" She noticed Wolfgang and her eyes practically bugged out of their sockets. She recovered in a blink, her lips curving into her trademark sex-kitten grin. "Well, well, well. Wolfgang Hessler, you've grown up."

Wolfgang's gaze zeroed in on Natalie's mouth before lifting to her eyes. "Do I know you?"

Somehow, Natalie made slipping off her leather gloves an art akin to pole dancing. "Sixth period, study hall, your senior year. I was the freshman who sat in front of you."

"Ah, yes, your hair was shorter then." Wolfgang rubbed his smooth-shaven jaw. "Natalie something."

"Beals." Natalie held out her hand to shake. "You were a lot thinner back then."

Wolfgang shook it. "And you weren't quite as curvy."

The jealousy bug nibbled on my ass. I shot Natalie a glare. "Nat, did you take a look under the back porch?"

Natalie shook her head, her eyes still gobbling up Wolfgang's gorgeous face, her hand still gripping his.

"Well, then, maybe you need to go check for termites and remember your sabbatical vow."

The word "sabbatical" made her recoil. She sighed and let go of his hand. "Damn, I sure picked a bad time to quit men."

Wolfgang watched Natalie stomp around the side of the garage and out of sight, then turned to me, his brows raised. "Quit men?"

I waved him off. "It's complicated."

He caught my arm and didn't let go, his smile mesmerizing. He must whiten his teeth. They couldn't be that blinding naturally, could they? "You haven't quit men, too, have you?"

Was he flirting with me? "Um, no." I'd just taken an involuntary layoff.

"Good." His thumb skimmed my wrist.

Okay, he was definitely flirting. A little voice in my head chanted my mantra of not mixing clients and sex—until I taped its mouth shut. Maybe just this once. It'd been too long. I was just mortal, after all.

I cleared my throat and pulled my arm free. "Addy. Why don't you go see if Natalie has something in her pickup to make a nest with." I handed Layne the baby bird and nudged him after his sister. "Take the bird and go help."

After they'd trudged off, I focused on Wolfgang again. "I hope you don't mind that I brought my kids along. I couldn't find a sitter." Or hadn't tried—almost the same thing.

"They're cute kids." He shoved his hands in his pockets, leaned his shoulder against the garage wall. "I didn't notice Natalie when I came around the house."

"She was probably down in the grass, inspecting your foundation. She's the only contractor I could find on short notice. Natalie has been working with her hands since she was a teenager. Her grandpa owned a contracting business out of Nemo. He just recently retired and moved to Arizona."

Jesus, I was babbling. I wiped my damp palms on my shorts, took a deep breath, and clamped my teeth together to cage my tongue before it spilled all of my dirty secrets.

"If you trust Natalie can do the job, then I'm a believer. My house is in your hands."

Wow, he knew just what to say to a girl. "Thanks."

"I'm planning on returning to San Francisco at the end of the month."

End of the month? Why so soon?

"Do you think Natalie will be able to have the place ready to sell before then?"

No way in hell. "Definitely."

"Good. What about inside?"

Excellent question. One to which I had no answer. "I'm working on that."

"Let me know when you want me to hire a moving company to remove the furniture and boxes."

"Okay." Wolfgang was all business now. I was beginning to wonder if I'd imagined that little flirting tango we'd danced a moment ago.

"I need to make a quick trip to San Francisco for a couple of days next week, so you'll have free rein of the house. You remember where the spare key is hidden, right?"

"Yep." After he'd signed the seller's contract yesterday, he'd shown me the key's hiding spot under a loose board on the bottom porch step. There was no need to get a lockbox for the place until I had it ready to show.

"I'll drop off a check tomorrow to cover initial costs."

"Sounds good."

"That leaves just one more thing."

"What's that?"

He reached out and tucked a stray curl behind my ear, his fingertips lingering on my jaw, his touch feather-light. Cobalt eyes locked onto my lips.

Oh, boy! We were dancing again. *He's a client.* The little voice was back.

"Will you have dinner with me Friday night, Violet?"

"To talk about your house?" I needed clarification. Should I spend the next two days preparing notes? Or trying on skimpy dresses? *He's a client.*

"I'd rather talk about you … and me … together."

He's a client!

Oh, what the hell. "Yes."

* * *

Thursday, July 12th

"Where's your shotgun?" I asked Old Man Harvey while climbing out of my Bronco.

Leaning against his porch rail, Harvey's gold-toothed grin was coat hanger wide. "I save Bessie for bill collectors, bank presidents, and four-wheelers."

Bessie? He'd named his shotgun after a cow? He was right; living out here alone all these years had warped him.

My sandals crunched on his gravel drive. The mid-morning sunshine had me squinting behind my sunglasses. There was something about being five thousand feet above sea level that made me feel like I could reach up and punch the sun.

The porch's shade still held a trace of coolness, keeping me from shedding the short-sleeved sweater covering my sleeveless paisley dress. I took a step toward Harvey and stopped, cringing. "What's that smell?"

Harvey checked the bottoms of his boots.

My eyes watered. "It's like heated vinyl and spearmint."

"Oh, that's my new cologne."

Noticing his greased-back hair under his weathered cowboy hat, I raised my brows. "You sprucing up for me now, Harvey?"

He hooted a little too loud for my self-esteem. Not very encouraging for a single mom midway through her thirties. "My cleaning lady came this morning. She's quite a looker."

I jumped on that like a hyena on fresh kill. "Who is she? Is she taking new clients?"

"I don't think Margo has any time for new clients. She seemed pretty frazzled this morning. She vacuumed Red and then raced off and left her cell phone behind."

Upon hearing his name, Red—Harvey's fat, yellow dog—lifted his head from the porch long enough to sneeze.

I sighed. Margo again. I should've known. Hers was about the only cleaning company in the Hills. "Isn't she married?"

"Who cares? I like to play the odds."

I did, too, lately. I pulled Mona's digital camera from my purse. "All right, Harvey. Let's take some pictures."

The inside of Harvey's ranch-style house smelled like fresh-baked cookies. I moved from room to room, snapping shots for the website. Contrary to his own scruffy, crusty exterior, Harvey's interior decorating skills were worthy of a *Good Housekeeping* spread. With leather furniture, butcher-block countertops, new bathroom fixtures, and a vase of fresh wildflowers on the maple, claw-foot table, I knew the house would show well.

The problem was Harvey's Timbuktu address. I had a better chance of winning this year's Ironman Triathlon than selling his place before Jane kicked me out on my hind end.

"You look like someone spanked your puppy," Harvey said as I stuffed Mona's camera back in my purse.

After searching his face to make sure that wasn't some weird sexual innuendo, I gave him a cockeyed grin. "Sorry. I'm just having a run of bad luck lately."

"Me, too. Fate must have brought us together." Harvey grabbed my arm as I turned toward the door. "Where are you going so soon? I made molasses cookies and opened a bottle of Kahlúa."

I really needed to hire Harvey a companion. Red, who'd managed to drag his sorry ass into the house and plop in front of his empty food dish, apparently wasn't filling the role.

"I wish I could stay." Warm molasses cookies would be the closest thing I'd had to an orgasm in two years. "But I have some appointments this afternoon."

"It's only ten." He dragged me over to a barstool and shoved me onto it. "Have a seat."

His eyes had a determined glint. I dropped my purse on the floor at my feet. I could use a glassful of courage, anyway. "Where are those cookies?"

He pulled a plate out of the stove and set it on the counter in front of me.

"Did Margo make these for you?"

Harvey shook his head. "My mama's own recipe."

Sweet gooey goodness drew a groan from my throat. The crazy old buzzard surprised me at every turn—including the small armory of shotguns and rifles I'd stumbled upon in his bedroom while taking pictures. How many guns did one man need? It's not like they were disposable. "So, you still hearing funny noises out behind your barn?"

"Yep. I found a mutilated deer carcass back there the other morning. A big, 12-point buck."

I wrinkled my nose. "Mutilated? Like by a poacher?"

"Nah. They'd have taken the antlers. That's an impressive rack." He grinned. "Kind of like your neighbor's."

"You mean Miss Geary?" Harvey had ogled Aunt Zoe's neighbor the evening we'd gone out to eat with the kids. She'd been weeding her flower bed wearing a tube top, short-shorts, and a pair of heels. I hoped my legs looked half as good as hers when I hit sixty.

"Damned straight. I have to get me some of that." Harvey growled and took a big bite of cookie. "So what's on tap for today? Anything fun?"

Chewing, I shook my head. Nothing I wanted Harvey to know about, anyway.

Last night after the kids went to bed, I'd snagged the previous Wednesday's copy of the *Black Hills Trailblazer* from Aunt Zoe's workshop, looking for any details I could find on the most recent missing girl, Tina Tucker. She'd made page two. Why not the front page? Did Deadwood's mayor have his boot heel on the chief editor's throat, squelching any tales that might tarnish the town's good-times reputation?

The article consisted of text only, Tina's 'Missing' poster's picture absent. A few short paragraphs explained how Tina had left her grandparents' house around seven Sunday evening to walk the four blocks home to her mom's place. She'd never made it. Tina's mother had gotten a flat tire on the way home from her job at a Sturgis diner. She'd pulled in the drive an hour later than usual and found the house empty, her daughter gone without a trace.

The police said they were looking into the matter. What that meant, I have no idea, but the "no current suspects" bit didn't make me feel warm and fuzzy inside. The mother was "not fit for an interview," per Tina's aunt, who also mentioned the little girl's "shocked and devastated" grandparents. I wondered why nobody brought up Tina's father. Was he dead? Or no longer in the picture like my kid's dad?

My gut ached after reading the story, my heart torn for the grief-stricken family. I'd checked in on Addy and Layne two more times before going to bed, wishing I hadn't sold my baby monitor with most of my other belongings when I'd moved back in with my parents last year.

All of my middle-of-the night fretting about missing girls had spurred me into action this morning. Before heading to work, I'd looked up Addy's new friend's address in the phone book, planning to drop by Kelly's house for a surprise visit after leaving Harvey's. If all was hunky-dory there, I'd consider letting Addy spend the night. While I didn't want to let Addy sleep out of my reach, I knew my daughter—there'd be no end to this when-can-I-have-a-slumber-party-at-Kelly's whining.

"Thanks for the picnic the other night," I said, grabbing another cookie. "The kids enjoyed themselves."

Harvey nodded while pouring me a Kahlúa. He topped it off with some milk. "That Kelly Wymonds girl sure was quiet the whole evening. You think her head is still all messed up from her little friend disappearin' last summer?"

I froze in mid-chew. "How do you know about that? Did Kelly say something to you?"

"Naw." He pushed the glass of Kahlúa my way. "I remember reading about it in the paper. That was the first girl gone missin', ya know."

For someone who lived in Boonieville USA, Harvey had his stethoscope on Deadwood's back, listening for any rattles.

"So I've heard. Do you know Kelly's dad?"

Snorting, Harvey said, "That dip shit? Sure, I do. He could have been a big-time football player. But after too much boozin', he didn't have the gumption to graduate. The local colleges didn't want him after he flunked out of school."

I sipped my drink and crammed half a cookie in my mouth. My picture of Kelly's dad was morphing. Now I could add "alcoholic" to the growing list of disparaging adjectives like *over-sexed* and *dim-witted.* Addy's chance of getting to spend the night at Kelly's was shrinking faster than a rain puddle in Death Valley.

Harvey gulped his Kahlúa and milk like it was a shot. "Hard to believe that knucklehead could produce such a cute daughter. She must take after her mama." He refilled his glass.

"How do you know all this about Kelly's dad?"

He shrugged. "Drinking holes are filled with homemade shrinks and drunken gabbers. You choose your role depending on how early in the day you show up."

I preferred playing the shrink. My dirty laundry didn't need airing, especially in such a small town. It'd taken me years to live down that damned incident with the cop in the movie theatre bathroom.

"I hear you're gonna try to sell the Hessler house," Harvey said, biting into another cookie.

Christ, the ink was barely dry on the contract. "If you're going to tell me it's haunted, you're too late. I've already heard about it."

"Haunted? That's old news." He slammed another glassful. "That Dame Hessler was sure one batty bitch. Her husband died when the kids were still young-uns. The doctor said his heart gave out; too much hard work down in Homestake's shafts for his scrawny body."

Once the largest and deepest gold mine in North America, Homestake Mine shut down operations at the beginning of the new millennium. Most of the old-timers in Deadwood, Lead, and the northern half of the Black Hills that I'd run into either had labored in Homestake's mines or had family who did.

Harvey rested his forearms on the counter, his voice lowering, secretive. "But we knew the truth."

"What truth?" I took Harvey's bait. There was nothing wrong with learning more about the man I'd agreed to have dinner with, I reasoned with my guilty conscience. Besides, it's not like he had any skeletons in his closets—I'd have seen them on Tuesday when I peeked in each of them.

"She poisoned him," Harvey whispered.

That sounded like some good old, bar stool gossip. "Why would she do that?"

"Her daddy didn't like him, and her daddy ruled her world. Hell, she never even took her husband's last name. Nope, kept her maiden name and gave it to the kids."

"Was her dad the same guy who started Hessler's Jewelry Designs in Deadwood?"

"Yes, ma'am. That's him, Mr. Hessler. Quite a dictator. Scared the bejesus out of us kids, threatening us with a broomstick beating when we'd roll a smoke out front of his store."

With that reputation, I could see why Wolfgang didn't want to be called "Mr. Hessler."

Pouring himself a third drink, this time mostly milk, Harvey continued. "Anyway, Dame Hessler became downright cuckoo after her daughter died. Holed up in that house day and night. Sent her son out for everything, and no amount of prying by the townsfolk would loosen his tongue about her."

Twenty-four hours a day, seven days a week in that house with all of those creepy clowns? That couldn't have helped bring her back from the edge. I swallowed the last of my drink. My heart twanged for Wolfgang—to be so young and all alone with a crazy mother. At least my kids had each other.

"How long ago did Wolfgang's mom die?" I asked, covering my glass when Harvey offered a refill.

"Nobody knows for sure."

"Why not?"

"Because nobody knows how long she'd been dead in the house before they found her. Rumor was the rats had been there and left long before."

Groaning, I smacked my forehead. That was just fucking great. I'd signed on to sell a haunted house belonging to a witch whose body decayed for God knows how long within those walls before someone carted her out. I threw down the remaining half of the cookie I'd been munching on, my appetite out the door and down the road, a cloud of dust in its wake.

Harvey gulped his milky drink, then set his glass by the sink. "No one had seen hide-nor-hair of her son after high school, not until he showed up for the funeral years later and took over the jewelry store."

I frowned at Harvey. "I suppose you're going to tell me that Wolfgang is as loony as his mother."

"Not as far as I can tell. That boy got his grandfather's looks and build, but his pop's personality. Seems as normal as you and me."

Which wasn't saying much knowing Harvey.

"Quite a handsome kid, too, after he filled out."

Harvey could say that again. Ever since I went against my No-Dating-Clients credo and agreed to have dinner with Wolfgang tomorrow, I'd been wringing my hands. Two years was a long intermission between dates. Last night, I'd stood in front of the mirror for twenty minutes, agonizing over lipstick colors—siren red or romantic pink, applying and reapplying until my lips looked like two inner tubes.

"He's loaded too," Harvey added, "by the looks of the gems in his store window."

Which meant wearing any jewelry from my bubble-gum machine collection was out of the question.

Harvey grabbed the remaining half of my cookie and chomped on it. "It's just too bad for all you womenfolk that he turned out to be as gay as a handbag full of rainbows."

Chapter Seven

Two snowmobiles, a muddy four-wheeler, and a Toyota pickup sporting beefy tires and a "Wish You Were BEER" bumper sticker sat in the Wymonds' front yard. The driveway was empty, except for potholes. I bounced to a stop and shut off my Bronco.

The engine ticked as I stepped onto the dirt-packed drive. The noon sun heated the top of my head, the smell of dust and baked pine thick in the still air. My sandals clapped along the front walkway, past several fly-covered garbage cans, past Kelly's pink Huffy bike, past a pair of dead Thuja saplings.

The Wymonds' single-story clapboard home reminded me of some of the houses up in Lead—the ones Homestake Mining Company threw together to accommodate some of their miners during the gold rush glory days. Unadorned little square dwellings lined up block after block, interspersed periodically by elaborate Victorian and brick neighbors.

Duct tape criss-crossed the Wymonds' screen door, holding the mesh together. The front door stood open. A booming voice rang out, shouting something about a wrestling "smackdown" coming up next on channel 7. The doorbell lay in three pieces in a dirt-filled flowerpot near my feet.

I shook off the urge to sprint to my Bronco and scurry back to the office. I owed it to Addy—and Kelly—to give the Wymonds family the benefit of the doubt. Not judge them by the single combat boot dangling from their gutter, nor the decapitated Barbie head nailed to their porch railing.

Straightening my shoulders, I knocked twice on the screen door and held my breath. Twenty seconds passed by with the only movement coming from a fly that found me interesting. I knocked on the screen door again, this time harder and longer.

"Kelly!" A gruff-sounding voice yelled out from somewhere inside the shadowy interior. "Get the goddamned door!"

I winced. Strike one against Addy's sleepover request.

I heard the slap of bare feet on linoleum, then Kelly's sad face appeared on the other side of the dust-crusted screen. I worked up a smile for her. "Hi, Kelly. Is your mom or dad here?"

Her round eyes widened. "Why? Am I in trouble?"

"Uh, no."

"Kelly!" The gruff voice hollered. "Who is it?"

"If it's about the kitten puke," Kelly said in a loud whisper, leaning closer, "I told Addy we shouldn't feed them the peanut-butter fudge ice cream."

"You fed them *my* ice cream?" I whispered back, my teeth grinding as I thought about Addy's denial of any knowledge on the whereabouts of my pint of ice cream.

"Kelly!" The voice roared, making us both jump.

"It's nobody, Dad." Kelly held her index finger to her

lips.

I choked down my Addy-instigated anger and whispered, "I need to talk to your parents, Kelly."

She shook her head, motioning for me to leave, going so far as to start shutting the steel door in my face.

"Kelly, wait," I said at my usual volume.

A large hand grabbed the door from the inside. I heard a squeal of protest and then the door opened. A grizzled-faced bear of a man in a stained white T-shirt filled the frame. Jeff Wymonds, I suspected, in the extra-large flesh. I could see hints of Kelly in his round eyes and narrow face.

"Who are you?" His voice sounded slightly slurred and full of suspicion, his eyes drilled me through the screen. "Did the sheriff send you?"

The smell of alcohol mixed with body odor slammed into me, knocking me back a step. Nice—drunk by lunchtime *and* expecting a visit from the law. Strike two, Addy dear.

My cheeks trembled with the effort to hold up my smile. "You must be Kelly's father, Jeff. I'm Violet Parker. My daughter is friends with Kelly. I've come to say hello."

His whole face crinkled into a glower. "Kelly doesn't have any friends anymore."

His reply surprised me so much that the niceties I'd practiced all the way there from Harvey's place jetted right out of my head. The only thing I could think to say was, "Is your wife here?"

His glower scrunched into a snarl. "She's at her mother's."

"Do you know when she'll be back?"

His laugh sounded harsh. "When hell freezes over, as far as I'm concerned."

Now I'd heard Deadwood winters could be pretty brutal, but I didn't think he was referring to the snowy season.

"Well, would you look at the time. I guess I'd better be going."

"Are you married, Violet Parker?"

Caught off-guard again, I told the truth. "No."

Jeff responded by gulping down the last of his beer and then crushing the can in his fist.

I tried to peek around his bulk. "I'll see you later, Kelly."

A faint "Bye" came from behind her father.

Backing down the first of two porch steps, I nodded. "It was nice to meet you, Mr. Wymonds."

He pushed his face against the screen. The mesh bulged as he leered at me, his scruffy beard sticking out through the screen in spots. His gaze crawled down to my sandals and then back up to my chest. "Come back soon, Violet Parker."

Shudders of revulsion made my arms and legs tremble. There was something wrong with his eyes, like something inside his big, messy-haired skull had gone sour. I couldn't believe Natalie ever shared a backseat with this inebriated hulk.

Barely keeping my feet from galloping, I fast-walked toward the safety of my Bronco.

"Hey, Violet Parker," he called out when I reached the driver's side door.

The way he kept saying my name had a cheese-grater effect on my nerves. I pulled open the driver's side door, pretending I hadn't heard him.

"I can see where your daughter gets her looks."

That knocked the wind out of me. How did he know what Addy looked like?

A finger of dread crept up my spine. I locked my door. That was it. Strike three. The asshole was out. Addy was just going to have to hate me for the rest of her life, because there was no way in hell she was ever setting foot in Jeff

Wymonds' house as long as I breathed oxygen.

As the engine rumbled to life, I stared at the steering wheel. Why was Kelly's dad at home getting wasted in the middle of the day on a Thursday? Why wasn't Kelly with her mom? Why had Jeff been expecting the sheriff? What exactly had the jerk meant when he said his daughter didn't have any friends anymore? Did he have something to do with Kelly's best friend disappearing? Did he have any connection to the other girls who were missing?

Back to the most important question of all, how in the hell did he know what my daughter looked like? Had he seen her at the pool? Riding her bike around town? Or had he sought her out because she was a petite, blonde, nine-year-old girl—just like the other three?

I glanced at the screen door as I backed out of the drive, expecting to still see the hulk's face. The sight of Kelly standing there alone on the porch, waving at me, made the back of my throat burn.

There was something wrong with that whole scenario. For Addy's sake, I needed to find out what.

***

Back at Calamity Jane's, Mona and Ray were arguing about the price of land in Mexico. I didn't have the time to find out if that was related to the price of eggs in China, my dillying at Harvey's and dallying at Kelly Wymonds' had me racing to make my house-showing appointment with Doc.

I paused long enough to download the pictures I'd taken of Harvey's house, return Mona's camera to her desk drawer, and wet my throat with a much-needed Diet Coke. Then I grabbed the MLS printouts I'd prepared for today's house-hunting adventure and scooted toward the front door.

"Where are you off to in such a hurry, Blondie?" Ray spoke with his usual demeaning tone.

Oh, how I longed to cram one of my sandals down his throat, but I was wearing my only pair of Anne Klein sling-backs, so I resisted. "To show some houses."

I'd hoped to see something akin to fear in his eyes, the realization that his nephew's future at Calamity Jane Realty was in danger. A smirk was all I got.

"You really think you have a fighting chance this late in the game?"

I backed against the door, pushing it open. Heat whooshed inside. "Kiss my ass, Ray."

The sound of his laughter followed me out onto the sidewalk, where Doc stood waiting for me. He had to be boiling in his black jeans and tan T-shirt, which hugged his broad shoulders.

"Hi," I said, squinting up at him. "I didn't realize you were out here. You should have come inside where it's cooler."

He shrugged. "I don't mind the heat."

I did, from both the sun and Ray. "You ready to go?"

"Sure." He followed my lead, quiet until we climbed into my sizzling Bronco—parked one teeth-grinding block away from my usual spot. "Ray likes to give you a hard time, doesn't he?"

That was a loaded question. Bad-mouthing a coworker to a client was on Jane's list of "No-Nos." I cranked down the window and started the engine, trying to come up with a nice, non-insulting answer.

"Ray can be …" *a huge asshole, a colossal dickhead, a gargantuan bastard.* "Let's just say Ray can be a little uncouth, sometimes. I'm sure he means no harm by it." If I had been made of wood and string, my nose would have been crossing the North Dakota state line right about now.

I could feel Doc's eyes on me as I wheeled onto the

street. I glued a smile on my face and pretended that working with Ray made swimming with blood-sucking leeches sound peachy-keen.

The first house on my list didn't look so bad, considering it was supposed to be haunted by a murdered prostitute named Lilly Devine.

When Mona had informed me of this well-known rumor early this morning, I'd debated striking the place from today's itinerary. However, she'd hushed my R-rated rant with one of her shoulder hugs and informed me that every other house in town was rumored to be haunted. With a history as greed-filled and violent as Deadwood's, the ghosts probably outnumbered the living.

If I believed in Casper and his wispy pals, Mona's pep talk would have had me jumping at every groaning floor board and creaking door hinge. Fortunately, my fear of things that go "bump" in the night ebbed about the time my period kicked in. However, that didn't mean I planned to broadcast to a client any superstitions about ghostly hangouts, especially when I was peddling the haunt to him.

Shutting off the engine, I stared at the brick, Tudor-style cottage, the looming chimney and steep roof both desperate for some TLC. "What do you think? You want to see the inside?"

"Sure." He pushed open the door and stepped onto the cracked concrete drive.

I followed him to the arched wooden door, handed him the printout detailing the property, and fished the key from the lockbox. The front door opened into a yellow living room carpeted in wall-to-wall, orange shag. I heard Doc inhale from behind me and peeked over my shoulder at him, expecting to see his nose wrinkled from the retro color choices or the odor of stale cigarette smoke.

He caught my gaze. A hint of a smile crossed his lips. "Just a beanbag and lava lamp away from 1975."

"Maybe there's hardwood under this." I stomped on the carpet, the underlying padding thin, as outdated as the style.

"Good try, Violet."

He stepped through the archway into the kitchen, pausing on the green linoleum covered with yellow curly designs. I trailed after him. The cabinets painted peach, the stove autumn gold, the fridge avocado. The built-in microwave appeared to be one of the pioneers of its kind.

Now I understood why the pictures on the MLS data sheet had been in black and white. As I tried to think of a way to sell this place on something other than its looks, we strolled into the master bedroom. I blinked twice, feeling like I'd stepped onto the set of the Brady Bunch's bedroom. Light blue, from the ceiling to carpet, filled every corner. The master bath boasted a bright pink toilet with a matching sink and bath.

"Whoever picked out these colors must have been color-blind," Doc said.

"At least the drywall is in good shape."

"Is that the best you can come up with?" Doc stared down at me, his grin wide, inviting my lips to play copy cat. When he smiled at me like that, I could almost forget about his whole human bloodhound routine. Almost.

"Well, the backyard *is* mowed," I answered. After wading through Wolfgang's yard, I thought this was at least a little improvement.

His gaze moved to the box window. "Interesting fountain. Does the water actually spout from the gnome's pen—"

"Let's check out the other bedrooms." I grabbed his arm and pulled him back into the hall.

The stench of stale cigarette smoke thickened as we approached the two bedrooms at the end of the dark hallway.

"If you rip the carpet out, I bet that smell would

disappear."

"What smell?" Doc asked.

I stopped. He'd been sniffing through the place as usual. How could he miss the odor? "Are you a smoker?"

He pushed open the door to the bedroom on the left. "Not since high school."

"Can't you smell the cigarette smoke?"

He inhaled deeper and longer than usual. "Sure, but it's not that bad."

I stood on the threshold and gaped at him. Yesterday, the light scent of gardenias had sent him running and gagging from the house. Yet here we were, swimming in burnt tobacco from yesteryear, and he just shrugged it off?

Treading after Doc as he moved across the hall, my shoulders tightened as he stepped into the last bedroom.

According to Mona, Lilly Devine had been strangled by her "John" in this north-facing bedroom. Vertical skinny stripes of red, white, and blue covered the ceiling and ran down the walls to the fire-engine red carpet. A wave of vertigo had me leaning against the open door for support. If the wallpaper had been the same back then, I had an idea what drove the murderer to do it.

"Whoa," Doc backed out of the room, covering his eyes. "That hurts."

I flicked off the light and followed him back to the shag-filled living room. "Sorry. This place looked pretty good in the black-and-white pictures."

"It has potential."

Sure, as a nightmare. "You want to check out the basement?"

"Lead the way."

I did. A light switch at the top of the stairs flooded the room with florescent light. I'd reached the bottom step before realizing Doc wasn't following me. I turned around and found him still standing at the top of the stairs. His face looked pale. Maybe it was the lighting. "Aren't you coming down?"

"No." His nostrils flared and he stepped back away from the top step until I could only see his head.

I sniffed. No gardenias, just the usual musty basement smell. What could possibly be wrong with that? "Why not?"

"I changed my mind. Come back up here."

I glanced around at the remodeled room, white-washed cement walls, dark blue carpet. "You should check this out, Doc. It's the nicest room in the house."

"Get up here now, Violet." His tone was edged with alarm.

Suddenly, I had a big hankering for fresh air. "Okay, okay. I'm coming." This sniffing business was for the birds—or the dogs.

Back in the lava-lamp living room, I asked the obligatory, "Are you interested in placing an offer on it?" A waste of breath, certainly, but part of the routine.

"Not at the moment, but I might want to come back here again."

Really? To this shithole? Why? "We'll leave it as a 'maybe' then."

"Good. What else do you have?"

Not much, unless a miracle occurred in Deadwood—or a mass exodus. I had one or two more up my sleeve, and then we'd have to discuss whether he'd consider commuting from a Lead or Central City zip code. "Let's go see."

Outside, I welcomed the warm blast of pine-scented air. My lungs felt like I'd spent a couple of hours leaning on the craps table in Vegas. We climbed into the Bronco.

After initially leaving the office, we had covered all of the small-talk subjects I could think of on short notice. Now the bouts of silence were heavy and made me want to drum my thumbs on the steering wheel.

Emboldened by his earlier smiles, I turned over the engine and asked, "How long have you been in Deadwood?"

"A while now."

Vague, but a start. "Are you renting a house or apartment?"

"Neither."

An RV? A pup-tent? A cave? What? Maybe I was going about this wrong. "What brought you to Deadwood?"

"A rumor."

I let that one sit for a breath to see if more was to come. Nope, nothing. I moved on. "Where are you from?"

"Back east."

"Like the East Coast?"

"Not that far."

Jesus! Prying open a can of pork and beans with my teeth would have been easier than getting a plain, clear answer from Doc. Whoever wrote the How-To book on forming open relationships with clients hadn't met D.R. Nyce. Was he hiding something? Or just toying with me for shits and giggles?

I idled at a stoplight behind an exhaust-belching, 1950s Ford pickup, searching for something to talk about. Then I remembered the scene in his office involving the mole and the magnifying glass. "So, Doc, what exactly do you do for a—"

In my rearview mirror, I saw my blonde-haired daughter riding her bike along the opposite sidewalk with a white chicken tucked under one arm. The rest of my question leaked out my ear.

Feathers floated behind Addy as she raced around the corner and pedaled hard out of view up a side street.

A honk from behind jerked me out of my stunned state. I hit the blinker and whipped a U-turn in the middle of the intersection, ignoring several more honks from on-coming cars.

Doc reached for the dashboard. "What are you doing?"

"Hunting chickens."

"What?"

I made a hard right onto the street Addy had ridden up.

"Is that a metaphor for something?" Doc braced himself as I floored it to the four-way stop.

"No." I looked left and right, no sign of Addy. Then I saw a white feather, floating across the road about half a block in front of us and I hit the gas. A BMW with a Michigan license plate shook his fist at me as I cut him off.

"It was my turn!" I yelled at him through my closed window.

"Remind me to drive next time we go out."

I ignored Doc's sarcasm and jammed on the brakes at the next Stop sign. Still no Addy. "Do you see any feathers?"

"What does that even mean?"

"There!" I pointed to the feather drifting toward the ground in the parking lot up ahead on the left and gunned it.

"Violet, are you on any kind of medication I should know about?"

"No." I should be, though, I thought as I rammed into the parking lot, and yanked the wheel to avoid careening into an Impala backing out of its spot. Another horn followed in my wake. I could see Addy's blonde hair ahead on the other side of the line of parked cars.

An RV rolled out of an alley and across my path.

"Hold on!" I stomped on the brakes.

Doc swore under his breath.

Son of a peacock! I was going to lose her. As the RV cleared out of the way, I cranked down my window and yelled, "Adelynn Renee! Stop right there!"

Lucky for Doc's blood pressure, my daughter heard and

obeyed. I zig-zagged through a couple of empty parking spots and pulled up next to where she stood straddling her bike, holding the chicken against her chest.

I slammed my door and rounded the Bronco's grill. "Where do you think you are going with that chicken?"

Addy's cheeks darkened under the red spots already coloring her skin. "Ummm, home?"

A second door shut behind me.

"No, you are not. You take that chicken right back where you found it."

"I can't."

"Why not?"

"Who are you?" Addy asked Doc as he approached.

"Never mind who he is, Adelynn. Why can't you take the chicken back?"

"Because I rescued it." Addy looked at Doc again. "How long have you known my mom?"

"A few days," Doc answered.

"Rescued it from where, Addy?" I had a bad feeling about this. Like last year when she'd sneaked that white mouse home in her lunchbox after her school field trip to the Reptile Gardens.

"From the chicken farm," Addy said, as if there were chicken farms on every corner in Deadwood. Her gaze returned to Doc. "Mom's single, you know. My dad ran off while she was pregnant, so you don't have to worry about him interfering."

My neck roasted, and it had nothing to do with the heat rolling off the asphalt. I grabbed Addy's chin and turned her face toward me. "Addy, dear, focus on me here." *And quit trying to pimp me out!*

She sighed and made glaring eye contact.

Had she not been of my own flesh and blood, I might have taken her to the post office right then and shipped her to the moon. "What chicken farm?"

"They were going to chop off her head, Mom. I just know it. I couldn't let them do it. She's too pretty. Please, can I keep her? She can share a bed with Checkers."

"Who's Checkers?" I asked.

"The kitten you said I could keep."

"I never said you could keep one of the kittens."

"Did too! You said, 'Yes, siree' last night when you were on the back porch drinking beer with Natalie."

"I said, 'We'll see.'"

A muffled chuckle from Doc won him my testicle-withering stare. He squeezed his lips tight and brushed some pine pollen off the hood of the Bronco.

"Please, Mom? Please, please, please." Addy used the sweet, innocent child voice she thought still worked on me.

Unfortunately, with Doc as an audience and the clock ticking on our afternoon of house viewing, I didn't have the time to deal with today's Addy-emergency. "Take the chicken home and put it in the garage. But—" I interrupted her whoop of victory, "that doesn't mean we are keeping her. We'll discuss this in more detail when I get home."

Addy frowned, but kept quiet. A wise child, considering that my head was about to explode. She climbed on the bike seat and adjusted the chicken tighter in her arms, receiving a squawk of protest in return. "Okay, Mom, but do me a favor."

I just stared at her, my hands clenched at my side.

"Try to keep an open mind about this."

This time, Doc's laugh was outright.

Addy smiled at him. "Mom loves daisies, peanut-butter fudge ice cream, Captain Kirk, and anything having to do with Elvis. Good luck!"

"Addy!" I yelled at her as she rode off.

A chicken feather floated to the ground between Doc and me.

"Sorry about that." I had trouble meeting his dark eyes,

so I focused on the cleft in his chin.

"She's cute. Reminds me of someone."

"Me?"

He chuckled. "Are you fishing for a compliment?"

This time, I blushed so hard my knees roasted.

"No, I just thought you were … I mean, I thought when you said she reminds you of … that you were offhandedly referring to …" I bit my tongue to stop it from talking gibberish.

"Ready to go?" I didn't wait for his answer and rushed around to my side of the Bronco.

Doc grinned as he slid in next to me. "Of course she has your good looks, but she's the spitting image of someone else I've seen."

Did Doc just say I was good-looking? I turned the key, breathing easier in the air conditioning even though Doc's off-handed compliment reminded me of Jeff Wymonds earlier comment about Addy's looks. "Maybe you've seen my son around town. They're fraternal twins, but they share some features."

"No, that's not it."

"Someone on TV?"

He frowned out the front window, shaking his head. Then his forehead smoothed. "Oh, it was—" He paused, swallowed, then said, "Never mind."

"Who?"

"Just someone I saw before."

Now he really had my curiosity standing at attention. "Come on, who?"

He looked at me, searching my eyes for who knows what before exhaling. "The girl from Deadwood who disappeared last summer."

Goosebumps soared up my arms.

* * *

Leaving the chicken feathers behind, I headed for the last available house within the city limits. I knew it was a bust from the moment I pulled into the driveway and Doc saw the pink paint and elaborate gingerbread gable ornaments.

I hesitated. "You want to go inside?"

"Sure." Although I could tell by his furrowed brow and the stiffness in his shoulders that he wasn't comfortable in the frilly surroundings, complete with window boxes brimming with pansies and shutters etched with ribbon-curls.

Not that I could blame him. As I unlocked the front door, I half-expected Hansel and Gretel to skip up the sidewalk and join us.

The interior reminded me of a doll house my father bought Addy for her fifth birthday. A bachelor pad, it was not. We tooled around inside for a bit, him sniffing, me still fuming about my daughter, the chicken lover.

"Well?" I asked without enthusiasm as we climbed back into my Bronco.

"I don't think so."

I shifted into gear.

"Do you mind stopping at that gas station up ahead?" Doc asked when we neared Main St. "I'm thirsty."

I turned into the parking lot of Jackpot Gas-n-Go, coasting past a Toyota pickup fueling up at the pumps. My breath caught when I saw the "Wish You Were BEER" bumper sticker stuck on the tailgate.

Crap! Jeff Wymonds—the last person I wanted to see.

I parked in a spot near the corner of the building, putting as much distance between Jeff's pickup and me as the lot allowed.

"Be right back." Doc hopped out.

Through the passenger-side window, I watched him stride along the walkway to the front glass doors. He pushed inside, and when the door swung back, Jeff stepped out. My heart dropped to my toes.

I cranked my rearview mirror to the side so I could spy on Jeff as he crossed the lot and climbed into his pickup. He looked less Neanderthal-ish with his hair damp and combed back, but he still sported the stained white T-shirt and blue jeans, the same facial scruff. As he rolled toward me, I slunk way down in my seat, my fingers crossed that he didn't recognize my Bronco.

I waited for the growl of his engine to disappear, but it didn't. Instead it rumbled up next to me, idling just outside my door. I heard his door slam.

Oh, fuck! I hit the door lock button and then waited for his face to appear in the window next to me.

Twenty seconds later, I was still waiting.

I inched my way up in my seat, peeking out the window. Jeff was marching toward the Dumpster in the back corner of the lot, carrying a big black garbage bag. As he neared the Dumpster, he looked left then right and then over his shoulder. Then he lifted the Dumpster lid and tossed the bag inside. I saw a hint of something pink before the lid crashed down again.

Someone knocked on the passenger-side window. I yelped and jerked, hitting my knee on the underside of the dash.

Doc stood on the other side of the glass, staring down at me with a furrowed brow.

I unlocked the doors and sat up, straightening my dress, avoiding eye contact as he climbed in next to me and held out a bottle of water.

"Oh, thanks. Let me give you some money."

He waved me off. "You feeling okay?" I could hear a hint of laughter in his tone.

"Yeah. Sure. I'm great."

The slam of a pickup door to my left drew my attention out my window. I looked over and ran smack dab into Jeff's gaze.

His eyes narrowed to a squint as he stared back.

My mouth went dry.

He pointed at me.

I locked the door again.

Jeff's crazed grin reappeared.

Holy shit. I grabbed Doc's arm, latching on tight.

Jeff winked and shifted into reverse, his tires chirping as he gunned it out of the parking lot and onto the street.

"Violet," Doc's voice spurred me to resume breathing. "I think you're drawing blood."

I let go, wincing at the crescent moons my nails had embedded in his skin. "I'm sorry."

"Don't worry about it." He nodded in the direction Jeff had departed. "You know that guy?"

I was too wound up to be anything other than honest. "He's the father of Addy's new best friend."

"He seemed fond of you."

I shivered with disgust and reached for the door handle. "I'll be right back."

There was something fishy about the way Jeff had been looking around before dumping his trash. Plus, he could have easily just thrown it in the garbage cans strewn around his place. Why risk getting busted for illegally disposing of his crap here?

Heat rolled off the pavement as I fast-walked over to the Dumpster. I flipped open the lid. The smell of rotting food and stale cardboard whooshed out of the bin, pushing me back a step. Jeff's untied black bag lay on the top, within reach if I stood on my tiptoes.

I hauled the bag out and dropped it on the ground. It fell on its side, spewing out a rolled-up, pink sleeping bag. I nudged the sleeping bag to the side and lifted the garbage bag by the bottom, emptying it. A pair of bunny-covered pajamas topped the pile. Under them was a girl's lace-edged shirt, some bright yellow jean shorts, one blue sock, and a nylon, purple jacket. Why was Jeff throwing away Kelly's clothes? They appeared to be clean, no grass stains, no holes, nothing.

I held up the jacket and turned it around so I could see the front. When I saw the initials *E.C.* written in permanent marker on the tag, I paused. Who was E.C.? Kelly was K.W.

I spun around and searched the lot to make sure Jeff wasn't lurking somewhere, watching. Doc was walking toward me, sporting a lazy grin.

I bent down and started cramming everything but the coat back in the garbage bag.

Doc picked up the sleeping bag and held it out to me. "So, do you go Dumpster diving often?"

"No," I fibbed and jammed the sleeping bag inside the black plastic. "Besides, last time I had no choice."

"Last time?"

"Yeah," I knotted the top of the bag. "He forgot to mention he was married and she took her jealousy out on my car keys."

He chuckled and lifted the Dumpster lid for me. "You're keeping the jacket?"

"For now." At least until I found out who E.C. was.

Back at my Bronco, Doc shot me another one of his infectious grins. "There's never a dull moment with you, Violet."

Said the kettle. I sniffed just thinking about Doc's quirk and grimaced at the smell of rotting garbage on my hands.

"I try my best to entertain." I tossed the jacket in the back seat and then cranked over the engine. "Just wait until you see what happens next time."

Chapter Eight

Fifteen minutes later, after dropping Doc off at his car (aka my parking spot), I walked into Calamity Jane's, my mind preoccupied with Jeff and the clothes. I stopped by the bathroom to wash the garbage smell off my hands, then headed for my desk. Mona greeted me with a big smile and a huge bouquet of daisies.

I didn't bother sniffing them. Daisies don't have the sweet scent of roses or the vanilla aroma of heliotrope. However, their happy yellow faces and white manes always make me feel like lounging in a field of grass under a cobalt sky. I must have been a cow in a past life.

"Are these from you?" I couldn't think of anything I'd done for Mona lately that would spur her to shower me with flowers.

"No. The florist delivered them a little while ago." She handed me a tiny purple envelope. "This came with them."

Tearing open the flap, I pulled out a small card with a cupid on it and read aloud:

Roses are red.
Violet is new.
I walk by your window,
Here's looking at you.

"Wow." Mona's chair creaked as she sat down. "That's kind of weird. Who's it from?"

"It doesn't say."

I read it again under my breath, and then stared out the blind-free front windows.

Were the flowers from Doc? He must have walked by the office many times, and Addy had told him that daisies were my favorite. However, that was just this afternoon, and I'd been with him until two minutes ago. Maybe he'd phoned them in.

Grabbing a vase from under the bathroom sink, I filled it with cold water. Creepy card or not, they were still daisies.

I set the flowers on the bookcase over by the coffee maker instead of on my desk, which didn't have much available surface area.

When I dropped into my chair, I noticed a white envelope with my name scrawled on it tucked partway under my keyboard. I recognized Jane's handwriting and tore the envelope open. A signed check from Wolfgang and a Post-It note with his cell phone number was inside. He must have stopped by while I was out.

I tucked the check into my wallet. I'd cash it and pass the money to Natalie later when we met at the Hessler Haunt, as she liked to call it.

"How's it going with our next-door neighbor?" Mona asked. "Any bites yet?"

"Barely a nibble." Mostly a bunch of sniffing.

"Well, your luck has turned," Mona said. "I have a gem that just landed in my lap."

"Is it in Deadwood?"

"A couple of blocks away from your Aunt Zoe's."

"Price?"

Mona rattled off a number that made me sigh. It was fifty thousand more than what Doc wanted to spend. "Think they'll come down any?"

"Maybe five grand. It's in great shape and located in a primo neighborhood."

It sounded perfect, except for the extra fifty thousand

bucks. "It's too expensive."

"You could still bring him by."

I could tell by the pinch of Mona's lips that she wasn't going to give up easily. "How about Sunday afternoon?"

Mona shook her head. "I won't have it ready for showing yet. If this is above his max, you need to wait until I have it all polished and shiny. I'll let you know when I'm ready."

My cell phone let out a muffled trill from my purse. I dug it out. Aunt Zoe's number showed on the screen. "Hello?"

"Are you coming home soon?" Layne asked.

"I need to take care of some paperwork and then I'll be on my way. Why?"

"I'm hungry."

"Make yourself a sandwich." The other end of the line seemed unusually quiet. "Where's Addy?"

"Out front."

"What's she selling this afternoon?" A white chicken, I hoped.

"Mittens for kittens that she made from some of her Barbie clothes."

That was it. No more new outfits for her Safari Skipper doll. "Put your sister on the phone, please."

"She's busy right now."

"Doing what?"

"Talking to that tall guy with the weird eyes again."

Every last drop of saliva evaporated from my mouth. "What do you mean 'again'?"

"He came by yesterday when she was selling doggie diapers and gave her a bag of taffy."

That explained the handful of wrappers stashed in her shorts' pocket that I found while loading the washing machine this morning. My hands trembled. Didn't she realize the boogeyman was roaming the streets, snatching up little girls just like her?

"Layne, take the phone out to your sister right now."

I heard the front screen door hinges squeak, followed by quick footfalls thumping on the wooden porch.

"Addy, Mom wants to talk to you." Layne's voice shook slightly. He must have been running.

A faint "goodbye" from Addy came through the phone. I crunched it tight against my ear, straining to hear any response from the candy man.

"You're in big trouble." Layne's tone was taunting.

"Give me that, you brat." Scuffling sounds made me pull the phone away several inches, then Addy's voice rang through. "Layne's lying, Mom."

"No, I'm not!" Layne yelled in the background.

"Adelynn Renee," I cut through their bickering. "Who was that man you were just talking to?"

"I don't know."

"What did he want?"

"To buy some mittens. He must have a dog, too, because he bought some diapers yesterday."

Still no mention of the candy. She was holding out.

"I don't want you selling stuff on the sidewalk, anymore." I'd save the "don't take candy from strangers" reminder for a face-to-face ass-chewing.

"Why not?"

Ah, the whiney tone. It strummed my neck muscles, which were already rigid as harp strings. "Addy, you know there's someone out there kidnapping girls."

"Yeah, but he only gets you if you're on a bike."

Childhood logic, so black and white. I guess I needed to sit down with both kids and spell out the danger. "No more sidewalk sales, Addy."

"C'mon, Mom. How am I going to make any money?"

"You're nine years old. What do you need money for?" Besides to place singles' ads?

"Stuff."

"I'll buy you whatever 'stuff' you need."

"But you don't have any money."

I winced, realizing how tuned in Addy was to my financial troubles. I was supposed to be providing for my kids, not putting them to work to help with cash flow problems.

"Listen, Addy. I'm not going to discuss this on the phone right now. I want you to take down your table and play inside the house or in the backyard."

"But, Mom—"

"I'll be home in ten minutes. If I catch you still out front, you're grounded." That was a first for me, but desperate times called for smothering actions.

"Grounded? From what?"

Good question. I glanced left and right, my brain stumbling for an answer. "Your bike."

Brilliant! That would keep her safe at home.

"Whatever!" she yelled, and the line went quiet.

I dropped my phone on my desk and followed it with my forehead.

"What's wrong?" Mona asked.

"Some guy is hanging around the house, giving Addy candy."

"Shit."

I glanced at Mona, her eyes round with the same question and alarm that had my legs weak at the moment. With three girls missing, now was not the time to play patty-cake with strangers bearing sweets.

"What are you going to do about it?"

"I don't know." Calling the cops seemed premature. After all, the candy hadn't been drugged or filled with any other nasty surprises. The only solution I could come up with at the moment was to remove Addy from the equation.

"I need to talk to Aunt Zoe." I shut down my computer, then grabbed my tote and purse. "I'll see you tomorrow morning at Billy's."

Jane liked to have brunch with her employees on Fridays at Bighorn Billy's, Deadwood's equivalent to Applebee's. It was her choice location for our weekly status meeting.

With a wave in Mona's direction, I fast-walked to my Bronco and sped home. Except for a pudgy gray squirrel, the front yard was empty when I pulled in the drive. Too bad, because I'd have loved the excuse to keep Addy off her bike for a week—or year.

Layne's peals of laughter from behind the house tugged me into the backyard. The sight of Addy chasing her chicken around the swing set, flapping her arms and clucking stopped me just inside the gate.

Tears filled my eyes without warning. Jesus! Whatever made me think I could raise and support two kids on my own? I was drowning here, and now there was a monster prowling nearby, possibly right outside my front door.

Straightening my sagging shoulders, I pretended that life wasn't shooting spit wads at me. "Hi, guys."

Layne ran over and welcomed me home with a waist hug.

Addy glared at me from the other side of the swing set.

Golly gee, being a parent was about as rewarding as getting kicked in the knee by a mule.

"Where's Aunt Zoe?" I asked, deciding to put off the verbal battle with Addy a bit longer. I needed to corral the fear still head-butting my ribcage before I could speak without screaming.

Layne pointed toward Zoe's workshop. "She's working. What's for supper?"

"I don't know. Natalie said she'd bring dinner tonight."

"Are we going back to that house?" Addy asked, her

face the envy of poker players everywhere.

"Yes."

"Can we check to see if the baby bird's momma rescued it?"

"Sure."

"Will Wolfgang be there?" Addy still showed no hint of emotion.

"Maybe." A girl could hope.

"Will you take me over to Kelly's afterward?"

Hell no! Especially not after catching Jeff Wymonds dumping little girl clothing in that Dumpster. He and the Candyman were running neck-and-neck as my prime kidnapper suspects.

I cringed mentally, imagining the fireworks sure to shoot from Addy's mouth when I denied her yet another want. "I don't know. I need to talk to Aunt Zoe."

Ducking my head, I darted into Zoe's workshop and shut the door behind me. Shafts of sunlight poured in through the west-facing window, spreading over a table covered with pipes, jacks, blocks, and other glass-blowing tools and equipment. The faint smell of something chemical hid beneath a cinnamon scent, courtesy of the air freshener Zoe kept plugged in.

Across the room, Aunt Zoe sat on a barstool, pencil in hand as she leaned over her table. "Hey, darlin'." Her smile reminded me of days-gone-by, when I used to help her blow and shape new glass pieces during my long summer visits. "How was work?"

"Promising," I lied. I came around behind her and peeked over her shoulder at the design she was sketching on her notepad. "Another new design?"

"Yep. I dreamed it up last night."

"They don't look like glass pieces."

"They're not. I've been wanting to try my hand at some kinetic art. These are wind activated."

"They'd be perfect for prairie dwellers."

"Bingo."

I moved over to the stockpile of *Black Hills Trailblazer* newspapers Aunt Zoe kept in an old cask barrel and started digging through them, the dry paper flimsy to the touch. "We have a problem."

The sound of Zoe's pencil scratching across the paper stopped. "I take it Addy told you about the twenty-two messages I cleared from the answering machine at noon."

I rolled my eyes. Sheesh! I'd have thought that after four days the replies to that damned singles' ad would slow. Turns out being single in Deadwood made me as popular as free pancakes at IHOP.

"Actually, no. I was talking about a new problem."

"Uh, oh."

"Layne says a strange man has been frequenting Addy's For-Sale table." Okay, so maybe "frequenting" was stretching the truth, but I didn't want Aunt Zoe to wave me off and tell me I was jumping at shadows—even if I was. "Yesterday, he gave Addy a bag of taffy."

"Please tell me she didn't eat it."

"I found the wrappers in her pocket." I skipped past the May, April, and March issues of the paper, hauled them from the pile, and dropped them on the floor. The February, January, and previous December ones followed.

"What was she thinking?"

When it came to Addy's sweet tooth, there was never much thought involved. November and October of last year joined the others on the cement. "I've banned her from selling any more stuff to your neighbors and ordered her to stay in the backyard or inside the house."

"Good. I'll try harder to keep an eye on her."

I shot Aunt Zoe a frown. "I hate to bother you more than we already have."

"Addy shares my blood, Violet. I don't want anything to

happen to her. Besides, I'm happy to have the company around here."

"Thanks." I flipped through September and slowed as I reached August's issues, my fingers now smudged with black ink. "Aunt Zoe, do you remember the little girl who disappeared last summer?"

"Vaguely. Why?"

"Did she look like Addy?"

Six folded layers down, a headline read, 'Another Girl Missing!' in big, black letters on the front page.

"Let's see, Emma had blonde …"

A rush of blood in my ears blocked out the rest of Aunt Zoe's answer as I stared down at a black-and-white picture of Emma, Kelly's friend. I gripped the lip of the oak barrel, fighting a wave of nausea.

Smiling up at me was a spitting image of Addy. While Emma's eyes were a little more almond-shaped and her lips not as full as Addy's, they could have been sisters with their similar hairstyles and oval faces. No wonder Addy reminded Doc of Emma.

Then I read the blurb under Emma's photo.

Emma Cranson. Last seen in front of the Piggly Wiggly on Saturday morning.

Emma Cranson. E.C. The jacket! Those were the same initials that were written on the tag. My knees trembled.

Oh, my God! What did that mean? Was Jeff Wymonds the kidnapper? Why else would he be throwing clothes away in a Dumpster? I needed to call the police and give them that jacket.

However, what if I was wrong? Kelly and Emma had been best friends. Maybe Emma had forgotten her jacket at Kelly's at some point, and Jeff was just getting rid of it. Surely the police had already looked into Jeff, since Emma had probably spent lots of time at the Wymonds' house. Plus, the jacket had been clean—no blood, no rips, no stains whatsoever.

Not to mention that if I did go to the cops, and they pulled Jeff in for questioning, he would know I was the tattletale. Then what? Was a jacket enough evidence to put the guy away? Probably not. I didn't need an angry, drunk, big-bear of a man as my number-one enemy, and I certainly didn't need him focusing any extra attention on Addy.

"Violet," Aunt Zoe's hand on my shoulder jerked me out of my frozen-lung trance.

I gulped down a breath.

Aunt Zoe's dark green eyes searched mine. "Are you okay?"

"I don't know." That was the honest truth.

I focused back on the newspaper, scanning the meat of the article, snagging on the words: *blonde*, *brown eyes*, *loves animals*, *avid swimmer*, *often find her at the Candy Corral*, and *last seen riding her bike*.

"Look at this." I pointed at the picture. "It's no wonder Kelly was drawn to Addy. Not only do Emma and Addy look alike, but their biographies read like they were freaking soulmates."

The workshop door banged open, bouncing against the wall coat rack. Aunt Zoe and I whipped around.

A pair of crutches came through the doorway with Natalie at the helm. Her hair frazzled, her cheeks red, and her lower right leg encased in a cast, Natalie grimaced. "We have a problem."

Chapter Nine

Friday, July 13th

Bighorn Billy's bustled with fanny-pack wearing tourists. My orange juice tasted a little bitter this morning. Either someone had slipped a few greenies into the juicer, or my shitty mood had soured my taste buds. Probably the latter.

Willie Nelson's "Whiskey River" poured out the overhead speakers, mixing with the clinks and clangs drifting through the kitchen's swinging saloon doors. The aroma of fried bacon had my stomach snarling out demands.

Mona sat across the table, looking very Grace Kelly-ish in her pink and white polka dot sweater. A matching silk scarf secured her auburn hair. Jane and Ray hadn't shown up yet.

"How did it go with Addy last night?" Mona asked.

The memory of Addy's volcanic reaction to my veto on the sleep-over idea made me sigh. "Same as usual. She hates me. I'm a mean, horrible mother. She wishes I'd never had her."

"Just because you banned any future sidewalk sales?"

"Because I *never* let her do *anything*." Lately, superlatives slipped off Addy's tongue like it was coated with butter. "Plus, I'm making her return the chicken."

"What about the kittens?"

"They have to go, too, probably." I hadn't had the heart to add them to the chopping block last night. Staring down

Addy's tears had been too tough.

"Any idea who Addy's candy man is?"

I shook my head. "Layne's description of him didn't spur any recognition from Aunt Zoe."

"Has he asked Addy to go with him anywhere?"

"No. The only thing she could remember—besides him talking about his niece's cat—was asking if her father was around."

"Hmmm. That's kind of suspicious—but not."

"Exactly."

I waited for the waitress to refill Mona's coffee and leave before continuing. "Natalie thinks he's probably just lonely, looking to make a friend."

However, Natalie had also been loopy from the painkillers, so what did she know—except not to walk on wet tin roofs while wearing cowboy boots anymore. Her newly fractured fibula had not only put her out of commission for a few weeks, but also sank one of my most promising battleships in the war against Ray and his nephew.

Stirring a packet of Splenda into her coffee, Mona raised her brows. "What do you think?"

"I think he needs to stay away from my daughter." Along with Jeff Wymonds.

After I'd lectured both kids last night about taking candy from strangers, I'd talked to them about the kidnappings—all of them. When I was finished, Addy had just stared at me, apparently speechless for once. Layne's only question had been if the police had checked Emma's bike for fingerprints—I should have named him Sherlock Jr.

"You figure out who your secret admirer is?" Mona asked.

"Not a clue." I had my fingers crossed that my chicken-rescuing cupid had let my love for daisies be known to

Wolfgang the other night while we were all at his place.

"Morning, Red," Ray said as he slid into the booth seat next to Mona. His yellow, button-up shirt emphasized his fake tan and light blue eyes. He smirked at me. "How's the Hessler house remodel going, short-timer? Has your girlfriend broken a nail replacing the gutters or windows yet?"

Mona leaned across the table, a frown on her glossy pink lips. "I thought you were just fixing up the inside and giving the lawn a manicure. You didn't mention exterior work."

It was my turn to frown. "Of course we need to fix the exterior. The roof is missing shingles, the eaves are rotting, and the paint is just flakes barely clinging to the wood in several spots." And that was just the easy stuff, according to Natalie.

"Oh, Vi. That's bad—"

"Any buyers yet?" Ray interrupted Mona with an unreadable glint in his eyes that made me feel vulnerable, like I was wearing one of those open-backed, paper hospital gowns.

"Maybe." I hadn't shown Doc the Hessler house yet, so there was still a tiny chance he wouldn't turn his nose up at it.

"Good morning, all." Jane dropped onto the seat next to me. Her floral and vanilla perfume drowned out Mona's jasmine scent. "Two coffees, please," she told the hovering waitress.

I sent Mona a raised-brows look, wondering why her happy vibe had faded at hearing about the work Wolfgang's house needed. She stared back, shaking her head.

Jane pulled out her magic task notebook and flipped to a page with today's date written in the top margin. My shoulders now tight, I sipped my orange juice and tried not to fixate on Mona's mood change. Out of the corner of my eye, I caught a glance of Jane's "To-Do" list and noticed my name in the number-two slot. The back of my knees started to sweat.

The waitress returned with Ray and Jane's coffees. I waited while she took each of our orders, wondering why I made Jane's list.

Jane clicked her pen and checked off the first task on her notepaper. "Ray, why don't you start with a status report."

While Ray, and then Mona, rattled off the potential and actual sales they had in-process, I stared at my orange juice and rubbed my finger over the cold sweat covering the glass. At least I had something to report on today.

A house, a ranch, and a buyer were all things to tout, especially the Hessler haunt. Once I had that place spit-polished, it was sure to land on Jane's "Big Winners" list; Harvey was all fired up to buy a bachelor pad in town after his place sold; and I'd found a new subdivision about ten miles northeast of Deadwood that I hoped was just up Doc's alley.

"Your turn, Violet." Jane's voice interrupted the locker-room pep talk I'd been giving my battered ego.

I sat up straight and spilled my three bits of news, ending with my golden goose—the Hessler house.

Mona patted my hand, her smile that of a proud mentor.

"About Wolfgang Hessler's place," Jane said, placing a checkmark next to my name in the number-two spot on her list. "We need to talk about something."

I stared at the checkmark. "We do?"

"Yes. There's a slight problem."

"What's that?" I dragged my gaze from the To-Do list and looked across the table at Ray, whose smirk now stretched ear-to-ear.

Jane poured some cream in her coffee. "As you already

know, the city of Deadwood is listed as a National Historic Landmark and a Historic Place on the South Dakota register. However, were you aware we also have a Historic Preservation Commission meant to protect the town's historic character and integrity?"

"No." *What was the problem?*

"This commission," Jane continued, "has implemented some strict rules and processes that everyone must abide by, including Realtors. Rules such as what color you can paint the house, what type of windows you can use to replace the old ones, and any other exterior changes you plan to make to the place."

"Crap." I sat back, my mind scrambling for a route around this road block. "Where do I find the guidelines for this kind of stuff?"

"They have a website with more details."

"Okay. I'll go online after breakfast and print the rules."

Ray snickered, seeming to enjoy some private joke on my account. I resisted the urge to stab my fork through the back of his hand.

"I like your attitude, Violet." Jane frowned at me as she lifted her coffee cup to her lips. "But that's not the problem."

My eye twitched. "What's the problem?"

"You don't have a Certificate of Appropriateness from the commission, so you can't work on the Hessler house."

Of course. I should have known there'd be some hoops to jump through with a historic agency at the helm. "Fine. I'll get one of these certificates and then start."

Ray laughed out loud. "You do that."

"You don't understand, Violet." Jane lowered her cup. "The Commission can take weeks, even months, with several reviews and sometimes public hearings before granting a certificate. There's no way you'll be able to put the Hessler house on the market before the end of the month," Jane finished just as the waitress arrived with our food.

Fuckity fuck! My appetite evaporated along with my optimism.

The rest of the Friday morning meeting was merely a drone of background noise for the tragic play, *Death of a Realty Career*, being performed in my head. As we filed out of Bighorn Billy's, I knew I couldn't go back to the office yet. Sitting there at my desk, listening to Ray schmooze his clients and pitch Benjamin to Jane would make me grind my molars down to little nubs, and I couldn't afford a visit to the dentist right now.

I needed a change of venue. Somewhere far from Ray and his taunting smirk, somewhere I could forget about needing to sell a house for a bit, somewhere I could hide while I focused on a part of my life where I had some control—like with my daughter.

***

I parked in front of the public library, a stately nineteenth-century gray-stone building fronted by four huge pillars. Perched just a block uphill from the historic Franklin Hotel and its stately front entrance, ornate decorations, and vintage furnishings, the library watched over Deadwood, chronicling transformations as the town cycled between seasons of bloom and wither.

The noonday sun sizzled my roots as I stepped out of my Bronco. A lone pickup shared the parking area with me, the surrounding streets quiet except for the faded growl of a chainsaw.

Last night, after a couple of glasses of wine, I had time to dwell on the kidnappings some more. The physical similarities between Addy and two of the three missing girls were not only undeniable, but also had my stomach twisted like a tie-dyed shirt. Until the police announced that they had a prime suspect sitting in their jail with indisputable evidence to back them up, my kid was a sitting duck.

I decided to take action, starting with reading up on the girl who disappeared in January, finding out if Addy was three for three. Since my budget didn't allow a computer at home yet, my options for finding information were limited. I could either try to sneak online at work, with Ray and Jane looking over my shoulder, or pay a visit to the library. The latter seemed my best bet.

Head down, I strode up the concrete sidewalk, my heels clacking up the steps. Next on the docket would be some sleuthing on Jeff Wymonds to see if I could tie him to each of the missing girls. The memory of sad-faced Kelly waving goodbye from her porch in the forefront of my thoughts, the picture of her best friend, Emma, in last August's newspaper a close second.

When I pushed open the heavy door, the smell of leather bindings, aged paper, and wood varnish welcomed me.

A pretty, young brunette sat behind the counter at the side of the room, her skin blotch- and wrinkle-free, her chest perky in a low-cut dress covered with plums. Compared to her, I was a saggy prune. It sucked getting older.

"Hi," I whispered as I approached the counter.

Miss Plum looked up from a celebrity-filled magazine she'd been perusing. "Can I help you?" Boredom edged her tone.

"How would I go about finding an old article in the *Black Hills Trailblazer* newspaper?"

"You need to fill this out." She handed me a piece of paper. "Then set up an appointment with us to come back later for a viewing."

Crudmongers. Did everything in this freaking town require paperwork and wait times?

"Oh, I forgot to mention," Miss Plum turned the page in her magazine, "there's also a search fee."

Of course there was. I stuffed the paper in my purse, wondering if Abe's Alehouse was serving hard liquor already.

"Unless you just wanted to view an article on microfilm. Then you can do it now for free."

It turned out that getting soused for lunch wasn't predicted in my horoscope for today after all. "That works."

"Cool. Follow me."

She led me past a table covered with computers and printers, through a narrow corridor lined with ceiling-high, book-laden shelves. Pausing in front of a closed door with a sign on it that read *South Dakota Room*, she asked, "Have you ever used a microfilm machine?"

"Sure." No, but how hard could it be?

Miss Plum pushed open the door and stepped into a small room. I followed, screeching to a halt at the sight of Doc sitting at a table, books stacked around him.

He looked up, his eyes widening when his gaze hit me.

"Hello, Violet." He shuffled some papers around, doing a rotten job of being discreet while trying to hide whatever it was he'd been reading.

Damn. The last thing I wanted right now was company, especially someone as distracting as Doc. I worked up a smile for him. "Hi, Doc. I didn't see your car out front."

"I walked here."

"It's hot outside."

"I took my time."

"They're calling for rain this afternoon." I sounded like an idiot. If I'd been wearing socks, I'd have taken them off and shoved both in my mouth.

"The hills could use the water."

"I hope you brought an umbrella."

"I dry easily."

I nodded, out of silly things to say about the stupid weather.

His dark eyes probed mine, making me squirm in my heels. What was it about this guy that made me feel like my bra was cinched too tight? Something that I couldn't put my finger on even if I wanted to—which for some reason, I did.

"How is the chicken?" he asked.

"Still a problem."

"And the kittens?"

"Up for adoption. You interested?"

He grinned, shaking his head.

I wondered if he had a girlfriend stashed away somewhere. Then I wondered where in the hell that thought had come from and why I cared.

Miss Plum cleared her throat. "Here's the machine."

I welcomed the interruption with my full attention.

She beckoned me over to the corner of the room.

Peeking at the stacks of books in front of Doc as I passed, I saw the words *Register of Deaths* and *City Directory*. What was he looking at those for? Researching his genealogy? Digging into Deadwood's infamous past? Or was he checking out estate sales? Looking up possible real estate investments?

Miss Plum pointed at a cabinet filled with tiny drawers, each labeled with a year. "When were you interested in?"

"Last summer," I murmured, keeping my back to Doc. I didn't want him to learn that I was chasing a paper trail for something that could just be a coincidence on Jeff Wymonds' part and a bit of over-reaction on mine.

Miss Plum pulled out a small spool and handed it to me. I stared at it like it was a toad waiting for a kiss.

"Here, let me help you." She plucked the spool from

my open palm. I watched as she stuck it in the machine and clicked a switch. A backlit newspaper page appeared on the screen. "There you are."

With a nod of thanks, I dropped into the seat and set my purse on the floor at my feet.

"If you need anything else, I'll be at the front desk." She left, closing the door behind her, leaving me alone with Doc.

Chapter Ten

I could hear Doc breathing in the silence. The back of my neck tingled as I pretended not to notice that he sat less than six feet away.

Staring down at the microfilm machine, I tried to keep focused on the task at hand—finding an article on the second "Missing" girl, the one who disappeared last January.

I pushed a big, green button on the front of the monitor.

Nothing happened.

I spun a knob just below the green button.

Nothing happened.

I pushed a button with a plus sign on it beside the knob.

The screen widened. At least I got a response that time.

I moved a lever under the knob to the left and right.

The screen's focus shifted left, then right.

The back of my eyeballs started to ache. Technology and I made cantankerous bedfellows. One of us usually stomped off in a huff after smashing the other into pieces with a club.

I tried to turn another knob that looked like a wagon wheel, but it wouldn't budge.

"Damn it." Maybe I could read the spool of film by holding it up to the light.

"Need some help?" Doc asked.

Not from him. "Yes, please."

As he came around behind me, I kept my gaze glued to

the monitor, catching his reflection in the screen. He leaned over my shoulder and grabbed a knob on the side of the machine.

I glanced at him, his cheek mere inches from mine. I hadn't remembered his eyelashes being so long.

"You smell good today," Doc said, his tone low, his voice just above a whisper.

He did, too—like sun-dried sheets instead of his usual woodsy cologne; but the fidgeting elephant parked on my chest kept me from telling him … and breathing. He was so close. Too close.

He inhaled. "Mmmmm. Makes me hungry."

I gulped. Had I heard him right? Was he really flirting so blatantly with me? I locked my fingers together and stared at a jagged scar below his elbow. It's not like I was new to flirting. I mean, I did have two children who weren't conceived due to any miracles. However, Doc was different, dangerous. I got the sense that behind his dark eyes lurked a beast I dared not pet, let alone poke.

"Do you have a date?" he asked.

How did he know about my dinner date with Wolfgang? My cheeks warmed, my skin tight and uncomfortable. "Umm, yes, but not until this evening."

The weight of his stare made my shoulder twitch. "Violet?"

I met his lazy grin. "Yes?"

"Am I making you nervous?"

"No." Standing so close, he had to be able to hear my heart pummeling against my ribs.

The brush of his fingertips across my wrist made me jump. His chuckle came from deep within his chest. "Liar."

Frowning, I whirled on him. "Listen, you're a nice guy."

He raised his brows. "Gee, thanks."

"And if you're the one who sent me the daisies, I appreciate the kind gesture."

His grin widened. "Daisies are your favorite."

"But getting personally involved with clients goes against my principles." Well, except when it came to Wolfgang—and Harvey—but he was just a friend.

"I didn't send you any flowers, Violet."

"Oh. Well, then good. I wasn't sure, being that Addy told you I like daisies."

"If I were going to send you flowers, they wouldn't be daisies."

What would they be? I clamped my teeth together to keep my tongue locked up.

"I agree with you," he continued. "We need to keep to the business at hand."

"Uh-huh." Roses were too cliché for Doc. Maybe he'd send tulips? No, too common.

"Sleeping with my Realtor is off-limits."

Sleeping with … His words sank in and my eyes widened. The image of our legs entangled in sheets, his whiskers scratching my bare stomach, his deep baritone voice groaning my name, whispering his wants and needs in my ear—all bundled in one breathtaking flash—ricocheted through my skull. My interest in Doc hadn't veered that far off the pavement. Until now.

He turned the knob on the side of the machine, the screen flickered with rolling images. "I'm not even sure what I'm doing that has you so skittish."

The heat in my cheeks spread down my neck, now fueled by embarrassment. Hold up! He was the one who started this. "You said I smelled good."

"You do."

"Then you said I'm making you hungry."

"You are."

I crossed my arms and glared at his profile. "How is that not coming on to me?"

He spared me a glance. "You smell like French fries and

bacon, and I haven't had lunch yet." His stomach growled next to my shoulder, as if on cue.

"Oh." The skin on my upper chest burned with mortification, too. "But you asked about my date tonight."

"I asked if you have a date."

"Same thing."

"A *newspaper* date for the article you're looking up."

I closed my eyes, wishing Scotty would beam me up right then. "Oh, crud. I'm sorry."

"Don't worry about it." The squeeze he gave my shoulder would have made me feel better if I could've run out of the room and avoided him for the next year. "So, you have a date?"

"Yes." My gaze now intently focused on the screen. "Last August."

He spun the knob faster, the images a blur. "Did Addy set you up?"

"What?"

"With your date tonight?"

"Oh. No." I peeked at him, noticing a second scar, this one very faint, above his eyebrow. "He asked me on his own."

"So, this is a first date?"

"Uh, yeah."

"I need more details."

What? Why was he so interested in my social life? Yet, my tongue kept rolling. "Well, I met him earlier this week, so I don't know much about him. He seems nice, though, and polite."

Sheesh. That made Wolfgang sound like Wally Cleaver.

Doc's body vibrated next to me, his laugh almost hidden by the whir of the microfilm machine. "I need more details about the article, Violet. Like what to look for in a headline."

My whole body broke into a sweat that reeked of

humiliation. Sitting so close to Doc was scrambling my brainwaves. I lunged out of the chair and put several feet of air between us. "I want to read about the girl that disappeared last winter. All I know is it happened sometime in January."

"It was January 10th."

The certainty in his tone froze my fiddling fingers. "You remember the exact date?"

He nodded.

Why? "Did any other girls disappear prior to last August?"

"Not recently. Not from Deadwood. No blondes."

I watched Doc as he scanned headlines, now turning the side knob much slower as he searched. Not only had he noticed the similarities between Addy and last summer's missing girl, he also knew the timeframe of the second girl's disappearance. Again, why?

"Here you go." Doc stepped back from the machine. "It looks like this one goes into a good amount of detail on it."

"Thanks for your help." I slid back into the seat, waiting until I heard Doc's chair scrape across the wood floor before letting my shoulders relax and diving into the article.

Jade Newel was the missing girl's name. She'd disappeared at the tender age of ten, most likely still pre-puberty, so I figured the chances of her having run away were slim.

The last place she'd been seen was in the very library in which I sat. One of the librarians had been interviewed (not Miss Plum, judging by the sophisticated word choices in the quotes), and said Jade had left shortly before closing time that Tuesday, which was eight o'clock.

The librarian remembered the girl as a quiet but happy child. Jade's outfit that evening had been a sweater covered with sunflowers and yellow snow boots. She'd been wearing a candy necklace, too, which the librarian made sure to stress was not really allowed in the library, but she'd made an exception that day. Jade had been one of her "favorites."

Like Emma, Jade had been a blonde. Her face was more heart-shaped, her hair longer, but she still had the general look of the others—and Addy. Jade's aunt described her as a polite, but shy girl. She hadn't had a lot of friends, only a handful and most from her swim class.

Her teacher used words like "good student," "smart girl," and "avid listener." The cops added quotes with "manhunt," "probably just lost in the woods," and "hope to find her soon."

The parents offered a sizeable reward, for which they thanked the community that had contributed. The article's author had ended with sentiments of hope and requests for prayers.

I sat back. The few remnants of breakfast I'd managed to choke down churned in my stomach as worries of Jade's fate, and that of all the other young girls in Deadwood—including my daughter—loomed.

I turned to Doc. His nose was buried in a book, the title shielded by his hand. "How do you print from this thing?"

He didn't look up from the page he was reading. "Push the green button on the front."

Ah. That was the green button's purpose. I pressed it and waited. "Nothing happened."

"The printer is by the front desk. The Off switch is under the knob I was turning."

"Thank you." Standing, I grabbed my purse. I'd like to have dug up more information on Jade's disappearance, but between my technological incompetence and the need to put a couple of walls and some fresh air between Doc and me, it was time to skedaddle.

"Did you find what you were looking for, Violet?"

"I'm not sure." The article was too fresh, my thoughts

drowned in details and images. I needed to let everything soak in and see what was left on the surface afterward. "Thanks again for your help."

He dragged his eyes from the pages and looked at me as I passed in front of him. "You're welcome. Are you available on Sunday to look at some more houses?"

I was available now if he'd quit sniffing around and actually bite into something. Anything. "Sure. What time?"

"One. Have fun on your date tonight."

I couldn't tell by his face if he was picking on me or not. "I'll try."

My hand was on the doorknob when his voice stopped me. "Wear green."

"Excuse me?"

His lazy grin was back. "You should wear something green to match your eyes."

Doc was a mix-master when it came to sending signals. His words seemed casual enough, but the intensity of his dark gaze had me nailed to the floor. I stood there, my tongue stumbling over itself, my face stuck between a blush and a frown.

"I'll see you on Sunday, Violet." Just like that, he returned his focus to the book in front of him and dismissed me without a second glance.

I closed the door behind me and leaned against it, my breaths swift and shallow.

What was wrong with me?

In five hours, Wolfgang would be pulling up in front of Aunt Zoe's house to take me to dinner. Undoubtedly, he'd be dressed in something drool-inspiring, his hair messed up just right, his cologne a notch above subtle, lighting pheromone firecrackers under my skin.

So, why was I standing here with my pulse pounding, imagining what Doc looked like naked as a jaybird?

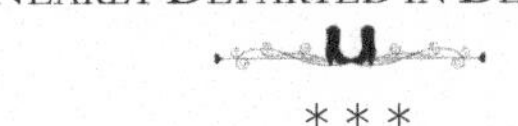

* * *

"He's here!" Natalie called from her post by Aunt Zoe's front window.

I gulped, nausea swelling up into my throat.

"Mom, your boyfriend is here," Addy sang as she came skipping into the upstairs bathroom, where I sat on the black-and-white checkered linoleum next to the toilet in my new, slinky green dress I'd bought at a consignment store in Lead.

"I heard."

If I were Cinderella, Addy would have been one of the little bluebirds today, whistling while she fluttered around me, helping me get ready for my date with Prince Charming. By the time I'd yanked up my stockings, she'd started planning the wedding.

I rolled onto my knees and gripped the cold toilet rim, the urge to empty my stomach bathing me in a fresh dew of sweat. The smell of ammonia drifted up from the sparkling bowl, which I'd cleaned after my first bout of nerves.

"What are you doing?" Addy asked, unwrapping a sucker. "You're going to get your dress all dirty."

"I'm getting ready for my date." I was also regretting that fourth latte I'd slammed this afternoon after leaving the consignment store. Too much caffeine mixed with a bucketful of nerves on an empty stomach had me kneeling at the altar of the Porcelain Goddess.

"You look like you're gonna spew." Sucker in her mouth, Addy pulled on a loose piece of door trim, letting it snap back against the frame over and over.

"Would you quit messing with that trim, Adelynn!" I didn't mean to bark at her, but patience wasn't exactly piloting the Mothership right now. "I've told you too many times, you're pulling out the nails."

"He's getting out of his car," Natalie hollered up the

stairs.

My stomach bucked.

"You should brush your teeth when you're done."

"Thanks for the advice, Sweetheart."

"Just in case he kisses you tonight."

"Nugghh," was all I could manage as I hovered over the open lid, swallowing as fast as I could.

"Do you think he'll kiss you?"

"I don't know." Kissing was the last thing my mouth was thinking about at the moment.

"Here, Vi," Aunt Zoe pushed past Addy and touched my shoulder. She held out a piece of bread. "Eat this, it'll help."

I didn't want to eat anything, but I shoved half the bread through my lips and managed to swallow. Then I choked down the other half and sipped from the glass of water she placed in my hand.

"He's coming up the sidewalk," Natalie reported.

Groaning, I sat back down on the floor. The clip holding my French roll in place clacked against the tiles as I leaned my head against the wall.

"Mom, can Kelly stay over tomorrow night?"

"I don't want to talk about this right now." Nor think about Kelly, Emma, Jade, or anything else having to do with the missing girls. This was supposed to be my night of romance. There was no way I was going to be able to get into "the mood" with worries and fears cooling the hots I had for Wolfgang.

"Adelynn," Aunt Zoe glanced over her shoulder, "go downstairs and help Natalie greet your mother's guest."

"I hope he slips you the tongue, Mom." Addy waved as Aunt Zoe nudged her out of the room and closed the door.

Forehead crinkled, I stared at the door. "Where'd she learn that?"

"MTV, probably." Aunt Zoe held out another piece of

bread. "You sure you're up to this tonight? I can go down and tell him you're under the weather."

The doorbell rang.

Stuffing my mouth full of bread, I pointed at myself and then gave Aunt Zoe a thumbs-up. There was no way I was going to put off this date. For one thing, my hair had participated and looked damned good. For another, I was planning on returning this fancy, green, lace-covered get-up as soon as possible in exchange for store credit. My bank account was looking a bit anorexic lately, and I couldn't afford to purge much more cash on non-essential items like expensive dresses—although it did erase twenty years and two kids from my cleavage.

I swallowed the bread. "I'm going on this date, even if it means carrying a barf bag in my purse and slipping off to the restroom every ten minutes."

"All right." Aunt Zoe offered me a hand up. "Then let's fix your lipstick and powder your nose."

The blonde staring back at me in the mirror didn't look like she'd spent the last half hour doing the Hokey Croaky. Hell, with all of the makeup Natalie had painted on me, the mirror could be a window to the past. Back before children had added frown lines, age spots, and gray hairs that only Clairol knew about.

A light knock on the door made Aunt Zoe and me both turn. The door opened wide enough for Layne to slip his head through. "Mom?"

"Yeah?"

"Wow! You look really pretty."

My son, my hero. I'd have to reward him with ice cream for that one. "Thanks, sweetie."

"Why do you have to go out to dinner with *him*? Can't you just eat here with us?"

Aunt Zoe and I exchanged grimaces in the mirror.

Layne had been doing a great impression of Eeyore

since I arrived home with my new ensemble in hand. He'd made it no secret that he didn't relish having his "man-of-the-house" status threatened.

"I thought you liked Wolfgang." I ruffled his hair.

Layne shrugged. "He's okay. A little odd, though."

He should meet Doc.

Opening the door wider, Aunt Zoe took Layne by the shoulders. "Come on, let's go downstairs. I made dirt pudding earlier and hid some treasures in it for you."

"Cool!"

With a "good luck" and a wink, Aunt Zoe steered Layne out the door.

I brushed my teeth, making sure to fill my mouth with enough minty-freshness to smell like an herb garden. Then I patched up my lipstick, interrupted only once by a counter-gripping ripple of queasiness.

The sound of crutches squeaking and clomping along the hallway announced Natalie's presence. "That dress was worth every penny," she said, leaning against the open door, her cheeks flushed.

I grinned. "It better be, because it took a lot of pennies to buy."

"The green makes your eyes look bigger, brighter."

"Thanks." An image of Doc's intense gaze when I left him in the South Dakota library room flashed in my mind. I blinked his face from my thoughts. I'd spent enough of the afternoon dwelling on his words and over-analyzing his signals. Tonight was about Wolfgang. Nice, no-hidden-messages, non-eccentric, gorgeous Wolfgang.

"So?" My brows raised, I stared at Natalie's reflection. "How's he look?

"Delicious. Drop a cherry on his head and I'd eat him for dessert."

I chuckled. "This sabbatical must be killing you."

Natalie ran her hand through her hair, tugging on it.

"God, yes. Maybe I could cheat, just this once."

"No way. He's mine, sister."

"Does that mean you are officially staking a claim?" Which had been our code words since we were teenagers for "back off, this one is taken."

"Yes."

"Fine." She tucked a loose curl back into my French roll. "Are you going to sleep with him tonight?"

"Natalie, it's our first date."

"So?"

"And I have two children."

"All the more reason to get it when you can."

Natalie's needs of the flesh ruled her actions more often than not, which explained why she had trouble finding the right guy. Handsome for her usually equaled heartache, not honor, truth, and happily ever after. My record in the relationship series wasn't much better, but I'd stopped trying and turned my focus on sexy men from the big screen who were either too old or too dead to break my heart.

I brushed away a smudge of mascara under my eye. "I'll just be glad to make it through dinner without dumping wine in my lap."

"You'll be fine. Just relax, be yourself, and he won't be able to resist you."

"Yeah, right. Until I have to cough up the fact that I won't be able to even start working on his house, let alone sell it, until September. Maybe even October." I wiped my hands on a yellow towel hanging over the star-covered shower curtain. "And that's if I still have my job by then."

"I'm sorry about that."

I squeezed Natalie's shoulder. "It's not your fault. It's all this damned red tape." I'd spent part of the afternoon jumping through the Historical Committee's bureaucratic hoops and submitting the mandatory paperwork. "Until the city gives me the green light, we're dead in the water—broken fibula or not."

"I'd offer to bribe someone on the committee with sex on your behalf, but I've taken this sabbatical vow, you see."

That made me laugh. "Thanks again for watching the kids. Aunt Zoe really needs to be at the shop tonight."

"No problem. I have big plans for the twins involving M&Ms, Twister, and a strobe light."

"They'll have seizures."

"Yeah, it'll be a blast." She loosened my spaghetti straps a bit, baring a hint more cleavage. "You ready, beautiful?"

I took a deep breath and worked my lips into a smile any parade queen would envy. "Now or never."

She stepped back as much as she could with her cast to allow me to pass. As I brushed against the frame on my way through the door, something tugged at my hip. I heard a ripping sound.

"Uh-oh," Natalie whispered.

I looked down. A dangling piece of lace flapped against my outer thigh, exposing a swatch of the green gauzy lining and a three-inch snag.

Natalie plucked a small strip of lace dangling from a nail that stuck out of the loose door trim. "Looks like you need a different dress."

I ran to my bedroom and slammed the door.

Chapter Eleven

The Wild Pasque was not only South Dakota's official state flower; it was also the name of Deadwood's sole hoity-toity, five-star watering hole. The menus came without prices, the wine included a corking fee, and the linens probably cost more than my fancy green dress, which now lay wadded up in the corner of my bedroom.

In spite of the rollercoaster start to my date, and my replacement dress being a decade out of style and a tad snug in the tummy, I made it through dinner without incident. White wine and Wolfgang's magnetism had my head buzzing by the time the waiter brought our tiramisu and espressos. Out on the dance floor, couples old and young swayed to a slow, jazzy, version of "Java Jive."

"You look beautiful in red." Wolfgang handed me one of the two dessert forks the waiter left behind. "In this light, your hair looks like strands of 14-carat gold, and your skin looks smooth as a pool of milk."

I grinned like a halfwit. How could I not? Across from me sat the hottest guy in the joint. "Thanks."

Natalie had been right. Wolfgang looked good—cotton candy, melt-in-my-mouth good. The flickering candle in the middle of the table painted his face in warm tones. His indigo shirt darkened his blue eyes while highlighting his blond locks.

I'd forgotten how intoxicating lust could be, especially when blended with alcohol, cologne, and unbridled charm. I found myself spinning thoughts about naked male flesh yet again.

"How long will you be in San Francisco?" I forked off a piece of tiramisu. I hadn't told Wolfgang the bad news about his house yet. I kept waiting for the right moment, and it kept not coming.

"A few days."

The taste of chocolate, mocha, and liquor all floating in a light cream dragged a moan from my throat. "This is heavenly."

His eyes held mine. "I'm glad you like it."

I took another bite, fumbling with my fork as I courted Natalie's idea of paying a visit to Wolfgang's hotel room tonight. "What time does your plane leave tomorrow?"

"Way too early."

A buxom sixty-something woman in a flower dress and rhinestone glasses paused on her way by our table. "Wolfgang Hessler. I'm so glad I noticed you sitting over here."

Wolfgang looked up at our visitor, a broad smile spilling onto his lips. "Hello, Mrs. Stine. You look lovely as usual. How are you this evening?"

She tittered under his charm. "Much better after finding out how bighearted you've been lately. The Deadwood Children's Shelterhouse can't thank you enough for your generous donation. Will you come over and say hello to my husband and let him thank you as well? We were great admirers of your grandfather."

"Well, I'm kind of busy." He glanced my way.

"Go ahead. I'll be fine." I dipped my fork into the tiramisu, my attraction to Wolfgang warming my body temperature several degrees after learning of his open-handedness when it came to a local kids' charity.

Dropping his napkin on the table, he pushed back his chair and followed Mrs. Stine. I couldn't help but admire his long legs, broad shoulders, and everything in between as he crossed the room.

"Hello, Blondie," a familiar voice said from behind me.

My shoulders tightened. I closed my eyes and hoped Ray was just an evil, hallucinatory side effect of too much booze.

"First Old Man Harvey, now Hessler. I see you're not above using your feminine wiles to lure clients."

Nope, Ray was the real thing. I opened my eyes and nailed him with a glare. "Go away, Ray."

His snicker made my jaw clench. He leaned in close, drowning me in a sinus-burning wave of Stetson cologne, lowering his voice. "Too bad sleeping with Hessler isn't going to get his house on the market any quicker."

"I'm not sleeping with him." Yet.

"You know, honey." The smell of liquor on Ray's breath made me shudder in revulsion. "I happen to be pretty good friends with a guy on the Deadwood Historical Committee. I might be able to pull some strings for you, get you a green light to start remodeling within a week instead of a month."

Tempting, but I knew better than to wag my tail and start panting. "What's your price?"

With his index finger, he drew a line up my bare arm. "Come over to my place after dinner and I'll show you."

I should have known. "I have plans."

"If you want to keep your job, you'll change them. I don't like sloppy seconds."

I laid my fork on my plate before I gave into the urge to bury it in his chest. I moved up close to his ear. "Go fuck yourself."

Ray chuckled and stood. "Your loss, Blondie. You'd better hit that unemployment office early Monday. I hear the line gets pretty long by lunchtime."

"Who's your friend, Violet?" Wolfgang asked as he stared at Ray. He'd returned just in time to keep me from launching myself at the asshole and scratching his eyes out. Lucky Ray.

"Good evening, Mr. Hessler." Ray held out his hand. "I'm not sure you remember me. I work with Violet."

Wolfgang was slow to grant a handshake, and quickly pulled his hand back, wiping it on his napkin afterward as he dropped into his seat. "Yes. Ralph, isn't it?"

"Ray, actually."

"Right. Are you here alone?"

"No. My nephew is sitting by the window. He's a real estate agent, too. We're celebrating a new job he's about to land."

"Good for you. He must be getting lonely." Wolfgang's eyes were on me now, his gaze searching. He reached across the table and squeezed my hand. His fingers were warm, tougher than I'd expected for a man who played with jewelry for a living. "Sorry about Mrs. Stine's interruption."

I smiled. "No problem."

"Feel like dancing?"

"Love to."

He kept hold of my hand as he helped me to my feet. "If you'll excuse us, Ralph," he said without looking in Ray's direction.

"Don't forget to pencil me into your dance card, Blondie." Ray threw out his parting shot as I walked away.

Chin held high, I followed Wolfgang onto the dance floor, relaxing into him as his arms encircled me. The spicy smell of his skin almost erased Ray's sleaziness from my mind. Almost.

"Have I told you how great you look tonight?" he said for my ears only.

I chuckled. "More than once."

We moved in silence around the dance floor for a few beats.

"What did he say?" Wolfgang asked.

"Who?"

"Your co-worker."

"Oh." I hesitated, shoving aside several nasty replies and the ugly truth. "He just complimented me on my dress."

"Liar." Wolfgang drew back and stared at me. "I saw your face when he leaned in close."

"Uhhh." The truth was too embarrassing. "He reminded me of something I need to tell you."

"Which is?"

The "right moment" I'd been waiting for all evening pulled into the station. I sighed. "I won't be able to put your house on the market before the end of the month."

"Why not?"

"Have you heard of the Deadwood Historical Committee?"

"In passing."

"Well, before we can fix up the exterior of your place, we need to get a Certificate of Appropriateness from them."

He grinned. Not the response I'd expected.

"It might take until the end of August before I get everything approved."

His smile widened.

I was speaking English, right? "Why do you look happy about this?"

"It means I'm stuck here in Deadwood longer."

"Exactly."

"With you as my Realtor."

"Yes." Well, maybe. That depended on Doc, my only buyer.

"I can think of worse fates."

Easy for him to say. He wasn't single and supporting two children in need of new school clothes.

"Unless you are willing to consider selling your house

as-is." I crossed my fingers behind his back.

If he took the bait, I could plant a For Sale sign in his yard tomorrow and send out word that there was a hell of a deal available in the Presidential district. If Wolfgang let me price it low enough, I might be able to attract other Realtors looking to flip the house in addition to regular buyers.

"As-is?" He frowned at me for several seconds.

I held my breath and hoped for an answer that could help save my job.

"No, I can wait longer." He pulled me close again, resting his jaw against my forehead. "It allows me more time to get to know you."

I groaned inwardly, wishing I was at home on the couch in my sweats with a gallon of peanut butter fudge ice cream in hand and Elvis' *Viva Las Vegas* on the boob tube. The hot and horny rumblings I'd felt earlier were now stilled by reality's cold, clammy grip.

My toes ached in my stilettos by the time the song finally came to an end. Wolfgang led me back to our table, where I dropped into my seat.

"Are you interested in anything else to drink?" The waiter asked as he made his rounds.

Wolfgang looked at me with raised brows.

Getting stone drunk sounded perfect right about now, but I shook my head and tried to hide my worries behind a fake grin. "No, thanks."

"Just the check, please." Wolfgang turned to me after the waiter left. "What's the plan now that remodeling has been placed on hold until the paperwork game plays out?"

"Well, the commission's rules apply only to the outside, so I think we should get started on cleaning up the inside."

"Sounds good. Mother will hate the idea of strangers in her house."

"*Will*?" I pointed out his slip of the tongue with a smile to soften it.

He waved off my question. "Sometimes it seems like she's still hanging around, cooking sauerkraut, telling me to mow the lawn. She was never the warm, loving type, but I certainly miss her apple strudel."

Not sure if I should dwell on the emotional moment or continue with business, I chose the most comfortable option. "I'll wait until the house is empty before hiring a cleaner."

Maybe Margo could fit me into her cleaning schedule now that I had a month with which to play. I'd have to give her a call tomorrow.

I tossed back the last of my water as Wolfgang paid for dinner, my stomach fluttery at the thought of a possible goodnight kiss. I should have listened to Addy and packed my toothbrush along, but I'd been too pissed at her for her part in snagging my green dress to even glance her way before we left.

As Wolfgang and I stood to leave, I gazed across the room at Ray and his nephew, whose back was to me. Was I willing to exchange sex for my job tonight? It was just bodily fluids, right? No kissing, no fondling, just in and out—literally. I could close my eyes, pretend I was with Wolfgang, maybe Doc. The old "take one for the team" mantra. How tough could it be?

Ray looked up and caught my stare. He blew me a kiss.

I recoiled, my alcoholic buzz replaced by Ray-induced queasiness. Nope, that was not going to happen.

Wolfgang placed his hand on my lower back. "You ready?"

The trip home was quick and quiet. Too soon, Wolfgang was strolling up the walk with me.

"Thanks for dinner. I had a wonderful time."

"My pleasure. Will you dine with me again after I return from San Francisco?"

"I'd love to."

The front window curtain twitched. We had an audience.

I stopped at the base of the porch steps. "Oh, I meant to ask, did you send me flowers yesterday?"

He shook his head, his white teeth gleaming in the feeble glow of the porch light.

If it wasn't Doc or Wolfgang, who was it? Harvey?

"Sounds like I have some competition," he said.

"I guess you do." The image of Doc's dark stare stirred my thoughts before I could blink it away.

Wolfgang took my hand and tugged me toward him.

My heart throbbed in my throat. Here it was, the magic moment—stars twinkling, crickets chirping, Aunt Zoe's honeysuckle blooms perfuming the night air. My pulse sped like a chipmunk on Red Bull, my lips tingled, my armpits dampened.

I hadn't kissed a man in almost two years, and that guy had smelled like onions and could have been the missing link between modern humans and the Neanderthals. I shivered, feeling like I was fifteen again, learning all about teenage hormones with Johnny Dean on a ten-minute break from Driver's Education class.

"I've wanted to kiss you all night," Wolfgang whispered.

"Ah, hah. My telepathic powers worked."

His chuckle vibrated in his chest. "Any objections?"

I raised my chin, ready and waiting. "Nope, but you'd better hurry. My kids already know we're out here. With Natalie in a cast, I don't know how long she can keep them penned in."

He touched my hair, twisting a loose curl around his finger. "You have beautiful eyes, Violet. Beautiful skin. Beautiful hair."

His wooing technique was a winner. I closed my eyes and opened my mouth, giving him the green light. Seconds ticked by. Then more seconds.

"I think we have an audience," Wolfgang said.

I opened my eyes, expecting to see my kids with their faces plastered against the window, but they weren't there. "We do? I don't see Addy or Layne."

"I'm not talking about your children." Wolfgang nodded toward the street.

I followed his gaze, squinting in the dark. Under a Ponderosa pine, about a half-block down the road, stood the shadowed silhouette of a man.

Somebody was watching us.

* * *

Saturday, July 14th

Old Man Harvey was on the prowl for houses—prematurely, in my opinion. However, Harvey wasn't interested in listening to what I had to say.

From the moment he'd burst through Calamity Jane's front door this morning, he'd been overflowing with piss and vinegar, cursing and swearing as he crossed the floor. Needing to pry his bony ass from the chair opposite my desk before Mona's VIP clients showed up for their appointment, I decided to take him on an impromptu tour of available homes.

The first place we checked out was located in a narrow gulley on the way up to Terry Peak. Several cars and a pickup sat in the drive. An Open House sign and the sweet smell of fresh-baked cookies drew us inside.

Upon entering, I nodded to the redheaded real estate agent who was acting as hostess, noticing her petite-yet-busty frame. Harvey did too. His whispered comment was flattering, admiring her tight silk dress; mine was a tad snarky.

We shook our heads at the mustard-colored living room

carpet and walked through the first doorway on the left—a bedroom.

Harvey let out a low whistle. "These pink walls remind me of a brothel where I used to hang my hat in Nevada."

I nudged him with my elbow, my face warming as a young couple over by the closet hit us with a pair of frowns.

Harvey ignored me. "What was the name of that beauty with the big bottom? Oh, yeah, Wet Willy."

I cleared my throat, glaring at him.

"She sure loved horses. She used to strap this saddle on my back and ride to town, whoopin' and hollerin' the whole time."

The couple was gaping now, disgust mirrored on their faces.

Criminy! I pushed him into the kitchen, where a batch of chocolate chip cookies cooled on a plate. I grabbed two when the redhead wasn't looking; Harvey nabbed three. They tasted pre-made. Figured. She didn't look like the Betty Crocker type. More like Jessica Rabbit with talons.

A gray-haired man with an anchor tattoo on his left arm entered the kitchen. Harvey's mouth kicked back into drive, his anecdote including a Navy buddy, an exotic Spanish dancer, and a handful of numbered ping-pong balls. By the time he'd finished, Miss Rabbit hovered, red lips squeezed tight, nostrils flared.

I took the hint and hightailed it out of there. Having learned my lesson on exposing Harvey to other clients, I headed to the house in which Doc had experienced his gardenia-inspired allergic reaction. When I pulled up in front and found no other cars in the drive, my shoulders sagged in relief.

Twenty minutes later, I stood next to the stainless-steel fridge while Harvey inspected the cupboard under the sink, confirming the new-copper-plumbing claim listed on the brochure. The smell of Pine-sol and Lemon Pledge wafted around me, making me wonder if the owner had an air freshener stowed somewhere.

My thoughts returned to last night's ending and the kiss that never happened. "You were wrong," I told Harvey, leaning against the counter with my arms crossed. "Wolfgang is not gay."

"Then he's the purtiest man I've ever seen," Harvey said from inside the cupboard. "What makes you so sure he's not?"

"I went out on a date with him last night."

"That doesn't make him straight."

"He kissed me good night," I fibbed, kind of.

Had Wolfgang and I not been interrupted by another of Aunt Zoe's neighbors, Mr. Stinkleskine, who was moonlighting as a Peeping Tom while taking his Chihuahua out for a potty break, we would have played some serious tonsil hockey. As it turned out, voyeurism was a major turn-off for both of us. Instead, all I'd gotten was a peck on the lips and a "see you next week."

Harvey grunted, backed out of the cupboard, and with my helping hand, returned to his feet. "With or without tongue?"

His question made me squirm for a second. "Harvey, that's none of your business."

He grinned. "Fine, but tell me this—was it just a single kiss, or was it several all lumped together."

I tugged on the collar of my sleeveless dress. Discussing the particulars with Harvey of a barely-existent kiss was not what I'd planned when I brought up the subject. "I don't remember."

"Bullshit."

"What? I was taken away by the whole moment."

His narrow eyes held mine. "Until you sleep with him, I'm not buying he's straight."

"Well, I'm certainly not going to call you with the details

if that time comes."

"What do you mean 'if'? Did you wear your hair down or up?"

"Mostly up." I pushed away from the counter and headed for the French doors leading into the backyard. I needed some air before the dew on my back turned into a full-on sweat.

Harvey followed me outside. "You should have worn it down. Men like long hair."

Next he'd be asking if my underwear had been lacy or satin. A change of subject was necessary. "Harvey, what do you know about the latest little girl who disappeared?"

"This yard is too damned big." Harvey grabbed my arm and dragged me back inside. As he closed and locked the French doors, he glanced at me over his shoulder. "You mean Tina Tucker?"

I nodded.

He headed back through the kitchen. "Her grandpa worked at Homestake for forty-plus years as a shaft sinker and drift miner, opening up new passageways, air vents, auxiliary tunnels, and shafts. Not a job for weenies. Her mama manages the Motherlode Diner in Sturgis. Her pa ran off with a carnie floozy who operated that ride that scrambles your guts."

None of that information did me much good when it came to pinning the abduction of the missing girls on Jeff Wymonds, my number-one suspect.

In the well-lit foyer, Harvey stopped and glanced at the stairs. The stained-glass windows dappled his skin with pink and blue-tinged tints. "Those stairs are too steep."

"They're the typical size."

"I'm too old for stairs. Show me a one-story house."

There was only one single-story house in town I could think of—Lilly Devine's haunt. The interior colors alone in that place might push Harvey over the Wacky state line, right into Bonkerville, the capital of Cuckoo County.

I opened the front door and held it wide for him to slip past me. "Do you think Tina Tucker knew Kelly Wymonds?"

He shielded his eyes from the late morning sun. "Probably. The kids from Deadwood and Lead all go to the same school. They're bound to have bumped into each other."

"But were they friends?"

"How would an old man like me know that? You think I hang out at the local playground to collect my gossip? Hell, no! You gotta hit the bar for the good stuff."

As we climbed into my Bronco, he added, "But I do know that Kelly's grandma and Tina's grandpa are kissin' cousins."

"So there is a link between the girls."

"Girl, most all of us old-timers up here in the hills share a little bit of the same blood. There may be a lot of land, but it's a small group of people living on it."

All the way back to the office, Harvey recounted bits of his family history, clarifying how many of the women he'd slept with over the years were distant relatives—too many in my book.

For once, Doc's Camaro wasn't hogging my parking spot. Ray's rig was instead. Bastard.

The blast of air conditioning as we entered Calamity Jane's via the back door cooled my face. I could smell Mona's jasmine perfume even though she was nowhere to be seen.

Ray snarled at me from his desk, his ear glued to his phone as he jotted down some notes.

"Woo-wee! Look what you got." Harvey pointed at my desk.

I followed his finger to a blue vase chock-full of daisies. Had someone moved the bouquet from the top of the filing cabinet? Nope, they were still there, showing hints of wilting in their smiling heads.

"Your new loverboy must really think you're something," Harvey said with a big grin.

Ray covered the speaker part of the receiver. "He's just paying for services rendered."

"Oh, go blow a goat," I said, not caring that Harvey heard me.

I walked to my desk, shooting a raised-brow look in Harvey's direction. "Are these flowers from you?" I knew the answer before asking the question, but I just wanted to hear it from his own mouth.

Harvey made a raspberry sound with his lips. "Are you kidding? Daisies are a waste of money. If you want to impress a lady, you need to buy her red roses. If you want to get her into bed, bring diamonds to the party. Every man knows that."

A small purple envelope sat on a stand tucked between the blossoms. I plucked it out and tore it open.

"Well?" Harvey peered over my shoulder. "What's it say, hot stuff?"

I read the scrawls aloud:

Your lips were red.
Your dress was, too.
I watched you dance last night,
What a beautiful view!

Trying to breathe through the panic welling up my esophagus, I fell into my chair.

Someone besides Mr. Stinkleskine had been spying on me last night. Who?

Chapter Twelve

I was still sitting at my desk, frowning down at the little love poem from my admirer, when my cell phone rang. I dropped the purple card and fished for my cell in my purse.

"I'm stepping out for lunch, Blondie," Ray said, jingling his keys. "Try not to make any sales while I'm gone. I'd hate to have to cancel the goodbye party I'm planning for you."

Harvey plucked one of my daisies from the bouquet as Ray headed for the back door. "You want me to fill his ass with buckshot?"

Yes! "Maybe later."

Aunt Zoe's number filled my phone's screen. Now what did Layne want for his archaeological dig? A sarcophagus? "Hello?"

"Mom," Addy's voice greeted me. "Can I stay at Kelly's tonight?"

Hell, no! I sighed. "Addy, can we discuss this later?"

Across my desk, Harvey glanced up from playing she-loves-me-not with the daisy, a smirk on his lips.

"No, Mom. You keep blowing me off."

I was not in the mood to be flogged by the Queen of Dramaland. "I'm not blowing you off, Adelynn. This is just . . ."

Never going to happen.

"Complicated."

Harvey dropped the flower and grabbed a pencil and a Post-It note.

My desk phone rang. I glanced at the phone number on

the LCD screen. A 415 area code greeted me. Wolfgang was calling me on his cell. My heart pitter-pattered a bit faster.

"And all you have to do is say, 'yes.'" Addy wrapped up, and I realized that the shrilling whine in my ear had been her arguing her point.

"There is more to this decision than you realize, Addy." I reached for the other phone as it rang again. "Honey, I have another call. I have to go."

Harvey placed the note and pencil in front of me and waved goodbye. I glanced at the words 'going next door' scribbled on the paper and looked up as he pushed open the front door and stepped outside.

Three rings.

Next door? The only thing next door was Doc's office. Why was Harvey going to Doc's?

"But, Mom!" Addy's voice sounded watery. "She's the only friend I have in the whole world."

I rolled my eyes.

"I promise I'll be good at her house."

Four rings.

"Please, please, please, Mommy. I'll even give away one of my kitties."

Bribery. I was tempted.

Five rings.

I caved—well, kind of. "Why don't you see if Kelly can spend the night with us tonight."

A scream of excitement made me wince as the phone rang for the sixth time.

"Addy, I'm hanging up now. Bye." I closed my cell while picking up my desk phone. The smell of Ray's Stetson cologne on my receiver made me yank the phone away and frown at it. The jerk probably licked it.

"Calamity Jane Realty." I was careful not to touch the hard plastic to my face. "This is Violet."

"Hi, Beautiful," the sound of Wolfgang's voice washed

away my frown. "How is Deadwood treating you this morning?"

"Like a fish that's starting to stink." I leaned back in my chair. "How's San Francisco?"

I pictured him standing on a cable car, a view of Alcatraz shrouded with fog behind it, Golden Gate Bridge towering off to the side. Having never been to San Francisco, my mental images were sponsored by Rice-A-Roni, with Dirty Harry in charge of promotion. I could almost taste the savory grains of rice.

"It's a bit lonely without you."

Aw, shucks. Even with a mountain range between us, Wolfgang could charm a girl's stockings off.

In the background, I heard *beep-beep-beep* and the diesel growl of a tractor. Not exactly the romantic moan of a fog horn, but I could still make it work in my San Francisco fantasy.

"How are things going with Mother's house?"

"Okay." I lied. "You'll be back on Wednesday, right?"

"Yes. I have an idea. How about we take your kids somewhere fun in Rapid City next week?"

"They'd like that." While Addy had warmed up to Wolfgang on sight alone (as her mother had), Layne's initial friendliness had vaporized upon finding out that Addy's song about Wolfgang-and-Violet-sitting-in-a-tree could become more than just a tease. Spending more time with Wolfgang might convince Layne to call off his hounds.

I'd like to try another ride on the dating train, too. This time, sans Ray and Mr. Stinkleskine.

My cell phone trilled in my other hand. I looked at it and cursed mentally at the sight of Aunt Zoe's number again. I wanted to cancel the call and keep pretending I was in San Francisco with Wolfgang, but the mother in me won. "Sorry, but my cell is ringing. I have to go."

"See you Wednesday, Violet."

"I'm looking forward to it." I hung up the phone and pondered dipping into my savings for a visit to the hair salon in anticipation of his return. I flipped open my cell. "Hello?"

"Mom?" Layne said.

I blinked in surprise, expecting Addy. "Yes?"

"We're out of glue."

He said it as if glue was one of the staples of day-to-day life. "I just bought a bottle a couple of weeks ago."

"I used it all on my cardboard tank. I need more."

"You're not sniffing it are you?" Dear God, I didn't have to deal with my kid trying to get high already, did I?

"What? No!"

"Good."

"Why? What happens when you sniff it?"

"Your brain melts and leaks gray slime out your ears." I was a firm believer in telling tall tales when necessary. A spiel of girl giggles interrupted our conversation.

"Layne, is Kelly over there?" Addy failed to mention that when she called.

"Uh, huh. Addy wants me to ask you if she can ride her bike over to Kelly's house. Kelly needs clothes and a toothbrush."

Warning alarms whooped. "Tell both girls to stay put. I'll go get Kelly's stuff."

It was a good opportunity to spy on Jeff Wymonds while under legitimate cover. I glanced down at the Post-It note on my desk. Maybe I'd drag Harvey along for protection.

"Okay. Bye, Mom." The phone went quiet.

Closing my cell, I blew out a long breath and stared at the daisies in front of me. They smiled back, clueless to the lack of sleep they'd be causing tonight. At least I wouldn't have to lie awake worrying about Addy snoring under Jeff Wymonds' roof.

After a few mental "I-think-I-can" push-ups, I stuffed my phone in my purse, moved the daisies over next to their droopy cousins on the filing cabinet, and tossed Harvey's Post-It in the trash on my way out the front door. I left the lights on and changed the "Open" sign to "Back in an hour." Ray would probably return from lunch before then. It wouldn't take long for the snake to swallow a rat or two.

Doc's door was unlocked. I pushed inside and found the front room empty. A hint of Doc's woodsy smelling cologne wafted around me. "Hello?"

Floorboards creaked from somewhere in back. Footfalls followed. Doc stepped into the room. "Hello, Violet."

The sight of his bare legs gave my tongue amnesia. I was used to seeing Doc in a T-shirt and jeans. In his green tank top, tan cargo shorts, and naked feet, he looked fresh off the beach. All we needed was some sand, a surfboard, and a hemp necklace, and I'd be California dreamin' again.

Doc's gaze journeyed down to my sandals and back up to my mouth. "Nice lipstick. It matches your toes."

"Oh." I swallowed the urge to lick my lips. "Thanks."

He sat on the edge of his desk, stretching his long legs out in front of him. "What can I do for you?"

"I'm looking for a friend."

He winked at me, his grin flirting. "I'm your Huckleberry."

My stomach fluttered like a chicken coup in a fox raid. "You're my what?"

"Huckleberry."

"The sweet or the tart kind?"

"Which do you prefer?" He crossed his arms over his chest.

I pretended not to notice his biceps and triceps. "The sweet."

"Ah, the lady loves sugar."

"It's my drug of choice." Why did my white, scoop-neck sundress now feel as warm as a fur-lined parka? Had the air conditioner died?

"I'll make a note of that."

"Are we still talking about huckleberries?"

His grin was now cockeyed. "Oh, no."

Doc was doing it again, running circles around me, tying me up in knots, lighting little fires around my feet. Just like he had at the library. "I didn't think so. What was my original question?"

"You said you were looking for a friend."

"That's right." However, my body was apparently looking for something more, and it was holding its own gigolo auditions whether my brain was on the judging panel or not. I really needed to have sex soon. Or devour several gallons of peanut butter fudge ice cream. Or sell a house. Something orgasmic.

The faint sound of a toilet flushing came from the back area. Harvey walked out, drying his hands on his jeans. "Whew! Almost waited too long."

I looked from Doc to Harvey. "I didn't know you two knew each other."

"We do now," Doc answered.

Harvey patted Doc on the shoulder as he shuffled by him. "Doc is going to fix me up good, aren't ya?"

"As long as you follow my advice."

As usual when in Doc's presence, I was scratching my head. I opened my mouth to pry about what it was he did for a living, but Harvey cut me off.

"So who's your stalker?"

"Stalker?" I blurted. Harvey's question left my brain stumbling in the dark for a second or two until I remembered the poem that came with the daisies. "Oh, you mean from last night."

"What happened last night?" Doc asked.

Harvey beat me off the line. "Some peeping Tom was

spying on her and her loverboy while they were dancing. He wrote her a little poem about how purty she looked in her red dress."

Wolfgang isn't my "loverboy," thank you very much, Harvey. Hell, I hadn't even made it to first base with him.

Doc's brows raised. "How was your big date?"

Discussing the sad state of my romantic affairs in front of Doc made me squirm. It was like inspecting my underwear for holes in the company of a stranger—a dark, attractive stranger with great legs.

"It was okay." I tried to play it down for some reason that I wasn't sure I wanted to explore.

"Just okay?"

"She didn't get any action."

"Harvey!"

He snorted. "What? You didn't. Not really." He grinned at Doc. "Her boyfriend is a bit light in his cowboy boots, if you know what I mean."

"He's not my boyfriend." That label required a lot more tongue action first.

"Fine. Your client with benefits."

Doc's gaze narrowed. "You went on a date with a client?"

"Sort of." My cheeks warmed, damn it. "Let's just drop this, okay. The flowers are no big deal."

"Bullshit," Harvey expressed his disbelief with his typical eloquence.

"It's probably just from one of those guys who saw the singles ad that Addy placed for me in last week's paper."

Harvey grunted. "Sounds like you need a bodyguard."

"No, it's nothing." I hoped.

"Did your boyfriend send you the flowers?" Doc asked.

"He's not my boyfriend," I reiterated, stressing that with an unyielding stare. "And no, he didn't."

Doc held my gaze. "Then it doesn't sound like 'nothing'

to me. Harvey's right. You could use a bodyguard."

"I'll volunteer," Harvey said. "Hell, I don't have nothin' else to do these days but watch the clover grow in the fields."

I knew the crazy, old buzzard well enough already to know a losing battle before I picked it. Besides, I wanted him along for the visit to Jeff Wymonds. Now I wouldn't sound like a coward in front of Doc. "Okay, Harvey. You're it." I hoisted my purse higher on my shoulder. "I need to go pick up some clothes for Addy's friend, Kelly. She's spending the night. Want to come along and watch my back?"

"Yes, ma'am." Harvey waved at Doc on his way to the door. "See you on Tuesday, Doc."

I followed Harvey.

"Violet," Doc's voice stopped me on the threshold.

I turned back. "Yes?"

"Is Kelly's dad the same guy we saw at the gas station the other day?"

"Uh-huh."

His forehead furrowed. "Be careful."

"I will."

"Don't let Harvey leave your side."

He must have been reading my mind. I nodded. "See you tomorrow at one." I backed out the door, holding his stare, wondering if he knew something about Jeff Wymonds that I didn't.

The trip to Kelly's house was filled with Harvey's ideas on different ways he could guard me, from spending the night on Aunt Zoe's front porch, camping in his pickup across the street every night, to sleeping with Aunt Zoe's spinster-turned-sex-kitten neighbor, Miss Geary, while he kept an eye on me.

By the time I parked my Bronco in front of the Wymonds' house, Harvey's plan had grown elaborate enough to include hand signals and bird calls. I'd had to nix the idea of me wearing a wire—mainly because Harvey's version required me being plugged into an outlet at all times.

Jeff's front yard still looked like the parking lot of a Rednecks Anonymous meeting. His screen door had been torn from its hinges since my last visit and now lay on the grass next to the porch. The front door was open several inches, the sound of a baseball game spilling onto the lawn. With Harvey on my heels, I knocked on the door hard enough for my knuckles to sting.

Several seconds passed, my breath held, and then I heard the faint slaps of footfalls on linoleum. A frizzy-haired, platinum blonde poked her head around the door. The bags under her eyes added a decade to her face.

"Who are you?" Her eyes seemed more suspicious than wary as she glanced back and forth between Harvey and me.

I smiled big and bright. "Hi. I'm Addy's mom. Kelly was supposed to have called for permission to spend the night at my house tonight."

At least, I'd assumed the girls had gotten permission from one of Kelly's parents. I peeked over the blonde's frizz, searching for a glimpse of Jeff.

"Oh, yeah." The blonde opened the door wide, her suspicious glint mellowing into an apologetic frown. "Sorry. You caught me off-guard."

"I would have called first," I lied, "but I didn't have your number." Calling ahead would have foiled my surprise plan.

"That's okay." She held out her hand. "My name is Donna."

"Violet Parker." Her handshake felt as firm as a watery Jello. I indicated toward Harvey. "And this is—"

"Sylvester Schwarzenegger," Harvey finished for me.

I choked on my spit, coughing into my hand, blinking away my tears. "Sorry about that. Swallowed wrong."

Donna smiled at Harvey. "You look really familiar. Are you related to the movie star?"

Harvey nodded. "We're third cousins on his father's side."

A strangled giggle escaped from my throat before I could corral it. "Uh, Donna. You have a very nice daughter. She's been great for Addy."

Donna's smile faded around the edges. "Thanks. I'm glad she's been behaving for you. Can you give me just a moment while I grab Kelly's bag?"

"Sure. No problem."

Donna disappeared, leaving the door open in her wake.

I hit Harvey in the shoulder. "What are you doing?"

He grunted from the blow. "If I'm your bodyguard, I have to be undercover."

"I thought you said everyone knows everybody else around these parts."

"By name, yes; but I haven't seen Donna since I grew out my beard."

Shaking my head, I leaned in the doorway, hungry for a glimpse of Jeff and Donna Wymonds' home. The front door opened into a small foyer, half-walls topped with skinny posts on the right and left divided it from the dining room and kitchen.

The house smelled of cigarette smoke and beer. A burst of applause came through an arched opening in the dining room.

Harvey stepped past me into the house. I grabbed his arm and pulled him back outside. "Where are you going?" I whispered.

"To check out the place. Aren't you curious if the inside is as messy as the outside?"

Actually, I had darker curiosities. "Of course."

"Come on, then." He pulled me inside.

"Harvey, stop it."

Donna walked through the arch in the dining room. She stopped at the sight of us.

"Can I use your restroom?" I threw out the first thing I could think of, guilt frying my cheeks over an open flame.

"She has a weak bladder," Harvey explained.

I shot him a glare for his help.

"Oh, sure." Donna pointed toward the kitchen. "There's a small bathroom in the utility room, past the pantry."

"Why don't you wait outside for me," I told Harvey. I didn't want him snooping around—with or without me.

"Fine." Harvey growled low in his throat. "But make it quick. It's hot out there."

"Can I get you something to drink, Mr. Schwarzenegger?" Donna followed me into the kitchen.

"A beer would be great."

Donna's laugh had a sharp edge. "You sound like my husband."

I turned down a short hall just off the kitchen, rushed past a washer and a half-opened dryer, and shut myself in a small bathroom. Unfortunately, I couldn't hear a thing going on in the other room between Harvey and Donna, which made my nervous perspiration turn into a full-on anxious sweat.

Where was Jeff? Where was Kelly's baby brother? And why hadn't Donna cleaned the toilet in the last year?

I hovered in the opposite corner of the corroded toilet and counted to twenty, then flushed with my shoe. Turning the doorknob through a protecting layer of dress, I tiptoed back into the laundry room.

As I walked by the half-opened dryer door, I froze on my toes. A suitcase sat on top of the Maytag, its top unzipped and half-filled with pastel-colored clothes. I crept over to it, taking a closer peek. They weren't little-girl clothes, as I'd initially thought. Donna was going somewhere, and in a hurry based on the way she'd just tossed in her clothes instead of folding them.

Did Jeff know? Maybe Kelly would.

I stepped back and glanced down at the trash can next to the dryer. The back of my neck prickled at the sight of a bouquet of mixed flowers crammed in with lint wads and dryer sheets. Red roses, yellow carnations, and white daisies stared up at me. A little purple envelope lay crinkled on top of one of the daisies. I reached into the can.

"What are you doing?"

I jumped at the sound of Donna's voice behind me. With my body drumming, fright and flight pushing and shoving inside me, I whirled around. "Sorry. I saw the flowers and …" flight won and my mind flew off with any good excuses. "Sorry."

"I gave Kelly's backpack to Mr. Schwarzenegger."

"Great." I squeezed past her into the kitchen, my arms wanting to flap on out of there, too.

Harvey stood by the open front door, drinking a can of beer. His gaze was questioning as I approached. I shook my head slightly. Something was definitely wrong at Kelly's house, and I couldn't escape to my Bronco fast enough.

The hot sunshine did little to remove the chill covering my back. "Thanks for letting me use the restroom," I said on my way down the steps.

Donna followed us outside. "Would you mind letting Kelly stay two nights with you?"

I nodded. Sure, whatever, just let me get the hell away from this place. "I'll bring her back Monday morning."

"Monday evening will work better for Jeff."

Where was Donna going to be Monday night? "Evening it is," I agreed from my driver's side door.

"Nice to meet you both." Donna waved and then

turned and shut the door. In the still air, I heard the deadbolt clunk.

Harvey looked at me over the Bronco's hood. "What happened in there? You looked like somebody pinched your tail feathers when you came out of the bathroom."

I waited until we were both inside the Bronco and I'd started the engine before answering. "I found a bouquet of flowers in the trash."

"So."

"From the same florist as the ones sent to me, purple envelope and all."

"Oh."

"It creeped me out. Makes me wonder if Jeff Wymonds is sending me flowers for some reason." The memory of Jeff's face pressed against the screen door, staring and sneering as he said my full name, made me shudder as I backed onto the street. My tires chirped on the pavement as we sped away.

"If flowers made you act like that," Harvey said, "maybe you should pull over for a second."

I glanced at Harvey. "Why? What do you mean?"

"I saw a poster board in Donna and Jeff's bedroom."

"When did you have time to go in their bedroom?" How long was I in the bathroom?

"They don't call me 'Mongoose' at the senior center for nothing," Harvey answered, grinning with pride. "Anyway, the poster was covered with pictures of all three missing girls."

I swerved into Deadwood Dan's Spuds and Suds gravel parking lot and hit the brakes. A dust cloud swarmed around us. "Really? Are you positive?"

"Sure am. They were the pictures from those Missing Girl flyers. Probably cut from them. There were several cutouts of each girl."

Goose bumps speckled my arms. "Jesus. That's weird."

"Oh, that's chicken feed, darlin'. Here's the gut-kicker," he paused and squeezed my shoulder. "A picture of Addy was on there, too."

Chapter Thirteen

Later that afternoon, perched on Wolfgang's back porch steps next to Natalie as the twins and Kelly played tag in front of us, I still had flowers and Jeff Wymonds on the brain.

The warm, waning sunlight held reign over the surrounding hills, while shadows hovered in the nooks and valleys, waiting for their turn. Sweat trickled down my cleavage and back, Wolfgang's shin-high grass now a thing of the past thanks to Aunt Zoe's lawnmower.

After several calls this afternoon, I learned that even with the added time until the Historical Committee would allow work to start on the Hessler Haunt, I was still on my own when it came to yardwork and housecleaning. When I'd said on my mass-mailer postcards that I'd go the extra mile for a sale, I hadn't realized I'd be pushing a lawnmower for part of it.

As we stared out at the backyard, abuzz with katydids, yellow-jackets, and other insects of prey, I spilled my thoughts about Kelly's dad to Natalie in hushed bursts. The scent of fresh-cut grass and the peals of kids' giggles took the shivers out of my suspicions.

"You're kidding me, right?" Natalie whispered for my ears only, her tone matching the disbelief wrinkling her brow.

"No. I'm totally serious." I shooed a wasp away from Natalie's shoulder. "How else do you explain the picture collage of the missing girls and the jacket?"

"I don't know. I just don't think Jeff is smart enough to pull off one abduction, let alone three. There has to be some other explanation."

I gulped the last of the lukewarm water from the bottle Natalie had brought me, tasting a hint of plastic, mulling over her objection. "Did you make the call I asked you to?"

Natalie nodded. "Rumor has it Donna is leaving Jeff because of another woman."

I gaped at Natalie. "What? Why? The guy has the sex appeal of a snail."

"Well, he's certainly no Doc Nyce."

Recalling the glimpses of Doc's bare skin that I'd snuck and not-snuck earlier today, I'd second that motion.

"Or Wolfgang." Natalie added with a wiggle of her eyebrows.

Or Wolfgang, I smiled. If only he wasn't halfway across the country sitting on the dock of the bay, wasting time we could better spend exchanging flirting glances.

"But Jeff cleans up decent and has a nice voice," Natalie continued, "and after a couple of beers, the stupidity pouring out of his mouth doesn't matter so much, anymore."

"You sound like you're speaking from recent experience."

Natalie's soft chuckle drew my gaze. "Almost, but I don't sleep with married men, even when I'm washing away the been-dumped-again blues with a pitcher of suds."

"All the more reason to continue with your sabbatical for at least a month."

"I don't know that I'd go that far." She leaned back, resting her weight on her hands. "Especially now that I've met Doc."

I frowned. First Harvey, now Natalie. Doc was worming his way into my world, and I wasn't sure I wanted him there. "You mean you've actually met Doc face-to-face?"

"Not yet, but I will soon. I called and made an appointment with him for this coming Wednesday. If things go as planned, we'll start out in his office and end up in my bed."

My gut twinged at the idea of Natalie and Doc leg-wrestling on her red satin sheets. Doc was on the way to becoming *my* dark, mysterious, forbidden fantasy, one I didn't want to share with my best friend. Unfortunately, having already staked a claim on Wolfgang, I couldn't rope off Doc, too. Natalie would call "Bullshit!" and rightfully so.

"Do you really think Jeff's the one sending you flowers?"

I shrugged. "The flowers started coming after I met him."

"He just doesn't seem like the flowers kind of guy."

"Harvey and I stopped by the florist this afternoon, but the clerk who took the order had left for the day and the flowers were paid for with cash—both times, so they had no record of the purchaser."

"Third time's a charm, right? You just have to wait for the next bouquet."

"I guess." Easy for her to say; she wasn't the one at the vulnerable end of a pair of binoculars. "Jeff may just be a local yokel to you, but I think there's something weird about him. Spooky, even." Possibly dangerous, too.

"You know, Violet, in some cultures, sending flowers is actually just a nice gesture."

"Smartass. If he's not a loony, why does he always call me by my full name?"

"Jeff always had an obsessive-compulsive personality. In school, he focused it on football. Now, it's on you."

"Splendid. I should buy him a voodoo doll with blonde hair." I stared at the ladybug climbing Natalie's cast. "Do you think his OCD explains why he has a picture of Addy pasted next to the missing girls' cutouts?"

"Maybe. Do you have any idea where he would have gotten a picture of Addy?"

"I've been thinking about that. Kelly may have had one of those disposable cameras with her at the Dinosaur Park last week. I believe I saw one when we were unloading the picnic stuff from Harvey's truck. It was that or a box of matches."

"Have you asked Kelly about the pictures?"

"I haven't had the chance. The girls have had their heads together since I came home, and I don't want to ask questions about Kelly's family in front of Addy."

"Well, I'm holding off judgment until you get a chance to drill Kelly on all of this."

"You're biased."

"Because he's an ex-football player who I sat next to in Woodshop class?"

"Because you don't want to have slept with a psycho."

"Oh, I have no problems with psycho sex. It's the normal guys who scare me."

"Mom," Addy came running up to us, holding out her blood-covered finger.

I winced. "Crap." I hopped up and grabbed her hand, taking a closer look. "What'd you do?"

"I fell on a piece of glass sticking out of the ground."

I couldn't tell how bad it was through the blood and dirt. "Come on, let's go inside and clean it up." I was thankful I knew where Wolfgang hid his spare key.

The quiet of the house felt thick and cottony in my ears after the buzz of the outside world. Shadows framed the sitting and dining rooms, the musty smell of stale varnish and dust heavy in the stillness. The house had trapped the heat of the day, the warm air rousing more sweat from my pores. I couldn't wait to hit the shower and scrub this place off of me.

Addy's thongs flopped on the hardwood floor as I led her into the kitchen.

"Cool!" She looked around at the clown paraphernalia as she sat on the counter next to the sink. "Wolfgang must really like the circus."

"You'll have to ask him about it when he comes back next Wednesday." I turned on the faucet, waiting through a low groan of the pipes before water spurted and then gushed out.

Addy's cut didn't look so ugly when clean. Just a small gash that some salve and a Band-Aid would fix. Unfortunately, I had neither on me and didn't know where to begin digging for either in the Hessler Haunt.

I opened and shut a couple of the drawers next to the sink. The first held silverware, the second a bunch of keys—mostly the old-fashioned, skeleton type—and odd tools. A pile of dish cloths and linens filled the third one down. Even the towels had garish clowns on them. Wolfgang's mother should have sought counseling.

"Here." I tossed a clown towel to Addy. "Wrap this around your hand for now. We'll fix you up with a Band-Aid when we get back to Aunt Zoe's."

After helping Addy to the floor, I grabbed another towel to wipe down the sink area.

"Can I go back outside now?"

"Sure. Just take it easy, Sweetie." I dropped a kiss on her forehead and smiled at her back as she flip-flopped out the kitchen doorway into the dining room.

I wiped down the counter and sink, stopping partway through the process to turn the clown-popping-out-of-a-barrel cookie jar so it wasn't watching me with those big, empty blue eyes and Joker-like grin. In the quiet of the clown-covered walls, my breathing sounded laborious. I really needed to stop using ice cream therapy to solve my problems. My clothes were going to start bulging soon.

A door slammed somewhere overhead.

I paused. The ceiling creaked, as if someone walked across the floor in one of the upstairs bedrooms.

"Addy?" I dropped the towel on the counter and stepped into the dining room, my ears straining. Why hadn't she gone back outside?

Something crashed upstairs.

"Damn it, Addy." Chewing my lip, I climbed the stairs two at a time. I hoped I could afford to replace whatever it was Addy had broken.

Three of the four doors on the second floor were closed. The fourth—the bathroom—at the end of the hall stood half ajar, dark inside due to it being windowless.

"Addy, where are you?" I tried to keep the anger out of my voice, using sugar, her kryptonite, to lure her out of hiding.

I turned the knob to the rose wallpapered bedroom. Inside, I thumped across the wood floor in my grass-stained tennis shoes. Dust particles swirled around me. The photo of young Wolfgang was where I'd left it on the night stand.

I yanked open the closet door and found no Addy. The sight of several frilly, girl-sized dresses hung on the narrow rack, small hat boxes piled high on the overhead shelf, and multiple pairs of black, patent leather shoes lined up on the floor had me frowning. These weren't here the last time I'd looked in this closet just days ago. Wolfgang must be storing them here for some reason. I ran my fingers down one lacy, pink sleeve, wondering what Wolfgang's sister looked like, imagining how devastating it would be to lose a child. How would I ever go on breathing, eating, living with a chunk torn from my heart?

My fingertips brushed over something hard. I lifted the sleeve cuff and stared at a piece of ribbon safety-pinned to the lace, knotted around a tuft of white-blonde hair. Wilda's hair? I dropped the cuff and backed out of the room, a wave of sadness followed by an eerie shudder spurring me.

Closing the bedroom door behind me, I moved on to room number two—the violet-papered boudoir.

"Addy?"

Again, agitated dust specks swarmed as I peeked under the bed and inspected the closet, which was empty except for a family of dust bunnies.

"Addy, I'm in no mood to play hide-and-seek right now." My voice pierced the stillness of my purple surroundings. I rubbed the back of my neck, grimacing at the grittiness I found.

I shut the door to the violet room. When I reached Wolfgang's bedroom, the knob wouldn't turn. I squeezed and twisted again, but the door was locked.

"Open the damned door, Addy."

No more sweet talk, I'd had enough. I leaned my head against the hard wood, waiting for the click of the lock. Nothing happened. The light leaking out under the door remained steady, no shadows, no sounds, no sign of life.

Maybe Wolfgang had locked the door before he headed for San Francisco. He could be using his room as storage for his mother's valuables, figuring I might be bringing a cleaning crew through while he was gone. Smart thinking on his part, wishful dreaming on mine.

That left the bathroom. The door's hinges squeaked as I shoved it wide. I pushed on the old-fashioned style button for the overhead lights, wondering if Wolfgang would need to update the electrical panel before selling the place.

No Addy in the bathroom, either. I walked over to the claw-foot tub and drew back the suspended shower curtain just to make sure. The tub bottom shined, squeaky clean to my touch. A faint bath water ring around the walls and a curled up spider by the drain were the only blights.

"Ewww." I grimaced at the dead spider, and then

looked into the mirror over the tidy sink. My curly spirals were escaping their bondage, sticking out all over like mini-antennas. Dirt streaked down from my temple and pooled in the creases of my neck. A big smudge covered the width of my forehead, a twin of the one on my forearm. "Double ewww."

The toilet gleamed at me, reminding me that I'd gulped down a bottle of water after mowing. I opened the lid, happy to see water in the bottom of the faded rust-ringed bowl. When in Rome, I thought and closed the door.

I glanced around the spotless white and black tiled floor while in the midst of "Rome-ing" it, realizing that besides the kitchen, the bathroom was the cleanest room in the house. Wolfgang must have scrubbed down both rooms before my first visit. A small, opaque crystal resting on a black tile near one of the tub's clawed feet caught my eye. Was that a rhinestone? Or a diamond? A jewel that had fallen out of Wolfgang's pocket while cleaning?

I stretched and grabbed it, noticing chips in the crystal upon closer inspection.

A door groaned open in the outside hall.

"Addy, freeze!" I shouted, pocketing the crystal, and then finishing up, flushing, and skipping the handwashing part in my rush to catch my kid in the act. I hauled open the door.

The hallway was empty.

Waning daylight peeked out from Wolfgang's room. Addy had left the door open in her haste to escape. That little shit was going to lose her candy privileges for a month.

I grabbed the knob, starting to pull it shut, but then curiosity got the best of me and I stepped into the room. The horses and groomsmen lining the hunter green walls chased after poor foxes without making sound. An old-fashioned skeleton key filled the keyhole below the inside doorknob.

I tiptoed around the queen-size bed, careful not to disturb the dust smothering the embroidered duvet. What had Wolfgang been like as a little kid? A teenager? A young man? The smell of bay rum lingered under the varnish.

A brass picture frame lay on the floor by the dresser. Frowning, I bent and picked it up, careful to avoid the broken bits of glass scattered around it. A black-and-white picture of a young woman with a long nose and blunt forehead stared back, her eyes steely, her lips thin, her hair dark.

Was this Wolfgang's mother? The woman Natalie and her school friends joked about being a witch? I could see a faint resemblance to Wolfgang in her cheekbones and jaw line.

The sound of another door slamming in the hall jerked me out of my scrutiny.

"Adelynn Renee!" I shouted and placed the picture on the dresser before stalking back out into the hall. "You're in such big tr—"

The sight of the other three doors standing wide open choked off the rest of my threat.

Didn't I hear a door shut?

I walked toward the window at the end of the hall, opposite the bathroom, glancing in the other two bedrooms as I passed. Addy still eluded me.

The window faced west, peering over the backyard. I stared out through the dirt-laden screen. Below me, Addy and Kelly ran circles around Natalie, who crutched her way toward the garage, where Layne kneeled, digging in the dirt. As I watched, Addy did a cartwheel, towel-wrapped hand and all, returning to her feet with a big grin for Kelly.

Behind me, a door clicked shut.

I whirled around, my arms tingling with goose bumps, my heart and lungs huddled together in my throat.

The door to Wolfgang's room had closed again.

"Hello?" I whispered, cleared my throat, then tried more loudly. "Is anyone there?"

Silence answered.

I tiptoed over to the door, my breath held as I grabbed the doorknob.

It wouldn't turn. Locked, again.

I stared down at the light spilling out from under the door, trying to come up with a rational, logical explanation for random door slamming in such an old house.

The floor creaked on the other side of the wood panel.

* * *

Sunday, July 15th

Eighteen hours later, standing in a new, never-lived-in-before house in a growing suburb about seven miles outside of the Deadwood city limits, I was still chastising my overactive imagination.

Doc waved his hand in front of my face. "Hello? Anyone in there?"

I blinked away a tired blur, my eyes burning from a sleepless night full of tossing and turning, of witches and clowns. "Sorry. Did you ask me something?"

"Yes, twice." Doc leaned against the kitchen island that had a built-in gas range and granite counter top. His grin was lazy—as usual. "Late night?"

"Long night," I corrected, squeezing the bridge of my nose. The new-carpet smell filling my sinuses was not helping to soothe the dull pounding in my head, a lovely side effect of counting ghosts until the wee hours of the morning.

I hadn't shared my experience yesterday inside the Hessler house with Natalie or Aunt Zoe—partly because I didn't know what to make of the whole thing, but mostly because of how red-faced I'd been later when I remembered my panic-stimulated, run-for-my-life reaction to the simple sound of a house settling in for the night. For a girl who didn't believe in ghouls and banshees, my imagination had sure jumped on the haunted-house party-wagon without even pausing to lift its skirt.

"Did you have another hot date?" Doc asked.

I held his gaze for several seconds, searching for mockery, cynicism, even hoping for jealousy, but found only brown eyes staring back at me. I contemplated telling Doc my door-shutting story, sharing my creepy secret. No, that was too nutty-sounding. "No date. Just the usual insomnia fun."

"That explains the dark rings."

I nodded.

"Red eyes."

I continued nodding.

"Wild hair."

"Hey, cut me some slack." I patted my hair. I knew I should have tucked it up again today.

Chuckling, he pushed away from the island and tugged on a curl below my temple as he walked past. "Just kidding. You look beautiful, as always."

The woodsy scent of his cologne trailed behind him, rousing my hunger for more—just one tiny touch—as I followed him into the cathedral-ceilinged living room.

I hesitated in the cushy shag carpet, still stewing on his *as always* comment. Something inside of me snapped. I crossed my arms over my chest. As far as I was concerned, we needed to keep things daisy-petal simple here. Either he liked me, or he liked me not.

Not that I should even care about Doc's likes, since Wolfgang was obviously interested in me. Unfortunately, I did care, at least my body did, in spite of the whole freaky sniffing thing Doc still did upon entering a house.

What was wrong with me that one man wasn't enough when no men had been just fine for the last two years? Maybe hanging out with Natalie so much since moving to town was beginning to affect my rusty libido. Maybe I was also into psycho sex now.

"Listen, Doc," I started, intending to clear the air between us once and for all. I was too tired today for any flirting games. "You and I need to talk about—"

The front door opened, cutting me off.

Pasting on a smile, I turned as a hippie-ish young couple stepped into the room. On their heels was the red-haired agent who'd shooed Harvey and me out of the open house yesterday. Jessica Rabbit's furrowed forehead as she glared at me told me she hadn't forgotten Harvey's parting remark regarding the tightness of her bony ass, and her pinched lips confirmed that she'd heard my answering laugh.

"Hello, again." While her voice was super-sweet, her smile was sour.

"Hi." I indicated where Doc stood near the stairs. "I think we're just about finished here."

As her gaze moved to Doc, her whole face flared bright pink right in front of my eyes.

"We're done now," Doc said, grabbing my arm and dragging me toward the open door.

"What are you doing?" I asked as he tugged me into the hot sunlight. I fished my sunglasses from the neckline of my satin tank. "You didn't even look at the master bathroom with the built-in sauna and soak tub."

"I don't need to." He still had my arm and was towing me down the sidewalk toward my Bronco at a full stride.

"So, I take it that's another 'no' today."

"Bingo."

"Wait!" A voice yelled from behind us as we reached the end of the walkway.

Doc stopped so fast I ran into his back. Rubbing my

nose, I turned around and watched the redhead stalk toward us.

"Oh, shit," I heard Doc mumble as she closed in.

"You!" The redhead's lips were pealed back in a snarl as she sliced Doc into tiny pieces with her razor-sharp glare.

"Hi, Tiffany." Doc said. "You're looking well."

Tiffany?

"You rotten bastard!" Before I could even blink at her words, the redhead slapped Doc across the face.

"Jesus!" Doc stepped back, holding his cheek. "What is wrong with you, woman?"

"What's wrong with me?" I swore her eyes were going to pop out of her skull. "You left without saying anything. You didn't call. You wouldn't return my calls. You even changed hotels."

I could have sworn I saw a hint of steam puffing out of her flared nostrils.

"You're overreacting." Doc sounded relaxed, but his tense jaw gave him away.

"You're a selfish son of a bitch."

Wow! My mouth was gaping and I knew it, but I couldn't seem to shut it, not with my ringside seat at the Doc vs. the Crazy Redhead Championship Fight.

"Tiffany, calm down."

She took another swing at him, but Doc dodged it this time, then captured her wrist in his grip.

"You're making an ass of yourself in front of your clients." The icy fury in Doc's gaze would have turned a regular mortal into a human Popsicle.

I glanced back at the doorway. The young couple stood there, their mouths hanging open, too.

"Fuck you!" Tiffany said. I could have sworn she followed it with a hiss.

"Goodbye, Tiffany."

"I hope you die a horrible death."

"Nice to see you, too." Doc let go of her wrist and grabbed my arm again. "We're leaving, Violet."

I stumbled after him down the curb and across the street to my Bronco, my mouth still catching bugs.

"Holy shit! I take it you two know each other," I said when I finally found my voice again.

"You could say that." He opened the driver's side door and pushed me inside.

"Intimately by the sounds of it." Not to mention the looks of it, judging by the fierce scowl that Tiffany was shooting in our direction from where she remained at the end of the walkway.

"That depends on your definition of *intimate*." He slammed my door shut and marched around to his side.

I waited for him to climb in and shut the door. "Intimate as in you've seen each other in your birthday suits."

I didn't know why I was digging for more details. Could be I was in shock. Could be I was a little jealous. Most likely, I just enjoyed seeing Doc squirm and sweat for once, instead of me.

He stared out the front window. "Then the answer would be *yes*."

I started the Bronco, the mystery of his relationship with the redhead clearing as my shock faded and a blast of warm air from the vents hit my skin. "I'm not your first real estate agent in town, am I?"

"Technically, yes. Her office is in Spearfish."

As we rolled through the housing development, I kept casting fleeting looks at him and his reddening cheek.

"I thought sleeping with your Realtor was off-limits." There, I said it. I couldn't help it. Something inside of me wanted to rub his nose in that, sting him just a tiny bit for rejecting me from the start.

He turned and caught my gaze. "It is."

I raised my brows as I stopped at the main highway junction, waiting for a long string of cars to pass before I could pull out and head back toward Deadwood.

"Violet."

Eight cars to go.

"Hmmm?" I glanced his way and my eyes got trapped by his.

"You're a much better agent than she was."

My neck warmed at his compliment, but my pride still smarted. "Thanks."

Six cars.

"If we have sex," he continued, "I'll have to find another Realtor, and I'm tired of living out of hotel rooms."

"I never said I wanted to have to have sex with you." That came out more defensive-sounding than I'd have liked.

"You don't have to say it."

My ears blazed. What was that supposed to mean? I'd had a couple of flesh-filled thoughts about him, but that was it. It didn't mean I planned to follow through on anything … probably. "You're not irresistible to all of the female species, you know."

Five cars.

"I know, but you date your clients."

Damned Harvey and his motor mouth! "Not usually. This is an exception. A one-time deal."

"Are you sure?"

Yes! No! Maybe. "I'm positive."

"So you say."

I drummed my fingers on the wheel, my focus now deliberately fixed out the front window. "Just because that crazy redhead couldn't keep her …"

Panties on.

"Her hands to herself," I continued, "doesn't mean I can't."

"Sure."

I snuck a peek at him. He was watching the last three cars coming our way, his lips curved with a hint of a grin. Damn him for turning this around so that I was the one hopping in the embers again.

Damn me for letting him.

"Besides, I'm seeing someone." Sort of, but not really—yet.

"You've had one date."

"I have another one planned for this week."

"Congratulations."

One car to go.

"I'm not going to sleep with you." My statement sounded feeble at best.

"Good."

The rest of the ride back to the office was quiet. I'd had one more house to show Doc, but after the fireworks and post-show, I decided to pass for today. I needed space and time to cool down and get my head back in the game.

We ran into Mona in the parking lot. She was nearing her SUV, which I'd parked next to, as we climbed out of the Bronco.

"Did you hear the news?" she asked, unlocking her door.

I glanced at Doc to see if he knew what she was talking about. His brow was wrinkled as he looked at Mona, his left cheek still angry from Tiffany's slap.

"What news?" I shielded my eyes from the unrelenting sun.

"About last night's kidnapping."

Chapter Fourteen

Later that afternoon when I parked the Bronco in Aunt Zoe's drive, Addy and Kelly were kneeling on the front porch. Between them sat one of the moving boxes we'd used this spring, "Layne's Books" scrawled on the side. Addy looked up from the box and waved as I killed the engine.

I shoved open the door, but stayed in my seat, letting my head fall back against the headrest as the aroma of warm pine and sun-cooked gravel filled the cab. Spending the last four hours listening to Ray schmooze his clients and reel in two new deals had renewed the pounding in my head.

I had two weeks until Jane pulled the plug on me, and the one person who could help take my job off life support kept turning his nose up at every house I showed him. The Sea of Failure had me trapped in its riptide, dragging me out beyond the buoys. It was only a matter of time until the sharks picked up the scent of fresh blood and had a frenzy on my sorry ass.

The slam of a screen door across the street interrupted my Life-Sucks monologue. I frowned at the sight of Harvey scurrying toward me down Miss Geary's front walk.

I hopped out of the Bronco as he crossed the street. Had the dirty old buzzard already worked his mojo on Aunt Zoe's neighbor? "Where's your truck?"

"In Beatrice's garage." Harvey scowled away my raised brows. "Did you hear about that little girl from Spearfish?"

"Mona told me." I kept my voice low, glancing at the

kids to see if they were listening. The flood of giggles flowing our way put my gut at ease. "I'm still shocked the girl escaped."

"You should get your kids a couple of those alarm-whistle dealies she used."

I closed my door and leaned against it. "I tried on my way home, but the Piggly Wiggly didn't have anything like that. They recommended a couple of hardware stores down in Rapid."

"Ever considered mace?"

"No way. They'd spray each other with it."

The creak of Beatrice Geary's screen door turned both of our heads.

"Willis?" Beatrice stood on the porch in a hot pink satin robe that reached her calves and showed off her high-heeled slippers topped with red fuzzy puffs. She smiled when she saw us. "Oh, hello, Violet. I almost didn't recognize you with your hair down. You look very smart in that shade of green."

"Thanks, Miss Geary." After my night of spinning in the sheets, mentally retracing my steps through the Hessler house ad nauseam, I'd dragged my hind end into the bathroom and found Medusa aping me in the mirror. The extra hour I'd spent ironing my shirt and skirt, trying to tame my hair, primping here and there, had made me late for work. In the end, Doc had barely noticed any of my hard work. That's what I got for dressing to impress.

Harvey squinted at me. "You don't usually leave your hair down. What's going on?"

I ignored Harvey's scrutinizing stare.

"Did you have an appointment with an important client?" Beatrice asked.

"Uh, yes."

"Who?" Harvey pressed.

"None of your beeswax."

"As your bodyguard, I'm making it my beeswax."

"Supper's ready, Willis," Beatrice said.

Whew! Saved by the dinner bell. As Beatrice sashayed back inside, I grinned at Harvey. "Willis, huh? You never let me call you by your first name."

"Yeah, well you never bake cherry pies for me."

"Baking is against my religion."

"Or let me butter your muffin."

I grimaced at a disturbing image of Harvey and Beatrice in a compromising position. "My muffin is off-limits."

Snickering, he patted my head. "I'll be over after supper."

After watching him bustle up Miss Geary's walk, I trudged through Aunt Zoe's front yard toward the girls.

"Hi, Mom. How was work?" An empty M&Ms wrapper lay behind Addy.

I propped my shoulder against the porch post and drudged up a smile—and a lie. "Pretty good."

"Did you meet any nice men?"

Kelly had yet to look up from the box, which had three of the four flaps closed.

"Nope. Where's your brother?"

"Gluing teeth into his horse skull."

Of course. "What's in the box?"

"Nothing."

I leaned over, catching sight of something that resembled a coiled up rope. "What is that, Adelynn?"

She reached in the box and pulled out the rope. Only it wiggled.

"Jesus!" I jumped back.

"It's just a baby, Mom." A forked tongue shot in and out as Addy held the green snake by the neck area.

"I don't care. Get rid of it right now."

"But, Mom!"

"Take it over there by those trees." I pointed to the

edge of the forest that divided Aunt Zoe's yard from Mount Moriah cemetery. "Now!"

Grumbling, Addy stomped across the yard toward the pine trees, the wriggling snake dangling out in front of her. Kelly watched Addy's progress with a frown on her lips.

I decided to use this moment alone with Kelly to dig for some details about her mom and dad.

"Kelly." I paused trying to use some delicacy in forming my question. "Was your mom going on a trip somewhere for a couple of days?"

She shrugged her bony shoulders.

"Do you know where your dad is?"

The Wymonds' house had been closed up when I cruised by this afternoon, the yard and drive empty of vehicles that still had all four wheels intact, the front door shut.

"Of course." Kelly shielded her eyes as she peered up at me. "He's at work."

I hadn't noticed any road crews out and about today. "On a Sunday?"

"Uh-huh. He needs to make more money."

"Is that what he said?" Or had Donna said that? Kids were excellent eavesdroppers and mimickers—mine in particular, especially when it came to swear words and finding-a-man conversations.

She nodded. "Mom can't work because of Johnny, so Dad works on the weekend now, too."

"That must be why he wasn't home when I picked up your clothes yesterday."

"Oh, he's never home on the weekends, anymore."

"Because he works so much?"

"No. Because he spends Saturday and Sunday night at Uncle Peter's place."

She made it sound so clear and simple, yet here I was in a fogbank. "Why does he stay there?"

"Because Dad's working on the new bridge they're building by Uncle Peter's house."

I didn't remember seeing any new bridge going in around town. "Where does your Uncle Peter live?"

"In Spearfish."

I took another step back, my chest winded like I'd been walloped in the bread basket with a frying pan.

Spearfish—where the girl was almost abducted last night. What a freaking coincidence. I needed to talk to Natalie.

"It's gone, Mom," Addy returned to her spot on the porch.

"Thank you."

She sighed. "Now what are we going to dissect tomorrow?"

Whatever happened to doll houses and playing dress-up? "How about you don't dissect anything?"

"That's boring."

"I thought Aunt Zoe was taking you hiking out by Custer Peak."

"Yeah, in the morning. We were going to cut open the snake in the afternoon."

"But the snake wasn't dead." While reptiles weren't my idea of cuddly calendar candidates, the idea of Addy slaughtering an animal just to examine its guts inspired a whole rash of parental-alert goosebumps. If memory served me right, Jeffrey Dahmer started off his serial killer career with harmless pets.

"Kelly knows how to kill snakes." Addy had missed my point.

Kelly's smile beamed. "My dad showed me. You just hold 'em down with your heel and chop off their heads."

"Okay." I was beginning to think Kelly was a few French fries short of a Happy Meal. Addy really needed to make more friends. "How about instead of playing

Operation with a poor snake, we go out to Pactola Lake tomorrow after lunch."

"Really?" Addy hopped to her feet, her smile wide, the snake apparently forgotten. "Will you come swimming with us?"

I'd sooner share a sleeping bag with Addy's snake than don a bathing suit in public, but how could I say 'no' to the excitement in her eyes. "Sure."

"Mom didn't pack my swimsuit," Kelly said.

"You can borrow one of mine." Addy grabbed her hand. "Let's go pick one out for you."

"Wash your hands, Adelynn," I yelled at the girls' backs as they ran inside the front door and clomped up the stairs. I followed them, minus the clomps, and detoured into the kitchen, where I found Aunt Zoe standing at the sink, staring out the window into the backyard.

I joined her and looked out at where my son's butt stuck up in the air. He looked like a turtle digging a nest in the sand as he widened the hole where he'd found the horse remains. "I thought he was gluing teeth in the skull."

"He was." Aunt Zoe pointed at where the skull sat on the picnic table. "But he's four short and determined to find them."

"Then what?"

"I guess the spine comes next."

"He'll tear up your whole yard before he's through."

She smiled. "I know."

"You want me to stop him?"

"No way. Who knows what else he'll find? I'm rather enjoying seeing what I've been living over all these years."

I hoped to be as open-minded as Aunt Zoe when I grew up. "I'll buy you new sod when he's done."

"Don't bother. Trying to keep grass green in these dry hills is a waste of water. Besides, I've always wanted to experiment with raised flower beds, just never had the time or energy to tear up the lawn."

Crossing the room, I opened the fridge and snagged a cold can of diet soda. "How well do you know Kelly's dad?"

"Only from the sports page back when he played football."

Cracking open the pop's top, I gulped down a mouthful of sweetened soda. I really needed to talk to Natalie. "Any more calls about my singles ad?"

"Not so far today."

"Good." Grabbing the phone, I punched in Natalie's number. Her phone rang four times before her answering service picked up. I hung up without leaving a message. "Damn. Where is she?"

My question pulled Aunt Zoe's gaze from the window. "Who?"

"Natalie."

"Oh, she called this morning. Her mom fell and hurt her hip. Natalie was heading down to Hill City to spend the night and then take her mom to the clinic in the morning."

"Falling must be contagious. Did she say when she'd be back?"

"Tomorrow night. She said something about a big date on Tuesday that she wasn't going to miss."

Her appointment with Doc. A tiny green monster stirred in my belly.

"Did you hear about the little girl in Spearfish?" Aunt Zoe asked.

Nodding, I dipped my finger in the yellow creamy sauce simmering on the stove. It was hot and tangy on my tongue. "It has to be the same guy, don't you think?"

"Probably, but the other girls were from Lead and Deadwood. And blonde. Why Spearfish? Why a brunette?"

I shrugged. "Maybe he's branching out."

"Or maybe it's a trick."

"What? Why?"

Aunt Zoe knocked my finger away as I started to double-dip and shooed me away from the stove. "So that people here will let their guard down. If the Boogeyman has left town, they'll let their kids play outside after dark again."

"People wouldn't let their guard down so soon, would they?" I wasn't going to.

"Not everyone."

I leaned against the counter and watched Aunt Zoe stir the sauce for a few seconds, dark worries shadowing my world, shooting chills down my spine. "I hope you're wrong."

Her eyes held mine. "Me, too."

* * *

Monday, July 16th

The day began with its usual sunny start, but by noon, a cool breeze blew in, and dark clouds flickering with flashes of lightning threatened to dump rain on our heads. After a few grumbles, the girls settled for a trip to the Deadwood Rec Center instead of risking electrocution out at Pactola Lake.

Layne opted to join Aunt Zoe at her glass shop for the afternoon. A thick book titled *The Archaeology of Mammal Bones* was tucked under his arm as he clambered into Aunt Zoe's pickup. I made a mental note to borrow the hardback the next time the insomnia bug bit me—I'd be asleep by the end of the Table of Contents.

The smell of chlorine welcomed us as we entered the Rec Center. The girls raced off toward the locker room. I signed us in and handed the gum-chewing front desk clerk a twenty-dollar bill in exchange for an afternoon of bathing-suit torture.

"Crap," the pony-tailed brunette said as she stared into her cash drawer. "I need more ones. I'll be right back."

She opened a door behind her marked *Office* and disappeared inside.

While I waited for my change, I glanced around the room. The walls were covered with framed pictures, some black and white, others in color, all filled with people. I walked over to one wall, taking a closer look at a photo that was more of a sepia color. The year on the bottom of the picture said "Deadwood - June 1943," the girls' swimsuits were modest one pieces with flaring mini-skirts and heart-shaped tops. Names were listed along the bottom of the picture, some of the last names the same as several current members of the chamber of commerce. Apples didn't fall far from trees around here.

"Here you go, Ma'am."

I winced at receiving the old-lady form of address from the teeny-bopper, resisting the urge to stick my tongue out at her as I grabbed the bills she held out for me.

After a quick shower and a full-face grimace at the sight of my body in my black-and-white polka-dot tankini in the locker room mirror, I pussyfooted out to join the girls.

The pool was alive with bobbing heads. Laughs and squeals echoed around me. I guess we weren't the only ones trying to fill an afternoon with some splashing. I scanned the human buoys, searching for a familiar blonde head.

"Do a cannonball, Mom!" Addy yelled. She and Kelly clung to the side in the deep end.

No way! The fallout would drown the preschoolers dog-paddling in the shallow end.

"Now that I'd like to see," said an all-too-familiar baritone voice behind me.

I closed my eyes and pulled my self-confidence up by the bootstraps. Of all the swimming pools in all the towns in all the world …

Smearing a smile on my lips, I turned around. Doc stood there, dripping in a pair of midnight blue swim trunks.

"Hello, Violet." His gaze took its usual trip down to my toenails and back. "Nice knees."

Trying not to stare at his bare chest, I zeroed in on the shallow cleft in his chin. "Hi. You come here often?"

"Often enough."

That might explain the T-shirt and shorts he'd been wearing on Saturday, and the rigid contours of his upper body—which I was determined not to notice.

"I haven't seen you here before," he said.

"I'm allergic to exercise."

He chuckled, water trickling down over his Adams apple. "My loss. I'd enjoy some one-on-one with you."

My face baked as I took that straight into the bedroom.

"On the basketball court," he clarified, his grin wide.

Nodding, I pretended I knew what he'd meant all along. "Sounds fun, but I haven't touched a ball in years."

No sooner had the words exited my lips than I wished I'd swallowed my tongue.

"Really. Not even one, huh? That's too bad."

I could hear the laughter in his voice.

"Are you coming in or what, Mom?" Addy came dripping up beside me.

A distraction, thank God! "Sure."

Addy eyed Doc under her spiky blonde lashes. "Hey, I know you."

"Yes, you do. How's the chicken?"

Shrugging, she brushed her wet bangs out of her eyes. "Okay. Mom's still making me get rid of her. Do you know of any nice chicken ranches around here?"

Out of the mouth of babes.

Doc's eyes twinkled as he met my smirk. "Nope, but I've heard there are several down in Nevada."

Addy frowned. "That's too far away. Oh, well, do you want to play Marco Polo with us?"

"Only if your mom's playing."

"You're playing, right, Mom?" She frowned at my hesitation. "Please play."

Cornered, I sighed. "Sure."

After a half hour of treading water and yelling "Marco" more times than "Polo," I hoisted my shivering limbs out onto the smooth, concrete ledge and declared that I quit. As I dangled my feet in the pool, I perused the other patrons, chewing on my lip.

Doc splashed out beside me and laid back on the ledge, his torso stretched out next to me, a visual buffet of olive-tinted male flesh. "You're a good sport, Violet."

"Thanks."

His long legs swished in the water next to mine. I noticed a faint vertical scar running up the outside of his calf. My fingers twitched, eager to touch, explore.

"But you could use some swim lessons."

I met his gaze with a raised brow. "You offering?"

"Sure. I'll take any opportunity to get close to a pretty girl in a bathing suit."

Doc had my core temperature fluctuating between hot and steamy again, melting away the last of my shivers. I closed my eyelids, disgusted with my inability to remain cool, calm, and in control. "Stop flirting with me."

His low chuckle right next to my ear made me quiver. "You make it so much fun."

I opened my lids to find him sitting up now, his shoulder almost brushing mine, his dark eyes inches away. Something simmered in their depths. The tips of my fingernails smoldered.

"Fun for you." He had his libido tightly reined. Mine kept bucking me off. "Some of us are a bit rusty at this game."

"Rusty? I don't think so, Violet. Not with the way you look at me."

"I don't know what you're talking about." Busted, I feigned innocence.

"Liar." He blinked and the heat was gone—except for the molten ball still in my gut.

I dragged my gaze away, my cheeks baked to a nice shade of embarrassment. Hot, horny, and humiliated in front of a good-looking guy—a flashback to my high school years when braces and padded bras made life awkward. Now two kids and a sagging body supplied the fuel.

"You should get Addy on the swim team here," Doc said. "She's a good swimmer."

I jumped on his change of subject. "Do they have tryouts?"

"I don't know. There's a sign-up sheet out in the lobby."

That reminded me of something Kelly had told Addy when they first met. Something Addy had repeated to me after our trip to the Dinosaur park about Kelly and Emma Cranson, the girl missing since last August, hanging out at the Rec Center all of the time.

I hopped to my feet.

"Where are you going?" Doc asked.

"I'll be right back."

In the lobby, the clerk was talking on her pink cell phone. She glanced up at me as I crossed to the wall covered with colored pictures, but kept talking.

I followed the dated trail of pictures until I came to last summer, which required a step stool to read the names at the bottom of the page. From my tip toes, I could see Kelly standing in the front row, third from the left. Her hair was longer now.

Three girls to the right was Emma, her oval, Addy-like face framed by her cropped blonde locks. My heart thumped in my ears. I squinted at the photo and tried to read the names of the other girls.

"What are you doing?" Doc had followed me.

"Looking for a link." I glanced over my shoulder at him. He stood a full head taller than me. "Can you read the names on this picture?"

"Sure." He read through the front row, confirming Kelly and Emma's appearance.

"Keep going." I used his bare shoulder to keep my balance as I went up on the very tips of my toes and placed each name with the matching girl.

Tina Tucker, the girl who'd disappeared earlier this month anchored the left side of the back row. Her blonde hair long and straight. Jade Newel, the girl who had left the library last January and not been seen since, was second from the right.

I rubbed my forehead. What were the chances of all three missing girls being on the same team?

"Hmmm." Doc frowned at the picture.

"What?"

"The coach is missing."

"Does it list a name at least?"

Doc nodded. "Jeff Wymonds. Kelly's dad. That's quite a coincidence, don't you think?"

Chapter Fifteen

"You can't go to the police," Old Man Harvey told me as the two of us sat outside at Aunt Zoe's picnic table in the twilight. Between us, we forked down the last few pieces of one of Beatrice Geary's homemade cherry pies.

I swallowed a glob of sweet cherry goo. "Why not?"

"You don't have enough proof."

"I'm not saying Jeff's guilty." At least not out loud in front of mixed company.

Shivering in the chilly air, I zipped my jacket up to my neck. The afternoon storms had sucked the heat from the hills and left a damp, wet-dirt-scented nippiness in its place. As I shoveled the second-to-last piece of pie onto my plate, I looked at Harvey. "I just want to see if the cops already know about the swim team connection."

"They do."

I did a double take. "How do you know?"

"I talked to Coop after you called me about that team picture. He says the police looked into the whole swim-team deal when the second little girl disappeared. Checked out every one of the parents, including Wymonds."

Coop? "Who's Coop? One of your bar buddies?"

"Nah, Coop's not much of a socialite. He prefers to drink alone." Harvey stabbed another bite of cherries.

"How does this Coop guy know so much about the case?"

"Coop is a detective for the Deadwood Police. He's also my nephew."

I paused, mid-chew, on that little tidbit. "Your nephew?"

"Yes, my nephew. As in my uppity older sister's youngest child. Anyway, Coop says that Wymonds has an alibi … of sorts."

"What do you mean 'of sorts'? That doesn't sound very definite. Maybe they didn't dig deep enough. Maybe they need to take a second look at Jeff." They probably didn't even know about the jacket back then.

Harvey pointed his fork at me. "You ain't in Rapid City anymore, girl."

No, I wasn't. I'd left that glum existence that had been filled with long hours at the dealership and no free time to spend with my kids, who'd been growing up without a mom, as well as a dad. I'd showed up late to way too many birthdays over the years to ever return to that chapter of my life, but I had a feeling Harvey was talking about something else.

"What's that supposed to mean?" I asked. Beware of flying monkeys and angry Munchkins?

"You can't go accusing a local kid of something without having definite proof."

"Define *definite*."

"Blood on his hands."

"What about the jacket?" I'd shown it to Harvey when he arrived with the pie.

"You know that's not enough. Besides, there's no blood on it."

I frowned at the image that conjured up, pushing aside the last of my cherry pie. "We don't even know what happened to Emma. What if I'm onto something."

He snorted. "Your theory is as holey as my favorite Fruit-of-the-Looms."

"I told you last night, your underwear as a topic of discussion is off-limits."

Grinning, he nodded at the remains of my pie. "You gonna eat that?"

I pushed the plate toward him. "This counts toward our deal, you know."

"What deal?"

"The dinner-once-a-week clause in your contract."

"You didn't even make the pie."

"No, but I bought the bucket of chicken."

"Fine, but next week you need to take me somewhere a little more fancy." He shoveled pie into his mouth, scowling at me as he chewed. "What if you're wrong about Jeff Wymonds?"

"The cops keep looking for the real kidnapper."

"Sure, after they've destroyed Wymonds' reputation. Do you really want to add to Kelly's family problems?"

Of course not. "I just can't shake this gut feeling about Jeff."

"That's just gas." He polished off the last of my piece of pie. "What about that girl from Spearfish—Cherry Cobbler?"

Harvey had cherries on the brain. "You mean Sherry Dobbler."

He grunted. "Same thing."

"What about her?"

"She wasn't on the swim team. Why did he go for her?"

"I haven't figured that one out yet."

"And why would Jeff be plucking girls from the team he coached? Anybody with half a brain knows not to piss in his own well."

"Yeah, but we're talking about Jeff. His antennae doesn't pick up all the channels, right?" According to Natalie, anyway.

"Sure he's hit his head one too many times, but that just makes him a bit dense sometimes. I don't know about you, but *thick-skulled* and *bat-shit crazy* don't share the same page in my thesaurus."

The fact that Harvey even owned a thesaurus gave me pause.

"Mom?" Addy called.

I turned around.

Addy's head was poking out the back door, a piece of red licorice hung from the corner of her mouth. "Kelly's dad just called."

"He must have felt you yanking on his chain," Harvey murmured for my ears only.

"He wants her to come home now."

"What should I do?" I whispered to Harvey.

Harvey scraped cherry sauce off the pie pan with his finger, licking it clean. "Personally, I'd drive the Bronco. The Wymonds' place is on the other side of town. But if you feel like pedalin' while Kelly rides on the handlebars, go right ahead."

"Smartass. I mean, should I take her home?"

"Sure. Unless *you* want to be thrown in jail for kidnapping."

"What if he's guilty?"

"What if he's just a father wanting to see his daughter?"

As much as the thought of returning Kelly to her home made my stomach cramp, I knew Harvey was right. I turned back to Addy. "Is Kelly all packed?"

Addy nodded.

"Tell her to go hop in the Bronco. I'll be there in a flash."

"I want to go, too." Addy's tone had a few drops of whine poured into it.

"Not tonight, Sweetie." Or ever, if I could help it. "I'll just be a couple of minutes there and back."

"Whatever!" The door slammed behind Addy.

I sighed. It was no wonder that lions sometimes ate their young.

"That one has your temper." Harvey snickered.

"I'm going to give her a little more of it if she doesn't knock off that attitude." Standing, I grabbed my plate. "You coming?"

"I'll ride shotgun."

With Harvey, that usually had a dual meaning.

The trip to the Wymonds' residence was quick and quiet. Kelly always seemed to hit the "mute" button when adults were present, yet I'd often heard her chattering away when Addy was her only listener—another one of the girl's traits that made my neck bristle.

When we pulled into the drive, the hood was up on Jeff's Toyota. Two jean-clad legs stuck out from under the truck. As Kelly hopped out of the back seat, Jeff wiggled out from behind the front tire.

After a "Hey, kid," and a kiss on Kelly's forehead, Jeff lumbered toward my open window. I reached for the button to roll it up, but Harvey killed the engine and took the keys before I could stop him.

"Hello, Violet Parker." Jeff rested his forearms on my door, his face so close I could see his pores under the black smear of grease that ran down his cheek. His big, burly body filled my whole window, blocking my closest avenue of escape. He gave Harvey a quick nod.

"Uh, hi … uh, Jeff," I said. He smelled like he'd spritzed himself with Penzoil and then dusted the sweet spots with powdered dirt. I didn't care if he had an Obsessive-Compulsive Disorder or not. If Harvey's hand hadn't been clamped on my wrist, I'd have crawled over the old codger, bailed out his window, and sprinted down the road to safety.

"Thanks for bringing Kelly home."

No sneers, no leers, no kooky gleam in his green eyes. Who was this man and what did he do with the monster from last week? "You're welcome. Thanks for letting her stay over."

"Are you available for lunch on Wednesday?"

"Uhhh." *No way! Huh, uh! Never ever!* Harvey squeezed my wrist—hard. "Yeah, I think so."

I flashed Harvey a glare that promised payback.

"Good. I need to talk to you about …" he hesitated, glancing at my ornery passenger, "something personal."

Oh God, he knows I took the jacket! I swallowed a shriek of panic and somehow managed to make my cheek muscles smile. "Okay."

"I'll pick you up at your office."

The only way I was going to ride anywhere alone with Jeff Wymonds was if I was hogtied and gagged with a gun pointed at my head.

"I have an early appointment." I grabbed a business card from my ashtray and handed it to him. "Why don't you just give me a call that morning and tell me where you want to meet."

"Sounds good." He pounded twice on my door frame with his fist, making me jump, and then pushed back and stuffed his hands in his pockets. A trace of the jeepers-creepers Jeff returned with his extra-wide grin that didn't quite reach his eyes. "See you on Wednesday, Violet Parker."

I nodded, the corners of my mouth trembling from forcing a smile for so long. If he called me by my full name throughout our whole lunch, I was going to stuff my napkin in his pie hole.

Afraid to take my eyes off Jeff for even a second, I practiced my ventriloquist act and muttered through frozen lips, "Give me the damned keys, Harvey."

Harvey obliged without comment—for once.

I started the engine and backed out of the drive.

"See," Harvey said as we reached asphalt. "He's harmless."

I shifted into drive. "Yeah, as harmless as a pissed-off rattlesnake."

* * *

Tuesday, July 17th

The next morning, the heat returned with the sun—both out on the street and in Calamity Jane's. As Jane filled the office with the scent of a dry-erase marker, writing in everyone's column but mine on her *Sale Pending* white board, Mona clacked away on her laptop and Ray worked his wheel-and-deal magic on the phone.

I spent most of the pre-noon hours trying to look busy with housing market research while really rummaging around online for more information on Sherry Dobbler, the little girl from Spearfish. It's not that I didn't want to be out showing houses or bartering on behalf of a client, but short of begging Ray or Mona for a handout, I was left twirling my hair.

For all of my surfing and digging, all I ended up with was the name of the store in Spearfish where Sherry's mom worked. Most of the local papers focused on Sherry's tale of capture and escape with hardly any personal details—on purpose and out of respect, I was sure. This far from Hollywood, reporters tended to be hungry for esteem rather than attention.

As eleven o'clock came and went, even my focus on the missing girls grew blurry. I stared at the plaster wall that divided Calamity Jane's office from Doc's. Not twenty feet away, Natalie sat doing God-knows-what with Doc. The urge to press my ear to the wall tugged on me. The need to squash my nose against his front window drove me out the back door to my Bronco.

Since Jane frowned on drinking alcohol at lunch, I

settled for a triple-shot latte at the Tin Cup Café. Natalie's appointment time crept by while I watched tourists through the coffee shop's plate-glass window as they ambled from casino to casino.

Worries over tomorrow's lunch date with Jeff had me nibbling on my knuckles. Harvey had offered to hide out at another booth or table, ready to pounce on cue, but I didn't think it was a good idea. Jeff knew Harvey. If he caught sight of the old codger in the restaurant, he might not feel like talking. Even though the idea of sharing a table with Jeff made my knees wobbly, I wanted to hear what he had to say.

At a quarter till twelve, my cell phone rang. I frowned at my work phone number displayed on my cell screen. Who was calling me from my own desk? "Hello?"

"Where are you?" Natalie asked.

"The Tin Cup. How was your appointment?" I held my breath as I waited for her answer.

"Interesting. I could use a cold shower."

"Sounds like you enjoyed yourself." My stomach churned with bubbles of jealous brew. God, I wished Wolfgang would hurry up and get back here to distract me from Doc.

"Oh, we're just getting started." I could hear Natalie's smile in her tone. "We have another appointment on Thursday."

I took several deep breaths to counteract my green-eyed monster's sucker-punches.

"You still there, Violet?"

"Yeah, sorry. My phone is acting up today."

"Anyway, Doc sent me over here looking for you."

"What for?"

"He wants to go look at a place this afternoon. He said to have you meet him at his car in twenty minutes. Do you know where he's parked?"

"Yes." In my spot.

"Okay. I need to head out to check on my mom. I'll stop by later tonight and give you all the juicy details."

"Great." I'd sooner get a bikini wax with a candle and tweezers. "Drive safe."

I closed my cell and tossed my half-empty coffee cup into the trashcan by the door. Ten minutes later, I stood next to Doc's Camaro SS, sweating under UV rays, wondering why he was driving instead of me, his Realtor. Probably just another way to get me twitterpated beyond coherent thought.

My cell phone trilled in my purse. I dug it out, shading the screen to see who was calling. Wolfgang's cell number scrolled across the screen. "Hello?"

"Good morning, Violet." Wolfgang's whiskey smooth voice crackled a little in my ear. "Actually, afternoon there, I guess."

I smiled. Here came the cavalry. "Hi, Wolfgang. You ready to come back to Deadwood?"

"I was ready yesterday. How are things there?"

Let's see, I have a lunch date tomorrow with a kidnapper and this morning I woke up to find a chicken roosting on the other half of my pillow. "Same as usual."

"How are things going with the house?"

"Fine and dandy." I'd stopped by to replace the laundered towel I'd used to wrap Addy's wound but had been too gutless to do more than inch open the front door and slip it inside. Then I'd scampered back to my Bronco, peeking over my shoulder at the upstairs windows the whole way, expecting to see someone standing there watching me. That what's-behind-door-number-one game still made my armpits clammy.

"Are you busy tomorrow night?"

"No," I said, assuming Jeff didn't have plans to stab me in the heart with his butter knife at lunch.

"How about having dinner with me?"

"I'd love to."

"Great. I'll pick you up around six. No need to dress up, I have a little surprise for you."

What kind of surprise? The sparkly kind from one of his jewel cases? No, that couldn't be. He'd want me in a nice dress if he was going to lavish me with diamonds. Wouldn't he? "I can't wait."

The back door to Doc's office opened. With a leather satchel in his hand, Doc crossed the parking lot, his eyes locked on me.

I almost dropped my phone, all thumbs suddenly. "Okay, then, see you tomorrow."

"Yes, you will," Wolfgang said and the line went dead.

"Another client?" Doc asked as he unlocked the passenger door for me.

I shoved my cell in my purse. For some reason, I didn't want Doc to know I'd been talking to Wolfgang. "Um. Sort of."

"Ah. Your boyfriend."

"He's not my boyfriend." I inspected my cuticles, avoiding his grin, hating how he could read me like a fifty-foot billboard.

"Planning date number two?"

"Something like that."

"Good."

I huffed mentally. The jerk didn't have to be so damned happy about me going on a date with Wolfgang. Hell, just the thought of Natalie sitting across the desk from him had me growling and pawing at the dirt for the last hour.

Doc held open the car door for me. The scent of heated leather mixed with his cologne floated around me. A gray plaid blanket lay folded on the seat.

"Just toss that in the back seat," he said.

I hesitated in the doorway, trying to wrestle my

pheromones back into submission.

"What's wrong? Are you allergic to plaid?"

I hit him with a glare.

He grinned in response. "Let's roll. He's waiting for us."

I flung the plaid blanket into the back and dropped onto the warm bucket seat.

As he crawled behind the steering wheel, I turned to him. "Who's waiting for us?"

"Mr. Harvey."

Adding the title in front of Harvey's name made him sound like an elementary school teacher instead of a dirty, old buzzard. "I thought we were going to look at a house."

"We are. Mr. Harvey's." Doc backed out of my parking spot.

"That's thirty miles out of town. You said you wanted to buy within the city limits."

"I do."

"Are you being enigmatic on purpose, or is this just a special Tuesday treat for me?"

"Mr. Harvey asked me to come out and take a look around, give him my thoughts on some stuff, and I agreed."

"What kind of stuff?"

Doc shrugged. "The usual."

Right. Doc must have a bachelor's degree in Vagueness, with a minor in Cryptic Retorts. "Then why do you need me?"

"Maybe I just like your company."

"Hey, what's that smell? Oh, yeah, it's just your brand of hogwash."

Chuckling, he said, "Okay, you got me. I needed a navigator. So, lead the way, please."

I made it until we reached the edge of Deadwood before asking the question burning my tongue. "How was your meeting with Natalie?"

"It went well."

"What did you two talk about?" I fished for some job information.

He spared me a glance as he wound his way up Strawberry Hill. "Mostly her. How long have you two been friends?"

"Since we were kids. I grew up in the house next to her cousins' down in Rapid City." As our parents grew comfortable with each other over time, Natalie would spend weekends with me down on the prairie or at Aunt Zoe's when I visited Deadwood for weeks at a time during the summer. During winter breaks, I'd hang with Nat's family out near Nemo, where her parents used to live before they retired to the bright lights of Hill City.

Doc rumbled past a hulking RV plodding along in the slow lane. "Has she always been so forthright?"

"Since birth, according to her mother." I tried to swing the subject back to his occupation again. "She says you're meeting again on Thursday."

"She invited me to lunch at her place."

My stomach felt like he'd bounced a bowling ball on it. "Oh."

"But I already have a lunch appointment that day."

Whew! I grinned in relief.

"So she's going to cook me dinner, instead."

Shitfire! My grin flipped upside down. I stared out the window so I didn't have to try to school my features while I beat back my hostility toward my best friend.

"Natalie is a good cook," was the only compliment I could spit out between gritted teeth at the moment. Jesus, I had to find a way to tame the jealous ogre clubbing around inside of me before Natalie's visit tonight, or she was going to catch on that I had a silly crush on the guy she was doing her damnedest to bed.

"Do you have any brothers or sisters?" Doc asked.

"One of each. My brother travels the world as a

photojournalist. His home base is in Rapid, but we usually only see him at Christmas and the twins' birthday, if he can swing it. Layne is a huge fan of his uncle Quint." I leaned my head back against the headrest. "I just wish he could hang around more. My son needs a male role model. I'm afraid living with three women is warping his young mind."

"What about your sister?"

"I don't know. I haven't talked to her since I caught her in bed with my boyfriend when the kids were toddlers."

"Ouch."

"Yeah, that's not the half of it." But now was not the time to reach into that pile of dung.

"Tell me about growing up in Rapid City," Doc said, apparently picking up on my unwillingness to explain the sister-subject in more depth.

The remaining half-hour trip to Harvey's whizzed by, along with the pine trees lining the road, as I talked about cold winters at home on the prairie and hot summers with Aunt Zoe in the hills.

Harvey banged open the screen door as Doc and I crawled out of the Camaro.

"Oh, Violet, I almost forgot." Doc grabbed his satchel and pulled a small, thin box wrapped in brown packaging paper from it. "This is for you."

I raised my brows. A gift? For me? From Doc? What was the occasion?

"It's not from me. Natalie stopped back by after her appointment and asked me to give it to you."

Oh, right. I smacked myself mentally for pipe-dreaming again and I took the box from Doc. Calamity Jane's address covered the front, *Attention: Violet Parker* was handwritten on the lower left corner. I fingered one of the taped ends as we walked toward the porch.

"What's that?" Harvey asked as I climbed the porch steps.

"I don't know. It must have come in the mail today."

"Well, quit diddling with it and open the damned thing."

Doc leaned against the porch railing as I tore open the package. Inside, I found a box of chocolates.

"Graceland's Finest," Harvey read the words printed on the box.

A picture of Elvis in his famous white, rhinestone-studded jumpsuit covered most of the box top. I opened the lid and found a yellow envelope with my name scrawled on it. Chocolates shaped like the King lay underneath, the smell of sweet cocoa hovered around me.

"Let me hold these for you." Harvey took the chocolates from me as I ripped open the envelope and withdrew a card with a field of daisies pictured on the front.

I looked up at Doc, my shoulders tense. There was no doubt in my mind who had sent these now. Doc frowned back, his dark brown eyes holding mine. He knew, too.

"What's it say?" Harvey asked through a mouthful of chocolate.

I opened the card and read aloud:

The roses will be red,
For Violet, who I'll woo.
The Wild Pasque, Friday at seven.
Join me—dinner for two.

"Woo wee, girl." Harvey whacked me on the back. "You just keep reeling in the weirdos and freaks, I swear."

"Yeah. Lucky me." I read the poem again, my left eye began to twitch midway through it.

"You're not going to go, are you?" The tone in Doc's voice made it clear what he thought of the idea.

I closed the card, my gut queasy, quivering. "I don't know."

"You don't know?" Doc's question rang with incredulity. He crossed his arms, his jaw clenched. "Have you considered that this admirer could be dangerous? Don't let the daisies fool you."

"Or the chocolate." Harvey grunted as he chewed. "Damn, this is good stuff."

I glared back. "You have any other idea on how to get him to stop watching me? Sending me these creepy poems?"

"Ignore him. He'll go away soon enough."

"He knows where I work. Finding out my home address would be simple. It's not like I'm in the witness protection program."

That shut Doc up for the moment.

"Don't worry," Harvey assured Doc, offering him some chocolate. Doc shook his head. "Me and Bessie will hang out in the parking lot. Make sure she makes it in and out of the restaurant in one piece."

"Who's Bessie?" Doc asked.

"His shotgun," I answered.

"Oh, Christ."

"You sure you don't want me and Bessie to come along tomorrow?"

Harvey held out the chocolate Elvis toward me, which I took and bit in half. I barely tasted the sweet chocolate or the raspberry filling as I chewed on the King's head.

"What's tomorrow?" Doc's eyelids were narrow as he looked back and forth between Harvey and me.

"A lunch date with Jeff Wymonds—her number-one kidnapping suspect." Harvey pulled open the screen door and leaned against it. "Come on, I need a drink. We can talk about this inside."

Doc didn't budge. A vein throbbed near his left temple. "Do you have some kind of a death wish, woman?"

"No, I just—"

"Hurry up," Harvey grabbed my arm and tugged me toward the threshold. "Before the flies get in."

Stuffing the card in my purse, I stepped inside Harvey's house, Doc huffing and grumbling on my heels.

"Welcome to my humble home." Harvey walked around Doc, who'd stopped short in the entryway. "What'll ya have to drink?"

"Something strong and burning," I answered. I wasn't driving, and Calamity Jane's was a half hour away—plenty of time to sober up before returning to my desk. *If* I decided to go back there today. "What's going on with the funny noises behind your barn?"

"Not much. Been quiet lately, but I set out some big ol' traps in the woods just beyond the barn. Unless it's a bear, those traps will catch whatever's sneaking around back there and hold on tight.

"Is that legal?" I asked.

A choking gasp came from Doc. I looked over my shoulder.

His face almost gray, his eyes fluttered shut, Doc swayed. I reached out to catch him as he started to fall, his weight sending me reeling backward into a coat tree.

"Doc, are you okay?" My shoulder blades burned where the coat hooks jousted me.

"Outside," he whispered, his whole body shaking.

"What in tarnation?" Harvey raced over and helped me steady Doc.

"Let's take him out on the porch, get him some fresh air."

A minute and lots of cursing and grunting later, Harvey and I eased Doc onto the porch swing. The chains creaked under our weight as I sat next to Doc, unsure where and whether to touch him while he held his head in his hands and took deep breaths.

"Go get a cold washcloth," I told Harvey, wanting a

moment alone with Doc. I waited for the screen door to slam before turning to Doc. "What in the hell just happened in there?"

"Allergies." He spoke through his fingers.

"Don't give me that allergy-baloney again." I crossed my arms, frowning at the back of his head. "Harvey doesn't have a single gardenia-scented air freshener in the house."

"Something else must have set me off."

He sounded like he was telling the truth, but my gut screamed "liar liar, pants on fire!" I clutched Doc's forearm. "Look me in the eyes and swear it was just allergies."

Doc lowered his hands and stared at me, his eyes red-veined, his cheeks and forehead still pasty. "I swear, it's just something I've dealt with since I was a kid."

I stared back, wanting to believe him.

I really did.

But …

Chapter Sixteen

Remember that gem I was telling you about last week?" Mona asked me after Doc ditched me back at Calamity Jane's.

I dropped my purse on my desk and swung by the coffee maker for a hit of caffeine to spur me through the last two hours of work. "Sure. It was about $50,000 out of Doc's price range."

Mona waved away my frown. "Don't worry about the price."

No problem. While we were visiting Fantasy Island, I'd like a million bucks and Salma Hayek's body, too, please.

"I'll have the place ready to show on Friday. Bring your client by at lunch."

"Okay." I sat down with my cup of coffee, flipped open my daytimer, and riffled through several empty pages.

When Jane hired me almost three months ago, I'd had big plans, and even bigger dreams. Looking back, I should have saved the thirty bucks I paid for the fancy datebook and gotten one of those credit-card-sized yearly calendars instead. At least the tip chart on the back might have come in useful.

I scribbled Doc's name on the page. I'd have to give him a call to make sure he wasn't going to be too busy sleeping with Natalie on Friday to view the place with me.

Meow! I sat back, lowered my pen. Whoa. I needed to cage that sabertooth tiger before she bit the wrong hand—like Natalie's, when she came over tonight to gush about

Doc.

My desk phone rang. I silently offered a certain chicken for sacrifice to the Realty Gods in exchange for someone calling to buy a home, a trailer, a tool shed, a dog house, anything. "Calamity Jane Realty, Violet speaking."

"Hey, Vi." Natalie said.

Damn. Addy's chicken would cluck and peck for another day.

"I was just thinking about you," I told her.

"Something good, I hope?"

"Of course," I lied.

"Sweet, because you're going to be upset with me."

"Why?"

"I can't come to dinner tonight. Mom just called. Dad has some kind of stomach flu, and with Mom's hip out of commission, she needs help. So I'm headed out to Hill City for the night."

Darn, no Doc-fantasy details. Woe was me. "That's okay. We'll do it another night."

"How about tomorrow?"

"No, Wolfgang asked me out."

"Where are you going?"

"I don't know, but he mentioned having a surprise for me."

"I hope it's something erotic and edible."

"I'd settle for just edible."

"Well," Natalie continued, "Thursday won't work for me. I'm having Doc over for dinner that night—and breakfast on Friday, if everything goes as planned."

Blah blah Doc blah sex blah blah. "That sounds fun."

"How about Friday?"

"I have plans." With a secret-admiring psycho. "Saturday?"

"It's a date. With any luck, we'll both have lots of juicy details to share by then."

"Definitely." *If* I was still breathing after my dates with Ted Bundy and the Son of Sam.

We shared goodbyes and I hung up to find Ray off the phone and grinning at me.

I scowled at him. "What?"

His grin spread toward his ears. "I'm just imagining what you'll look like wearing a McDonald's uniform."

"Jesus, Sunshine," Mona said, disgust lacing her tone. "Can't you just lay off Violet for one day?"

"I'd sooner lay on her, but I don't dawdle with the help." He laughed at his own joke. "Although, she'd probably fill out a French maid uniform nicely—in the hips, anyway. Those miracle bras do wonders." He winked at me. "You should try one."

I reached for my cup, planning to poach his trouser trout with some steaming coffee, but I heard Jane's office door open just as my finger wrapped around the handle.

"Violet," she said, "are you available this afternoon?"

I carved a smile onto my cheeks. "Sure."

"I need your help. The old Sugarloaf building in Lead is for sale. I want to know more about it. Can you run over to the library and see what you can dig up?" She held out a Post-It with an address on it.

Oh, God, the end was near. Jane was using me as her personal errand girl now. Shouldering my purse, I stood and took the address from her. "Will do."

"I have an appointment in Sturgis this afternoon, so just leave whatever you find on my desk."

I followed Jane into the hallway that led to her office and the back door, flipping Ray the bird behind my back as I walked. The sound of him blowing me a kiss almost made me turn around and go poke him in the eyes Three-Stooges style, but I straightened my shoulders and stormed to my Bronco instead.

During the short ride to the library, I practiced

perfecting my comebacks and insults for my next round in the ring with Ray. The sight of Doc's Camaro parked in front of the library made me frown. I pulled in behind it. What was *he* doing here—again?

Doc had recovered from his allergic reaction at Harvey's after a glass of lemonade, but he'd stuck to the porch swing the rest of the visit, requesting a rain check on Harvey's offer to show him the house. Harvey had supplied a plate of cold-cut sandwiches for lunch, and later handed off a thick folder to Doc as we climbed into the Camaro.

Our trip back to Deadwood had been filled with lots of useless small talk on my part about Aunt Zoe's glass shop—the only neutral subject I could think of to pass the time since Doc had made it clear back on the porch swing that he wasn't going to elaborate on his so-called allergy issues no matter how much I prodded him.

I climbed out of my Bronco and ascended the concrete stairs. The century-old library greeted me with the smell of wood varnish and musty paper. I paused inside the threshold, counting three other patrons lounging in chairs. Miss Plum, the young brunette from my last visit, was nowhere to be seen—neither was any other official-looking person, thank God. With my hide still stinging from Ray's sharp teeth, I felt about as sociable as a hemophiliac at a vampire convention.

Stealing across the creaky wood floor, I pushed open the door to the South Dakota records room. Doc looked up from the table as I stepped inside. I held my finger to my lips, shushing him until the door clicked closed behind me.

He leaned back in his seat, crossed his arms over his chest, and smiled. "Are you on another top-secret mission, Special Agent V?"

"Maybe." I glanced down at the book laid out on the table before him—the *Register of Deaths* again, this time spread open and splayed across a large map. "What are you looking at?"

Doc's smile slipped a little around the edges, but he didn't try to hide anything as I leaned over the table. "Just some local history."

"That's right." I remembered the thick, Wild Bill Hickok book. "You're a big history nut."

"That's one way of putting it."

"What part of the hills is this?" I bent over the USGS topographical map, tucking some loose curls behind my ear as I scanned the curvy contour lines.

"North Central." He scooted forward, nudged my arm aside, and touched a spot near the left edge. "Here's Custer Peak."

"And there's Harvey's place." I pictured his place in my mind, orienting myself, and noticed a mark on the contoured hill behind where Harvey's barn was located. "What's this sideways Y symbol mean?"

"A cave opening or mine tunnel."

I thought about Harvey's "funny noises." Was something living in the cave or mine above his barn? Was that what'd left the deer carcass behind?

"What's wrong?"

I looked at Doc. God, I hoped Harvey didn't get it in his stubborn brain to go exploring up there on his own. Bessie by his side or not.

"Violet, what?"

I debated on telling him about the noises and deer, but logic weighed in and I decided against it. It was probably just a cougar. "Nothing. It's nothing."

My eyes returned to the map, and I noticed something else. "I didn't realize there was a cemetery out by Harvey's place." I glanced at the *Register of Deaths*, putting two and two together, and then looked up at Doc. "What exactly do you do for a living, Mr. Nyce?"

He raised his gaze from the map, his long black lashes

close enough for me to count, his eyes hooded. "Make an appointment with me and see for yourself, Ms. Parker."

"Are you always this secretive?"

"More often than not."

"When can you fit me in?" For what, I had no idea, but I was tired of trying to listen through walls, wondering what was going on in the office next door.

"I'm open Friday."

Friday.

"Oh, yeah." I blinked back into real estate agent mode. "That reminds me. Mona has a house in the Presidential district coming on the market. Are you available Friday around noon?"

"I think so. Let me take you to lunch afterward."

I frowned. "Why?"

"Because."

Two could play this ambiguity game of his. I strolled over to a bookshelf full of South Dakota-related titles. "I might be busy. I'll have to check my daytimer."

A glance Doc's way showed his eyes still on me. I ran my fingers along a row of book spines. "Now where would I find a book on historic buildings in Lead?"

"I saw your daytimer when it fell out of your purse today, Violet." His chair scraped on the floor. "It has a lot of white space in it."

Damn him for noticing. "I do have a date that evening."

"With your secret admirer, I know."

I pulled out a book called, *The Merry Days of Lead* and flipped through pages filled with a lot of print and very few pictures. "If I say 'yes' to lunch, will you come clean?"

Footfalls behind me made the floor creak. "What makes you think I'm dirty?"

I gulped as his breath warmed the back of my neck. I was playing with matches—but lighting them with Doc was so intoxicating. "I can see it in your eyes."

"What else can you see?"

That sounded like a dare. I turned. The objects in question were very close. The musky aroma of his aftershave lured me even closer. I locked my knees. "You're hiding something."

"I'm hiding a lot of things." He placed both hands on the bookshelf behind me, imprisoning me.

Oh, shit. "Like what?"

"There's no fun in telling." He lowered his head.

He was too close! Warning alarms whooped in my head. The matches I'd been playing with caught fire low in my belly, flaring white hot. I dropped my gaze to the center of his chest, staring at the cotton weave on his dark blue T-shirt.

"I'd rather show you," he whispered, his lips hovering near my ear.

"Oh." It came out as a croak as I struggled to breathe.

"Violet?"

Every muscle rigid, I waited for his touch. "Yes?"

"Is this what you're looking for?" He grabbed my hand. The feel of something cool and hard against my palm made me blink. I looked up.

Doc grinned down at me, a twinkle in his eyes. In my hand, he'd placed a book titled, *Lead—From Then to Now.*

The flames in my stomach climbed up my neck and cheeks, undoubtedly branding the words, *World's Silliest Fool,* on my forehead for all of Deadwood to see. "Uh, sure. Thanks."

He nodded and stepped back, lounging on the edge of the table like he hadn't just played yo-yo with my libido. "Shall we go to lunch before or after we see the house on Friday?"

I wanted to throw the frickin' book at him, would have, too, if I didn't want him to buy a stupid house through me. "I don't care."

"Then we'll eat after."

"Fine." Yanking out a chair, I plopped down at the table and flipped open the book on Lead.

Doc had been spot-on, damn him. The pages were filled with "Then" and "Now" pictures of buildings in the old mining town. I gave him my best Clint Eastwood squint as he returned to his seat across the table from me.

"Is there something in your eye?" His grin still rounded his cheeks.

"No." I flipped several more pages with an extra dose of attitude.

"Where are you going to lunch tomorrow with Jeff Wymonds?"

"I don't know. He's going to call me in the morning and tell me where to meet him."

"I wish you'd let Harvey join you."

"I'm a big girl. I can handle Jeff on my own." That sounded tough. I just hoped I felt an iota of that gumption tomorrow when I sat across from Jeff and tried to stuff food down my throat while acting as if I wasn't sharing a table with a serial kidnapper.

"Like you just handled me?"

That earned him another glare. "You're different."

"Thanks. You're different for me, too." The fervency in his dark gaze seized my attention for several breath-held seconds.

What exactly did he mean by that?

Instead of trying to pick his words apart and find meaning where there probably wasn't any, I tugged my mind back to the task at hand—digging up tidbits on the Sugarloaf building.

"Mr. Harvey mentioned that you were trying to make a connection between the girl from Spearfish and the other three missing girls."

"Harvey has a bucket mouth." That came out surly, but

I couldn't help it. Doc's teasing had left me grinding my teeth.

"I don't know Harvey well enough yet to confirm that, but I do know something about Sherry Dobbler."

His matter-of-fact tone made me look up from a page of Lead's past.

"Her sister is a lifeguard."

I frowned. Not exactly part of the same swim team, but still a water-related trade. It had potential as a link. "Did they mention that on the news?" If so, I'd missed it.

"No."

"Then how do you know about Sherry's sister?"

"Because she works weekends at the Rec Center. I've seen both her and Sherry there during open swim—many times."

I slammed my fist down on the book. "Bingo!"

* * *

Wednesday, July 18th

I drove to work with the windows down, whistling along with the blue jays under the bright mid-morning sunshine. The earth smelled fresh: mowed grass, heated pine pitch, baked asphalt. Walt Disney couldn't have arranged a more cheerful opening to my day.

For the first time in over a week, I had a full night of sleep under my belt. I'd awoken alone, without burning eyes, a throbbing headache, or a molting chicken. Not even the sight of five yellowish-brown horse teeth soaking in a glass next to my toothbrush could make me cringe. Nope, not today. Nor had I screamed or yelled after stepping barefoot on the red toy train lying in wait at the bottom of the stairs.

My lavender blouse hadn't needed an ironing, my white

pants felt a little loose, and my purple boots didn't have any little green army men hiding in them when I slipped them on. Life was good.

For once, Doc's Camaro wasn't in my parking spot when I pulled into the lot behind Calamity Jane's. Ray's SUV wasn't anywhere to be seen either. I locked my Bronco and practically skipped across the parking lot.

Mona clacked away on her laptop as I dropped my stuff on my desk then detoured to pour myself a cup of coffee.

"I spoke with Doc yesterday," I told her as I loaded my brew with plenty of cream and sugar. "We'll be there Friday at noon to see the place."

"Great."

I dropped into my chair and flicked on my computer. "You're going to be there to give us an official tour, right?"

"Of course." Mona stopped clacking and smiled across at me. "Trust me, Vi, I'm going to make this place impossible for him to resist."

"My fingers will be crossed." I sipped my sweetened coffee.

My cell phone trilled. Aunt Zoe's number filled the screen. "Hello?"

"Hi, Mom," Layne said.

"Hey, sweetie. What's going on?"

"When are you coming home today?"

"The usual time."

"Okay." He paused. "I guess I'll see you then."

"What is it, Layne?"

I could feel his hesitation through the line. "The newsman said the kidnapper tried to get another girl."

I leaned back in my chair, hating that I couldn't guarantee safety for my children. "That's true."

"But she got away, right?"

"Yeah, honey. She did."

"I knew it. Addy didn't believe me. She said Kelly told

her the girl was gone."

"Kelly was wrong."

"Sweet! Addy owes me a dollar. I love you, Mom. Bye."

"Oh, hey!" I tried to catch him before he hung up.

"Yeah?"

"You need to pick up your toys. I bruised my foot this morning on that train you left at the bottom of the stairs."

"I didn't leave it there. Addy's kittens must have been playing with it."

"Where did you get that, anyway? You didn't have Aunt Zoe buy it, did you?"

"No, Mom." He said it as if that was my tenth stupid question of the morning. "Addy found it in Wolfgang's yard, remember? Near that trap door."

That train had been black. He must have painted … wait! "What trap door?"

"The one by the back of the garage. Natalie told me not to open it."

"Natalie was right." It was probably an old root cellar, and with all of Homestake's underground blasting over the years, the roof on it was likely one good shake away from caving in.

"I couldn't open it, anyway. It had a blue padlock on it."

"Good." Smart thinking, on Wolfgang's part. That door was just a lawsuit waiting to happen.

"Gotta go, Mom. Aunt Zoe's looking for me. Bye." He hung up before I could say anything else.

I flipped my phone closed just as Ray stepped through the back door, his boot heels thumping my way.

"Hey, Red," he said to Mona as he passed her desk.

I kept my back to him, pretending to be neck deep in an Internet search to avoid any interaction with him.

"Nine days and counting, Blondie."

No such luck. I glared at my screen, struggling not to tackle him, tie him up, and scrub his teeth with the office toilet brush.

"What's wrong, Blondie?" Ray dropped into his chair, which whooshed and then squealed in objection. "Am I being too rough on you this morning?"

Maybe fitting him with concrete shoes and dumping his lousy ass in the middle of Lake Pactola was a better idea.

"Your delicate little feathers can't take so much ruffling?"

Better yet, lock him up in a well-used port-a-potty and roll it down Strawberry Hill.

"Here, Ray," Mona clonked a glass down in front of the sleezeball. "Shut up and drink your orange juice."

"Thanks, Red."

I could feel Ray's eyes on me as he gulped down his drink. I smiled as I read through the new MLS listings in the area, knowing that within a half-hour, Ray would be relocating to the commode as Mona's fiber-filled elixir worked its magic.

My desk phone rang. "Calamity Jane Realty, Violet speaking."

"Hello, Violet Parker." Jeff Wymonds hadn't forgotten about our lunch date. Damn.

"Good morning, Mr. Wymonds."

"Are you still available for lunch?"

"Sure. Where and when?"

"The Purple Door Saloon at eleven-thirty."

It figured that Jeff would pick the one place in town famed for being the best whorehouse east of the Rockies for the first half of the twentieth century.

"Sounds good. I'll see you there." That gave me almost two hours to work on keeping my bladder leak-free and knees steady when I sat down across from him.

"Goodbye, Violet Parker." The phone went dead.

I was beginning to hate the sound of my name.

"Violet?" Jane clomped out from her office, her gold

heels matching her shiny gold blazer. "Thanks for that information on the Sugarloaf building. That was exactly what I needed."

"You're welcome."

"Will you do me another favor?"

My stomach tightened. I didn't want to be Jane's gopher girl, but I couldn't see that I had much choice. "Sure."

"Here are the names and addresses of two more buildings I'm considering purchasing. One is in Hill City, the other is in Sturgis. Will you run over to the library and see what you can find on each of them?"

I took the two Post-Its that she held out. "I'm having lunch with a client today." No harm in lying this late in the game. "Can I bring you the information this afternoon?"

"Of course." Her smile reached her blue eyes. "Good luck at lunch."

Ray snorted as soon as she was out of earshot. "Looks like Jane is making you into her little errand bitch, Blondie. How about picking up my dry-cleaning while you're out. Oh, and if you bring me back some lunch, I'll throw in a nice tip."

Slinging my purse over my shoulder, I paused by his desk long enough to whisper, "Asshole says *what*."

His eyebrows pulled together. "What?"

"Exactly." Whistling, I strolled out the back door.

Head down as I crossed the parking lot, I fished my keys from the bottom of my purse. I'd reached the back bumper of my Bronco by the time I'd finally freed them. I looked up and stopped short. "Goddamn it!"

Ray had parked practically on top of me.

I side-stepped between the two vehicles and unlocked my door, but his SUV was so close there was no way I could squeeze inside. Tempted to key his sparkling SUV, I glared in through his passenger window. His beige leather seats shined in the sunlight filtering through his moon-roof.

A nest of papers covered the passenger side floor—probably his For Sale flyers.

A peek into the back seat area found more papers, some with torn edges. Several pieces were flipped right-side up, looking like he'd driven with his windows down. I shielded my eyes and squinted through the back window. As I looked from one paper to the next, I frowned. *What the hell?*

Why was Ray's SUV filled with "Missing Girl" posters?

Chapter Seventeen

The Purple Door Saloon had a red front door. Either, Sherwin-Williams had been out of purple paint or the exterior decorator had smoked a joint before slipping into his coveralls. Whatever the reason, I had to quit procrastinating and go see what Jeff Wymonds wanted to talk to me about—alone. My palms clammy, my heart pitter-pattering, I pulled open the door.

Across a shadowy, tin-ceilinged room filled with clusters of square tables, I saw Jeff's furry head bent over a mug of beer. The Cowboy Junkies' haunting version of "Sweet Jane" echoed from the jukebox in the back of the bar, next to the two empty pool tables. Wisps of cigarette smoke eddied around me as my boots clomped across the well-worn, plank floor. A bald bartender watched me with narrowed eyes, his tight-lipped stare reminding me that I was not yet a tried and true *local*.

"Hello, Jeff." I hesitated next to the table, wondering how offended he'd be if I sat on the other side of the room.

He raised his head out of his beer, his eyes red-rimmed and glossy. "Violet Parker, you came."

Marvelous. I was lunching with a drunken Mr. Hyde. "How long have you been here?"

"Since I called you." He kicked out the chair opposite him. His version of chivalry, I guessed. "Let me buy you a drink."

I eased onto the edge of the seat, ready to sprint back outside if necessary. "You don't need to do that."

"I insist." There was no slur in his voice, nor did he act tipsy or wobbly as he pushed to his feet. Either he held his liquor well, or the red eyes represented something else. What that was, I'd probably find out soon enough. "What'll you have, Violet Parker?"

I hesitated, craving a rum and Coke, but knowing I might need my wits about me to make it through this lunch with all four limbs still attached. "Just a Diet Coke, please."

As Jeff shuffled to the bar, I glanced around the room, counting seven other customers—one leaning over the jukebox, and three couples scattered throughout the tables. A brunette waitress weaved between the chairs with a tray of burgers and fries in yellow baskets.

"Here you go, Violet Parker," Jeff placed a glass brimming with brown foam in front of me and then sank into his chair. "If that's your real name."

Huh? What was that supposed to mean? I decided not to bite on that hook and sipped on my fizzy drink instead, the spritz of Diet Coke tickling my nose. I searched for a neutral subject. "How's Kelly doing?"

Jeff shrugged with his whole upper body. "Kelly is—" He paused and nailed me with a hard stare. "Why? Did she say something last weekend?"

His question caught me off guard. I'd thought we were just going to trade small talk while we waited for the waitress. "About what?"

"About things going on at home? Anything odd?"

Besides the bit about how to kill a snake, the girl hadn't said more than a teacup full of words to me during her stay. However, Jeff didn't need to know that.

I swirled my drink, buying a few seconds, trying to figure out how to use this ace card to my advantage. "She did mention something about you being in Spearfish a lot lately."

"For a weekend job." He sat forward, his tone

defensive.

Right, and it just so happened that Sherry Dobbler's attempted kidnapping was also a weekend job.

The bald bartender sidled up to our table. "What do you want to eat?"

The frost in his steel-gray eyes almost made me shiver. I got the feeling I'd done something to piss him off and I hadn't even opened my mouth yet. That had to be a new record for me.

"I'll have my usual," Jeff said.

His usual? My hackles raised. I'd thought I was meeting Jeff on neutral ground. Turns out this little chicken had strutted into the fox's den.

The bartender crossed his arms over his chest and cranked up his glare from piercing to blaring. "What about you?"

I hadn't even had a chance to peruse a menu. "Ummm, I'll have some chicken strips." I had poultry on the brain.

He snorted and stormed off.

"Don't mind him," Jeff told me, nodding at the bartender's back. "He hates women these days—especially blondes."

Lucky me. I sipped my drink. Movement over Jeff's shoulder caught my attention. Back by the pool tables, Doc stood chalking up a pool stick cue, frowning at me.

I inhaled Diet Coke.

"You're supposed to drink that, not sniff it." Jeff leaned across the table and landed a stinging whack on my hunched back as I coughed up a lung.

"I'll be …" a couple of more coughs erupted from my throat, my eyes watered, "right back …" I pointed toward the back of the room. "Bathroom."

"Good idea. Your nose is pretty red and shiny. It could use some powdering."

Nice of him to point out my resemblance to Rudolph

while I was choking to death. It was no wonder his wife was leaving his sorry ass. Shouldering my purse, I stomped toward the pool tables, still coughing up Diet Coke.

Doc cued up for a break shot as I neared. "Swallow your tongue, Boots?"

Boots? I frowned down at my purple cowboy boots, then shrugged. I'd been called much worse just a short time ago. "What are you doing here?" I said for his ears only when I could breathe freely again.

"Shooting some pool." The pool stick slid through his fingers, the white ball slamming into the nine racked balls with a *crack*. The one- and seven-balls dropped into the opposite corner pockets. "What about you?"

"You know damned well what I'm doing here."

A smile hinting at the corners of his lips, Doc bent over and lined up another shot. "Making any progress?"

"Yes." I lied, then regretted it. "No." Then I remembered Jeff's concern about what Kelly might have told me. "Maybe!"

Another clack of pool balls followed Doc's shot. The two-ball dropped into the side pocket. His grin lazed on his lips. "You sure about that?"

"Oh, shut up." These days, the only things I was sure of anymore were the sun, the moon, and Bugs Bunny. "Did you follow me here?"

Doc bumped me aside and aimed at the three-ball. "It's a small world."

"Not that small. Did Harvey put you up to this?"

"No." He knocked the three-ball into the four-ball, sinking both of them in the same corner pocket. "I thought you might need some company."

"I told you yesterday, I can take care of myself."

"I'm sure you can, but I'd rather make certain."

Enough to go to the trouble of stalking me today? I could be wrong, and I often was these days, but that seemed a bit over the top for a guy who insisted on keeping a working-relationship-only wedge between us. "Why is that?"

Doc looked up from the table. His gaze traveled down the v-neck of my lavender blouse, following the buttons down to the waistband of my white pants before returning to my face. "Nice opal."

I fingered the single opal hanging from my necklace, but refused to be sidetracked. "Why, Doc?"

He lined up for a shot at the five-ball. "Good Realtors are hard to come by in this town."

"Yeah, right." Teeth grinding, I shoved his pool stick as I pushed past him toward the bathroom and jarred him in mid-shot.

"Hey," he complained to my back.

I kept walking, growling under my breath, frustrated with wanting something he wouldn't give. He was lucky I didn't break that pool stick over his stubborn head.

The bathroom hummed with florescent lights. Jeff had been right. My nose was red and shiny. Damn him. I powdered it back to a dull sheen and washed my hands, wringing my fingers in the cold water while I built up the nerve to return to the table.

When I stepped out from the Ladies' Room, Doc was racking up another game of Nine-ball.

"Violet," he said as I passed behind him.

The edgy tone in his voice made me turn. "Yes?"

"You need to change seats."

I must have heard him wrong. "Come again?"

"When you return to the table, sit in the chair on Jeff's right."

"Why?"

He hit the cue ball, breaking up the other balls, sinking three of them. "Never sit with your back to the door in Deadwood."

"Are you mediating for Wild Bill's ghost now?"

He took aim at the four-ball. "He never played poker in here."

"How do you know?"

"He told me." He took the shot, the four-ball dropped into the pocket.

"Oh, okay. What else did he say? No, let me guess. Something about aces and eights, right?"

"Just trust me. Sit in the other chair."

"Are you serious?" When he didn't crack a grin or look up from lining up his next shot, I weaved my way back toward Jeff replaying that conversation over in my head, making no more sense of it than I had the first time around.

A yellow basket overflowing with fries and chicken strips awaited my return. Wow, I must have dawdled in the bathroom longer than I thought.

Jeff frowned around his mouthful of burger as I pulled out the chair on his right and sat.

"This one has a window view," I explained, still wondering why Doc had insisted I switch chairs. More importantly, why had I even listened to him?

"How do you know that guy?" He pointed in Doc's direction.

I glanced at Doc, catching him watching me. He nodded and then returned to his pool game. "He's a client of mine," and nothing more, according to him.

"He hangs out at the Rec Center a lot."

I couldn't have asked for a better segue. "How long have you been a swim coach?"

The wrinkles spanning Jeff's brow deepened. "A couple years, why?"

"Just curious. What made you decide to coach?"

He stuffed a bunch of fries in his mouth before answering. "Kelly's little friend joined the team and talked Kelly into signing up, too. The coach at the time got a job in Wyoming. He knew I'd been a lifeguard back in school and asked me to take over." He swallowed a visible lump of fries. "One season rolled into the next."

The *little friend* must have been Emma. I dipped a chicken strip in the tub of BBQ sauce nestled amongst my fries. "It must be hard for you, what with three girls from your team disappearing in the last year."

"Hard?" He threw back his head and laughed—not a Shirley Temple giggle, more like a Charles Manson cackle.

I squirmed on the hard wooden chair and glanced at Doc, who stood watching us, his lips thin, his eyes narrow.

"You've no idea, Violet Parker." Jeff grabbed my chicken-free hand and squeezed too hard for comfort, his greasy fingers pressing into my skin. His blue eyes locked onto mine. "No idea."

Forcing a smile, I patted his arm while trying to pull my hand free. My heart pounded against my ribs, trying to hammer its way out and bounce to safety. I struggled to keep my voice even. "Why don't you tell me about it." *And why you threw those clothes in the Dumpster.*

"Tell you what?" He loosened his grip so he could pour beer down his throat. "What do you want to know?"

If you kidnapped the missing girls. I shoved my hand under the table and sat on it so he couldn't hold it hostage again. "If there is anything I can do to help."

"Well," he chewed on another bite of burger for several seconds. "Funny you should ask."

"Why?"

"Donna left me."

I froze, chicken chunk midway to my mouth. While that was no surprise to me, his bringing it up was. "Oh."

"For another woman."

I almost dropped my chicken. I'd had that fact backwards. Now that Jeff had straightened it out for me, I didn't know what to say besides, "That sucks."

"Yep. On top of that, Kelly won't stop talking about death, even after I've forked out a shitload of money for shrink visits over the last year."

The whole bit about how to kill a snake popped into my brain again, followed by the need to have a talk with Addy about what Kelly had been saying to her behind closed doors. I bit off half of the chicken strip, the salty morsel as appealing as deep-fried cardboard at the moment.

"And if my wife has her way in court, I'll get to see my son for one day every other weekend." Pain scrunched his face.

I reached toward his arm, then pulled back, uncertain. He was the villain in my suspicions, I wasn't supposed to feel this ache in my throat for him. "I'm so sorry."

"My boy is going to be raised by a pair of lesbos."

I winced at his offensive choice of terms, and searched for a positive spin. "At least he'll have three parents. A lot of kids don't have any." Hell, my kids had only me.

"You like men, don't you, Violet Parker?"

"Sure." I glanced Doc's way again. Some more than others, damn it.

"You and I should go out," he said through cheeks packed with burger. "You're pretty enough. We could be like the Brady Bunch."

Or like John and Lorena Bobbitt—butcher knife included. "Uh-huh," was my noncommittal reply. "Is that why you asked me to lunch?"

He shook his head. "I need your help."

I doubted my one psychology class at Rushmore Community College was going to cut it. "With what?"

"My house. I want you to sell it."

* * *

I walked around Deadwood a bit after lunch, craving some alone-time to rehash my suspicions before returning to face my bare desktop—and Ray. Warm breezes tainted with exhaust fumes trailed down Main Street. The growl of creeping traffic blocked out most of the dings and pings of slot machines, muffled behind plate-glass windows. My sunglasses offered shelter from eye contact with strangers.

Jeff's admissions about his home life had left me scratching my head. Desperation had choked off my *Hell, no!* reply when he'd requested my Realtor services, so we'd spent the last part of lunch buried in shop talk.

I'd learned that he had to sell in order to pay Donna for her portion of the house's value. Lucky for him, he'd bought the place back before gambling came to town and house prices had quadrupled. His ambition was to move to Spearfish, closer to his brother. Kelly would be joining him—her mother unable to handle the little girl's slippery slide into depression.

Jeff hadn't even blinked when I'd mentioned the percentage he'd have to pay me if I could find a buyer, nor the amount of cash he'd need to invest to clean his place up so it didn't look like the site of a redneck kegger. I'd walked away from lunch with heavy feet—not at all what I'd imagined before stepping into the Purple Door Saloon.

The hot sunshine drove me inside Fancy Fannie's, a casino with life-sized, black-and-white pictures of showgirls lining the walls. Chilled air cooled my neck and arms, cigarette smoke burned the back of my throat. Plopping in front of a Triple 777 slot machine, I fed it a ten-dollar bill and hit the Spin button. Sevens and cherries blurred in front of my eyes.

Why had Doc insisted I change chairs? What was the deal with him and the crazy bit about Wild Bill?

The tumblers landed on a single seven, a blank spot, and a double seven. I hit Spin again.

Why had he been looking up information on dead people again, anyway? A morbid curiosity? Something work-related?

Why the cemetery out behind Harvey's place?

The tumblers stopped on a triple seven, a single cherry, and a blank spot. I punched Spin.

Did Doc suspect that Harvey had something to do with the missing girls? No, that couldn't be it. Harvey was crusty on the outside, but inside, he was just a big glob of goo. Although, he was partial to Bessie. Okay, maybe he had the potential to smack a puppy or two, but hurt a little girl? Surely not. Right?

Double seven, single seven, and two cherries.

Who was Doc to be pointing a finger, anyway? He wasn't exactly above suspicion. He sure spent a lot of time at the Rec Center. Probably almost as much as Jeff over the last year, now that I thought about it. He must have seen all of the missing girls at some point. He'd already admitted to knowing Sherry Dobbler … and her sister.

Single seven, single cherry, blank spot.

However, there was something about Doc that made me wave away any mistrust—in spite of his need to sniff the corners in every room he entered and say the oddest things. Maybe it was the way he seemed to be watching out for me whether I liked it or not. Or the way he grinned so easily. Or the way he listened when people talked, as if he was focusing on every single syllable uttered.

Triple seven, double seven, double cherries.

A glance at the clock on my cell phone made my chest twang with guilt. It was two-thirty, and I should probably head to the library to dig up that information for Jane. Then I needed to get back to the office and fill out the contract for Jeff's place. This would give me three houses on my plate, with the Hessler haunt the rough-cut diamond in my rhinestone tiara.

Single seven, single seven, double seven.

Thinking about Wolfgang's house still gave me the heebie jeebies. Just the thought of those stupid clowns with their manic grins made me shiver. I needed to convince Wolfgang to paint over them before we showed the place. Surely he knew how tacky they would look to a potential buyer, especially one who could afford the price we'd be asking.

Double seven, two cherries, single cherry.

I sighed. Ah, Wolfgang—my gorgeous, fair Lancelot. So comfortable to be around compared to Doc, who always had me jumping around on hot coals. Wolfgang with his sexy blue eyes and Don Juan smile. Maybe I should wear that little backless, black satin number tonight that Natalie bought me for my birthday. No wait, he'd said not to dress up.

My cell phone rang. I reached for my purse.

Double seven, double seven, double seven.

The slot machine lit up, bells clanging for a couple of seconds. As I hauled my phone from the bowels of my purse, I scanned the legend at the top of the machine, searching for how much I won as the number of credits climbed.

"Hello?"

"Violet, where are you?" Aunt Zoe asked.

The slot machine quieted, its victory dance over too soon. Two hundred credits. What was that in quarters? "Downtown, why?"

"You need to come home."

"What has Layne done now?" I hit the Payout button. The machine spit out a paper receipt.

"It's not Layne. It's Addy."

"What about her?"

"She's missing."

Chapter Eighteen

I rocketed through three Stop signs on the way to Aunt Zoe's, every muscle trembling, my hands clenched on the steering wheel. Addy's sweet, freckled face filled my head, fear for her life fueled my panic. I skidded into the driveway and scrambled out of the driver's seat before the engine stopped sputtering.

Harvey burst through Aunt Zoe's screen door. "Let's go!"

"Where?" He caught me off guard. I had expected Aunt Zoe's worry-lined brow, not Harvey's grizzled cheeks.

"You tell me." He rounded the front of the Bronco. "Where does Addy like to hang out?"

"Ummm," I struggled to wrap my brain around his question while climbing back into the driver's seat and turning the ignition key.

His hand clamped on my arm. "Violet, look at me."

I obeyed, my chest heaving, as if I'd sprinted all the way from downtown Deadwood.

"Take a deep breath," Harvey ordered.

I tried, but fear seemed to have my lungs locked in a bear hug. "I can't," I gasped.

Harvey pinched the back of my upper arm—hard.

"Owwww!" My eyes watered from the sharp pain. I slapped his hand away and rubbed my stinging skin. "What the hell did you do that for?"

"Where does Addy like to hang out?"

"The Rec Center."

"Then let's start there."

Oh. Now I understood. I shifted into reverse, my arm still throbbing. "You didn't have to pinch so damned hard."

"I'd have slapped your ass, but you were sitting on it."

Yet another reason to keep my head tied to my shoulders at all times around Harvey. "Why were you at Aunt Zoe's?"

"I wasn't. I was at Beatrice's fiddling with her … uh … her plumbing."

That explained the lipstick smudge on his earlobe.

"Your aunt sent Layne over to get me. Wanted me to help you search for Addy while she stayed home with Layne—in case Addy returns."

We rolled into the Rec Center parking lot a minute later. Harvey caught up with me in the lobby, where I stood scanning the Sign-In register. I wiped away the sweat dewing on my upper lip.

"Is she here?" Harvey asked.

"No, but Doc is." He'd signed in at three o'clock, just five minutes ago. I'd seen him slink out the back door of the Purple Door Saloon when I'd been giving my "call you later" spiel to Jeff after our long lunch.

"I'll go get him," Harvey said.

"Why?"

"He can help us look."

"I don't know."

"What's to know? With this thing going on between you two, he'll want to help."

"There's nothing going on between us." Doc was making sure of that.

"I may be an old fool, girlie, but I'm not a blind one." Harvey crossed his arms. "I don't understand why you kids like to play these silly games. In my day, we just parked up at Mountain Goat Lookout, knocked boots in the back seat, and then tied the knot when the baby started to show."

"Listen, Doc is my client, that's all. Now let's just go look for Addy."

Harvey shook his head. "Nope. Not without Doc."

"Damn it, Harvey. We don't have time for this shit."

"Time for what?" Doc said from the Men's locker room doorway.

I growled in my throat. "Happy now?" I shot at Harvey.

"Hey, Doc." Harvey grinned at Doc as he joined our little party at the desk. "We were just talking about you."

"Really." Doc's gaze searched my face. "What's wrong?"

"Violet's daughter is missing." Harvey blurted out.

"How long?" Doc asked.

I looked away, my eyes blurring, my throat too tight to speak.

"She took off on her bike this morning," Harvey answered for me. "Should have been home a couple of hours ago. I'm gonna take a gander at the pool, make sure she's not there."

The cacophony of children's laughter and screams waxed and waned as he shoved through the double doors leading to the pool.

"Where have you looked so far?"

Swallowing the lump of fear and worry trying to choke me, I faced him. "This is our first stop. The library is next, then Kelly Wymonds' place. After that, I don't know where to look."

"I'll cruise around town, see if I can find her." He dug his car keys from the pocket of his navy cargo shorts.

I pointed at his fingerless, weight-lifting gloves. "You're busy. Harvey and I can take care of this."

"Shut up, Violet." He cupped my face, his leather-covered palms smooth against my cheeks. He leaned close enough for me to see little gold sparkles in his irises.

"Um, sure." My voice sounded husky, tears dammed

behind it.

"Now listen to me. Addy is okay. We'll find her."

The dam cracked. My eyes welled up again. I glanced down, trying to blink away the tears. Why did I have to be hard-wired like my mother, all damp and melty when I needed to be sturdy and strong?

The pool doors whooshed open.

"She's not in there," Harvey said, his eyebrows raised as he approached us.

Doc dropped his hands and stepped back. He jangled his keys between us. "Keep your cell phone on."

I nodded and he pushed out the front door.

Harvey stared at me, his grin banana-split wide. "Nothing going on between you two, huh?"

"Oh, stuff a sock in it." I grabbed him by one of his suspenders and tugged. "Let's go."

Almost two hours later, Harvey and I sat in the parking lot of the century-old Fremont, Elkhorn & Missouri Valley Railroad Station. A call to Aunt Zoe left me chewing on my fingernails, an old habit that usually reared up after the shit had already passed through the fan blades and shot out the other side.

Still no Addy. No sight, no word, no call, nothing.

Harvey and I had scoured the library, pummeling Miss Plum, the young librarian, with questions and pictures. She admitted to knowing Addy by sight, but said she hadn't seen her in days.

Next, we'd visited the Wymonds' property. The drive had been empty. Dented trash cans lined the curb, Kelly's bike lay on its side in the yard, the front tire flat and hanging off the spoke wheel like a necklace.

I'd banged on the door. Silence had responded, followed by loud buzzing as a pair of yellow jackets harassed me.

After fighting off my sting-happy attackers, we'd

trampled through the overgrown grass into the backyard, peeked in the dirt-rimmed windows of Jeff's tool shed, and frowned at the baby-doll head floating face-up in the brown water of a kid's pool.

We'd left and headed back to town, raced through the aisles of the Piggly Wiggly, poked our heads in the Adams Museum, marched through the headstones up on Mount Moriah, waded through children at the mini-amusement park at the south end of town, and even stomped around Wolfgang's yard, making sure the root cellar door remained locked up tight. All for naught.

Addy seemed to have disappeared off the planet. I gnawed on my thumbnail. My stomach roiled, nauseated, the remains of my lunch threatening to crawl up my esophagus and escape screaming out of my throat. "How long until I can go to the police?"

Harvey shrugged. "Honey, you can go to the police any time."

Doc's Camaro rolled into the lot. I was out of the Bronco and standing beside his car door before he shifted into Park.

"Anything?" I stood back as he pushed open his door and climbed out.

He didn't need to answer. The lines criss-crossing his face said it all. "Sorry. I checked in the casinos, too, and talked to some of the floor-walkers. Nobody has seen her."

"Oh, fuck!" I covered my face with my hands. My heart ached from being ripped in half. "Where is she?"

A pair of arms wrapped around me. I lowered my hands and buried my nose in the soft cotton of Doc's T-shirt, his woodsy scent cocooning me. "She'll show up, Violet."

"What if *he* has her?" I whispered, my voice trembling. "I just want my Addy back,"

"You'll get her back." Doc's voice sounded so certain as he stroked my back.

"How do you—"

"Violet," Harvey called from the Bronco's passenger side window. "You have a phone call."

I pulled back from Doc and squinted in the late afternoon sunlight at Harvey. "Who is it?"

"He didn't say."

"Tell whoever it is I'll call him back."

"He says he needs to talk to you immediately."

I strode back to my Bronco, Doc on my heels, and grabbed the phone from Harvey. "Yes?"

"Hello, Violet Parker," Jeff Wymonds said in my ear.

"Listen, Jeff, I don't have time to talk right now."

"I think you're going to want to hear this."

"Really?" If this was more about his soon-to-be ex or death-obsessed daughter, I wasn't in the mood to play psychiatrist. "What is it?"

"Your daughter."

I gasped. "What about her?"

"I have her."

* * *

The Northern Hills Hospital had served the communities of Deadwood, Lead, and the surrounding silver and gold-mining settlements through boom and bust since the 1870s. I had often imagined the famous and infamous patrons that had dragged themselves through its doors, bleeding from bullet wounds, knife gashes, and all of the other violent ways to end a crooked card game or saloon brawl.

Not once had I imagined myself following in their footsteps. Yet here I was, Bronco tires squealing as I skidded into a parking spot and stomped on the brakes.

I didn't wait for Harvey to peel himself off the dashboard, nor for Doc, who rolled in behind me, as I ran across the asphalt and shoved through the Emergency Room's double doors.

Addy sat in the corner of the room, her arm in a makeshift sling. Kelly lounged in the chair next to her.

"Oh, thank God." I swallowed the coconut-sized lump in my throat and jogged across the carpet, indifferent to the stares of the handful of other patrons waiting for their turn with a doctor. I squatted in front of Addy, wanting to squeeze her tight against me, but holding back due to her arm. "Hi, Sweetie. I'm so glad you're safe."

Her brow was wrinkled as she looked up, her lower lip quivering. "Mom, I lost Elvis."

Huh? The king of rock n' roll? "Elvis?"

"My chicken."

Oh. I needed to start writing down these kinds of things. "Addy, your chicken is a girl."

Her eyes filled with tears. "I knew you wouldn't understand."

Jesus! I'd just spent the last few hours having my heart and soul ripped out through my throat while *what-if* demons stripped years from my life. Excuse me if I struggled with working up a snuffle or two for a freaking chicken who used the hood of my Bronco as its own personal outhouse.

"Sweetheart," I had trouble keeping the terseness from

my tone, "I'm sorry you lost your chi—Elvis."

"Me, too," she whispered.

Her fat tears weathered away my rough edges. I brushed the wetness from her cheeks. "Maybe we'll see about getting you another one."

What? Who said that? It wasn't me, because the last thing I wanted was another chicken roosting on my pillow every night. Although snuggling up to a pet snake would be worse.

"No, I don't want another chicken. Just Elvis."

Well, thank the poultry gods for that. I kissed her on the forehead, soaking up the feel and taste of her skin against my lips.

"Hello, Violet Parker."

I stood, smiling at Jeff Wymonds without effort for the first time since meeting him. "Thank you so much for your help."

"No problem." He patted Kelly's head and then sat in the seat across from her. "I just hope these two numbskulls understand now why that old mine was barricaded and plastered with No Trespassing signs, and don't pull this kind of shit again." He shot a glare at his daughter. "Next time, I might not be around to fish either of you out of a shaft."

"We know, Dad." Kelly's sigh could have won her an Emmy for the *Best Dramatic Scene in a Daytime Soap Opera* category. "You lectured us all the way to the hospital, remember?"

Addy's forehead was puckered as she looked up at me. "We wouldn't have gone in if Elvis hadn't squeezed between the boards. It was a rescue mission, Mom, see?"

A tap on my shoulder made me turn. Doc stood behind me, holding out a can of Diet Coke.

"Thanks," I took the cold can and cracked it open. "Jeff, this is my …" I paused, not sure really what role Doc played in my life. "My friend, Doc Nyce."

"Yeah, the pool player." Jeff remained seated but held out his hand toward Doc while giving me a raised-brow look. "I thought you said he was a client."

Oops, I'd forgotten all about our lunch conversation.

"Violet likes to mix business with pleasure," Doc said, his grin teasing me as he released Jeff's hand. "Nice to meet you, Mr. Wymonds."

"Where's Harvey?" I asked Doc and dropped into the seat next to Addy. Coming down from my adrenaline rush left my legs weak.

"He said something about needing to use the facilities." Doc ruffled Addy's blonde hair. "Good to see you again, Squirt. I hear the doctor says you're going to need a cast."

"Yep. It's going to be purple, too."

"Cool. I can't wait to see it."

Sipping on my Diet Coke, I patted the chair next to me, not ready to break the bond that I'd forged with Doc this afternoon. While he'd made it clear I couldn't act on this crush I had for him, which was mushrooming out of control by the minute, there were no rules about feeding a friendship.

Doc obliged, stretching his long legs out in front of him. "How did you know where the girls were?" he asked Jeff as he draped his arm over the back of my chair.

Good question. One that might have popped into my brain had I not been so busy trying to figure out if Doc's hand had just brushed my ribcage on purpose.

"Kelly—"

"Whew!" Harvey ambled into our corner of the waiting room, wiping his hands on his jeans. "My prostate must be as big as a grapefruit today."

I winced. I was quickly learning that there seemed to be no topic off-limits in Harvey's repertoire.

"What's a prostate?" Addy asked.

"It's a saloon girl who likes to sleep with dirty boys," Kelly answered, her tone factual.

Jeff grinned. Doc chuckled, his hand skimming my ribs again.

"No, that's a prostitute," Harvey clarified.

"The prostate is a gland, Sweetheart," I answered, trying to figure out how to keep this conversation from plunging into a squirming pool of discomfort. In my family, there were three topics we didn't explore in mixed company—religion, politics, and bodily functions. "It's nothing important, Adelynn," I added, using my motherly, end-of-discussion tone.

Harvey grunted. "It is when you're my age."

"What does it do?" Addy pressed, avoiding my glare.

"Makes it hard to take a piss."

Splash! I squirmed in my chair, bumping into Doc's hand, and kept my focus fixed on Harvey.

"Howdy, Jeff," Harvey plopped into the seat next to Jeff, his blue eyes moving from me to Doc and back to me, his lips forming into a know-it-all grin.

I shot him a scowl, but my neck roasted, anyway.

"Hey, Harvey," Jeff nodded at the big-mouthed old bird. "How's life treating you?"

"Viagra is a wonderful drug."

That said it all. My blush climbed to my cheeks as I wriggled in my seat again.

Doc's fingers strummed my ribcage.

I stilled as my body tightened, inside and out. Turning, I met his dark brown eyes. He winked and strummed again, this time slower, his fingertips lingering on each rib.

Such a small touch, no more than a leisurely sweep really. Yet a shudder registering around magnitude eight on the Richter scale rumbled along my nerves, which were still recovering from the side effects of hours of adrenaline rush. Did he have any clue how aware I was of every breath he took at this moment?

"Mom?" Addy's voice yanked me back to the ER waiting room.

I tore my gaze from Doc's. "Yeah, sweetie?"

Addy pointed at the doorway. "Look who's here."

Following her finger, I gasped at the site of Wolfgang standing there, smiling at me with those dazzling white teeth. With his indigo blue camp shirt unbuttoned at the neck, his faded jeans hugging his form, and his hair looking like he'd combed it with his fingers, he could have been the newest cover model for a Stetson cologne ad.

I groaned inwardly. I'd forgotten about our date.

I met him halfway across the room. "I'm so sorry, I—"

He took me in his arms and dropped a quick kiss on my lips, surprising me into silence. I'd forgotten that we'd made it to the kissing-cousin level in our relationship.

"Don't worry about it." He said, stepping back. The spicy aroma of his aftershave lingered around my head. "Your aunt explained everything to me. I'm just glad to hear Addy is okay."

I glanced toward Addy, then Doc. His poker face would have made Wild Bill Hickok envious. "Why don't you come join us? We're waiting for Addy's cast fitting."

"Sure, but first," Wolfgang grabbed my hand and raised it to his lips, his cobalt eyes locking onto mine. "Let me just look at you for a second."

I fidgeted under his stare, knowing my makeup had been rubbed off several hours ago and my hair was spiraling out all over my head.

"I couldn't stop thinking about you while I was gone."

"Same here," I lied, wishing it were the truth. I tugged my hand free. "Come on. Addy will be happy you came."

I had trouble meeting Doc's eyes as we joined the group, so I started the introduction with Jeff. "Wolfgang, this is—"

"Jeff Wymonds," Wolfgang finished for me.

"Oh, that's right." I'd forgotten Wolfgang was a local. "You two went to school together."

Jeff's smile didn't reach his eyes. "How's the jewelry business, Hessler?"

I glanced at the back of Jeff's neck to see if it was bristling, but his scruffy hair covered any evidence.

"Booming," Wolfgang's grin dazzled as usual. If he was picking up on Jeff's surly undertone, he hid it well. "How's your wife?"

Alarm whistles blared in my head. I pointed at Harvey. "This is my friend, Willis Harvey."

Wolfgang followed my lead without a hiccup. "Mr. Harvey. Didn't you used to frequent the casino next to my store?"

"Sure did. I was dating one of the cocktail waitresses there—until her husband found out."

I heard a quiet laugh come from Doc. "That must have put a kink in things."

"Might of," Harvey snickered, "if her old man had gotten a hold of my wedding tackle. His trick hip gave me the edge."

"What's wedding tackle?" Addy asked.

"A kind of fishing pole," I answered, skirting the subject again, practically twirling as I danced through introductions.

Harvey snorted and smacked his leg.

"And this is Dane Nyce," I turned to Doc, unsure why I chose to use his real name. "Another … friend of mine."

Doc shot me a one raised-brow stare, then stood and held out his hand toward Wolfgang.

"Are you from around here, too?" Wolfgang asked.

"Nope." Doc pulled his hand free and indicated toward the chair he'd just vacated. "Have a seat."

"No, thanks," Wolfgang said. "I don't plan on staying

long. I just wanted to make sure Addy was okay and give her this." He pulled a small pink box from his pants pocket and held it out to Addy, who blasted him with both dimples and grabbed the box.

"Addy," I chastised. "What do you say?"

"Thanks, Wolfgang." With Kelly's help, Addy tore open the box. She squealed down at a rhinestone-covered unicorn broach.

The broach reminded me of the crystal I'd found in his bathroom and pocketed. Unfortunately, Aunt Zoe had washed my lawn-mowing clothes the next day and I hadn't seen the crystal since. I had a bad feeling the washing machine ate it, and unless I came across the crystal again, I wasn't going to bring it up to anyone, especially Wolfgang.

"Also," Wolfgang continued, turning toward me. "I wanted to see if her mother wanted to reschedule our date to Saturday night."

It took me a couple of seconds to realize he meant me. Saturday? Wasn't I doing something that night? Feeling the weight of all six pairs of eyes on me, I just smiled like an idiot. "Sure. Same time, same place?"

Wolfgang nodded. "Wear that red dress again. I have something special planned for you."

"I need to get going," Doc said, digging into his pocket and coming out with car keys. "See you later, Squirt," he said, winking at Addy, like he had at me not five minutes ago, but without the heat.

Her dimples appeared again. "Bye, Doc. Will you sign my cast later?"

"You bet, kid."

Relief and disappointment churned in my gut. While having both Doc and Wolfgang in the same room made me feel like I was juggling lit torches, I didn't want Doc to leave.

I grabbed Doc's arm as he passed in front of me.

"Thanks for your help today."

His grin flashed so fast I would have missed it if I'd blinked. "Anything for a *friend*, Violet."

I watched his broad shoulders as he strode away, my teeth gnashing at the frosty edge in his tone. What was that supposed to mean? He's the one who'd laid down the no-sex law.

"Addy," Wolfgang said from behind me. "How about you and your friend join me for a tour of the gift shop's candy rack?"

"Can I, Mom?"

I turned, smiling for everyone's benefit when what I really wanted to do was lie on the floor, kick my feet, and scream for five minutes. "Sure, but only one piece of candy this time—and a milk carton of Whoppers does not count as one item, Adelynn."

Wolfgang and the two girls strolled off down the hall that led to the gift store. I sighed, dropping into my chair.

"Well," Harvey said, mirth in his voice. "That was fun."

"How do you know Wolfgang Hessler?" Jeff asked me, his eyes narrowed with a hint of suspicion.

"He's a client," I said, then added, "and a friend."

"Really?" Jeff rested his elbows on his knees.

I frowned at the leer in his tone. "Yes."

"Well then, Violet Parker," Jeff said in a hushed voice that had Harvey and I both leaning forward to hear it. "I'm already a client, so how do I get to be one of your so-called …" he made quotation marks in the air with his fingers, "*friends*?"

The glint in his eyes as his gaze traveled down my throat and lingered on the top button of my blouse made me cross my arms over my chest.

"And do you charge your clients by the hour or by the job?"

Harvey's bark of laughter echoed through the room.

Chapter Nineteen

Thursday, July 19th

Another bouquet of daisies greeted me at Calamity Jane's early the next morning. They lay across my desk, their perky petals beginning to wilt. I wanted to throw them on the floor and jump up and down on them.

I glanced over at Mona, who seemed to be battling the rooster for sunrise bragging rights lately. Her fingernails clackity-clacked away on her laptop, as usual. Her jasmine-scented calling card drifted around me, competing with the aroma of fresh-brewed coffee. "When did these flowers arrive?"

"Yesterday afternoon." Mona looked at me, her eyebrows spiked, her rhinestone-studded reading glasses resting on the tip of her nose. "Speaking of yesterday, where were you?"

"In hell." I cast a glance at Jane's closed office door. Light leaked out through the bottom crack. I'd forgotten about the property information that Jane had asked me to dig up until I had Addy settled at home with her new cast.

Grateful for the library's extended summer hours, I'd grabbed Layne and raced across town. Disappointment had tightened my chest when I didn't find Doc sitting in his usual chair in the South Dakota room. I'd spent the next half-hour scanning books, all the while lecturing myself about why I needed to pluck this crush I had on Doc before its roots dug in.

I pulled the information I'd copied for Jane from my

tote and asked in a lowered voice. "Did Jane notice I didn't come back from lunch?"

"Of course, but I told her you were showing some houses."

"Thanks. I owe you."

Mona waved away my gratitude. "So spill. What happened?"

I retrieved the pink envelope from the bouquet and then dumped the flowers in the trash. "You'll never believe it."

"Does it involve a horse skull or a chicken?"

The fact that my life was now predictably threaded with equine and poultry subplots made me want to throw back a couple of Zoloft and chase them with a splash of Southern Comfort. "The latter. Addy followed her chicken into a mine, fell down a shaft, and broke her arm."

Actually, Addy informed me after we left the ER that she had tripped over Kelly's foot *by accident* and stumbled into the shallow, test shaft. Later, long after Addy's eyelids had drifted closed, I tossed and turned in the quiet dark of my bedroom, wondering if I should have been focusing on Kelly instead of Jeff all this time.

Could Kelly's obsession with death have had anything to do with the disappearance of the other girls from her swim team? Maybe her morbid fixation, born last summer, had just taken a while to float to the surface. Maybe she'd lied about what really happened to her best friend, Emma Cranson, on that fateful August day. Maybe the other girls had also fallen *by accident* into shafts in some of the many mines littering the outskirts of Deadwood—shafts too deep for anyone to be fished out of alive.

"How's Addy doing today?" Mona's question tugged me out of my shadow-filled thoughts.

"When I left home, she was supervising Layne. He's helping her build a chicken trap." Addy was determined to rescue Elvis from the mine, even though I'd grounded her from entering any holes in the earth for the next six months.

I stared down at the tiny envelope in my hand, running my finger over my name scrawled in purple ink. Anticipation and dread tightened my stomach.

Mona's fingernails returned to their key-pecking routine, but her gaze bounced between her screen and me. "Did you have a nice lunch with Jeff Wymonds?"

Mona knew of my suspicions about Jeff and the missing girls. She had never agreed on a *guilty* verdict, her jury was still open to hearing more evidence.

"It turns out he's pretty torn up about his wife leaving him, needs to sell his place to pay what she's demanding in the divorce settlement, and wants to hire my services." *In bed as well as in real estate.*

My cheeks warmed at the memory of his misconception about my profession. However, as Harvey had so kindly pointed out on our way to the Bronco after Addy's cast-fitting, I now had a career to fall back on when I ran out of unemployment benefits.

"That's good, right?"

"I guess."

"Is he still on your list of suspects?"

"I don't know." My jury had begun deliberations. While I was swaying toward him being innocent, I wasn't willing to let him leave my line-up just yet.

I tore open the envelope and extracted the card. My secret admirer's latest poetic stab filled the front of it.

The roses will be red
On our table with a view.
Reserved under "Adelynn,"
I'll be waiting for you.

The sight of Addy's name made my legs shaky from the neck down. I slumped into my chair.

"What's it say?" Mona hovered over me, her forehead crinkled with concern.

I handed the card to her and scrambled for my cell phone.

She scanned it. "How does he know Addy's name?"

"I don't know." How in the hell was I supposed to keep my little girl safe with so many monsters prowling throughout this damned town? I punched in Jeff Wymonds' phone number. It rang twice and then I heard a click. I didn't wait to hear his voice. "Jeff, it's Violet. Have you been sending me flowers with little notes?"

"No," he answered. "Why? Should I be? Is that how I become one of your special *friends*?"

"No. Goodbye, Jeff." I ended the call and sighed. "This can't be good, can it?"

"What can't be good?" Jane asked, pouring a cup of coffee.

I'd been so busy gnawing on my knuckles, weighing the pros and cons of shipping my kids to boarding school in another state, I hadn't heard the clomp of her heels on the floor. "Uhhh."

"The city planners' idea to add another stoplight on Main Street," Mona said, covering for me … again.

"Oh, right." Jane joined us at my desk, her gaze locked onto me. "How did it go yesterday afternoon?"

"Pretty well." I knew she was referring to my supposed house-showing jaunt, but Addy was alive and breathing, Wolfgang wasn't pissed at me for standing him up, and Harvey had landed a date with one of the hospital's blue-haired candy-stripers. All in all, Lady Fortune's umbrella had shielded me and mine from what could have been a real downpour. "Here's that information you wanted."

"Thanks." She took the copies I held out. "So where

did you go yesterday?"

I sat up in my chair, doing my best not to fidget. "All over Deadwood." No lying there. Harvey and I had covered the town from one end of the gulch to the other.

"Any bites?"

"Just a nip," I answered, thinking of Doc's stinging *anything for a friend* chomp. "But today is a new day."

"I like your attitude, Violet."

"Thanks." I smiled. Mona had taught me during my first week at Calamity Jane's that optimism would carry me a long way with the boss toward the sweet land of good graces.

"I'd like it even more if you had something to show for it." Jane nodded her head at the Sale Pending board.

Me, too! I gulped, but kept my chin held high. "I will."

"I hope so, Violet. I really do." Jane squeezed my shoulder. "Let me know if there is anything I can do to help get your name on the board."

I waited until Jane had returned to her office and closed the door before crawling under my desk and huddling there with my arms wrapped around my knees.

Mona rolled aside my chair and peeked in at me, her reading glasses dangling from her neck. "Vi, what are you doing?"

"Hiding."

"From whom?"

"The world."

"Sweetheart, you're going to need to find a better hiding spot to accomplish that."

The sound of someone clearing his throat spurred Mona upright. I peered out from under my desk and spotted a pair of black boots draped with blue jeans standing smack-dab on the front door's threshold.

"Hi," Mona said, all polish and business. "Can I help you?"

I heard a sniff, then a deep, all too familiar voice. "I need to talk to Violet."

I closed my eyes and groaned mentally. Why him? Why now?

"She's unavailable at the moment," Mona said without hesitation. "Can I take a message for her?"

"Okay." I could hear the grin in Doc's tone. "But isn't that Violet under her desk?"

Mona shuffled her feet. "It might look that way, but—"

"I'm coming out now, Mona." I crawled out under the fluorescent lights and hauled my sorry ass to my feet. Doc's lazy grin was supersized this morning, reaching from one ear lobe to the other. I straightened my shoulders. "Don't ask."

His brows lifted, but he obeyed. "I need to talk to you."

Brushing floor dust from my orange capri pants, I rolled my chair back in place and pointed at the one across from my desk. "Have a seat."

"No."

The sharpness in his voice stopped me mid-sit. It was my turn to do some brow lifting.

"Let's talk outside."

I stood, but held my ground. What was Doc's issue with sitting inside Calamity Jane's four walls? As I stared at him, his gaze flickered behind me toward the coffee maker.

"Why outside?" I asked.

He glanced at Mona, who'd returned to her laptop. "It's private business."

Liar. "All right."

I grabbed my sunglasses and joined him under the cloudless, cerulean sky. The smell of pine trees and exhaust surrounded me. A warm breeze ruffled my collar and plastered Doc's faded red T-shirt against his chest.

"How's Addy?" he asked, as soon as the front door closed behind me.

"She's well, thanks for asking." Hands on hips, I waited for what he really had to say.

Doc glanced toward Calamity Jane's door, then seized my arm and towed me around the far side of the building where a mostly empty parking lot was our only audience.

I was in no mood to be jerked around this morning. My back to the brick wall, I demanded, "What's going on, Doc?"

"I was thinking about Jeff Wymonds a lot last night."

That made me pause. I thought I was the only one who laid awake obsessing about Jeff. "Well, he is a handsome man."

Doc opened his mouth, then closed it. His eyes drilled mine. "You think so?"

"Not really."

His smile rounded the corners of his eyes. "Good."

Good? Peachy, another mixed signal to spend hours analyzing. "But Natalie does." I couldn't resist the dig.

He shrugged. "Her tastes seem quite eclectic."

"You don't know the half of it." Then I remembered with a twang in my gut that he'd be paying her a house call this evening. "Although, you will after tonight."

"Probably," was his vague response to my little jealous poke. "Anyway, I want you to take me to Jeff's house."

"Why?"

"I want to see it."

"How did you know Jeff was my client?" I hadn't even drawn up the contract yet.

"I overheard you yesterday at lunch."

"Oh, yeah." I kept forgetting about lunch.

"And Harvey called me last night." Doc's eyes twinkled with mirth. "He told me about Jeff's proposition in the ER."

My neck flash-burned. "Harvey has a bucket mouth."

"So you've said before."

"Well, I can't show you Jeff's house yet. It's not ready. We have a lot of cleaning up to do first." A garbage truck's worth of cleaning.

"I don't care. I want to see it."

As thirsty as I was for a sale, I wasn't seeing any palm-tree-lined mirages in this housing desert. "You're up to something, Doc."

"I'm just curious."

"What do you think you'll find at Jeff's?"

Doc shrugged. "He's still not above suspicion."

I agreed, but was too stubborn to let Doc know. "He's going through a nasty divorce."

"Harvey mentioned that."

"His daughter is having serious issues with depression."

"You feel sorry for him now?"

"Not to mention that he saved Addy's life." Well, that was a bit of an exaggeration, but he did rescue her.

"All of which makes him a more sympathetic person-of-interest."

Doc wasn't going to budge on this one, I could tell. Sighing, I tucked a breeze-loosened curl behind my ear. "Trust me, his house is not your style."

"Really." Doc caught my hand and didn't let go. "What is my style, Violet?"

"Ummm." I stared at the circles he was making on my palm with his thumb, feeling reverberations from his touch in too many places to count. He was scrambling my brain. "Blue."

"Blue?" His laugh was low, deep. "I was thinking it was more vibrant, more … I don't know … *violet*, perhaps."

I looked up into his dark eyes. "You're flirting with me."

"You noticed, huh?" His thumb moved to the inside of my wrist, still circling.

"What are you doing, Doc?"

"Something I shouldn't."

"Then you'd better stop."

"I know." His fingers climbed up my forearm. He leaned closer, his breath quickening, matching mine.

"You're not stopping." Nor did I want him to, not until he'd reached my toes.

"You mess with my head, Violet."

"You say that like it's a bad thing."

"It is."

"I don't understand why."

He let go of my arm and stepped back, the fire in his eyes banking. "I want to see Jeff Wymonds' place."

His ability to snap in and out of lust made me want to beat him with my shoe. My inferno still raged, my breath still labored, my heart still galloped. No fair!

I gave in. "Fine, but I'll have to call Jeff and see how he feels about it." Maybe I'd figure out a way to ask why he'd tossed those clothes in the Dumpster while I was at it. We seemed to be on much friendlier terms now that I was his agent— and therapist.

"Thanks."

Whatever. I stared over Doc's shoulder, across the parking lot, not wanting to look at him any more if I couldn't touch him. He sure knew how to suck the helium right out of my balloon. "Anything else?" I asked.

A flicker of sun-glare by the Mudder Brothers Funeral Parlor caught my eye. I squinted through my sunglasses, recognizing Ray's vehicle parked behind the two-story building, the back of his SUV wide open.

"Yes. Are you still going to dinner tomorrow night with your secret admirer?"

I dragged my gaze back to Doc. "Of course."

"Don't."

"I have to." I had no choice now. He knew Addy's name.

One of the funeral parlor's double back doors opened. As I watched, Ray walked to his driver's side door, leaned in, and grabbed a pair of gloves. He slid them on, looking left and right, and then marched back inside the building.

"No, you don't, Violet."

"Well, I am. End of discussion."

"Fine." Doc's tone said it was anything but. "You'll let me know when you get the *okay* from Jeff?"

Both of the funeral parlor's back doors swung open.

"Uh, sure."

This time, Ray had company—a short, beefy guy, with a white buzz cut. Together, they hauled a big, wooden crate out through the double doors and hefted it into the tail of Ray's SUV. The weight of the crate made the vehicle's springs bounce.

"What is *that*?" I whispered.

When Doc turned and followed my gaze, I realized I'd spoken out loud. "What?"

First the Missing posters, now a heavy crate from a funeral parlor. Something told me Ray was up to no good, and I was not going to get much sleep until I knew what degree of *no good* it was. However, I didn't need Doc harping on me about this, too. "Never mind. It was just a coyote."

"Violet, your nose twitches when you lie."

I covered my telltale appendage with my hand. Before Doc could drill me with any more questions or glares, I tossed out an "I'll call you later," and raced back to Calamity Jane's.

Mona's fingernails were still tapping away when I dropped into my chair. I shot a sideways peek at Ray's desk. Somehow, I needed to get everyone out of the office, because before the day was through, I planned to do a little rummaging.

* * *

An hour after Calamity Jane's closing time, I sat alone in the office, staring at the key lying on my desktop.

All afternoon I'd been in and out, running petty errands for Jane, managing to sneak some peeks in Ray's desk drawers here and there. Unfortunately, the only thing I'd found besides the ordinary desk-drawer paraphernalia was a Rec Center Programs' schedule. While this piece of evidence had a possible tie-in to the pool, it wasn't exactly a bloody knife.

Jeff had stopped by during one of my ins, signed the sales contract I'd typed up, and left his house key. He'd begged a favor—babysit Kelly tonight. Something about his brother over in Spearfish needing his help.

I'd agreed. For one, Kelly was already at Aunt Zoe's, according to the last call I'd received from Layne requesting spaghetti for supper. Her spending the night caused no hardship for me and meant I could keep a close eye on her and my daughter. For two, I'd thought more this afternoon about Emma's jacket, the one that Jeff had thrown out, as well as Doc's description of Jeff—*a sympathetic person-of-interest*, and recognized a golden opportunity when it landed on my desk.

Jeff hadn't blinked an eye when I'd asked his permission to pay a visit to his house this evening to assess what we'd need to do to prepare it for sale. Now, the only question was, did I have the guts to follow through and go play Miss Marple?

I flipped open my cell phone and dialed Harvey's number. He picked it up on the third ring.

"Harvey, it's Violet. I got Jeff's house key, and I'm thinking about heading over to take a peek inside." I'd feel more comfortable snooping while my backup sat waiting for me in my Bronco, his shotgun by his side. "What are you doing right now?"

"Talking to the cops."

That made me blink. "What? Why?"

"I caught something in one of my traps. So I called Coop. He brought some friends to the party."

"What did you catch?"

"An ear."

Ear? "Like a coyote's ear?"

"No. A human ear."

I had to have heard that wrong. "Come again?"

"Part of the scalp, too. Looks like the trap tore it right off."

I cringed. "Oh, Jesus."

"But there's something funny about it."

"Besides the obvious?"

He grunted. "There's no blood."

"No blood?" I was still having trouble bending my mind around the first tidbit. An ear?

"Nope. It's like it's been licked clean."

Yuck! My stomach clenched. "What the hell?"

"And it took the damned squirrel I used as bait to boot." A voice mumbled something in the background. "I gotta go, Coop needs me out back." The phone went quiet.

I sat there listening to the silence for another minute, wondering what was hiding in the hills behind Harvey's barn and who was missing an ear.

Shaking the bizarre conversation with Harvey from my thoughts, I returned to the question at hand—was I going to go search Jeff's place or not? As much as I hated to admit it, I wanted to call Doc, but he was at Natalie's, having dinner. I didn't want to think about what was for dessert.

I took a deep breath, grabbed my purse and the key, and headed for the back door.

As I climbed Jeff's front porch and hauled open the

duct-taped screen that had been hung back up, a cloud covered the sun. Figured. Just what I needed. Mother Nature to add some special effects to my task.

I steadied my hand, shoved the key in the lock, and turned the knob. The door popped open. The shadowed foyer waited beyond, exhaling stale cigarette smoke.

Coughing, I pushed the door wide. "Hello? Anyone home?"

The thump of the door against the wall behind it was my answer. I stepped inside. The screen door's spring rasped with a metallic creak as it closed behind me, the latch clicking shut. I could have sworn it echoed.

I fumbled with the light switch, breathing easier under 60 watts. The kitchen meandered off to my right. I'd seen that room before, and the laundry and bathroom beyond it, so I veered left, through the dining room, through the archway, into a living room.

A leather recliner held court in front of a TV cabinet filled with electronics galore. The chair's sweat-stained armrests and scarred seat cushion, along with the worn, dirty carpet at its base, reminded me of its owner. A lumpy sofa leaned against the far wall, below a long window exposing the tattered backyard. I could see the dirty water in Kelly's kiddie pool from my vantage point. The only thing suspicious in this room was the fluorescent green circle painted on the wall next to the TV.

I tiptoed deeper into the house, passing a small nursery on my left. Tiny clothes were stacked high on top of a changing table. The crib disassembled, leaning against the wall. Donna must not have come with a moving truck yet.

On my right, another bathroom. I didn't want to look in there after what I'd seen in the toilet in the other bathroom on my last visit.

Next on the right, Kelly's room. I flicked on the light, barely able to see the pink carpet under the piles of scattered clothes and dolls and stuffed bears and books. A picture of Addy sitting on a green dinosaur was tacked to the wall above Kelly's headboard. I weaved through the mess and leaned in close to see it. Addy was waving at the camera.

The front screen door banged shut.

I gasped, my knees buckling, dropping onto the bed. *Shit!* Was Jeff home? I held my breath, listening with every muscle.

"Violet?" a baritone voice called.

I almost fell off the bed. Stumbling to my feet, I found Doc in the kitchen, sniffing. Wearing a pair of khaki pants and a white, rolled-sleeved, Oxford shirt open at the collar, he made my breath catch again. I shoved aside my stupid lust and asked, "What in the hell are you doing here?"

He crossed his arms, a muscle ticked in his jaw. "You shouldn't have come here without me? It's not safe. Why didn't you call?"

"I forgot." I lied with a straight face.

His lips thinned. "You forgot to call me, but you remembered to call Harvey?"

Ah, that explained Doc's sudden appearance. Damned Harvey. "I didn't want to interrupt your date with Natalie."

"It's a business dinner," he clarified.

Not according to Natalie. "Why are you here instead of there?"

"I rescheduled."

"Why?"

"Something came up."

"What?" I pushed.

His stare pegged me to the wall. "You."

"What's that supposed to mean?"

"You figure it out." He grabbed my wrist and tugged me toward the dining room. "Come on, give me the tour."

He didn't let go as we moved from room to room,

retracing my steps more slowly, breathing deeply throughout. In Kelly's room, Doc noticed the picture of Addy. "Is that what you looked like at her age?"

"Basically, but my hair was curlier. I wish I had Addy's straight hair."

He tugged lightly on one of the curls that had escaped my French knot. "I like curls."

"Thanks," I said when I extracted my tongue from my throat.

"Let's go check out the shed." He towed me back out into the hall.

I played anchor, dragging him to a stop in front of the recliner. "Wait! We haven't checked out Jeff and Donna's room."

"There's nothing in here."

"What? How do you know?"

"Because I …" he stopped, glanced out the window overlooking the backyard, and frowned. "Just trust me, I know."

"But Harvey found a collage of missing girl pictures in Jeff's bedroom."

"What was he doing in Jeff's bedroom?"

"Don't ask."

"It doesn't matter. The only thing that smells fishy in this house is the carpet." He looked at the recliner. "And probably that chair."

It was my turn to nail him with a stare. "What aren't you telling me?"

"Things you don't want to hear." He pulled me toward the door. "Now come on, let's get out of here."

My teeth gritted, I locked the door on the way out and allowed him to lead me around back to the shed. While I didn't like being brushed off yet again, I liked the feel of Doc's warm palm pressing against my skin. I wanted him to touch elsewhere, too, damn it.

The shed was unlocked, shadow-filled, crammed with more crap, and stunk like grease and dirt. Again, an extension of Jeff.

"Well?" I asked Doc. He'd been sniffing out the corners, picking up and putting down tools, car parts, plumbing accessories, and old calendars covered with bikini-clad babes and chromed-out Harleys. "Is there anything in here?"

He shook his head. "Are you still thinking Jeff might have killed those missing girls?"

I didn't remember ever voicing that suspicion to Doc. It also must have leaked out of Harvey's big mouth. "Maybe."

"Well, if he did, he didn't do it here."

"What are you? Clairvoyant?"

"No."

"Then how can you know that?"

He stared at me, his forehead crinkled. "I can …" he looked away, brushing his hands together. "I can just tell."

"Do you work for the police? Are you some kind of undercover detective?"

"No, and I'd prefer we kept this to ourselves."

"Why are you helping me? Why are you here? Did you know one of the girls?"

"I want these kidnappings to stop, just like you."

I sighed, wanting to hurl a car part at him. I'd have better luck scratching my way through a cement wall than getting a straight answer out of Doc.

We strolled back out front toward my Bronco and his Camaro in the lengthening shadows of the surrounding hills. I remembered he was a client and Jeff's messy abode was about to become another yoke for me to bear. "I don't suppose you're interested in placing an offer."

Doc chuckled. "No. You have your work cut out for you on this one."

Ha! I should drag him around Wolfgang's place.

"I'm sorry you had to cancel your dinner date."

He shrugged. "Business can wait."

"Did Harvey tell you about the ear?"

"Yes."

"What in the hell is going on out there?"

"I don't know. Maybe the police can figure it out." We'd reached my Bronco door. "You want to go get something to eat?"

Yes! "I can't. Layne's expecting spaghetti. You could join us."

He seemed to think about it, then frowned. "Maybe I should just go play some pool."

"Right." I opened my door and climbed inside, disappointment burning in my chest. "Because I'm your Realtor."

"Exactly." He shut my door. "See you tomorrow, Violet." With a wave, he was gone.

Chapter Twenty

Friday, July 20th

Blurry-eyed, my hair tucked up with a clip, I stumbled into Calamity Jane's the next morning and hit the coffee pot first thing. I needed caffeine to clear the fog clouding my brain.

Last evening's fun and games with Doc at the Wymonds' place had stayed in my thoughts long after I'd climbed between my sheets, and the resulting frustrations had triggered another bout of insomnia. I'd laid there, staring up at my shadow-cloaked ceiling, replaying the tour through Jeff's house, wondering what Doc was hiding from me. The fact that he'd come racing to my rescue at Jeff's house hadn't escaped me, but dwelling on that only upset me more.

I'd tossed and turned, wishing I could stop thinking about Doc so much, fretting about growing old alone. Would I end up like Harvey some day—ornery, horny, and full of blusters and rants? Why couldn't Doc offer more than just flirting glances and touches? Why couldn't Wolfgang's charm and good looks be enough?

Then there was the whole ear situation out at Harvey's. That alone ate up another hour full of questions, anxiety, and dumbfoundedness.

I'd heard the downstairs clock strike three before finally drifting off to sleep.

I headed for my desk, coffee in hand, noticing that Mona and her laptop were both missing in action. Jane was gone, too, thank God. I had a feeling she wouldn't appreciate me being two hours late with nothing more to show for it than shadows under my eyes and furry teeth. It was just my luck that Aunt Zoe had packed up all three kids at the butt-crack of dawn and gone fishing at Lake Pactola. Without any children or chickens to wake me, I'd overslept and woke panic-filled and scrambling for clothes.

Ray was talking on the phone with his feet propped on his desk. His Stetson cologne burned the back of my throat. His voice droned into the background as I turned on my computer, pulled up the newest MLS listing for all of the Black Hills area, and started scrolling through houses and properties.

While I slurped down my sugar-filled, lukewarm, giddy-up-and-go juice, I tried my damnedest to keep my focus on saving my job. However, my brain had other ideas, and before I knew it, I found myself searching for any tidbits on Eddie and George Mudder, the owners of the Mudder Brothers Funeral Parlor.

"Blondie, you're late." Ray's voice ripped me from an article about George Mudder's very public, very messy divorce from the great-granddaughter of one of Deadwood's early pioneers.

"I had an appointment," I lied, avoiding Ray's stare.

He snorted. "In whose bed?"

Why did everyone around here think I was some kind of call girl? I glared him down. "Do you look in the mirror every morning and practice being a gigantic asshole, or does it just come naturally for you?"

"Whoa there, Medusa. You're the one wearing the tell-tale sleep lines."

"Oh." I covered my cheeks, which warmed with guilt.

"So pop a Midol and pay attention," Ray laced his fingers and cracked his knuckles, "while I show you what a successful Realtor at work looks like."

I wanted to bash in his pearly whites with my coffee cup. Instead, I hit him with a question that had been replaying in my head for days. "Why are all of those Missing Girl posters in your back seat, Ray?"

His smirk slipped.

Why stop there? "What was in the crate you hauled out of Mudder Brothers yesterday?"

Dark red spots mottled his face.

"And what's with all of your extracurricular activities at the Rec Center lately?" I had no evidence to support that last one, but I was a good bluffer.

Nostrils flared, Ray leaned toward me, his hands fisted. "You should really mind your own business."

I picked up my stapler, just in case he lunged. "Minding yours is so much more fun."

The slam of the back door made us both turn. Mona's smile faltered as her gaze bounced between us. "What's going on?"

My cell phone rang, saving me from having to answer her. I turned my back to Ray as I flipped open my phone. "Hello?"

"Hey, girlfriend," Natalie said. "You have a minute?"

"Sure, hold on." Avoiding two pairs of eyes, I slipped out the back door into the sizzling sunshine. I weaved through the parking lot, my skirt swirling and swishing, my boots clomping on the asphalt as I headed toward the shade of several large ponderosa pines. "What's up?"

"I can't watch the kids Saturday night."

Saturday night? What was going on Saturday night? Damn, I needed to start injecting ginkgo biloba straight into my veins. Oh, that's right—my date with Wolfgang. "Crud."

"I'm really sorry, Vi, but I made plans for that night before remembering that I'd told you I'd babysit." Her tone overflowed with apology.

"That's okay. I'm the ditz who forgot that you and I had made girls' night plans and dumped you for Wolfgang." Some great friend I was.

Natalie continued. "I'd call and reschedule …"

Maybe I could get Harvey to hang out with the kids. It's not like he had to change diapers or anything.

"But I really want to have dinner with Doc."

"Doc?" The sound of his name brought me to an abrupt stop next to a yellow VW bug.

"Yeah, Doc Nyce. He had to cancel last night. Something about a friend needing his help at the last minute."

"Oh, really?" Hmpff! *Friend*, huh? For the record, I certainly hadn't needed Doc's help. I kicked the VW's front tire.

"To make up for cancelling," Natalie said, oblivious to the fact that I was looking for something to break, punch, or throw, "he said he has a special gift to give me Saturday night."

Don't ask, don't ask, don't ask. "What is it?" The jealous troll in my stomach asked.

"He wouldn't say. He wants it to be a surprise."

I swallowed a groan.

Natalie giggled. "I can't wait."

"I bet."

"I think he's the one, Violet."

No! Falling back against the bug, I hugged my stomach with my free arm.

"The one who will help you finally get over Mr. Clean?" I misunderstood on purpose, not wanting her to mean what I was 99.9 percent sure she meant.

"No, silly. The *one* one."

The last time Natalie had found *the one*, it had taken her two years to fall out of love with the jackass, in spite of his blatant on-and-off-again affair with a barmaid out of Custer.

"Oh, that one." I bent over, practically kissing the white parking line, waiting for my light-headed feeling to pass.

"Yeah, that one." Natalie giggled again. The sound of it made me cringe.

"Aren't you jumping the gun a little here, Nat?" Breathe, breathe, breathe. "You're supposed to be on sabbatical. You barely know the guy."

Neither did I, but so what. Doc was mine. We'd flirted, laughed, talked about sex, scoped out a possible suspect's house together. Hell, we were practically dating.

"I know enough. He's kind, giving to his friends, drop-dead sexy, and runs his own business. I'd bet my lucky G-string that he is a god in bed. How could he not be with that body? Right?"

"Right." No argument there. After all the time I'd put in fantasizing about Doc's body, just the sight of his naked bits and pieces would glaze my pastry.

"Plus, I got this vibe from him when I was at his office."

I knew about the vibe, too. Doc was a regular electrical substation.

She sighed in that Scarlett O'Hara, dreaming-about-Rhett way. "I can't explain it exactly. I just know he's the one."

"So, you're staking a claim?" My aching gut already knew the answer.

"Definitely. Consider him staked."

Fuck! Much more of this conversation and my ears would start bleeding. "That's great, Natalie. Listen, I have to go. Mona needs me."

"Sure. Oh, one more thing. Your blind date is back in town."

"What blind date?" The ache in my gut seemed to be scrambling my memory.

"You know, the Trekkie. I gave him your number

yesterday. He said he'd get a hold of you soon."

"I can't wait." My tone said otherwise.

"Don't be that way, Vi. You're going to love him. If it makes you feel better, Doc and I could double with you two on your first date."

Oh, Jesus! What sweet torture that would be. "I gotta go."

"Call me later."

No. I couldn't. I needed a break from her Doc-filled sonnets. "Will do. Bye."

I snapped my phone closed and hurled it into the stand of pine trees. Then I remembered that Jane had given me that phone my first day on the job. "Hells bells!"

I chased after it.

* * *

When I pushed open Calamity Jane's back door at noon, Doc was leaning against the trunk of his Camaro, waiting for me, wearing the same khakis and white button-up shirt he'd had on last night. He still looked positively scrumptious, and I still couldn't do anything about it. Clamping my teeth together to keep my tongue from panting, I paused to slide my sunglasses on and shield my peepers from his prying gaze. The man saw way too much for my own good.

"I love those boots," he said as I approached.

"Thanks." I pretended to fish for something in my purse to avoid his eyes. "You ready?"

"Sure."

He led the way to the passenger side and held open the door for me—damn him. The aromatic mix of leather and cologne filled my lungs as the door shut behind me, spurring a rash of goosebumps up and down my arms.

Frickin' frack! What was wrong with me? I was acting like a backseat virgin. Doc was just a client, and I was just a single mom who couldn't stop drooling over tasty man flesh. I needed to focus on Wolfgang and rekindle my lust for his golden locks.

Doc crawled behind the wheel. "Are you cold?"

"No." I needed a space suit to hide in. I crossed my arms, trying to cover my goosebumps with my hands. "Mona is waiting for us at the house."

"What's going on, Violet?"

I shoved a smile on my lips and glanced at him. "Nothing. I just have a lot on my mind right now."

He stuck the key in the ignition and the Camaro rumbled to life. "Are you worried about tonight?"

Tonight? Oh, that was right. The Wild Pasque, seven o'clock, reservation under *Adelynn*. My secret admirer. "A little."

He backed out of the parking spot. "You should let Harvey hang out at a nearby table."

I didn't want to discuss my pending date unless Doc wanted to take my secret admirer's place across the table. I pointed toward the street. "Take a left at the Stop sign."

Doc obeyed without comment, but the little chirp of his tires after he turned and hit the gas spoke volumes.

"Take another left up here onto Cemetery Street."

He followed, his knuckles white on the steering wheel.

"Left on Lincoln."

My seatbelt tightened as he stomped on the brake pedal harder than necessary.

"Right on Jackson."

A muscle ticked in his jaw.

"There it is." I pointed at the yellow Victorian that matched the description that Mona had given before she headed out of Calamity Jane's thirty minutes ahead of me.

Doc pulled up in front of the white picket fence and cut

the engine. "Listen, Violet—"

"There's Mona." I scrambled out of the car before he could finish lecturing me again on how my obstinacy was going to land me in a mountain of trouble. As if that was something I hadn't figured out by the ripe old age of ten.

I heard Doc's door slam behind me and forced my feet to walk rather than sprint up the sidewalk.

Mona stood on the front porch, a smile spread across her face, her red hair and redder lipstick immaculate. "Hi, guys. Do you prefer lemonade, soda, or something stronger?"

Lemonade would be the safest, I figured. "Got any rum?"

"Uh," Mona blinked twice, but held her smile. "Sure. You want me to cut it with a Coca-Cola."

No. "I guess so."

"I'll just take a Coke," Doc said as he crested the top porch step. He held out his hand toward Mona. "I don't think we've officially met. I'm Doc Nyce."

"Mona Hollister." Mona shook his hand. "Do you want to take a look around outside before we go in?"

I glanced around the porch, biting back a whistle of appreciation. The gabled and gingerbread architecture screamed nineteenth-century splendor, but the hanging bench swing and lounge furniture were modern and in mint condition.

"No, I've seen enough out here," Doc said.

For the first time since exiting the office, I took a close look at him, trying to read if there was any meaning behind his words.

As his agent, I probably should have established some kind of secret codeword system on the way over here. Some way of letting me know if he liked the place or would rather roast marshmallows over it as it burned to the ground. Unfortunately, I was an idiot with a crush the size of Texas on the guy my best friend believed she was in love with—the guy who just also happened to be my only buying client. I'm sure after I explained that to Jane, she'd understand why Doc requested a real estate agent who was able to separate her job from her bed.

Doc locked gazes with me, his brown eyes inscrutable, then he held out his hand toward the screen door Mona had opened wide. "Ladies first."

I stepped into a large, open foyer, filled with caramel-colored wood accents. Doc followed, inhaling, as usual.

The house smelled like vanilla and lemons. Mona must have made the lemonade herself. Johann Pachelbel's "Canon in D Major," my mother's favorite, floated in from the living room on the right, where plush chocolate carpet melted into buttercup walls. A cushy suede sofa and loveseat surrounded a round coffee table, on which a platter full of finger-sized sandwiches were laid out in a flower pattern.

To my left was a formal dining room. The rectangular cherry table set for an elegant dinner for two, silver candlesticks and matching napkin holders included. The polished wood floor was covered by a burgundy Oriental rug that probably cost more than my Bronco.

Mona closed the door behind Doc, shutting out the hot breeze that tried to shove inside. "I'll just leave you two on your own to take a look around while I go pour some drinks."

As soon as she was out of earshot, I whirled on Doc. "There's something I haven't told you."

His lazy grin appeared. "There are lots of things I haven't told you."

As if that was breaking news. "I'm talking about this place."

Doc quirked an eyebrow. "What about it?"

"It's expensive." I didn't want him to fall in love with it

and then hate me later when I dropped the extra fifty-thousand-dollar price-bomb on him.

"I'm not surprised."

I wrung my hands. "I should have told you sooner, but Mona thought I should get you here first, and she's a better agent than I am. A much better one by the looks of it. I mean, check out those sandwiches. Who has time to cut the crust off bread? And I bet the curtain rods alone in this place cost more than I used to make in a month, not to mention the china place settings. You think that's real gold leaf around the edges? I bet the kitchen is state-of-the-art, with expensive appliances and a flower arrangement perfectly placed on the counter. Wow, that fresh bouquet over on the mantel must have cost her a fortune. Oh my God, is that a Ming vase replica?"

Doc's laughter interrupted my nervous ramble.

I glared at him. "You think this is funny? I'm standing here, realizing how inadequate I am as a real estate agent, and you're enjoying the show."

"You're not inadequate, Violet." He grabbed my hand and tugged me toward the stairway. "Hopelessly stubborn, maybe. Lacking in common sense sometimes. But never inadequate."

I followed him up the stairs, my eyes locked on his hind end—what could I say? I was weak.

There were three upstairs bedrooms and one large bath. Every room was immaculate, every piece of décor, chic. Who owned this place and why were they wanting to sell it? This was the kind of place I'd find in one of those fancy architectural magazines for people who had money growing out the ying-yang.

Doc and I moved from room to room, him sniffing in closets and knocking on walls while I "oohed" and "ahhed" over the damask curtains, crown molding, and silk-like wallpaper.

In the smallest of the three bedrooms, a narrow door opened to an even narrower staircase. Doc's shoulders rubbed the walls as we descended into the shadows. At the bottom, my nose bumped into his spine. I backed up a few steps.

"Is it locked?" I whispered. The soothing sounds of violins muffled by the door below.

"No." Doc hunched his shoulders and managed to turn around. "Why are you whispering?"

"I don't know," I whispered again, feeling about eight years old. "It just seems appropriate, don't you think? I mean, here we are, sneaking down the back stairs in the dark."

His eyes glittered in the feeble light leaking down from the open doorway above. As we stood there, staring at each other, the easy-breezy atmosphere between us grew heavy. So did my breathing.

"Violet." He grabbed my wrist and pulled me down a step. "Skip dinner tonight."

That again? Boy, when Doc sank his teeth into something … "I can't."

He towed me down another step. "Why not?"

Our eyes were now level. So were our lips. I gulped. "Because his last poem had Addy's name in it."

"That son of a bitch." His grip on my hand tightened painfully for a split-second. "Why didn't you tell me?"

"What difference would it have made? This is my problem. Not Harvey's. Not yours."

"Violet, I know you're a very independent, strong-minded, capable woman."

"Yeah, right," I said with a sarcastic buffer, but my insides warmed at his compliments. Most days I didn't feel qualified to brush my hair, let alone raise two children on my own.

"Add hard-headed to that list." Doc tugged me down to

the penultimate step. One big breath and our shirts would be touching. "However, there is one important attribute you are missing."

Just one? Hell, I could name ten off the top of my head. Which one was he referring to? "What's that?"

"This." He leaned down, his cotton shirt rustling against my silk blouse.

Holy moly, he was going to kiss me. I couldn't let this happen. Shouldn't let it happen. Natalie had staked her claim. I closed my eyes and pushed up onto my tiptoes to meet his lips halfway.

Only I kissed the air as Doc squeezed my upper arm. I opened one eyelid.

Doc was no longer leaning. Instead, he was grinning down at me in the shadows. "I was referring to your lack of muscles for hand-to-hand combat."

"Oh." Well, didn't I feel like the silliest sucker this side of the Mississippi? My core started to overheat, embarrassment steaming out my pores. "I am a girl, you know."

"Believe me, I know." He crossed his arms over his chest and propped his shoulder against the wall. "Did you think I was going to kiss you?"

"No. Of course not." My whole body blazed with humiliation. I hoped Mona wouldn't hate me forever after I spontaneously combusted and burned down her client's beautiful house.

"Liar." He stared at my lips. "If I had kissed you, would that have been a good thing or bad thing?"

"Bad." I fanned my blouse, thinking about Natalie and how quick I was to toss my life-long loyalty to her out the window in exchange for just one kiss. "Really bad."

He grabbed my hand, the one I was using to cool my neck and chest. "Then that's a problem."

I frowned up into his suddenly serious face. "Why?"

"Because of this." He hauled me against him and covered my mouth with his.

He tasted salty, his lips soft at first, hesitant, coaxing; then hard, demanding. I sagged against his warm chest, my mind reeling. This was Doc. Dark, mysterious, dangerous Doc. I was kissing Doc. *Finally!* Well, he was actually kissing me, but that was something I planned to change right away. I wrapped my free hand around the back of his neck and pulled him down lower, closer, and took control of the kiss, my tongue teasing his into a response.

His fingers squeezed my hand, his breath jagged, mirroring my own. "Violet," he rasped and shoved me back against the wall. "You're right."

I pulled my hand from his grasp; eager, impatient, wanting to touch and explore, nibble and lick. I had scars to examine, skin to study. "About what?" I asked, my hands tugging at his shirt while my mouth surveyed his jaw line, trailing toward his ear. His cologne filled my head, sending my sense and sensibilities floating up to the ceiling.

His hands hovered around my stomach, hesitating. "It's really bad." He groaned as I sucked on his earlobe.

"I know." I grabbed his hands and moved them north, planting them on my chest. His palms scorched me through my shirt and bra.

"Jesus, woman." He growled against my neck. "Your hair smells like peaches." His fingers came alive, fondling, caressing, rubbing. "I love peaches." His teeth left a trail of fire along my collarbone.

Any last qualms about Natalie, my job, and my principles burned up in the inferno roaring between us. I wanted Doc, now, right here in this dark stairwell, while Mona's little sandwiches grew dry and crusty in the living room.

Doc's body crushed mine, my shoulder blades digging into the plaster wall. I lifted my leg and pressed my inner thigh against his hip, rubbing my boot up and down his leg as I dragged his mouth back to mine and thoroughly investigated his lips, nibbling. "You do things to me, Doc."

"I want to do more," he said against my mouth, between long, wet, searing kisses. He hooked his hand under my knee, inching my skirt up my thigh while his hips ground into mine.

"What's stopping you?" I sure as hell wasn't.

He braced his hand on the wall beside my head. "We need to stop."

I nipped his lower lip, then kissed it better as my hands found hot flesh covering a ripple of abs. I didn't think I could stop. I'd been too long without sex, too hungry for Doc's hands and mouth on my skin. "You first," I challenged him.

Doc tore away from me so fast I almost fell down the last step. He backed up, bumping into the door behind him.

I shook my head, feeling like I'd just been stampeded by a crash of rhinos. "What the hell?" I hadn't expected him to take me seriously.

"Mona," Doc whispered, his chest heaving. "She's calling your name."

Then I heard her as the blood rushing in my ears faded. "Vi? Where are you?" Her voice was muffled, but growing louder.

Panic spread a fresh layer of dew on my skin. I looked at Doc. "What should I do?"

He reached out and adjusted my shirt, fastening the top two buttons again. "Answer her."

"I can't go out like this." I touched my lips, blood still pounding in them. They felt swollen. "You go."

Doc chuckled and glanced down at himself. "This might be kind of *hard* to explain."

I admired his problem.

"That's not helping the matter any, Violet."

"Vi?" Mona sounded like she was upstairs now, nearing the open door above us.

I heard a rattling sound and then I was blinded by a gush of daylight from behind Doc. I shielded my eyes.

"Oh, look," Doc said, pushing the door all the way open and dragging me into the light. "You were right about the kitchen."

After adjusting my skirt and shirt, I left Doc in the kitchen to cool off. I reached the main stairs just as Mona was coming down.

She hesitated at the sight of me, her eyes searching my super-sized smile for several seconds. "Where were you?"

"Checking out the house." And the inside of Doc's mouth.

"Natalie called." She came down the last steps and handed me her cell phone.

Natalie's number showed as a missed call. Damn. Guilt slammed into my gut like a battering ram.

"Where's your phone?" Mona asked.

"It's on the fritz." After colliding with a pine tree and then crashing onto a boulder, I was experiencing a few technical difficulties. I handed her phone back. "I'll call Nat later." Much later—after I'd washed the smell of Doc off my hands and rinsed the taste of his skin from my tongue.

"You okay?" Mona asked. "You look …" she wiggled her fingers in the air around her face. "Flustered."

Frustrated was more like it. My body wanted to finish what Doc started. "I'm fine, just thinking about Doc." *Naked.*

"You think he'll bite?" Mona asked.

I knew he would. I could still feel his teeth marks on my collar bone. I wanted a matching set on my inner thigh. However, about the house, I wasn't so sure. "I hope so."

I headed back to the kitchen where Doc stood leaning against the counter, his smile lazy once again, his feathers all smoothed down and ruffle-free, his body looking finger-licking good.

I turned my focus to the state-of-the-art kitchen, marveling at the high-quality accoutrements along with Doc. Next, we admired the multi-level deck and manicured backyard through a pair of French doors, peeked into a granite-tiled three-quarter bathroom, and then made our way back into the living room, where Mona waited for us. Drinks sweated on a silver platter next to the sandwiches.

"So, Doc," Mona said as I dropped onto the couch next to her and reached for my rum and Coke, needing it even more now than ever as guilt and desire arm wrestled in my belly. "What do you think of Deadwood summers?"

"It's colder than where I grew up and warmer than where I came from last."

I swished my drink, smiling. Nobody could dodge a question like Doc.

A half-hour later, Doc had charmed more of Mona's life history out of her than I had in three months, and I had finally collected all of my wits and X-rated thoughts and tucked them safely back into my underwear. We thanked Mona for the tour, drinks, and appetizers, and then headed to the car.

"Well?" I asked as the Camaro rumbled to life, trying to remember I was still his Realtor first and foremost. Hashing out what happened in the back stairs could come later when I wasn't just an arms-length away from reaching over and unbuckling his belt. "Did you like that one?"

"What wasn't to like?" Doc shifted into gear. "What's the asking price?"

When I told him, he didn't flinch at all. Just nodded and steered toward Deadwood. I wasn't sure if I should dance a jig at this point or not.

"Hey, can you stop in front of that rundown house up on the left for a minute?" I asked as the Hessler house loomed in the front windshield.

The night of Addy's cast-fitting, I'd driven by Wolfgang's place on the way home from the library and noticed a light on in the upstairs, violet-themed bedroom. I'd figured Wolfgang was in there, but later realized I hadn't seen his car in the drive. The light was still on last night, when I purposely cruised by on my way home from Jeff's. Again no car, no sign of life. Just the light, which made me wonder if I'd left it on when I was up there last week playing the creepy door game.

Doc parked in front of the rusted gate and looked at me, his brows raised behind his sunglasses.

"This is Wolfgang's house," I explained.

His jaw tightened. "A bit of a fixer-upper, I see."

"Nothing a little paint and a lot of love couldn't help."

"Or just a lot of paint."

"Right." I grabbed the door handle. "You want to come in?"

"Why?"

Because I was too scaredy-pants to go inside on my own, even in broad daylight. "You could take a look around, admire the nineteenth-century details. You never know, maybe you'll fall in love with it." Especially the clowns. They were definite selling points.

"All right, let's go." He shut off the car. "Listen, Violet," he said as he pushed open his door, "about what happened back there—"

"Not now, Doc," I cut him off, avoiding eye contact. While I currently had a firm handle on my lust for the guy, my feelings about the whole shebang—or lack of shebang—still had my panties in a bit of a twist.

"Okay." He shut his door. "But it can't happen again."

Natalie's voice singing *he's the one* replayed in my head. "Tell me about it," I said and led the way.

The squeaky gate made sure the neighbors knew we

were opening it. Doc followed me up the walk. If he had any comments to make on the condition of the yard, he kept them to himself.

After a glance for any looky-loos, I lifted the floorboard on the bottom step. "You don't see this," I told Doc. If it were anyone else, I'd make him turn his back while I fished the key from its hiding spot.

"See what?" he replied, but his eyes confirmed he understood what I meant.

Doc sniffed as I stuck the key in the lock, but said nothing. The tumbler clinked and the door inched open.

"Let me put this back before I forget." I returned the key to its hiding spot. When I stood up, I noticed how pale Doc's cheeks were. "Are you okay?"

He frowned at me. "What? Yeah, it's just the heat."

"If you say so." I led the way into Wolfgang's front foyer. "Hello? Anyone home?"

I didn't expect an answer, but my chest felt tight as I listened, nonetheless.

The floorboards creaked as Doc joined me in the entry.

"I just need to run upstairs and shut off—" A choking sound behind me made me spin around.

Doc stood just inside the door, his eyes rolled toward the ceiling, his whole torso convulsing as he gasped for breath.

"Oh, my God!" I grabbed his arm, his muscles contracting spasmodically under my grip. "Doc?"

His shudders grew violent, his body shifting as he started to tip backward.

"Shit!" I tried to use my weight to keep him upright, but his knees gave out and we both tumbled to the floor, me on top of him. I scrambled up onto my haunches. "Doc, are you okay?"

His legs were trembling now, but his eyes made contact with mine. "Outside," he gasped.

I didn't waste any time. Grabbing him under the arms, I dragged him over the threshold, grunting and huffing the whole way, and out onto the porch. His shoulders had cleared the first step before I realized he was trying to tell me something.

"What?" I asked, dropping onto my butt and holding his head in my lap. "What is it? Are you okay?"

His nod was slight. His grin a ghost of its usual gusto. "S-sorry 'bout that."

"What happened in there? And if you try to tell me that you're allergic to one more thing, I'll drag you back inside and leave you."

He closed his eyes and sighed.

My heart beat loud enough to hear down in Rapid City. "What is it? Is it terminal?" Brain tumor? Cancer? Epilepsy?

"You could say that." His dark eyes open again. He struggled to sit up, using my shoulder for leverage.

"Christ, Doc. You're killing me here. What is it?"

He took another deep breath and then turned to me, the intensity of his stare making me sit back a bit. "Someone died in that house."

"How do you know about that?" Had he read about Wolfgang's mom in the death registry?

"She just showed me."

Chapter Twenty-One

When it came down to the nitty-gritty, nothing had changed. From the start, I'd thought there was something peculiar about Doc. Now, the only difference was that I *knew* it.

Did I believe that he'd seen the ghost of Wolfgang's mother? That she'd communicated with him from the *other side*? No. Not really. At least I didn't think so. However, as I drove toward Aunt Zoe's, his words replayed in my head. I was still trying to make sense of what I'd witnessed, of what he'd told me—which wasn't much, seeing as how he was the same cryptic Doc he'd been before we'd stepped into the Hessler house.

I swung into Aunt Zoe's drive and cut the engine. Layne frowned at me from the front porch, where he sat scrubbing on a bone as long as his arm—using *my* foot scrubber. Damn it!

I slammed my door and strode toward him. "Layne, didn't I tell you to quit using my pedicure tools on your artifacts?"

"Sorry, Mom. I forgot." At least he had the decency to look sheepish for a second or two. "What are you doing home already?"

Doc and I had decided to skip lunch after what had happened at Wolfgang's place. His excuse had been exhaustion, mine a lack of appetite. We'd both avoided eye contact on the ride back to the office, the rumble of his engine the only sound in the car.

"I decided to take the afternoon off." I dropped onto the hard step next to Layne. The smell of bleach made my nose itch. I nudged his bucket of sudsy water a few inches away.

"Cool. You want to help me glue the spine together?"

"Sure." I could use an Elmer's-glue high this afternoon to take the edge off. My hands were still shaky with adrenaline aftershocks.

The screen door squeaked open.

"Layne, where's my chicken leash?" Addy did a double-take when she saw me. "Oh, hi, Mom. When did you get home?"

"Just now."

She let the screen door bang shut and joined us on the top step, a small bag of M&Ms in her hand. Her pinkie toe popped out of the side of her yellow canvas tennis shoe as she sat down. "I called you earlier but you didn't answer."

"What did you need?"

"Kelly asked if I can go school shopping with her and her mom tomorrow morning." She dumped some candy in her mouth.

I still had a wheelbarrow full of doubts about Kelly in regards to the missing girls, but with nothing more than middle-of-the-night suspicions flapping around in my belfry, I knew better than to ban Addy from hanging out with her friend. Besides, what could possibly happen in a crowded shopping mall?

"Sure. You can take the early birthday money your Grammy sent and buy some new tennis shoes." I wondered if Kelly's mom's girlfriend would be joining them. I'd have to pump Addy for answers when she got home.

"Sweet!" She rested her purple cast on her bent knees and smiled at me like we shared a secret. Her teeth had chocolate bits in them. "Are you excited about tonight?"

I squinted at her. "What do you think I'm doing

tonight?"

"Going to dinner with a man."

Earlier this week, when I'd informed the kids I'd be absent for supper for two nights in a row, I'd blamed work. Tonight's dinner was supposed to be a class on mold spores, tomorrow was an open-house party with Wolfgang. While lying to my kids would blow my chance of winning a World's Best Mom award for yet another year, the last thing I needed was Addy finding out I was on two different dates. Next, she'd have me signed up for the Singles Bingo Night at the Elks.

"Who told you I was going to dinner?"

Addy picked at the hole in her shoe. "I accidentally overheard Aunt Zoe talking to Natalie on the phone earlier."

Accidentally? Right.

"You're going out with a man tonight?" Layne's tone overflowed with disapproval.

Layne was the other reason I'd lied about my dates. His man-of-the-house anxiety didn't need any more fuel.

"She's going out with Wolfgang tomorrow night, too." Addy told him, and dumped the last of the M&Ms into her hand.

Thanks, big mouth. I stole a yellow M&M and popped it into my mouth. "Yes, but just to an open house. Remember?" I squeezed Layne's wet hand.

The wrinkles lining Layne's forehead multiplied. "Mom, you're not going to get married, are you?"

I blinked, fighting back a grin. "Not this weekend."

"Do you love Wolfgang?" he pressed.

"No." Honest truth there. I wasn't even sure if I lusted after him any more. I'd find out that answer tomorrow night. "He's just a friend."

"Like how Doc is your *friend*?" Addy asked.

Not really. Doc was a different beast all together—even

more so after today. "Sure."

Layne's gaze bounced back and forth between Addy and me. "Who's Doc?"

"He's a client of mine, Honey."

"If Wolfgang is only your friend, how come you kissed him at the hospital?" Addy tossed down the last of her candy.

I squirmed under her grilling. "Officially, he kissed me."

"How could you let him?" Layne accused more than asked.

"Listen, sometimes friends kiss," I explained to both of them. "It doesn't mean they are in love with each other and going to get married. It's just something adults like to do. It's not a big deal."

"Do you and Doc kiss?" Addy asked.

My neck heated up. "Uhh, no," I lied, kind of. What had happened in that back stairwell had been too frenzied—too carnal—to be labeled a kiss.

Addy leaned closer. "Why not?"

Wow. As if I hadn't chewed on that question over and over before today. "Doc doesn't want to kiss me." *At least he says he doesn't.*

"Do you want to kiss him?" Layne asked, his nose crinkled.

"Okay, that's enough of this Barbara Walters' interview for today." I grabbed my purse and stood. "Where's Aunt Zoe?"

"In the kitchen," Layne answered.

"Who's Barbara Walters?" Addy asked.

"I need to ask her something." I kissed both of their foreheads. "Be good."

I found Aunt Zoe in the kitchen, humming under her breath, surrounded by tin-foil muffin cups and the mouth-watering aroma of banana bread. My stomach growled, my appetite back now that I was wrapped in the comforts of home and family.

I grabbed one of the cups from the baking rack, the tin still warm, and peeled a muffin free. "These smell wonderful."

Aunt Zoe lifted an eyebrow. "You're home early."

"Things were dead at the office." At Wolfgang's house, too, according to Doc. I'd have laughed at my own joke if the memory of Doc's convulsions wasn't so fresh in my mind.

"Natalie called." Aunt Zoe returned to the task of filling another muffin cup. "She can't watch the kids tomorrow night."

"Yeah, she got hold of me at work," I mumbled through a sweet bite of muffin.

"I can close the store tomorrow night and stay home."

"No, you're already doing that for me tonight. Let me talk to Harvey, see if he can come over. Hell, he's at Miss Geary's house every other night as it is. They can just watch Jeopardy over here—if that's okay with you."

"Sure," she glanced at me over her shoulder, her eyes sparkling more than usual. "But don't you want the option of having the whole night free?"

"Why?" Oh, duh—sex. "No, it's just dinner tomorrow."

"Okay, but if you change your mind, just holler." She opened the oven door and pulled out a sheet of puffy muffins. "Harvey called, too. He wondered if he needed to babysit you tonight at dinner, or if Doc was."

"Doc?" He hadn't mentioned joining me, just asked me not to go.

"That's my question." She stuffed another tray of muffins into the oven and shut the door. "Who's Doc?"

I swallowed the last of my muffin and grabbed another. "A client of mine."

"You're going to take a client along on a blind date with your secret admirer?"

"Well, Doc's kind of a friend, too, and I'm not going to take him. He's just worried about me being alone with my admirer."

"Really?" Aunt Zoe tossed her oven mitt on the counter and planted her hands on her hips. "And he's just *kind of a friend*?"

"Uh, huh," I said through a mouthful of muffin.

"Is he good-looking?"

I pretended to examine the accordion design on the muffin tin, hiding my eyes behind a cluster of loose blonde curls. "My admirer? How should I know?"

"You know I'm talking about this *Doc* friend."

I sighed and crumpled the muffin wrapper in my hand. "Yes. He's very good-looking. Too good-looking."

He also claimed to be chummy with the dead, which should affect my attraction to him, yet it didn't—not even a little bit. I should probably talk to a psychiatrist about that.

"But you're going out with Wolfgang tomorrow night."

"Yep."

"Interesting."

"Not really." More like depressing. I stole a third muffin and crammed it all into my mouth.

I wanted a man I couldn't have, and had a man I didn't want. There, I'd laid it on the table. Wolfgang was drop-dead gorgeous and mine for the hands-on ogling, yet here I was peeking over Doc's fence, checking out how green his grass looked. I definitely needed psychological help.

"I'm worried about tonight, Violet." Aunt Zoe dumped the empty mixing bowl in the sink. "Maybe you should let Doc join you."

"No." Although a part of me hoped he'd show up at the restaurant. He knew where and when.

"What about Harvey?"

"Absolutely not." I waved off her exasperated glare. "I'll be in a public restaurant. What could happen?"

"Promise me you'll call as soon as dinner is over."

"I will." Or not, being that my cell phone was in three pieces at the moment. "I'm going to go change and help Layne. Thanks for the muffins."

Several hours and three-quarters of a horse spine later, I stood in front of my bedroom full-length mirror wearing the sapphire, calf-length dress I'd worn in my cousin's wedding two years ago. Always a bridesmaid, always an unwed mother, never a bride. My evening loomed in front of me, my nerves seeping out through my armpits.

Still no word from Doc. Not that I'd expected him to come around, banging down the screen door, wanting to talk. I mean we'd only almost had sex this afternoon and then shared one of those life-and-death type of moments, after which he made me solemnly swear to never tell a soul about his ability to have tea and crumpets with the dead. Silly me, I'd kind of felt like we'd reached a new level in our so-called friendship.

After a dab of lipstick and a pep rally with my mirror, I kissed the kids goodbye, hugged Aunt Zoe, and headed downtown.

The Wild Pasque's parking lot overflowed onto the street, typical for a Friday night. My heels clicked across the asphalt, my eyes searching for Doc's Camaro as the sun slipped behind the surrounding hills.

I climbed the grand stairway to the restaurant's entrance. The stuffed-shirt host found the *Adelynn* reservation without a problem. Scanning the other patrons as he led me through a maze of tables toward large windows overlooking Main Street, I sought a familiar face with a cleft chin and pair of dark brown eyes, but found only strangers.

Two place settings awaited me at the table, the linen napkins fanned out next to the silverware. My date had yet to arrive. Good. I needed time to gulp down some liquid courage.

The host held my chair and waited for me to settle in before taking my drink request. Merlot sounded good. Fruity with a bite—kind of like Harvey. As I waited for my date and drink to arrive, preferring the latter first, and the former never, I studied each passerby on the street below. If Doc was down there, he'd hidden himself well.

The waiter stopped by to introduce himself and drop off my wine. He looked all of sixteen, in spite of his fat-Elvis sideburns, and tossed out several 'ma'am's as he told me about the evening's specials. Had I not been wearing my only pair of Jimmy Choo heels, which were given to me three Christmases ago by my mother, I would have crammed my shoe down his acne-dotted throat for making me feel like an old maid.

Sipping on my wine, I searched the upper windows of the buildings across the street. Maybe Doc had decided to dine vicariously this time. Alas, no sight of him. I knocked my fan-shaped napkin over.

"I was worried you wouldn't show up," a man said in my ear.

I jumped, splashing red wine on the white table cloth.

"You look stunning, Violet." He dropped into the seat opposite of me. "As usual."

I gaped at him.

No. Fucking. Way.

"Blue looks even better on you than red."

I finally heaved my jaw up off the floor. "*You* are my secret admirer?"

"Surprised?"

If my nose broke off, landed in my glass of merlot, and blew out a stream of bubbles, I couldn't be more shocked. "A little."

"Good." Benjamin Underhill, Ray's nephew, chuckled. "I hate to disappoint."

I gaped at him, noticing his eyes were different colors—one icy blue, the other light green. They'd both been blue in the picture on Jane's desk. "But, I thought your eyes …"

"I wear a colored contact usually. It keeps people from staring."

"Oh." I gulped down a mouthful of merlot, staring, and debated on making a run for the hills. However, since I already lived in them, I forced my feet to stay planted and asked, "How do you know my daughter's name?"

"Addy?" Her nickname rolled off his tongue way too easily for a mother's comfort.

Our waiter, Elvis Jr., approached, holding an open bottle of merlot.

"She's quite a sidewalk saleswoman. I bought some mittens for my niece's kitten from her."

"You did?" I frowned, then remembered Layne's phone call about Addy selling stuff to the guy with *weird eyes*. I drained the rest of my wine, not sure if I should feel relieved or more frightened. Benjamin could be the kidnapper. If Ray knew, that would explain why he was collecting Missing Girl posters.

Benjamin nodded as the waiter filled his wineglass. "Along with some other pet paraphernalia."

My wine glass clunked on the table, empty, ready for more. I waited until the waiter had refilled my glass and departed before asking, "Did Ray tell you where I live?"

"No, I followed you home one night." He raised his glass for a toast. "Here's to a long, successful partnership."

I almost swallowed my tongue.

* * *

Saturday, July 21st

I whipped into the Deadwood library's parking lot and

parked next to Doc's Camaro. Mid-morning sunshine ricocheted off his side mirror, making me squint behind my sunglasses. The lingering effects of last night's wine throbbed with fresh zeal. After killing the engine, I dry-swallowed a couple of aspirins before shoving open my door.

I'd waited over an hour for Doc to show up at work, leaving nose prints all over his front window, sweating and pacing outside his door. Finally, I'd decided to hunt him down—Deadwood had only a handful of places to hide. After a quick run through the Rec Center, here I was; and here Doc was, too.

I climbed the library steps, my sandals flapping on the concrete. A musty smell rushed to greet me as I stepped through the door. Miss Plum looked up from behind her desk.

"Can I help you?" she asked as I strode past her toward the South Dakota room.

"No, thanks. I know exactly what I'm looking for."

I pushed open the door and found Doc sitting in his usual place, surrounded by his usual stack of books—death registry, cemetery listings, etc. It all made sense now. I closed the door behind me, dropped into the chair opposite him, and leaned my elbows on the table.

"Hello, Violet." His grin was absent today, a frown acting as its understudy.

"We need to talk."

"How was your date last night?"

Mind-blowing. "The wine was good."

"How about the company?"

While it turned out Ray's nephew and I had several things in common besides the desire for my job, and he seemed as harmless as a gnat, I couldn't get past him sending me those creepy poems and following me. No matter how much wine I poured down my throat.

"You weren't there."

"Was I missed?" He looked tired, emphasized by the shadows under his eyes.

I didn't want to admit to anything. Besides, this meeting wasn't supposed to be about me. "Mona wants to know if you're interested in the property."

He raised his brows. "Only Mona?"

"Are you?"

"Maybe."

"As in maybe we're going to make an offer?"

Scratching his chin, he shrugged. "It's a lot of money."

"It's a one-of-a-kind house. You won't find anything comparable to it in Deadwood. At least not anything available."

Doc leaned back in his chair and crossed his arms over his chest. "Where are you going for dinner tonight?"

I blinked at his curveball. "Wolfgang hasn't specified."

"What are you wearing?"

"He requested my red dress. What about you?"

"I would have requested something green."

So he'd mentioned before—and I hadn't forgotten. "I meant, where are you taking Natalie?"

"She told you we're having dinner?"

My ears still rang from her shouts of joy. "She mentioned it in passing."

"I'm not taking her anywhere. She offered to cook for me. What kind of wine does she prefer?"

"Any with alcohol in it."

"So she's easy to please?"

"You could say that." That was a polite way of putting it. I didn't want to ask, but couldn't stop myself, "Are you going to kiss her goodnight?"

His grin finally made an appearance. "Who wants to know?"

"Harvey," I lied.

That made him laugh. "Is *Harvey* jealous?"

Being eaten alive by it. "Yes."

"He's not alone."

It was those kinds of comments from him that left me spinning long after the merry-go-round stopped, but I didn't want to talk about Natalie and Doc, anymore. I had enough heartburn for now. "What do you do for a living, Doc?"

"Make an appointment with me and you'll see."

"I tried that route already and got booted because of a dead person."

"You were the one looking at me like I had antennas growing out of my head."

"Well, it's not every day that a client informs me he just shook hands with a house's dead owner."

"I'm back to being just your client, huh?"

"Client, friend, psychic. You choose the title." I wanted *lover* even though I shouldn't, but Doc's wall was back between us after yesterday's hiatus.

"Are you going to see your secret admirer again?"

"Undoubtedly." Most likely, he'd be sitting at my desk in my chair if Doc wouldn't put an offer on Mona's gem. "Are you going to sleep with my best friend?"

Whoa! I hadn't planned to go there, but I was having control issues today—as in a lack of it.

His grin grew wider. "I haven't worked out any details."

I sat back, his answer a burr in my butt. "Try not to hurt her."

"What about you?"

"What about me?" I was already hurting.

"Are you going to have sex with Wolfgang tonight?" His question sounded bored, but his stare stole my breath.

I wanted to sound all cool and Fonzie-like about casual sex, but I settled for honesty. "No."

"Why not?"

"Contrary to what the men in this town think of me, I don't just hop into bed with anyone who buys me something to eat."

"Good."

"Although I'm weak around hot fudge and whipped cream."

"I'll remember that," he said, then his grin disappeared. His eyes took on the haunted look I'd seen for the first time yesterday. "Violet, be careful in that house."

I tried to laugh off his warning, but I was all off-key. "Because an old woman who died a decade ago told you she doesn't like my company?" Hell, those damned clowns gave me worse nightmares.

"Something like that." He rubbed the back of his neck. "I'm still working out the details."

Details he thought he'd find in the books in front of him? As far as I was concerned, the only important *detail* was that I had a rundown house to hurry up and sell. "Doc, I don't believe in ghosts."

His smirk didn't match the intensity in his dark eyes. "Well, I do. And this one is very pissed off about being dead."

Chapter Twenty-Two

Back in front of my bedroom mirror, hiding behind a veneer of hair gel, red lipstick, and my too-snug red dress, I frowned at the broad in the mirror.

Violet wears red,
Violet wears blue.
Violet is befuddled,
With no clue what to do.

To sell or not to sell? That was the question I'd been volleying since Doc had warned me earlier at the library to be careful at the Hessler haunt.

I sucked in my gut and lifted my chin. Maybe a little more light to offset the harsh shadows of the setting sun would help. I flicked on the lamp next to my bed and returned to the mirror. Nope, that made it worse. I sighed and tugged out the pins corralling my curls.

It wasn't Doc's ghost that had me wading in a pool of self-doubt, it was the idea of working so closely with Wolfgang over the next couple of months. If his being easy on the eyes wasn't enough to make my engine hum tonight, we were going to slide into an awkward tailspin when he hit the gas at the same time I yanked on the parking brake.

The rumble of a car engine rolled through my open window.

Speak of the devil. I peeked out through my curtains and saw a white Mercedes cozy up to my Bronco's back bumper.

Standing there with bated breath, I watched as Wolfgang pushed open his car door. Something small and blue—a shade lighter than his cobalt shirt—fell to the ground as he stepped out onto the drive and shut the car door. He glanced down at the blue thing, his leg blocking it from my view, then stared at the front of Aunt Zoe's house.

I took a step back from the window, but still peeked out and admired his finely-shaped backside as he picked up and pocketed whatever he'd dropped. Trying my damnedest to jump-start my libido, I tried to imagine what he'd look like sans his black trousers. Unfortunately, my stubborn body refused to play along and my pulse kept its slow, steady beat.

I dashed back to the mirror, combed my hair with my fingers, and then spritzed my neck and the back of my knees with my favorite sweet, musky perfume. I might look like I'd been wrestling monkeys, but at least I wouldn't stink like it.

The doorbell rang.

"Mom," Layne hollered up the stairs. "He's here."

"Coming," I yelled back, rolling my eyes at the lack of enthusiasm in my son's tone. I grabbed my matching, red-beaded purse from the bed while I slipped on my Jimmy Choo heels. After one last grimace at my finger-in-the-light-socket hairdo, I clomped down the hall toward the stairs.

The living room was deserted. I heard voices coming from the kitchen and stole across the carpet to the arched entryway.

Harvey lounged against the counter, a half-eaten banana muffin in his hand, crumbs in his beard. It was the first time I'd had a chance to talk to him since our phone conversation about the ear. I wanted to prod him for more details, find out what Coop had to say, see if there were any more *funny noises* going on behind his barn. However, now was not the time.

As I hesitated in the doorway, he glanced my way and jumped in surprise—not the most flattering of reactions for my self-esteem. "Well, Lord love a duck! Look at you, girl."

My face now matched the color of my dress. Perfect. I wanted to race back upstairs, bar my bedroom door, and hide under the bed. Instead, I smiled at Wolfgang, who stood by the kitchen table, admiring Layne's horse spine while my son stood stiff-shouldered next to the refrigerator and glowered.

"Hi, Wolfgang."

Wolfgang's blue eyes widened at the sight of me. "Wow."

He stepped back, his gaze crawling over me as he crossed the room and took my hand. "You look stunning with your hair down."

Aw, shucks. "Thanks." I stood up straighter and sucked in my stomach, wishing I had a shawl to hide my soft spots.

He raised my hand to his lips. "I'm a very lucky man."

He was even more handsome close up in his silk shirt and pleated trousers. With his blond locks messed into a bad-boy hairdo and his teeth dazzling as usual, charisma practically gushed out his pores. I could be happy with this man. Right?

I just wished my heart was as convinced as my eyes.

The back door crashed open and Addy barged in, her cast banging on the door frame as she carried the small cage she and Layne had built to catch Elvis. She lowered it to the floor and smiled at Wolfgang. "Here it is. You think it will work?"

Wolfgang released my hand and walked over to Addy, squatting next to the cage. He lifted the door and let it drop. "Definitely. What will you use as bait?"

"I don't know." Addy's forehead puckered. "What should I use?"

"Chicken feed, I guess." Wolfgang looked at Layne, whose glower now included crossed arms. "What do you think?"

"I don't care."

I sighed and aimed a glare at the little monster.

Harvey reached over and ruffled the back of Layne's hair. "Show some respect, young man."

"Sorry," Layne muttered, scowling at his shoes.

"It's okay," Wolfgang let Layne off the hook with another dazzling smile.

"How about some worms?" Harvey said to Addy. "My chickens love digging for worms."

"Really?"

"Sure. After your mom leaves, how 'bout we go hunting for some juicy night crawlers?"

"Okay!" Addy jumped up and down, her excitement bubbling over.

Layne nodded, his sheepish grin replacing the frown.

Wolfgang stood. "That sounds like our cue to leave, Violet. You ready?"

Ready to get this night over with. "Yep."

I stepped back for Wolfgang to pass into the living room. I started to follow on his heels, then paused. "I'll be right there, Wolfgang."

Back in the kitchen, I kissed and hugged Layne goodbye first.

"Mom," he whispered, clinging to me. "Don't go."

I unwound his arms from my neck. "Sweetie, stop—"

"I don't like him."

"You barely know him."

"He's weird."

Spoken by a boy who once crammed Mexican jumping beans up his nose in hopes of bouncing to the moon. "Give him a chance, Layne." At least until I unloaded his house. "Wolfgang was kind enough to let you have that toy train.

The least you could do is be nice in return."

Layne's gaze dropped, his lower lip protruding a bit. "Fine, but he can't move in with us."

"Of course not." Sharing my bed with a man under Aunt Zoe's roof would be like skinny dipping in holy water. I ruffled Layne's hair and turned to Addy, who beamed at me.

"I'm not too old to be a flower girl, Mother."

"Dream on, daughter." I hugged and then kissed her.

"Do I get a kiss, too?" Harvey snickered.

I pointed at his beard. "You have some crumbs."

"I'm supposed to. I'm an old man."

"Not that old." I patted my crazy curls and adjusted my spaghetti straps. "I'll be home before nine."

"What?" Harvey's bushy brows shot skyward. "That doesn't leave you much time to fool around with Russell."

Russell? Didn't he mean Wolfgang? "Who?"

"Russell, the one-eyed muscle." His shit-eating grin almost reached his ears.

Both of my kids turned to me, their mouths opening.

"Never mind!" I poked Harvey in the chest. "Keep it PG tonight, you ol' buzzard."

"What? That was PG."

"I'll see you in a bit."

"Get a piece for me!" He called to my back.

Wolfgang waited for me at the front door, holding the screen open. "A piece of what?"

"Cake. Harvey likes cake."

Our shoes crunched along the gravel drive. The aroma of fresh-cut grass blended with Deadwood's usual pine-tree potpourri in the still air. In spite of its fading hold, the sun continued to dole out warmth, keeping the goosebumps at bay.

As we backed out of the drive, Wolfgang glanced at me. "You're quieter than usual. Something on your mind?"

Yes. He had dark brown eyes and was wining and dining with my best friend at this very moment. "No, I'm just enjoying being here with you."

"Good." He squeezed my hand. "I can't wait to show you my surprise."

If it was Harvey's buddy, Russell, I'd exit sprinting.

"I can't wait to see it." I tried to make that sound genuine, adding as much inflection as I could muster. Wolfgang was a nice guy—giving, good to my kids. Why wasn't that enough?

"Before we go any further," he reached under his seat. "I want you to put this on." He held out a black satin sleeping mask. When I just stared at him, he tweaked my chin and added. "I'm serious. It's part of the surprise."

I complied, slipping on the lavender-scented mask and sliding into darkness, but remaining stiff in my seat as he hit the gas.

"Did you ever find out who was sending you flowers?" he asked.

He had a good memory. I'd forgotten I'd told him about the daisies. "Yes, actually."

The car shifted as we turned left. I clutched the seat.

"Do I have some competition?"

"No." I threw in a chuckle to camouflage my lie.

The car swung right, then left a little farther up the road, then left again after a bit longer.

"Good. I'd hate to lose you."

I was ninety-five percent sure I was already lost.

The car slowed. I heard gravel crunching under the tires. Then we stopped, the engine idling.

"I'll be right back," he said and I felt the air pressure change as he opened his door. True to his word, he returned in a jiff. "We're almost there."

"Almost where?" We had twisted about enough that I couldn't tell if we were close to downtown or somewhere in the boonies.

"You'll see."

We rolled forward slowly, then he parked and killed the engine.

"Can I look now?" Curiosity had me sitting forward. I fingered the satin mask and hoped my mascara and eyeliner hadn't smeared. I doubted Wolfgang would find me so attractive when I looked like Beetlejuice's twin sister.

"Not yet."

His door clicked shut. I waited, trying to rally some enthusiasm so I could appear as excited as I should be.

I heard my door open.

"Okay, darling, just a little further." His palm warmed my upper arm as he helped me out of the car.

The slam of my door echoed, like we were inside a building. Yet gravel crunched under my shoes as I stepped away from the car. I opened my mouth to ask where we were and the ground under my feet turned soft and lumpy—grass.

"Hold on a second," he said, and let me go. In the midst of a ruckus of caws from a murder of nearby crows, I heard a creak and then a thump behind me. What was that? Some kind of door? Then Wolfgang was back, leading me along the grass.

"Three steps up." He saved me from falling on my face when my toe collided with the last step. "You okay?"

"I think so." Although, I'd heard a rip from somewhere south of my neck, and that couldn't be good, especially since the red undies that matched my dress were still at home in the dirty clothes hamper. My heels clomped across a wood floor.

He had me pause for a second, then said, "One more small step here."

I obeyed, and my soles came down on something smoother than the wood I'd been walking on. The aroma of roasted chicken enticed me along as the crow caws became muffled. My stomach gurgled awake, curious as well, now.

Wolfgang led me across what felt like linoleum underfoot. The melodic sound of a piano accompanied by various stringed instruments grew louder as we walked. I didn't recognize the tune. My mother must not be a groupie for the composer.

We turned right twice and then stopped.

"Here we are." Wolfgang lifted off my satin mask.

I blinked in the flickering light. My mouth gaped after my eyes finally focused. Surrounded by what must have been fifty candles, we stood in the breakfast nook in Wolfgang's house—the place where we'd first had lunch together weeks ago.

"Surprised?"

For the second time in twenty-four hours, I had to rummage around for my tongue. "Uh, huh."

I peeked at the ceiling. A bit freaked out, too, in spite of the calming music. If I heard one thump overhead tonight, I'd be donning my Speedy Gonzales shoes and disappearing in a cloud of dust.

Wolfgang pulled out a chair for me. I lowered into it, pretending to tuck under my dress while checking the seams for a tear. I found the hole mid-hip, no bigger than my fingertip. My shoulder blades loosened. I didn't relish Wolfgang seeing London, France, and my mint-green underpants.

The feel of Wolfgang's lips brushing my shoulder cinched me right back up.

"I'll be back with some wine and appetizers," he whispered in my ear and then dashed out of the room.

I'd barely had time to admire the pattern on the china place settings and scan the room for any clown paraphernalia before he returned with a narrow tray of toasted baguette slices topped with bruschetta. The tiny tomato and mozzarella chunks made my mouth water.

"Did you make these?" I asked as I scooped up one and shoved it in my mouth. I'd expected a heavy garlic hit. Instead, the fresh tomato and basil cleansed my palette and made my tongue waggle for more.

"Yes." Wolfgang placed a glass of white wine in front of me and then eased into the opposite seat. "I took a cooking class last summer."

A classy dresser *and* handy in the kitchen. I chomped down another slice. Why couldn't his kisses leave me pining as much as his cooking?

He sipped his wine. "The candlelight makes your hair look like golden threads."

I swallowed a mouthful of tomatoes, wishing we were in a loud, public restaurant so I could find something to distract me from the lack of magic in this moment. "Umm, thanks."

He just stared into my eyes.

I fidgeted with my silver spoon, searching for a diversion. "We need to talk about your house."

"Tonight? Can't it wait?"

"Not really. It's important."

Wolfgang leaned back, his brows arched. "What is it?"

Your mother doesn't like me. I kicked Doc and his ghost nonsense out of my head. "I don't think I can sell this place."

He didn't even blink. "Why not?"

"Well, for one thing, it's going to take months to get all of the reconstruction plans approved by the historical committee."

"So it takes longer than we originally planned. That's no reason to concede defeat."

I couldn't think of another convincing excuse, so I tried my hand at a bit of honesty. "I don't know that I'll still have a job by then."

His eyes narrowed. "What is it you're not telling me?"

"If I don't sell a house in the next week, I'm fired." There. Whew! It felt so good to have that out on the table. I grabbed another baguette slice. Now if only I could be so open about my lack of hankering tonight for any flesh other than roasted poultry.

"You're joking."

"No. Girl Scout's honor." I chewed on the crusty bread for a moment. "If I don't hand my boss an accepted offer on a house in the next week, she's going to give my job to another Realtor." Who also happens to be my poem-writing secret admirer. Such is the circle of my life.

"So you see …" I pointed at the last slice of baguette on the tray. "Are you going to eat that?"

Wolfgang shook his head.

I grabbed the toast and continued. "The chances of me still being a real estate agent by this winter are pretty slim."

"Am I your only client?"

"You're one of four." I shoved the last bruschetta in my mouth. God, it felt great to be so honest.

"You don't have to work for Calamity Jane Realty to sell my house, do you?"

"No, but I'll be out of money long before that, so I'll have to move back into my parent's basement and mooch off them for another six months to a year until I can get back on my feet." I frowned at the empty tray, wondering if he had more bruschetta in the kitchen. "It's very likely I won't even be in the area to make the sale."

If I had to return to Mom and Dad's, at least Addy would be out of reach of the kidnapper's net.

Wolfgang said nothing, just sipped on his wine.

"I can recommend another agent for you." Mona would polish this lump of coal into a regular Hope diamond.

"What if I don't want another agent?"

"You don't really have a choice."

Setting his glass down, he said, "Hold that thought. I'll be back in a second." He grabbed the tray and pushed to his feet. "Drink your wine."

He left me there, staring at the wine flute in front of me. I scratched my head and blew out a breath of relief. I'd done it. I'd spilled my guts. No more popping Tums because of this house and its creepy clowns. I felt like kicking off my heels and doing the Charleston. Would the table hold me?

I picked up my glass and swallowed a light, fruity sip.

By the time Wolfgang returned a couple of songs later, I'd drained every drop from my glass as well as his and needed a refill. However, my shoes were still on.

He frowned at the sight of my empty glass and lowered a tray of roasted chicken surrounded by potatoes and sprigs of rosemary to the table. "You're supposed to sip wine, dear."

I giggled, my head partying solo. "I chugged."

"Would you like me to dish up your plate?"

As I looked up at him, he split into two Wolfgangs. I blinked him back into one. "Whoa. That was weird."

"What?" Two Wolfgangs asked in unison.

I blinked again and rubbed my eyes. When I opened them, the twins were still there. "Something is wrong with my eyes."

"What is it?"

The world turned on an axis and began to whirl. I reached for the table and missed, listing away from both Wolfgangs. "I'm a little dizzy."

"Violet."

I shook my head, trying to clear it, and made myself tilt further. "I think I need to sit down."

"You are sitting." The Wolfgangs squatted next to me.

"Oh. Then I'm in …" my eyelashes felt like tiny anchors. So heavy. My lids plunged. "Trouble."

The chair bucked me off. My head thumped on the floor.

There was pain, dim in the shadows. Then darkness.

* * *

Something was stabbing me in the neck.

I moaned. Everything was muddled, echoing, dark.

I leaned my head to the side, stretching. Pain! Shooting into my brain. *Jesus!* Inhaling sharply, I gagged. *What was that rancid smell?*

I opened my eyes, blinking as my pupils adjusted in the flickers of dim light, and stared across a table … at the stitched-shut eyelids of a corpse.

Sucking in a gasp, I choked on the underlying stench of what must have been decaying flesh.

I tried to look away, but my watery eyes devoured the dried face—skin stretched tight across cheekbones, two holes that used to be the nose, lips sewn closed. Tangled blonde hair was matted against the small skull.

Panting, my tunnel vision widened. I now saw corpses on either side of me, tied to their chairs, just like the one across the table.

Cramps buckled my stomach.

The small one on my left was losing its blonde, wavy tresses in clumps, its bony skull visible in several areas. The skin resembled flat, tan-colored jerky; the eyes also sewn shut with what looked like black fishing line; the nose missing; the lips sealed with black cross-stitches.

I gulped down a wave of nausea clawing its way to the surface.

The corpse on my right appeared to be fresher, the skin not as withered, the long, straight blonde hair pinned back with barrettes. Another young girl. Her eyelids sewn, her nose shrunken in, and lips thin in death under the sutures. Just sleeping. That's all, just sleeping, I told myself; and this all was a very bad dream. It had to be.

Then I recognized her. The last picture I'd seen of her had been black-and-white. The words *Missing Girl* across the top of the page.

My heart thumped hard in my chest, hammering in my ears.

No! My gaze darted to the other two mummified girls, my memory matching clothing descriptions, my brain finishing the puzzle. *No! No! No!*

Somebody was screaming.

A hand crammed a rag in my mouth, and the screaming

stopped.

I tried to sit forward, to free my voice. A sharp pang in my shoulders stopped me. I whimpered and tugged at my hands, which were tied behind my back.

"Now, Violet." Wolfgang kneeled next to my chair, stroking my hair. "If you're going to make such a commotion, I'm going to have to tape your mouth shut. Do you want me to do that?"

I wanted to get the fuck out of here! What was he doing? Why wasn't he screaming, too?

I saw the wallpaper behind him and froze. Violets.

My face grew cold as the blood drained from it. Holy fucking shit! He had me in the upstairs bedroom.

Wolfgang tucked a curl behind my ear. "You promise not to make a peep if I remove the cloth?"

I nodded, trying to focus on his blue eyes, wanting to forget the three dead girls sitting at the table with me. A table covered with pink tissue paper, a tiny teapot, and child-sized cups and saucers. A grisly tea party for four, and I was the only living guest.

His teeth gleaming in the candlelight, Wolfgang pulled out the gag. He waited, watching my mouth, then stood. "Good girl."

I swallowed the taste of cotton and frowned up at him. "What am I … why did you …" I paused, found my left brain, and then with what little calm I could apply to my vocal chords said, "What the fuck is going on?"

He pointed at the nearby dresser. A cake sat on the top, a pink plastic tiara next to it. "It's a going-away party."

"For me?" My voice squeaked. I didn't want to go anywhere. Just home, please. Now!

"No, for Wilda."

Wilda? Wasn't that his dead sister? "Why am I here?"

"Wilda insisted." He grabbed the tiara and placed it on my head. "You're the guest of honor."

Chapter Twenty-Three

Son of a bitch! I wiggled my hands, testing the rope holding my wrists hostage.

This couldn't be the end for Violet Lynn Parker. Not so soon. Not before I got to ride roller coasters with my kids, swim naked in the Caribbean, have sex on the top of Mount Rushmore, run with scissors.

Oh, no. There was no way in hell I was going to die in a violet wallpapered room while wearing green underwear.

Tugging and pulling on the rope, I watched Wolfgang's back as he hauled a Piggly Wiggly shopping bag from the closet.

"Ah, Violet." Wolfgang pulled a can of lighter fluid from the bag. "My beautiful Venus with tresses of gold. Your hair is so much like hers, you know."

Like whose? The dead girls sharing the table with me?

"How I hate to do this to you." He popped open the cap.

I paused, my wrists stinging, my breathing shallow, my eyes locked on the can in his hands. "Do what?"

He dumped lighter fluid over the dried corpse across the table from me. "Burn you."

The fuel's pungent odor covered the stench of decomposing flesh and seared my nose. I cowered into my chair, trembling so hard my teeth chattered. I couldn't become a human torch. The smell of burning hair always made me gag. "How about we skip the barbecue? Charred meat has been linked to cancer, you know."

Chuckling, he moved to the sleeping girl on my right. "Always the jester. That's one of the things I love about you."

"You should see me juggle." I reared back, trying to avoid being splashed as he squeezed out the last of the can's contents. "Untie my hands and I'll show you."

He set the empty container on the dresser next to the cake. "Do you believe in love at first sight, Violet?"

No, but I'd experienced lust at first light. Did that count? My eyes began to water. "Sure. Who doesn't?"

"Me, too." He reached into the shopping bag and pulled out a second can of lighter fluid.

A soprano voice in my head screeched in terror. I twisted my wrists with new purpose, ignoring the burning and tearing of my skin.

"I knew the first moment I saw your golden curls on your postcard that you were the one."

Not *the one* again. I decided to play dumb, buy more time. "The one what?"

How about *the one who got away*? I was all for that.

"The one I will love forever." He added a couple of more squirts to the sleeping girl.

Finally, a man who would spend eternity pining for me and he was going to turn me into a shish kabob. I coughed on the fumes, my throat tingling, my lungs aching.

"The one who would free me from her," Wolfgang added, showering the third corpse with lighter fluid.

"Her?" The rope felt slicker now, wet, sticky. I told myself it was just sweat, but the tearing pain on my wrists said otherwise. I pulled at my right wrist, my shoulder cramping. Looser. Closer. "Are you talking about your mom?"

"Mother?" The harshness of his laugh made me flinch. "She was an angry, old bitch."

"Angry at you?" I should've taken more notes in Psych

101.

He tipped the can of lighter fluid upright, the top still open, and set it on the dresser next to the other empty can. "Angry at death, for stealing her daughter and leaving her son."

I stopped struggling whenever his gaze was on me. "Did she hurt you?"

"Hurt? Ha!" His grin scared me as much as my dead tea party mates did. "She told me every day how she wished I'd died instead of Wilda. She plastered the walls of my room with rose-covered wallpaper, made me wear dresses and play with dolls, buried my toys in the backyard."

"So that rusted toy train Layne found …"

"A Christmas present from my grandfather."

I might have had a lump in my throat for little Wolfgang had I not been trussed up and about to be marinated in liquid fuel by the bastard. "Did she hit you?"

"She knew better. Wilda wouldn't have liked that."

"Is your mom hurting you now?" Did he have her dried, rat-chewed corpse sitting in a rocking chair in the basement? Did he like to wear a wig and pretend to be her?

"Violet." He looked at me like I was a silly ninny. "Mother has been dead for years. How could she hurt me now?"

Well, excuse me for confusing the *nearly* departed with the *dearly* departed in his psychotic hallucination.

He lifted the cake and set it on the table. Then he pulled a square piece of paper from his shirt pocket and placed it in the center of the cake. I crooked my head to the side, squinting in the candlelight at the black-and-white photo. A curly-haired, blonde girl glowered back at me.

He stuck a clown candle next to the picture. "Wilda has always loved clowns," he explained.

Wilda? Sitting back, I continued to stare at the picture, everything falling into place. From Wolfgang's fascination with my hair to the clowns plastering the rooms downstairs, it all made sense now—twisted as it was. Neither Wolfgang nor his mother could let go of Wilda. She'd possessed them both long after her death.

I glared at the waxen fool jammed into the icing. There wasn't anything the slightest bit funny about his rainbow suspenders, big shoes, or the wick sticking out of his top hat. I wanted to mash it with a sledgehammer.

"Mother hated me, but the penalty she doled out eased with time." Wolfgang squirted the cake with some lighter fluid. "Wilda's vengeance keeps growing stronger, more painful."

I wanted to raise my hand and remind him that she was dead, too. At least I thought she was. I glanced over my shoulder, checking for a young girl, coiled up in a corner, waiting to strike, but found only shadows. "I thought Wilda was gone, too."

"Oh, no, Wilda is still here." The surety in his tone made my limbs quiver harder.

I jerked on my bindings, my right hand close to freedom. If I could just get some leverage.

"She refuses to leave me alone." He held the can of lighter fluid toward me. "Unless I kill the one I love."

Expecting to get squirted, I shrank away. "Why kill?" I couldn't keep the panic from my voice. "Can't you talk her into a minor maiming instead?"

He frowned and dropped to his knees beside me, placing the lighter fluid on the floor. "No. She's the eye-for-an-eye type."

"But I didn't do anything to her."

"I did, and she won't leave me alone."

"What did you do?"

"She was a bad seed, Violet, sprouting thorns early. I had to stop her before she could murder anyone else."

"Who did she murder?"

"My father."

I turned to him, my eyes wide. He had my full attention now. "I thought your mother poisoned him."

Wolfgang shook his head. "You've been listening to rumors. It was Wilda. I was five, she was seven. He wouldn't let her join the swim team, wanted to punish her for feeding the neighbor's dog a bunch of Alka Seltzer tabs for no reason other than the pleasure of seeing the animal suffer." He captured a strand of my hair, rubbing it between his fingers. "So she poisoned him. Mixed Diazinon with the coffee in the canister he took down in the mine every day."

Damn. Wolfgang's whole family had been cuckoo for Coco Puffs. "So you killed Wilda?"

"I didn't intend to kill her, just hurt her." His eyes were dry, his voice steady. "Wilda had said she was going to poison the only girl on her swim team who was faster than her in the backstroke. I tried to stop her, threatened to tell Mother. She'd swore she'd cut off my ear if I tattled. So I pushed her down the stairs and told everyone she'd tripped."

My mouth fell open. "How old were you then?"

"Eight."

"Oh, God, Wolfgang. You were just a kid."

"Mother always knew I was to blame for Wilda's death. She'd stare at me, hatred in her eyes."

And I thought the Liberace records my mom used to make me listen to were torture.

"Wilda died that day," he continued, "but she never really went away. At first, she followed me around the house, always there, always silent. But ever since Mother died, Wilda has become irate, loud, even violent." He rubbed his temples, his face crinkling as if the agony was crushing him. "She won't leave me alone. She screams at me nonstop, blaming me, threatening to destroy all of the good in my life."

"Is she screaming now?"

He stood and picked up the can of lighter fluid, his gaze focused over my head. "No."

Goosebumps streaked up my spine, scattering shudders along the way. I peeked over my shoulder and saw nothing but the bedroom door. "What is she doing?"

"Just watching. Making sure I follow through."

Had she noticed that my right hand had just slipped free of its binding? Because Wolfgang hadn't.

"I have to get rid of her, Violet." He continued to stare at the bedroom door. "She's driving me insane."

Driving? I glanced at the corpse across from me. I'd say he'd already arrived at Looney-town and was setting up shop.

"Why did you kill *them*?" I nodded toward my tea-mates, unsure how they fit into this grisly tale. "Did Wilda tell you to?"

"Of course not. She doesn't even know them."

There went my only theory. "Then why?"

"I thought they would appease her, since they all swam the backstroke." He shrugged as if their deaths were incidental, just flies stuck to a sticky strip. "Calm her down. Stop the screaming."

What? Like goats to lure and feed an angry troll? *Jesus!*

Speaking of luring, I asked, "How did you get the girls to come to you?" To get within reach?

"Most little girls love sparkly crystals and gems, especially in the shape of a pretty flower bouquet or cute pink teddy bear and offered with a friendly smile. I see the desire to touch and possess time and again in their wide eyes as they stare through my store's front window with chocolate smeared on their hands and mouths. Even Addy couldn't resist, I'm sure. How is she liking that rhinestone unicorn? I made it special for her, you know."

Oh, God! I recoiled at the memory of Addy's glee when

she opened the unicorn gift at the hospital. I'd throw that broach down a mine shaft if I made it out of here breathing.

So he'd enticed the girls with jewelry. No wonder they'd fallen into his hands.

They were innocent little girls with their whole lives ahead of them. How could the same man who showed such kindness and compassion to my daughter so easily snatch the breath from these girls and prop them up at this table like macabre dolls?

I blinked back more tears, my eyes aching from the fumes and the truth. Maybe they were just dolls to him. Like those his mother made him play with instead of the train.

He petted my head. "Only you can placate Wilda, my beautiful Violet, because it's only you I love."

That was just swell. What an honor. I wanted to bite his hand. The fool didn't love me, he loved his sister. Some twisted, psycho, almost incestuous type of love. I just had the bad luck of having curly, blonde hair like hers.

"I don't want to burn to death, Wolfgang. Did Wilda specify how I had to die?"

His brows drawn, he stared down at the lighter fluid in his hand as if he'd forgotten he was holding onto it. "What? Oh, no. I'm not going to burn you alive, darling. That's just cruel."

What part of sacrificing me was humane? "Then how are you going to kill me? With more roofies?"

"That wasn't Rohypnol I gave you. It was Burundanga." He walked over to the curtains and sprayed them with lighter fluid. "It's a popular trance-inducing drug from Colombia."

"Explain the difference." While his back was to me, I picked at the knot tying me to the chair.

"Do you remember what happened before you woke up in here?"

I frowned as my fingers worked on my bindings, trying to remember how I got here. Unfortunately, everything prior to waking up at the tea party was a fuzzy bundle of memories. The taste of tomatoes on my tongue and the smell of roast chicken was all I could recall. "No."

"Exactly. If the correct amount is administered, it won't even fully knock you out."

"But I was knocked out." Hadn't I been?

"I didn't expect you to drink your wine so fast."

"How long was I out?"

"A couple of hours," he emptied the second can of lighter fluid on the bed. "Not long enough to interfere with my plans, though."

Nice of me to be so considerate of his schedule. "Now what?" I asked, stalling for another minute or two.

He tossed both empty cans in the shopping bag. "Now, you have to die."

"I was afraid of that."

"It's the only way I'll be free." He opened the bedroom door. I heard the cans clink as he dropped the bag in the hall. "After you're gone, Wilda will go, too, and I'll burn the house to the ground around you. With all of the dry rot in these walls, the fire will burn so hot it will take them weeks to find any trace of you and the others in the ashes. Then, like a Phoenix, I'll rise, reborn, my life fresh and unmarred."

I'd like another plan, please. One that didn't involve seared flesh. My heartbeat echoed in my fingertips and toes. "They'll come looking for you."

"Of course they will." He leaned over me. "However, I'll be long gone by then. A new man, a new identity, free from her at last."

The crazed glitter in the depths of his blue eyes made me gulp and recoil.

"I'll always love you, Violet." His lips hovered over mine, his fingers entwined in my hair. "So divine, even in death."

Hold the phone! My ticker might be knocking like an angry landlord, but it was still pumping adrenaline through my limbs. I wasn't ready for a dirt nap, yet.

His lips covered mine, the taste of wine faint on his tongue. I slinked down in my chair under the weight of his kiss, my mouth open for whatever he had to offer as my fingers found the knot and tore at it.

So close, just a bit longer.

He pulled away. "I'll make it quick."

Crap! "Can I have one last request?"

"That's so cliché, dear."

"I know, but give a girl one last wish."

"Maybe." He crossed his arms. "What is it?"

"A chicken leg."

"What?"

"A leg from that roasted chicken you made for dinner. I want one."

"You can't be serious."

"Why not? I don't want to die hungry. Let me at least have the dignity of dying with a full stomach."

For a second, I didn't think he was going to relent. Then he smiled. I wanted to kick in his white teeth.

"All right. A leg of chicken it is." He closed the door behind him, leaving me untied and alone—not counting the three corpses staring at me.

Or Wilda.

Chapter Twenty-Four

I sprang from my chair so fast I had to catch it to stop it from tipping over. Yanking off the stupid tiara, I jammed it in the cake next to the clown candle. Then I slipped off my heels and headed for the window. I knew the drop to the backyard below had to be twenty feet—an ankle-breaker, but my options weren't plentiful at the moment.

The curtains reeked of lighter fluid. I pinched the edge of the thick cloth, trying to keep my skin fuel-free. When I peeled back the fabric, my stomach plummeted. Boards covered most of the window, leaving peepholes here and there. I peeked out through one gap. Stars twinkled overhead. An orange glow off to the right pinpointed downtown Deadwood, but darkness shrouded the yard below.

I let go of the curtain and wrung my hands. *What now?*

The door beckoned, escape just a staircase away.

I scurried past the tea party, my eyes on the doorknob, my brain already outside on the front lawn, and my foot connected with one of the chair legs. I grabbed the dresser as I fell to keep from thudding onto my ass and alerting Wolfgang.

Pulling myself upright, my forearm bumped one of the lit candles. I lunged to catch it … and missed.

The candle clunked as it hit the floor. I cringed. In an instant, the lit wick found the fuel-coated floorboards, igniting a whoosh of fire that sent me back-pedaling toward the door. I twisted the knob and wrenched open the door just as the flames licked Emma Cranson's ankles. A fireball shot to the ceiling with a roar. I shielded my face with my arms, my skin roasting. The stench of burning hair and flesh made me retch.

Coughing from the billowing smoke, I stumbled toward the staircase and saw Wolfgang running from the dining room. He halted at the bottom, his eyes wide as he stared up at me, my every muscle stiff with panic.

The fire crackled as it spread. With another whoosh, heat spilled into the hall.

"You're out of your chair," he accused.

The sound of his voice spurred me to life and I sprinted down the hall to the bathroom. The pounding of his shoes up the stairs chased me along. At the last moment I veered and skidded into the green bedroom, the one I'd been locked out of last week—his mother's room.

I slammed the door, turning the skeleton key in the lock just as the knob twisted in my blood-slick palm. I held my breath and stared down at the key. A loud thump on the door sent me screaming backwards onto the queen-sized bed.

"Violet," Wolfgang's muffled voice crooned through the wood. "Open the door, darling."

Searching the room, I hunted for something … anything … to use as a weapon.

The knob rattled. "Come on, Violet. The fire's getting hotter."

I grabbed the picture of his mother off the dresser, the glass still broken, and hefted the brass frame in my hands.

A volley of bangs rumbled as Wolfgang hammered on the wood. My heart mirrored the tempo.

"Open the goddamned door!"

"Fuck you!" I yelled back, my voice rusty, but steady.

"Fine. We'll play it your way."

Silence followed. I ran to the door and pressed my ear

to the wood, cool against my face. A door slammed, followed by the retreating stomp of Wolfgang's shoes on the stairs.

Where was he going? Then I remembered the drawer full of keys in the kitchen. *Oh, God!*

My wrists stinging, I wiped my blood-covered palms on my dress and leaned against the door. I had to think, think, think.

My gaze landed on the window across the room. I ran over and tore open the curtains. Boards covered most of the glass, just like in the violet room. I tugged on the boards, none budged.

"Damn it!"

Maybe there was something in the closet. I yanked open the door. The smell of bay rum was strong in the small space. Drab-colored dresses swayed on their hangers, shoes my grandma would've loved lined the floor. The purses stacked on the upper shelf were my only weapon choices.

I needed more time.

Racing across the floor, I tapped the knob with my fingertips—the metal was still cool. I squashed my ear once more against the wood and heard only muted crackles and pops. After a peek under the door for Wolfgang's feet, I turned the key and inched it open.

The hall was empty, except for the roasted chicken that the psycho had abandoned on the hallway floor.

I stepped out, shut the door quietly, and then locked it, pocketing the key. Wolfgang had enclosed the fire in the tea-party room, but it wouldn't stay caged for long. Black smoke already seeped out the seams around the wood panel and eddied near the ceiling.

To mask which room I was in, I closed the bathroom door, too, and tried the key in the lock. It worked. I crept forward, hesitating at the top of the stairs, listening, staring down at the front door. I tested my foot on the first step down, but Wolfgang's approaching footfalls locked my knees. *Fuck!*

Heat radiated out from under the tea party room's door, stinging my bare feet as I tiptoed past. I slipped inside the doorway of the third bedroom—Wolfgang's room.

His footfalls crested the stairs. "Come out, come out wherever you are," he taunted. He'd unlock the door and find his mother's room empty. Then it would be a game of hide-and-seek.

A loud groan echoed from the violet-walled room, then a *boom* and *crash* in the hall. A deep roar followed, twice as loud as before. Heat rolled in through the open door, baking my ankles.

I wanted to peek out, see what was happening, but I wasn't sure where Wolfgang was.

The fire snarled louder, angrier, closer. The door apparently was no longer a barrier. Flames now blocked me from the staircase.

With a fresh coat of sweat lacquering my skin, I shut the door and turned the key in the lock, sealing my own tomb.

I flicked on the overhead light, not sure if it would even work, anymore, and lucked out. Across the room were two windows. If memory served me right, one faced the side yard, the other the street. I tried the street window first, expecting to find boards. Sure enough, Wolfgang had made sure I couldn't jump out. I tugged at the two-by-fours, my eyes blurring, and cursed under my breath.

At the second window, he hadn't been as meticulous and left wider gaps between the boards. I braced my foot against the wall and yanked, crying out when one of the boards near the bottom creaked and gave a little. A bent nail only half-buried in the sill was its Achilles' heel.

Scanning the room, I zeroed in on the skinny torso of a brass lamp on the dresser next to the door. The cord, plugged in behind the dresser, came free on the second jerk.

Back at the window, lamp in hand sans the shade, I popped the board free of the sill, letting it swing to the floor. The window pane was no challenge for the brass base of the lamp. The shattering glass made my heart flutter with hope.

I kneeled next to the six-inch tall strip of freedom, inhaling sweet, fresh, Black Hills air, and listened for the sound of fire engines over the jackhammer in my ears. However, the sizzles and hisses from across the hall drowned out anything else, and the gap was too narrow to slip my head through.

Back on my feet, I leveraged the lamp behind another board.

A loud screech came from the other side of the door.

I whipped around.

The wood panel seemed to shudder, the door knob turning, and then there was a click and the door popped open.

I grabbed the lamp and held it out in front of me like a light saber.

The door swung wide and Wolfgang stepped into the room, a crowbar in his hand, his hair and shirt smoking. His toothy smile scared the breath out of my lungs.

"Hello, darling." He closed the door and leaned against it. "I've been looking for you."

A mewling whine crawled out of my throat. I tightened my grip on the lamp.

"That was very clever of you, locking all the doors, hiding in my bedroom."

He laid his crowbar on top of the dresser and grabbed the four-drawer cabinet by the edges. The feet scraped over the wood floor as he pulled it in front of the door, blocking me in.

I backed around the bed, putting it between us.

"But I'm tired of playing games now."

He picked up the crowbar and walked toward me as his smile slid from his face. His nostrils flaring, he rounded the end of the bed. I dove across the pillows and rolled over the duvet. My feet touched the floor on the other side at the same time he caught me by the hair. With one hard tug, he hauled me back onto the bed. He raised the crowbar over my face; I screamed and wrenched my body to the side as it came down. It thumped onto the duvet, just missing my ear.

His grip still tearing my hair, he raised the crowbar again. Then I remembered the lamp in my hand. I swung up as he brought the bar down. Brass clanked against steel, knocking the crowbar sideways, burying the hooked end into the bed again.

Before he could take another shot at my skull, I turned and smashed the lamp down on his crowbar wrist.

He howled and let go of my hair, clutching his wrist.

I spun away, falling off the other side of the bed onto the floor, dragging the duvet with me—my zipper caught. I tore free of the duvet's hold and scrambled to my feet.

Wolfgang ran around the end of the bed. He charged me, an angry cry contorting his face.

I raised the lamp, wincing, anticipating his blow.

As his feet came down on the duvet, he skidded sideways, landing on his back. "Oof!"

I heaved the lamp like a sledgehammer. The brass base smashed into his forehead with a sickening *thunk*.

I hoisted the lamp again, ready to strike.

Wolfgang's eyes rolled up into his head, his mouth gaped, and the crowbar clattered onto the floor as his grip slackened.

I fell back against the wall, my body shaking so much I almost dropped the lamp. A crash from the other side of the door reminded me that I wasn't free to skip on home yet. Smoke poured into the room from under the door.

Giving Wolfgang a wide berth, I dashed to the dresser

that blocked the door, heaved it aside, and hopped about on the wood floor now sizzling under my bare feet. The door knob was probably searing, but thanks to Wolfgang's crowbar work on the jamb, I didn't need to touch it.

Using my fingertips, I inched open the door. Flames crammed the hallway, slathering the walls, blackening the ceiling. Heat blasted my hair back, scorching my face and chest.

I was so screwed.

I closed the door and shoved the dresser back in front of it. After a quick check on Wolfgang to confirm that the beast still slept, I crept to him and grabbed the crowbar. The window was my only shot. Just one more board and I could fall to freedom.

Wrestling the board, my sweat-and-blood-slick hands lost hold of the crowbar, which clattered to the floor just missing my toes. I wiped my hands on the bed sheets and returned to the window. This board fought me, its nails buried deep; but I refused to give up and one side of the board splintered free.

I whooped in victory.

"Violet!"

I screamed and turned. Wolfgang was still sprawled on the floor, his eyes still closed.

The dresser scraped across the floor a couple of inches. The door banged against it.

"Violet, move the damned dresser!" Doc yelled through the crack in the door.

I raced over and shouldered the dresser aside.

He stumbled into the room, wrapped in the gray plaid blanket from his car. He lowered the cover, his face streaked with soot and sweat. After a glance at Wolfgang, he frowned at me. "Are you okay?"

"I've been better."

"You don't look so hot."

Well, I hadn't had time to freshen up, yet. "Give me ten more minutes and I'll be smoking."

His eyes narrowed. "Didn't I warn you about this house?"

"Oh, shut up!" I noticed the red canister in his hands. A fire extinguisher. I planted my hands on my hips. "Are you here to rescue me or lecture me? Because if it's the latter, I'm jumping out the window."

He grinned and lifted the cover. "Get under here, smartass."

I hesitated, my gaze bouncing between him and the window.

"What?" he asked.

"I don't have any shoes." I'd sooner free-fall than dance across hot coals.

A crash boomed over our heads.

Wincing, I stared up at the ceiling, which creaked and groaned. A fracture appeared near the interior wall and streaked toward the front of the house, plaster raining down in its wake.

"That can't be good," Doc said.

Another bang resounded from above; I flinched and ducked. A flaming beam busted through the ceiling, dividing the room in half, Wolfgang on the other side.

Doc tugged on my arm. "Get on my back."

He didn't have to tell me twice. I hiked up my dress and climbed on, wrapping my arms around his neck.

"I need to breathe, Violet."

Oops. Loosening my hold, I helped pull the plaid cover— wet, warm, and heavy—around my shoulders and over my head.

"Ready?" Doc yelled over the snarling flames.

"Let's go!" I tried not to choke him as he opened the door, stepped into the inferno, and sprayed a path through the flames.

The blanket did little to shield the heat. By the time we reached the stairs, I thought my skin was going to melt off my shoulder blades and leave a sticky trail. The stench of smoke and burnt plastic made me cough, my throat scalded by the acrid air.

Doc paused at the top of the stairs, then threw the fire extinguisher aside.

"What are you doing?" I cried.

"It's empty," he shouted back. "Hold on tight. The staircase is about to collapse."

I dug my fingers into his shoulders, squeezed his hips between my thighs, and buried my face in his neck. There was no way he'd lose me. Shaking off a tick would be easier.

He grabbed me behind the knees and started down what was left of the stairs. I snuck a quick look over his shoulder halfway down and nearly screamed. Flames surrounded us, eating the wood banister, licking the walls, gobbling up the ceiling. Down below, past the flames, the front door stood wide open. Darkness beckoned from beyond.

An explosion rumbled behind us, rattling the house. The staircase groaned and tipped. Doc stumbled, his shoulder bumping into a flaming wall. I cringed and yanked my hand away, waiting for the wood underfoot to give way and take us down with it.

A growl reverberated through Doc. He shrugged me higher on his back, then flew down the remaining steps two at a time and shot through the entry. He didn't stop until we'd reached the front gate. He tore off the steaming blanket and I dropped to the dry grass, coughing and gagging, gasping for oxygen. Doc bent over me, sucking in fresh air.

When I found my voice, I said, "Wolfgang is still up there."

A crash rang out through the open front door. We both

stared into the inferno.

"That was the staircase." Doc kneeled next to me. "I can't get to him."

I rolled onto my back and gazed up at the stars. Sirens wailed in the distance.

The image of Wolfgang lying on the floor haunted me. Would he feel the pain as the flames devoured him? Would I hear his screams of agony through the broken window? Or would he suffocate before the fire reached him?

Why did I care after all he'd done to me? To those poor little girls? To this town?

"Violet." Doc leaned over me and brushed back my hair. His fingers trailed across my forehead, down my cheekbones, over my lips. His dark gaze held me captive. "I—"

"Here comes the cavalry!" Harvey crowed from the sidewalk. The front gate shrieked open.

Doc snatched his hand back and sat up. Whatever he'd been about to say was his secret now.

"Hey, Harvey," my voice croaked as I spoke, my vocal chords like brittle taffy. I tried to wave at him as he approached, but my hand was trembling too much.

"It's good to see you breathing, girl." Harvey blinded me with a flashlight. "Shit. Where are your eyebrows?"

Chapter Twenty-Five

Sunday, July 22nd

I dragged my sorry ass out of bed the next afternoon feeling like I'd spent the last ten hours tumbling around in a clothes dryer. Every muscle ached; my throat was scratchy, skin too tight, hair frazzled, eyes dry, ears clanging, and forehead bruised and pounding from when I'd fallen head-first out of my chair.

A splash of cold water didn't cut it, so I tossed back a couple of aspirin and crawled into the shower, shuddering to life under a freezing spray. After standing in front of my closet for several minutes, I grabbed a sleeveless dark-green denim dress with copper snaps that ran the length of it, ending at my shins, and slipped on my favorite cowboy boots. I scrounged through my underwear drawer and found a pair of terry-cloth wristbands from my racquetball days of old to cover my bandaged rope burns. Brushing my curls hurt too much, so I shoved a couple of hair combs into the rat's nest and called it good.

The smell of fresh-baked brownies lured me downstairs and reeled me into the kitchen. Aunt Zoe stood at the sink washing the brownie pan.

"Morning," I mumbled as I stumbled across the linoleum. Halfway to the coffee maker, I noticed Aunt Zoe had company.

"'Bout time you rolled out of bed, Wonder Woman!" Harvey hollered.

I cringed and poured myself a tumbler of black brain

juice. My head hurt too much to handle the sound of Harvey's voice, especially when he had the volume cranked up.

"Nice wristbands, Chris Evert." He kicked out the chair next to him as I approached. Always the gentleman. "Hey, your eyebrows are back."

Not really. His eyesight just wasn't so good. I'd penciled in the scorched parts after camouflaging my head bruise with cover-up.

Avoiding his gaze, I dropped into the chair and gulped down half of the cold, bitter dregs. Aunt Zoe slid a plate of brownies under my nose. I grunted my thanks. Maybe warm chocolate would soften the effects of Harvey's crusty personality.

Harvey stole a brownie from my plate. "Coop called for you this morning?"

"What does Detective Cooper want?"

Aunt Zoe pulled out the chair across from me. "He has a few more questions for you."

Hadn't we talked enough last night at the hospital while I was being checked out for smoke inhalation and having my wrists wrapped? I'd told him my story three times already. Did he think a few hours of sleep would change the ending?

"I'll call him on the way to work. Can I borrow your cell phone today?" I asked Aunt Zoe. "Mine's under the weather."

"Sure, but you're not going into the office today, are you?" Aunt Zoe frowned at me over her glass of iced tea. "Not after all you went through last night."

I nodded, swallowing some brownie. "I don't have time to play victim. I have a house to sell." Neither rain, snow, sleet, nor psychotic murderers could keep me from trying to save my job. Besides, I wanted to see Doc. With luck, I'd find him in his office.

Harvey wiped his hands on the napkin Aunt Zoe handed him. "Coop says they found where that nut job stored the bodies."

I raised one brow, which was all I could manage at the moment.

"He said something about chunks of hair and scalp in the root cellar," Harvey snatched another brownie, "and a bad smell."

Grimacing, I dropped the rest of my brownie on my plate.

"Coop also mentioned that they found evidence of several big bags of rock salt in what's left of the basement. He figures Hessler was gutting and stuffing the bodies with the salt, then packing them in it to dry out the corpses."

"Packing them? Where? Like a barrel?"

"Cooper thinks Hessler used the tub. It's one of the few things that survived the fire."

The crystal! My hands grew clammy. Holy frickin' moly, I bet that was rock salt I'd found in Wolfgang's bathroom that day I was searching for Addy upstairs. That would explain why the crystal disappeared after being through a wash cycle.

"Maybe we should talk about this later," Aunt Zoe suggested.

"That's okay," I said and sat back in my chair. "Keeping quiet now won't change what happened. Besides, it's better coming from you two than Detective Cooper."

"You sure you're up to it?" Aunt Zoe searched my face.

"Sure, she is," Harvey answered for me. "She's no shrinking Violet."

Especially if I keep eating brownies for breakfast.

"Look at how she took out Wolfgang on her own," he added.

My cheeks warmed. Not entirely on my own. The duvet deserved most of the credit, I just delivered the knockout blow.

Harvey patted my head as though I was a good bluetick hound who'd treed a raccoon. "And Doc Nyce told me that she was about to jump out the window when he found her."

More like dangle from the sill and scream bloody murder until the neighbors came running, but I liked Doc's version better.

"Speaking of Doc." I set my empty cup on the table. "How did you two know where to find me? Or to even come looking?"

"That was Layne's doing," Aunt Zoe said.

"Layne?"

Harvey nodded, grabbing the penultimate brownie from my plate. "That's one smart kid you got."

I'd known that since back when he'd asked Santa for a thesaurus and a set of training wheels, but, "How did *he* know?"

"When you didn't show up by nine," Aunt Zoe explained, "he called me at the gallery, insisting something was wrong. By the time I closed up and drove home, he'd phoned just about every restaurant in Deadwood and Lead looking for you."

"There was no talkin' the kid out of it," Harvey added. "He insisted you were in trouble. Turns out the little shit had been spying through the curtains with a pair of binoculars earlier when Wolfgang arrived and he'd seen a padlock fall out of Wolfgang's pocket when he'd crawled out of the car."

"A blue padlock," Aunt Zoe continued. "Layne remembered it from the root cellar door in Wolfgang's backyard."

I remembered talking with Layne about that root cellar door—and the padlock. It all made sense now. The memory of Wolfgang standing in this very kitchen and talking to my kids with that padlock in his pocket made me shiver.

"By that time," Harvey said, "Layne had Addy all buggered-up about you being in danger and she begged me to call Doc."

"Doc?" I asked, sitting forward. "Don't you mean Natalie?"

"No, she insisted on Doc. Said he would rescue you. Even knew his cell phone number."

My eyes narrowed. Somebody must have nosed through my purse when I wasn't paying attention. Little Miss Matchmaker and I were going to have to have a talk about boundaries again.

"Lucky for me, Doc had his cell phone turned on," Harvey continued. "He picked me up and we cruised by the Hessler house. The place was dark, but we'd promised Layne we'd check out that root cellar door. While we were monkeyin' around in the back, we heard glass break out front. By the time we got around the house, you were up there squealing like a half-castrated pig."

I scowled. He could've come up with a more flattering simile.

Harvey stood and grabbed a beer from the fridge. "You should have seen Doc go at Hessler's front door. His shoulder is gonna hurt for days."

I'd be happy to kiss it better. It's the least I could do.

Aunt Zoe looked at me, her brows raised, suspicion glinting in her eyes. I hurried to change the subject. "What did Coop have to say about the ear?"

I'd filled in Aunt Zoe about Harvey's creepy visitor yesterday. Her gaze flew back to Harvey. "Surely somebody missing an ear has shown up at one of the hospitals around here by now."

"Nope, not a one. Coop mentioned that the ear had been sent off to some lab to be looked at." He cracked open the can. "He and some of the sheriff's deputies checked out that mine up behind my barn. They found a few things. Something made a nest."

I shivered clear through my toes. "What kind of things?"

Shrugging, Harvey said, "Broken glasses, an old boot, dirty skivvies, a half-eaten possum. Oh, and teeth."

"Teeth?" Aunt Zoe asked, reading my mind.

"Coop says they look human. He mentioned something about bones, too. Didn't say from what."

"Jesus, Harvey." I sat back, feeling a bit winded.

"Something's been diggin' in that old cemetery on the back end of my property again, too. At first I thought some mountain goats had broken through the fence, but it's still up."

"Maybe you shouldn't be staying out there alone for awhile," I said. "At least until Coop figures out what's going on."

"There's room in my basement," Aunt Zoe offered.

"Nah. I'll be fine. Bessie is good company. Besides," he winked, "I wouldn't want to upset the good thing I got goin' on next door, and whatever whangdoodle was up there is long gone."

"Whangdoodle?" Aunt Zoe and I asked in harmony.

"That's what my pappy used to call the crazy kooks who'd wander too far from Slagton."

"I thought that town was abandoned decades ago," Aunt Zoe said. "After that big mining accident."

"Nope. There are quite a few stragglers still holding out, living in the surrounding hills."

The back screen door opened.

"Natalie's here," Addy shouted as she galloped inside. She skidded to a stop at the sight of me sitting at the table. "Oh, hi, Mom. What's wrong with your eyebrows?"

"I'm trying a new look." It was called almost-burned-alive. "What do you think?"

"You should stick with your old look. How was your date with Wolfgang?"

I glanced at Aunt Zoe, who said, "After Harvey called me last night, I let the kids know that you were fine and had just lost track of time."

"Thanks." I'd need to explain the truth to Addy and Layne sometime soon, but not until I could talk about it without trembling. I turned to Addy. "I've had better dates."

"Oh." Her smile dimmed a few watts. "Are you going to see him again?"

Only in my nightmares. "Probably not."

"That's too bad. He seemed really nice."

Yes, he had. I'd been blinded by his ultra-white teeth. I fluffed her hair. "There are a lot more nice guys out there."

"Like Doc?" she asked, her eyes twinkling.

"Like Doc what?" Natalie walk-rolled into the kitchen, her cast resting on a little cart with handle bars. She stopped next to the table, extracted an iced latte from her tote bag, and handed it to me. "I figured you might need this."

"You're an angel." I sipped from the straw and shuddered as cold, sugared caffeine poured down my throat. I pointed at the cart. "Where'd you get that contraption?"

"It's my *special gift* from Doc."

"He gave you that?" Not the most romantic gift. Very practical, very generous, but a bit odd. Kind of like Doc himself. Maybe I'd ask him about it sometime.

"Isn't he the most thoughtful guy?"

I swallowed my gag and changed the subject. "How are your parents?"

"Jeez, Vi. You look like you're wearing a turtleneck." Natalie leaned over and unsnapped the top three snaps on my dress, exposing an eyeful of cleavage. "There, that's better. My parents are fine, but Mom's worried about you."

Natalie's mother had taken me under her wing when I was a fledgling. Yet another reason I needed to keep my talons off Doc. Disappointing my pseudo-mother would be almost as bad as making my best friend cry.

Harvey held out his chair for Natalie, which she fell into with a sigh. "How sweet is it that Doc rescued you?"

The hair on the back of my neck bristled at her cooing tone. Doc was my white knight battling the fire-breathing dragon in my fairy tale—not hers.

"What does she mean Doc rescued you?" Addy asked. "From what?"

"I'll tell you later."

"Nobody ever tells me anything," Addy bemoaned.

"I promise I will." I squeezed her hand. "But I need you to do me a favor right now."

"Fine!" So much attitude for such a small body. "What?"

"Go get the twenty-dollar bill out of my wallet, grab your brother, walk to the Candy Corral, and buy whatever you want."

Addy's mouth fell open, her eyes bugged. "Really? Can we?"

"Just be careful and don't talk to strangers." Especially any offering sparkly jewelry. I'd searched for Addy's jewelry box for her unicorn broach late last night and come up empty. She must have it stashed somewhere else. I'd have to keep an eye out for it so I could make it magically disappear. "And get back here as soon as possible," I added. No need to completely let go of the reins, exterminated monster or not.

She squeezed me around the neck with her cast-free arm. I wrapped my arm around her and clutched her against my side, turning and inhaling her fruity-sweet smell, blinking back an ambush of tears. I'd come close to losing this. Too close.

"Mom, you're squishing my cast."

"Oops." I sniffed and released her. "Now get out of here."

"Okay. Be back in a bit!" She ran out the back door screaming her brother's name.

With Addy out of earshot and my eyes no longer leaking, I turned to Natalie. "Sorry we interrupted your evening with Doc last night."

A white lie on my part, nearly transparent in the daylight.

"Oh, you didn't interrupt anything. Doc was saying goodbye when his cell phone rang."

Did that goodbye involve any kissing?

"Are you two going out again?" I ignored the pointed look that Harvey was giving me.

"I hope so."

"You haven't made any plans, though?" Much more pressing on my part and I'd be leaving fingerprint bruises on her.

"No. He said he'd call." Her smile seemed wistful. I wanted to smear brownie goo all over it. "He's such a great guy. Do you think I should wear a white dress at our wedding?"

I inhaled latte. Harvey snickered as I coughed and gasped. Aunt Zoe watched us both with a gunslinger stare. Natalie's smile faltered.

The phone rang. *Thank God!* I practically ran to it. "Hello?" I covered the mouthpiece and coughed off to the side.

"Hello, Violet Parker."

I cringed mentally. "Hi, Jeff. What's going on?"

"I heard about last night."

Already? It hadn't even been twenty-four hours yet. "How?"

"It's a small town."

"So I'm told."

"You sure add excitement to this place, Violet Parker."

"Thanks." I think.

"I'm calling to see if Kelly can stay over there tonight. I need to be in Spearfish at dawn and her mother is too busy with her girlfriend to watch her."

"Sure." After identifying Wolfgang's charred remains last night before Doc drove me home, my worries about Kelly's psychosis had faded. Although, not entirely. "Jeff, is Kelly okay?"

There was a hushed pause from his end.

I continued, "With her therapy … well, after her therapy … assuming she is done with therapy," I took a breath, untied my tongue, and started again. "I saw the collage of Missing Girl pictures in your bedroom when I was there last." Another lie, but if Doc hadn't showed up, I would have seen it, so close enough.

"Right, that." Jeff's voice sounded tired. "The counselor thought it would be a good idea for her to put that together."

"Did it help?"

"I don't know."

There was one other question that I cringed at the thought of asking, but now that I knew Jeff wasn't the kidnapper, I needed to hear the answer. "Why did you throw a garbage bag of Emma's stuff in that Dumpster at Jackpot Gas-n-Go?"

"Wow, you don't miss much, do you?"

I waited quietly, hoping I hadn't pushed too far.

"Emma had been staying at our house the weekend she was kidnapped. With all of the commotion after she disappeared, everybody forgot about the clothes and sleeping bag she'd left at our place. By the time things had quieted down, Donna and I didn't know what to do with the stuff. A few weeks later, Kelly built a weird little shrine with it all in her bedroom, along with candles and pictures, and I knew I had to get rid of it in order to help her move on with life. If Kelly had seen that stuff in the trash, she would have flipped out, so I just bagged it and took it to the gas station."

"Oh." Here I'd conjured up a much darker, more sinister explanation. My father would tell me there was a lesson in this—something about not sticking my nose where it didn't belong. "How is Kelly now that you got rid of Emma's stuff? Is she moving on?"

Another pause. "I'll be straight with you. If you're asking if I think Kelly has some nutty hang-ups still, then yeah, I do. But she hasn't cried herself to sleep since she started spending time with your kid, and she's eating again instead of just picking at her food."

My heart twanged for both Jeff and Kelly.

Jeff cleared his throat. "I think Addy has done more to help Kelly through this bullshit than that lousy hundred-bucks-an-hour counselor."

"Good," I said, smiling for the first time since waking up. I was done grilling Jeff. "Do you want me to pick Kelly up, or are you going to drop her off?"

"How about I bring her by around five today?"

"Sure."

"Great. Thanks. Oh, and—"

His hesitation lasted so long I thought he'd been disconnected. "Yeah? Hello?"

"I was wondering if you'd like to go out on a date sometime. We could get a burger, maybe see a movie."

Yikes. How was I going to dodge this bullet? Jeff was not only the father of my daughter's best friend, but also my client; a man whose wife left him for another woman; *and* a guy who'd worked up the nerve to ask me out in a nice, non-prostitution-like manner. This required some expert-level pussyfooting.

"How about we sell your house first, then we'll try a date?" That seemed safe with less than a week until I lost my job.

"You mean like go out to celebrate?"

"Yes."

"Okay."

"Goodbye, Jeff." I hung up and turned to find three pairs of eyes drilling me.

"Was that Kelly's dad?" Aunt Zoe asked.

Natalie leaned forward. "Did he just ask you out?"

Harvey grinned. "How much are you going to charge him for sex?"

"I have to go to work now." Grabbing my latte from the table, I nodded in their general direction and darted.

Chapter Twenty-Six

I called Detective Cooper with Aunt Zoe's cell phone on my way to Calamity Jane's. "You have some questions for me?"

"Yeah. You said something about Mr. Hessler having traveled to San Francisco last week."

"Right."

"Did he ever mention his departure airport?"

"No. I just figured it was Rapid City." Public airports didn't exactly grow on scrub bushes on the prairie. The next closest was four hours away.

"Hmmm. Did he mention a particular airline?"

"I didn't ask. Why?"

"We're having trouble finding any record of him flying out of the area."

Maybe he hadn't left. I thought about Sherry Dobbler, the girl in Spearfish who'd escaped a kidnapper's clutches. Had Wolfgang stuck around and tried for one more girl? Or had that been his way of distracting the police, like Aunt Zoe had predicted, keeping the heat off him for a while longer?

"You said you'd talked to him once while he was in San Francisco." Detective Cooper's voice cut through my thoughts.

"Yeah, he called from his cell phone just to see how things were going." Also, to offer to take my kids on a date. Thank the stars that never happened.

"That was it?"

"Yes." No need to expound on my gargantuan gullibility to the detective.

I pulled into the parking lot behind Calamity Jane Realty, parked three cars down from Doc's Camaro (parked in my spot, as usual), and killed the engine.

"Did you remember any background noise during that phone call with Mr. Hessler? Any city sounds? Anything at all?"

I remembered the beep-beep-beep of something backing up. "Just some construction sounds. Can't you check his cell phone records?"

"We're looking into that."

"Did you ask Ray Underhill why he had all of those Missing Girl signs in the back of his vehicle?" I'd tattled on Ray during the post-inferno interrogation.

"Yeah. He claims they were detrimental to his realty business, so he took it upon himself to remove them before they scared off buyers."

Damn. Ray had to be the biggest asshole this side of the Mississippi.

"Are you available tomorrow for lunch?" the detective asked.

My breath caught. "Are you asking me out on a date, Coop … I mean Detective Cooper?"

Christ! Was I in heat and didn't realize it?

His laughter left my cheeks burning. "No, Miss Parker. I'm thinking about relocating and need a real estate agent. Uncle Willis says you're helping him sell his ranch."

Uncle Willis? Oh, right, Harvey. "Of course, an agent. Sorry." I pulled out my organizer and flipped to tomorrow's page. Where had all of these wanna-be clients been a month ago back when they could have saved my job? "Do you want me to meet you at the station?"

"No, I'll pick you up in front of your office at noon."

"Okay, noon it is." I penciled him in and realized he'd

already hung up on me. Nice. He'd learned his manners from his uncle.

I locked the Bronco and crossed the heat-soaked parking lot to the back door, my headache easing as the tag-team of caffeine and aspirin beat it into submission. Jane's office door was closed when I passed, light spilled out from under it. I paused inside the office long enough to drop my purse on my desk and wave at Mona, who pointed at me and frowned while she talked on her phone. She must have heard about last night, too.

I heard the toilet flush behind me and beelined out the front door before Ray saw me or Mona had a chance to corral me.

Doc's front door was unlocked. I deadbolted it behind me. Mr. Nyce and I had some shit to hash out, and I didn't want to be interrupted until I was satisfied.

I strode through the empty front room, my boots clunking across the scarred wood floor, and headed down the short hall. A doorway to my right led to a bathroom. The one to my left opened into a small room lined with mostly-empty, wall-to-wall bookshelves. An overhead bulb was the only source of light, an upside down five-gallon bucket the only seat.

It was here that I found Doc standing next to a ladder that was attached to tracks in the ceiling and floor. He had a thick book open in his hands. His cargo shorts and T-shirt beach attire left a lot of olive skin available for admiring. The scent of his woodsy cologne teased my sinuses … and libido.

I leaned against the doorframe. "Hey, Doc."

His forehead furrowed, he closed the book. "You should be home resting."

"Good to see you, too." I nodded at his book. "What are you reading?"

He held the book up for me to see. I read aloud, "*Ghosts*

of Deadwood's Past."

Doc dropped it on an empty shelf. He stared at me, his jaw clenched, his gaze guarded.

"Anything about the Hessler family in there?" I asked.

"I thought you didn't believe in ghosts."

"I don't."

"In spite of what you told the police Wolfgang said about his sister haunting him, telling him to kill you?"

I shrugged and spun the copper head of one of the snaps midway down my dress. "The man murdered little girls, mummified them in his bathtub, and stored them in his root cellar. He was a Grade-A wacko. The voice he thought was his sister's was probably one of the many in his head. You know, like that *Sybil* movie."

"You mean Dissociative Identity Disorder."

The name rolled off his tongue too easily. My eyes narrowed. "Yeah, that."

"So, in your theory, it was another personality in his own head that instructed him to kill the one he loved in order to quiet the voices?"

"Yes." That sounded about right to me.

"Had he succeeded in taking your life, do you think he'd be free of the voices now?"

"Of course not."

Doc rubbed his stubble-covered chin. The raspy sound filled the small room. "So, was this other personality encouraging him to commit suicide?"

"What do you mean?" I was going to need another latte to keep up with Doc if he pursued this subject much further.

"Well, would you say that Wolfgang loved himself more than anyone else?"

"Probably."

"You two had only one date prior to last night, right?"

"Uh-huh."

"So the chance of him actually falling in love with you after just one date is probably slim."

My neck heated. "You may not realize it, but I can be pretty charming when I try."

"You don't have to try."

I skipped over his comment. "Wolfgang told me when he saw my picture on my Realtor postcard, it was love at first sight."

"You believed him?" His tone had a hint of incredulity.

"Well," I said, sputtering, indignant, "my hair was down and looked damned good in that picture." I didn't share the small detail about my hair being just like Wilda's. It wouldn't have helped my cause.

Doc grinned at me.

"And I was probably a little high on lighter fluid fumes at the time he said it, but yes, I did believe him." He loved me in his own twisted, incestuous way.

He nodded, then gave me a thorough once-over from the floor up, pausing on my open neckline. "You look great in green."

"Are we changing the subject now?" If so, I'd prefer to turn the spotlight away from me.

"It appears so." His gaze dipped to my feet. "Those sure are sexy boots."

I tried to push aside the memory of the last time I'd worn these boots and found myself alone in a small, dark space with Doc, but my gut quivered anyway. Straightening my shoulders, I plowed forward. "Do you really believe you can see ghosts?"

His focus returned to my face, his eyes darker than usual. "No."

"Oh." He derailed me before I could get up a head of steam. "But I thought—"

"I can sense them."

"Come again?"

Crossing his arms over his chest, he said, "You heard me."

"Sense how?"

"Well, the only way I can describe it—and you're going to think it's crazy—is that I can smell them."

He was right, it was crazy. "Smell? What do you mean?"

He touched his nose.

"You're purposely being evasive," I accused.

He shook his head slowly, squeezing the back of his neck, staring at the floor. "It's complicated, Violet. The best way I know how to explain it is that it's an odor, only more, but not in the usual sense. It affects me in ways that I don't understand—yet, but I'm working on it."

I couldn't think of a single thing to say to that.

He blinked and looked over at me. "Do you believe me?"

I hesitated. This was Doc, my client, my white knight, my friend, but I couldn't lie to him. "I don't think so."

"Yeah, I didn't really expect you to. That's why I didn't want to tell you. You'd think I was deranged."

"Wolfgang was deranged. This is just a little … nuts."

His lips twisted into a wry smile. "Right. Can I trust you not to mention this to anyone?"

I couldn't think of one good thing that could come from spilling it, especially in my line of work. "Yes."

"Thank you."

"However, let's just say there were such things as ghosts and you could sense them."

He lifted his brows and waited for me to continue.

"Why do you think Wolfgang's mother's ghost was hanging around the house? Haunting it?"

"I never said it was his mother. You just assumed that."

"Oh. Then you saw—I mean, smelled, his sister?"

"Something like that."

"You'd said she was angry about being dead."

"Very."

"Why?"

"Because her brother had killed her when he shoved her down the stairs."

My mouth gaped. I hadn't shared that part of Wolfgang's story with anyone last night. Not Detective Cooper, not Harvey, not Doc. I didn't know why, probably to protect the little boy inside the monster, the poor child whose cruel sister had stolen the light from his life and left him in darkness.

"How did you know about that? Who told you?" I asked.

"Wilda sort of showed me how she died the first time I went into the house, but I wasn't sure who'd pushed her until I did some research and deciphering."

I shivered, chilled by his words. This had to be some parlor trick of his. He must have read something blaming Wolfgang for her death at the library. "How were you able to go back in the house during the fire? You couldn't even step inside the foyer on Friday without collapsing."

"I knew what I was facing. I could prepare up here," he tapped his temple, "for her."

The conviction in his voice gave me pause. He really believed he could sense dead people. Where on earth had he come from? More importantly, "What brought you to Deadwood, Doc?"

"Nothing brought me. I was just passing through on my way out West."

"But something convinced you to stay. What?" I remembered his knowledge of the details of Emma Cranson's disappearance, which occurred about the same time he claimed to have come to town. "Was it the first missing girl? Did you think you could help find her?"

"No. Not initially. That came later, after I started learning more about Deadwood's history and experimenting."

"Experimenting with what?"

"The past."

The past? What? "How?"

"It's easy around here. There's lots to work with."

He was being about as clear as chocolate pudding. "Okay, if it wasn't the kidnapping that made you decide to stick around, what then?"

He stood there looking at me, his lips thin, squeezed tight. For a moment, I didn't think he was going to answer me. I lifted my chin and refused to budge. I wanted an answer.

He exhaled loudly. "Wild Bill."

"Hickok? Really? You're *that* big of a fan?"

"No, I mean Wild Bill convinced me to stay. Literally. I ran into him in town."

I laughed. When he didn't even crack a smile, I stopped. "You're serious?"

He nodded slowly.

I stared into his brown eyes, searching for something that would show he was pulling my leg. That it was all a hoax. That I didn't have a Titanic-sized crush on a human bloodhound who believed he could sniff out ghouls and banshees.

Doc stared back, giving no ground. "If you want to walk out of here and never look back," his tone was low, somber, "I'll understand."

He was offering me an out. A sweet gesture, but … I stepped inside the room and closed the door. "It's not that easy to get rid of me, Doc."

His eyes narrowed as I strolled toward him. "I never said I wanted to. Decent Realtors are hard to come by."

I stopped an arm's length away from him. We shared a secret now. A doozy of a secret. Whether I believed in it or not didn't matter. I smiled up at him. "Why won't you step inside Calamity Jane's?"

"I don't like the smell."

I raised my brows. "You think it's haunted?"

He shoved his hands in his pockets, his shoulders hunched, tense. "I thought you didn't believe in ghosts."

"I don't, but humor me."

"Either you believe or you don't."

We'd reached a stalemate, a typical ending to our usual dance routine. I sidestepped. "What about the Purple Door Saloon? You made me switch chairs that day I had lunch with Jeff. Is there a bad smell in there, too?"

He broke eye contact. "Something like that."

His discomfort with this subject couldn't be more obvious, yet he wasn't shutting me out. That made my stomach all tingly. Since he was in the sharing mood, I asked, "What do you do for a living, Doc?"

"I'm a financial planner."

"Really?"

His gaze came back to meet mine. "Surprised?"

I nodded. "I guess I hadn't expected you to do something so …" *boring.*

"Mundane?"

"Yeah."

"Not all of us can handle the wild roller coaster ride of realty, Violet." The corners of his eyes crinkled with mirth. His body didn't seem so rigid anymore.

"I could use a financial planner in my life." As soon as I got some finances to plan.

"You don't even know if I'm any good."

I had no doubt—on many fronts. I grabbed a handful of his T-shirt and tugged him toward me. "You can show me."

Doc took my hands in his, running his thumbs over my palms as he frowned at the cloth wristbands. "How are the rope burns?"

"Healing." I squirmed under his feather-light touches. "How's your throat? Still scratchy?"

"A bit. Yours?"

"The same. Thanks for saving me."

"I didn't. I almost got you killed. I should have figured out Wolfgang's connection to the girls on the swim team."

"The police hadn't, and that's their job."

"But a big clue was right there on the Rec Center walls, and I'd been in there almost every day."

"Yeah, but Detective Cooper said Wilda was missing in the team picture, only her name mentioned."

"I should have tried harder after you took me to Hessler's place on Friday, but I couldn't think straight."

"Because of the house?"

"Because of you. You mess up my head."

I took that as a compliment and towed him closer yet. "How was your date with Natalie?"

His lips curved. "She's a good cook."

"She's a woman of many qualities."

"What about you?"

"I'm a lousy cook." If he didn't kiss me soon … I captured his thumbs in my fists, stopping them, trapping them. "Are you going to have dinner with her again?"

"I don't know. Are you going to go out with your secret admirer again?"

"Not if I can help it."

"Good."

I entwined my fingers with his. "Addy thinks you're a nice guy."

"What about her mother?"

"She thinks you have potential."

He leaned into me, his eyes on my lips, his eyelashes at half-mast. "Potential for what?"

I thought of Natalie's wedding dreams, Layne's man-of-the-house worries, Addy's hunger for any kind of father figure. "To cause a lot of trouble in her life."

"Tell Addy's mother the feeling is mutual."

One big hiccup and my lips would touch his. The warm, scent of his skin had me panting, itching for a bite. "Are you going to kiss me or what?"

"I shouldn't."

I angled my head, lining up with his mouth. "Why not?"

"You're my Realtor. I have my rule."

"Fuck your rule." I yanked on his hands and his mouth came down on mine.

This time there was no hesitation for either of us. The water had already been tested and found boiling. My tongue danced with his, twisting and turning, entwined in our own steamy samba, our breathing a mix of gasps and groans.

He broke the kiss way too soon and put several feet of cold air between us. His chest heaved; his eyes dark, obsidian pools in which I wanted to skinny-dip. "I want to put an offer on Mona's house."

I blinked. "You do?" Damn, I was a better kisser than I thought.

"Yes." His gaze raked over my face. "How soon can we close?"

"I don't know." I was having trouble grinding my brain out of lust and into real estate. "If we push hard and fast enough," I paused, smiling, enjoying the image of Doc, naked, his body thrusting into mine, "maybe two or three weeks."

"Perfect."

That meant I had exactly one week to get Doc and the seller to agree to everything and scribble their signatures on the dotted line before I could submit all of the necessary paperwork to Jane. Only then could I put my *X* on Jane's Sale Pending board and save my job—and my ass. "I'll need you to sign the offer letter today."

"No problem." He was staring at my lips again, so I

licked them.

"And if you're game to do whatever it takes to get the seller to sign and accept our offer before the week is up, I'll take you to dinner."

He closed the gap between us and grabbed the lapels of my dress. "Oh, you'll do more than that." The surety in his tone made me shiver.

I gave him a wicked grin. "You ever hiked around Mount Rushmore?"

"Stop looking at me like that, Violet." He tugged on each lapel. The snap just above my chest popped open.

I raised an eyebrow and baited, "Like what?"

He tugged again, another snap popped, exposing the little rose on my lacy purple bra. "Like you want me to tear your dress off."

I scraped my fingernails along his muscled forearms. "Then what would you do?"

Three more snaps popped open, my belly button now able to peek out. I sucked in my gut, wishing the light was a bit dimmer.

He leaned forward and whispered against my lips, "I'd touch you."

Ooh la la. "Where?"

"Hmmmm, let me see." His fingers traced the contours of my breasts, then skimmed down my ribcage, hovered at my hips. With one yank, he tore open the last five snaps.

My dress hung around me like a green drape, framing my body for his eyes to devour—which they did.

I covered my stomach with my hands, suddenly feeling bashful. "I've had twins."

He looked up into my eyes, his pupils dilated, his face slightly flushed. "I know."

"I don't look like I did when I was twenty."

"Neither do I."

"I have stretch marks."

"I don't care."

"And things sag more than I'd like."

He grabbed one of my hands and placed it on the front of his shorts. "Feel that?"

Boy, did I. A thrill rocketed through my veins at knowing that I did that to him. I nodded, burning up inside.

"I want you, Violet. Every tempting part of you."

I grinned like an idiot, I couldn't help it. Doc wanted me, warts and all. "You should probably seek counseling about that."

"I'd rather try some hands-on therapy first." He lifted my palms to his lips and kissed them. "Now where were we?"

I placed his hands back on my hips. "You were going to tell me where you'd touch me."

"Right." He dropped to his knees before me, his hands sliding around my behind, cupping my hips through the purple satin and lace. "I'd start here." He leaned forward and drew a circle around my belly button with his tongue.

"Then I'd probably go here." My knees trembled as he trailed a string of kisses down to the top of my panties, the stubble on his chin grazing, tickling me deep inside.

I started to feel lightheaded and realized I wasn't breathing. "Then what?" I gulped, clinging to the ladder behind me.

"Then I might kiss the inside of your knee," which he did. "Or your inner thigh." Again, his lips followed suit.

"Holy shit, Doc!" I panted. It had been too long since I'd had an orgasm for me to stay in this game much longer. All he had to do was touch me right …

"Or this spot here." His mouth moved higher, and his finger slipped inside my underwear, caressing, playing hide-and-seek.

There! The shudders started in my toes and rumbled all the way up to my neck. I gripped Doc's shoulders, rocking as wave after wave slammed into me, moaning, writhing, floating while Doc continued to kiss and touch, lick and stroke.

When I landed back on earth, I sighed and opened my eyes. "Is the ride over already?"

Doc rose, unbuttoning his shorts. "Hell, no. We're just getting rolling."

"I'm on birth control," I blurted, "and clean." Might as well get the awkward stuff behind us. "You?"

His grin grew Cheshire-cat wide. "As a whistle."

Yippity do dah! I started to kick off my boots.

"Leave your boots on."

"Kinky—nice." I barely managed to get one foot free of my underwear when he grabbed me around the waist and hoisted me up on a ladder rung.

"Wrap your legs around me," he commanded.

I obeyed, locking my ankles together as he positioned himself against me.

"Look at me, Violet," his voice was hoarse, strained; his eyes black, hypnotic. "I've fantasized about doing this since you tripped over my box of books." Then he plunged into me, making me gasp. He stopped halfway in and pulled back an inch. "God, you're tight."

"It's been awhile." Hell, I was surprised it hadn't closed up for good.

"This is so much better than I'd imagined," he whispered against my lips.

I adjusted, relaxing my muscles so I could take all of him. "Prove it."

He thrust again, this time buried. A groan tore from his throat. "You have no idea," he said, getting a delicious rhythm going, "how much you light me up."

Talk like that was going to turn me into his own personal sex slave, chains and all. I captured his bottom lip in my teeth and then trailed my lips to his ear as I dug my boot heels into his flesh. "Harder, Doc," I ordered, between gasps, and bit his ear lobe. "Don't hold back."

"God, Violet!" He slammed into me, fast, the muscles under my hands rigid, all control gone. I spiraled with him, squeezing my legs tight, burying my nails in his skin, sinking my teeth into his shoulder to keep from crying out. My body clenched, pulsing around him.

He roared against my throat, his body stiffening, then racked by shudders.

When the shudders stopped, he looked at me, his grin surfacing. Our breaths mingled, ragged.

"Wow." I shifted so I could rub the spot where the ladder had dug into my back. "That's gonna leave a mark." Both the ladder rung and Doc's touch.

"Tell me about it." Doc glanced at the teeth marks on his shoulder and winked. "Wild thing."

Below my marks were several nasty bruises spreading around to his back. He'd used his shoulder to bust open Wolfgang's front door, Harvey had said. Without thinking, I brushed a kiss over his bruised skin.

The tenderness in his eyes when I looked back up at him made me want to do things to him—fun, naked things. "Did I hurt you?" he asked.

I felt branded, not hurt. "Only in a good way."

"I have no control when it comes to you." He pulled out.

I missed him already. That couldn't be good.

I slid to my feet, my boots clunking on the floor. "Welcome to the club." I pulled my dress together, feeling vulnerable all of a sudden, snapping as fast as I could. "What are we going to do about it?"

He zipped his shorts. "I don't know."

"Maybe we just needed to get that out of our systems," I suggested.

He laughed. It rumbled in his chest. "As if once will do.

All I have to do is hear your name and I get hard."

That made me flush, in a feel-good-all-over kind of way. Then I thought of Natalie and nearly gagged on my guilt. I snatched up my undies and climbed into them. "So, what? We keep meeting here until we're dried-up prunes?"

He reached out and fixed my crooked snap job, his knuckles brushing my breasts through the jean fabric. His hands grew still and his eyes met mine. "You need to leave."

I winced. "You're not very good at after-glow chit-chat."

"Yes, I am." He tugged me toward the door. "But if you don't leave, I'm going to have to take your dress off again."

"Oh." The beast inside me perked back up. *Down girl!*

Doc opened the door and led me out into the hall. "Go get the paperwork started."

He dragged me toward the front door, my feet stumbling, my body lovesick. It wasn't until he'd pushed me out under the warm sun that I found my voice. "I forgot to tell you, Harvey said the police found some kind of nest up in the mine behind his barn."

Doc leaned against the doorjamb. "He mentioned that last night at the hospital while you were getting your wrists wrapped."

"You had a pretty strong reaction to something at Harvey's place."

Doc crossed his arms over his chest. "Yes, I did, but you don't believe in ghosts, remember?"

"I'm not saying this was a ghost. I'm just wondering if you might have smelled this thing when you were there." That half-eaten possum had to have left a sticky stench on whatever was living there with it.

"No, that's not what I detected."

"You sure?"

Nodding, he said, "Harvey's not alone out there, but

what I ran into has been dead for a long time."

I just stared up at him, speechless. He reached out and tugged on a loose curl. "Come back in an hour, Boots, and I'll take you to lunch."

I'd rather take another trip to the moon.

He closed the door in my face and clicked the deadbolt. After a wave in my direction, he disappeared into his back room.

"Holy frickin' moly." I pinched myself. Nope, this was the real thing. After taking a moment to pat down my curls and straighten my clothes, I wandered back into Calamity Jane's.

Mona's fingers paused. "What happened?"

Criminy! JUST HAD SEX! must be blinking in neon lights on my forehead. "Nothing. Why?"

"You're beaming."

Oh, well, what could I say? Sex with Doc had side effects. I closed my mouth to keep the sunshine from pouring out of it.

Ray glanced up from clipping his toenails, his crumpled sock on his desktop, his sneer loud and clear. "I heard you burned down your ace in the hole, Blondie. I'd offer to help pack your desk, but I have houses to sell."

I locked gazes with the dickhead. While Ray was off my radar as a possible kidnapper, I hadn't forgotten about that crate at Mudder Brothers. However, today I didn't feel like fishing for trouble. "I'm not going anywhere, asshole."

Ray's upper lip crinkled. "What makes you so sure?"

"Doc wants to put an offer on Mona's client's house."

Mona clapped and cheered.

Scowling, Ray stood. "An offer doesn't guarantee a sale."

Jane came out of her office. "What's going on?"

"Violet got a sale," Mona answered.

Jane's eyes lit up. "You did?"

"Well, that depends on Mona's client. Doc's going to sign an offer letter today."

"Congratulations!" Jane squeezed me with a big hug, enveloping me with the scent of vanilla and flowers. I hoped she couldn't smell sex on me. "When you get Mona's client's signature, I'll take you out to celebrate."

I waved playfully at Ray over Jane's shoulder. "Can Ray come, too?"

He growled and kicked his desk with his bare foot.

Mona laughed as he howled and hopped around on his shod foot.

Aunt Zoe's cell phone trilled from my purse. I ran over and dug it out. "Hello?"

"Mom, where are you?" Layne, my other knight in shining armor, asked, his voice a tad breathless.

"At work." I could hear a loud, squawking noise in the background. A cloud covered my sun. "What's that sound?"

"Elvis. Harvey just came back from the mine with him. Our chicken trap worked."

My heart started beating again. "Oh, that's good." Except for the fact that I had finally cleaned the last of the chicken feathers from my velvet comforter. "What do you need, Honey?

"You have to come home now!" he whispered.

"Why?" I whispered back, playing along.

"I found a foot."

Duh, his horse again. "They're called hooves, Kiddo."

"I know that, Mother. I'm not talking about my horse skeleton."

I plugged my other ear to block out Ray's cursing. "I don't understand."

"It's a human foot."

"Human?" I dropped into my chair. I must have heard that wrong.

"Yeah, hanging in a tree. It's missing two toes."

I laughed. It came out as more of a queasy cough. First Harvey's ear, now a foot? Were body parts falling from the sky? "You're kidding me, right?"

Silence issued from Layne's end of the line.

"Right? Layne?"

THE END … for now

Five Fun Facts about Ann Charles

When I was fifteen, I got lost in the Black Hills (back near Galena) one summer day because I'd come across a bull standing in the road while out on a walk and I was too chicken to try to skirt around it. For five hours, I wandered the forest, trying not to panic as dusk neared, until I came across a cute little cottage filled with a kind, older couple who took me in, fed me some cookies, and then drove me home. Turns out, I'd ended up on top of Strawberry Hill–only two freaking miles from my mom's house. My brother, Chuck, later bought me Stephen King's book, *The Girl Who Loved Tom Gordon*, as a trophy for getting lost in the forest and making it out alive.

* * *

I have an irrational fear of zombies and cows (the latter explains the first fun fact listed). Both give me the heebie jeebies!

* * *

I am a huge fan of roller coasters, amusement parks, and carnival rides. Cedar Point Amusement Park in Sandusky, Ohio is my favorite!

* * *

I use nicknames for my immediate family members. If you hear me talk about Mr. Biddles, Beaker, and Chicken Noodle, that's them.

* * *

My dream job would be a Coke Slurpee inspector for the 7-11 Corporation. I would travel around the United States on their dime, testing Coke Slurpees in the various franchises, and giving rewards depending on the Slurpee's smoothness, flavor, and liquidity. And I would be paid hundreds of thousands of dollars every year to do this, of course.

Sneak Peek!

Want a sneak peak at Ann Charles' second book, *Optical Delusions in Deadwood**, in the Deadwood Mystery series?

Synopsis:

Word has it single mom, Violet Parker—Deadwood's most notorious Realtor—likes to chitchat with ghosts.

With her reputation endangered, her bank account on the verge of extinction, and her career threatening to go up in flames, Violet is desperate to make a sale. When the opportunity to sell another vintage home materializes, she grabs it, even though this "haunted" house was recently the stage for a two-act, murder-suicide tragedy.

Ghost or no ghost, Violet knows this can't be as bad as the last house of horrors she tried to sell, but charmingly irresistible psychic, Doc Nyce, has serious doubts. Her only hope of hanging on to her job is to prove that the so-called, ghostly sightings are merely the eccentric owner's optical delusions. But someone—or something—in the house wants her stopped … dead

Chapter One begins on the next page.

Chapter One

Deadwood, South Dakota
Wednesday, August 1st

Some jackass has been talking shit around town about me chitchatting with dead folks.

I didn't believe in ghosts, or haven't since I started wearing a training bra, anyway. But a couple of weeks ago, a psychotic serial killer tricked me into being the guest of honor at his macabre tea party with his sister's ghost and three of his decomposing victims. Since then, my reputation had suffered.

Normally, I'd just shrug off the stares, whispers, and snickers of sidewalk onlookers and fellow Piggly Wiggly shoppers, but I was relatively new in town—and even newer at this real estate agent venture. With two kids to support, big smiles and friendly service were my bread and butter.

Lucky for me, my fellow diners this morning at Bighorn Billy's were mainly tourists chattering away about what was on their day's agenda. With the infamous Sturgis Motorcycle Rally right around the corner, the Black Hills were crawling with chromed-out bikes.

I stirred cream and sugar into my steaming coffee, happy as hell to be upstaged by the leather-clad crew for the next couple of weeks. My stomach growled, antsy from the aroma of fried bacon and eggs thick in the air. A glance at the Harley Davidson clock on the wall made it growl again.

My breakfast date was late, and if he didn't get his

ornery old butt here soon, I was going to order without him.

A shadow fell over my table. "Excuse me, are you Violet Parker?"

That depended on if the woman standing over me with the owl-eye glasses and squeaky voice was one of my ghoul groupies. Her silver-blue eyes were magnified by lenses thick enough to read *War and Peace* etched on a grain of rice; her hair a helmet of brown, frizzy curls. My gaze lowered to the gray turtleneck sweater and long wool skirt covering her from neck to toe. Somebody should tell her it was August outside.

I smiled extra wide, always the saleswoman. "That's me. What can I do for you?"

She seemed harmless enough, but I'd recently learned the hard way that looks could be deceiving. My eyebrows were just starting to fill back in after that lesson.

She pushed her glasses higher up on her nose. "A gentleman from your office told me we could find you here."

Gentleman? My smile almost slipped. I had only one male coworker at Calamity Jane Realty. He hated my guts for stealing this Realtor job from his nephew and had made it his personal mission to destroy my career before it could even get one wheel off the ground. We'd hit it off like a sledgehammer and old TNT right from the start.

"I'm Millie Carhart," the woman said. "My mother would like to hire you to sell her house."

I peeked at the woman cowering behind Millie. With her white hair twirled up into a bun on top of her head and her ample bosom restrained in a faded, red gingham dress, she looked straight out of *Little House on the Prairie.*

My gaze returned to Millie's magnified irises. "Is your mother's place in Deadwood?" I assumed they were local, but with all of the tourists around, it didn't hurt to double-check.

"No. We live up the hill in Lead."

Lead was Deadwood's golden-veined twin. Its history books were filled with mining tales rather than gambling legends.

I had no issues with selling a house in either city. Money was money, something I had very little of, but I wasn't agreeing to anything until I took a look at the place. Again, past lessons learned; last contracted dwelling burned to the ground—blah, blah, blah. "When's a good time for me to come take a look at your house?"

"As soon as you can."

Nice, a motivated seller. Now if I could only find a buyer half as eager. Hell, just find a buyer—period. "How about this afternoon at two?"

"Good." Millie pulled a piece of paper from one of the folds in her sweater and placed it next to my coffee cup. "Here's our address. We'll be waiting for you."

Before I had a chance to fish one of my cards from my purse, she left, her mother trailing after her. They passed my tardy breakfast date on their way to the door.

"Sorry, I'm late." Old Man Harvey slid onto the seat across from me, his grizzled beard in desperate need of a trim. "I was putting out a fire all night."

Another fire? I frowned. "At your ranch?"

His grin was broad, his gold tooth gleaming. "Nah. In an old flame's bed. I left her smoldering."

I choked on an involuntary chuckle and sipped my sweetened coffee to wash it down.

I'd met Harvey and his 12-gauge shotgun up-close and personal about a month ago. After we'd straightened out that I was a Realtor interested in helping him sell his ranch and not a banker bent on taking it, we'd tossed back some hard liquor over a listing agreement. He'd confessed he was lonely and then proved it by insisting I include a once-a-week-dinner-on-me clause. Desperate, I'd agreed.

"What's for breakfast?" Harvey opened his menu. "After all of that bumping and grinding last night, I could eat a herd of elk."

Grimacing, I set my cup on the table. "Stop. You're going to kill my appetite."

He snorted, then buried his nose in the plastic pages. "What did the Carharts want?"

"You know them?" I shouldn't have been surprised. Harvey had grown up in the Hills. The dirty bird liked to brag about all of the cousins he'd kissed.

"Wanda was a few grades ahead of me in school," he said.

"They want me to sell their house."

Harvey squinted at me over the menu. "And?"

"And what? I'm paying them a visit this afternoon."

He leaned across the table, his forehead puckered. "What are you thinking?"

I blinked. Had I missed the memo? "What do you mean?"

"Are you really going to take them on as clients?"

"Sure." If their place wasn't a pit. "Why not?"

He tossed his menu on the table. "Maybe because six months ago in that very house, Millie's brother bashed her father's head in with a rolling pin and then blew his own brains out."

I swallowed wrong, hot coffee searing the back of my tongue. "You're kidding me."

"I wish I was." He crossed his arms. "If you take this job, you might as well plug your nose and hold your breath, because your career is gonna go swirling down the damned crapper."

About the Author

Ann Charles is an award-winning author who writes romantic mysteries that are splashed with humor and whatever else she feels like throwing into the mix. When she is not dabbling in fiction, arm-wrestling with her children, attempting to seduce her husband, or arguing with her sassy cat, she is daydreaming of lounging poolside at a fancy resort with a blended margarita in one hand and a great book in the other.

Connect with Me Online

Facebook (Personal Page):
http://www.facebook.com/ann.charles.author

Facebook (Author Page):
http://www.facebook.com/pages/Ann-Charles/37302789804?ref=share

Twitter (as Ann W. Charles):
http://twitter.com/AnnWCharles

Ann Charles Website: http://www.anncharles.com

Made in USA - Kendallville, IN
96097_9781940364148
03.27.2024 1119